ABOUT THE AUTHOR

Janet Gover grew up in outback Australia, surrounded by wide open spaces, horses … and many, many books.

She is a self-confessed 'bit of a geek girl'. When not writing novels she works in IT—in really dull places like Pinewood Movie Studios, Puerto Rico and Iraq.

When her cat lets her actually sit in her chair, she writes stories of strong women, rural communities and falling in love. Her novel *Little Girl Lost* won the Epic Romantic Novel of the Year Award presented by the Romantic Novelists' Association in the UK, and she has won or been shortlisted for awards in Australia and the USA.

As Juliet Bell, in collaboration with Alison May, she rewrites misunderstood classic fiction, with an emphasis on heroes who are not so heroic.

Her favourite food is tomato. She spends too much time playing silly computer games, and is an enthusiastic, if not always successful, cook.

Janet loves to hear from readers—so do drop her a line.

www.janetgover.com

www.facebook.com/janetgoverbooks/

Twitter: @janet_gover

JANET GOVER

The
LAWSON
SISTERS

mira

First Published 2020
Second Australian Paperback Edition 2021
ISBN 9781867218395

THE LAWSON SISTERS
© 2020 by Janet Gover
Australian Copyright 2020
New Zealand Copyright 2020

This is a work of fiction. Names, characters, places, and incidents are either the product of the author's imagination or are used fictitiously, and any resemblance to actual persons, living or dead, business establishments, events, or locales is entirely coincidental.

Published by
Mira
An imprint of Harlequin Enterprises (Australia) Pty Limited (ABN 47 001 180 918), a subsidiary of HarperCollins Publishers Australia Pty Limited (ABN 36 009 913 517)
Level 13, 201 Elizabeth St
SYDNEY NSW 2000
AUSTRALIA

A catalogue record for this book is available from the National Library of Australia
www.librariesaustralia.nla.gov.au

Printed and bound in Australia by McPherson's Printing Group

MIX
Paper from
responsible sources
FSC® C001695

For Michelle ... chef, chauffeur, reader, pug mother and my friend.
Thank you for always being there.

CHAPTER

1

Elizabeth Lawson never cried. Never.

She could remember the last time she'd cried. It was four days after her eighteenth birthday, and not all that far from where she now sat at the wheel of her tractor. That was just over fifteen years ago and in all those years, she had not shed so much as a single tear.

But today … today it was hard.

A drop of moisture fell onto the black steering wheel, fading as it dried instantly in the late morning heat. Sweat, she told herself firmly. It was sweat. One of these days, she'd buy a new tractor with an air-conditioned cab. But that was pretty unlikely. New tractors cost money, and money was something she didn't have. She was even less likely to have it after today.

Liz jammed the hat back on her short dark hair and reached for the ignition. There was nothing wrong with the tractor she had. It had a few years on it, but it was reliable and exactly what she needed to cultivate lucerne on the river flats or cart hay or shift muck from the stables.

Today it was exactly what she needed to dig a grave big enough to bury a horse.

She blinked furiously. It was only the dust in her eyes. She closed her work-roughened hands firmly around the control levers, and started pushing the loose soil into the hole, covering the dark shape that lay there.

It was well past midday when Liz parked the tractor in the machinery shed. As always, her first thought was for her horses. Some needed feeding, others hadn't been exercised. She also had to clear out the stallion stall, which was now empty. She slumped against the tractor. She really didn't want to face that empty stall right now.

And it looked like she wouldn't have to. Her eyes narrowed as she watched a car approaching up the long gravel drive trailing a small cloud of dust. It stopped by the homestead and the driver got out. He was carrying a briefcase. That was not a good sign. He paused for a few moments, looking up at the building in front of him. Liz knew he wouldn't be seeing the beautiful lines and proportions of the historic building, with its wide verandas and arched windows. Nor would he be admiring the grace of the wrought-iron railings or the elegance of the fountain in the centre of the circular drive. All he would see was the flaking paint and the stains on the stone. That's all everyone saw now. Everyone except Liz.

'G'day,' she called as she walked towards the house.

The driver of the car turned to her. He was probably in his early forties, with neat hair and a suit and tie. She recognised him immediately, and her heart sank a little further.

'Miss Lawson.' He offered her his hand.

Liz wiped her hand on the thigh of her jeans before shaking.

'I'm Richard Walker. I'm the loans manager—'

'At the bank in Tamworth. Yes, of course. I recognise you. What brings you all the way out here?'

'It's about the Willowbrook loan account.'

'I thought it might be.'

'You're very hard to get on the phone during business hours. I had a meeting in Scone. As you are so close, I thought I'd come by in the hope of a chance to talk.'

'Then I guess you'd better come inside.'

She could feel him assessing her home as she led him past the wide stone front stairs and around to the back door, could almost hear him adding up the dollars and cents. She knew exactly when he looked up at the dark windows of the second floor. Windows that hadn't been opened in an age. She bristled. What gave him the right to judge? Was he judging her too? Was he thinking that she looked as run down as the house, with the lines in her sun-browned face, the hair that she cut roughly herself and the creases between eyes that viewed the world so cautiously?

The door led into the kitchen. She didn't take him through to the front of the house. She didn't want his critical eye looking at those unused rooms. Nor did she lead him through to her office, because that was also where she slept most nights. Instead she indicated a chair at the wooden table in the centre of the kitchen.

He sat and opened his briefcase.

It wasn't a long conversation, nor was it an easy one. Liz had pretty much known what Walker was going to say. Despite that, the papers he left on her kitchen table were devastating.

'Please don't leave it too long to get in touch with me,' he said as he got in the car. 'I knew your father. I liked him. Respected him. I'll do whatever I can to help. But I have to answer to my bosses. And at some point—'

'Thank you, Mr Walker.' Liz shook his hand and sent him on his way as quickly as she could.

Before the car had even vanished down the driveway, she was striding towards the stables. Several elegant heads appeared as Liz walked past, but she didn't stop to talk to any of them. She paused at the tack room long enough to collect what she needed, and carried it outside to a small paddock behind the main stable block. A bay horse saw her coming and walked over to meet her at the gate. There were grey hairs on his muzzle and around his eyes. He was pretty much retired, and spent most of his time dozing under the trees. But right now Liz needed to ride, and she knew better than to work any of her young horses when she was upset. And besides, Zeke was part of the memories that were driving her.

A few minutes later, she swung herself up onto his back and urged him on at a fast trot and then a canter. She had to stop to open a gate, but then she pushed the big gelding into a gallop, wanting the feel of the wind in her face and the sound of hooves on the rich black soil.

But even that couldn't wash everything away.

Zeke was breathing heavily when they reached the highest spot on Willowbrook. Liz swung herself out of the saddle and looked across her home.

This was her favourite place in the whole world. Her heritage was here. A long curving line of stately river gums marked the creek. There were no willow trees on Willowbrook Station. Her Irish great-great-grandfather had named the place after the past he had left behind. He had embraced his new world and new life and ordered that no willows should ever be allowed to grow by the creek. To this day, none had.

The original wooden shack that Patrick Lawson had built by that creek was long gone, replaced by a two-storey building of soft golden stone that was considered one of the great houses of the Upper Hunter Valley. The house had grown and been extended by his descendants, mapping the rise of Willowbrook from a struggling one-man operation to one of the most famous horse studs in the country. From this distance, Liz couldn't see the shabbiness that now marked its decline.

Between this high point and the house, sloping green pastures were dotted with dark shapes. Brood mares and yearlings. Australian Stock Horses all of them. Their bloodlines were among the best in the country. Willowbrook horses had won show championships and proven their worth in high country musters over and over again. There were far too few horses in those paddocks now.

When Patrick Lawson died, he asked to be buried on the highest point of the place he loved. His grave was the oldest in the small graveyard on the hill, where many of his descendants also rested. Liz had stood in this place with her father so many times, talking about the family and Willowbrook, it felt like he was still with her. In a way, he was. She tore her eyes away from the view to look at the two most recent stone crosses.

'The land will never let you down, Lizzie.' She could almost hear her father's voice in the rustle of the breeze in the tall gums. 'Respect it and treat it well. As long as you have this place, you will always have a home. When times are tough, even in the worst drought, hold on to the land. Sell your stock. Sell the shirt off your back if you have to, but never, never sell the land.'

Reluctantly she looked to the far side of the creek, feeling the usual tug at her heart, but today the pull was so much stronger. Through the trees she could see a cluster of buildings, and a small house, painted white. Those buildings and the land around them, land that had once belonged to Willowbrook, represented her greatest failure.

If only she could simply ride down the hill, cross the creek and knock on the door of that house. She so longed to lay her head on a strong shoulder and let someone else take the burden. Let someone take the pain away.

But she had given up any right to lean on that shoulder a long time ago.

She gently laid her fingers on the top of the nearest of the stone crosses.

'I'm sorry, Dad,' she whispered.

Something nudged her in the middle of her back, and she staggered forward a step. 'All right, you don't have to nag.' She gathered Zeke's reins and stroked his forehead. 'Let's get you back. You need a good rub down. And those youngsters need tending to.'

And then she was going to do something she hadn't done in a very long time. She was going to talk to her sister.

CHAPTER

2

'It makes me look fat!' The bride's chin began to wobble and Kayla reached for the box of tissues.

'Not at all,' she spoke quickly, before the waterworks could start. 'You look beautiful. In that dress, you look like a fairy tale princess. Like Cinderella at the ball, and you know how well that ended.'

'Do you think so?' With a rustle of silk and tulle, the bride twisted her body so the mirror no longer displayed the growing bump that had probably prompted this rather rushed wedding.

'Absolutely,' Kayla assured her. 'Not everyone could wear a dress like this, but on you it looks amazing. I wouldn't be at all surprised if ...' she searched her mind for the right name, '... David sheds a tear or two when he sees you walk down the aisle.'

'He will, my darling, I'm sure he will. You look wonderful.' The mother of the bride wiped the tears from her eyes.

Kayla didn't mind the mothers crying, but she needed the bride to keep herself together long enough to at least say 'I do'.

'Now, let's get your veil on,' she said. 'It's such a lovely veil, with all those sparkles.'

As the harried-looking hairdresser was setting the clip in the bride's tastefully styled blonde hair, there was a discreet tap on the door. Kayla opened it. Her boss, Pascale Bonet, stood outside. She gave a nod to indicate it was time. As Pascale disappeared down the hotel corridor, Kayla returned to the suite to see that her bride was now ready.

'There you go. Perfect,' she said brightly. 'Now, let me fetch your father.'

Kayla opened the connecting door to the adjoining room and found a tall, grey-haired man straightening his cravat in the mirror. The father of the bride was usually as nervous as the bride. She went to his side and took over.

'There you go, Mr Andrews. I must say, you look rather dashing.' She smiled in a slightly flirtatious manner. That always helped.

'Thank you.' The gentleman preened ever so slightly.

'Your daughter's waiting for you to walk her down the aisle. She looks beautiful. Are you ready?'

He swallowed and nodded. Kayla directed him to the doorway and stood back. It was important for her not to intrude on this special moment between father and daughter. If the truth be told, she hated this moment, because it was something she had always dreamed of, but would never have.

Giving her clients those few moments of privacy also gave Kayla time to catch her breath and run through her mental checklist. Planning a large society wedding was a complex, if lucrative, business. Elite Weddings was normally brought on board at least a year before the big event. She and Pascale had organised this wedding in just six weeks. At first, Kayla had doubted they could do it, but it was amazing what could be done if you could throw money at every problem. Elite stood to make a substantial profit for their time.

She took a deep breath and stepped through the door into the bride's retreat. This penthouse suite in one of Sydney's best hotels had a glorious view of the harbour and plenty of room for a girl in a huge tulle cupcake wedding dress.

'Well, I think it's time,' she said. 'Mrs Andrews, if you'll come with me, one of our staff is waiting to escort you to your seat. And I'll be back in a moment to take our lovely bride to the ceremony.'

Kayla gave the mother of the bride plenty of time to get into the lift before she escorted the bride and her father in the same direction. As directed, and paid for, a hotel staffer was holding the main lift for the bride.

The dress fitted into the lift—just.

Once on the second floor, Kayla gave the bride a few moments to compose herself, before catching Pascale's eye. Pascale nodded. They were ready. The team had turned the large terrace overlooking the harbour into a wonderland of flowers and silk and fairy lights. The guests were seated on velvet chairs, and the arch of the Harbour Bridge would form a backdrop for the ceremony. Not even Pascale could manage to hang lights from that structure, but the ceremony was timed for sunset, so the bridge lighting would perform the way she wanted even without her influence. From the terrace, a lone violinist played the first bars of the tune guaranteed to bring a tear to the eyes of any bride. Beaming widely, Mr Andrews placed his daughter's hand firmly on his arm and stepped through the doors.

That was Kayla's cue to move on to the next phase of the operation: the post-wedding canapés and drinks followed by the wedding dinner. She turned away from the terrace and headed for the kitchen, taking a deep breath before stepping into the midst of chaos.

More than a dozen kitchen staff darted about, laden with pans and trays and all manner of cooking implements. On the massive stove tops, pots of sauces boiled away, releasing delicious aromas into the room. Huge ovens gave off waves of heat as the doors were opened and dishes added or removed. Waiting staff hovered by the door, trying to keep out of the way.

At the centre of the chaos, dressed in immaculate chef's whites, Lachlan Henderson was standing stock still. As always when he was in his kitchen, his handsome face was alive with energy and passion. When he snapped instructions at his staff, his voice was loud and decisive. He looked like he was about to explode, but Kayla knew him better than that.

'Chef?'

'Thank God you're here.' Always the drama queen, Lachie flung his arms in the air. 'We are on the brink of disaster.'

'Then I'll fix it.'

'This woman is wonderful,' Lachie declared to the world as he followed Kayla out of the kitchen.

Once they were in the hallway, Lachie glanced around to make sure they were alone, then pulled Kayla to him for a lingering kiss.

She gave herself up to it for a few seconds, then pulled away. 'We're supposed to be keeping this a secret,' she told him. 'Now, what's the disaster?'

'There's no disaster, I'm just keeping them on their toes. And besides, I wanted to kiss you.'

Kayla wasn't sure whether to laugh or blush. Lachie was a famous and fabulous chef, dynamic and sexy and fun—pretty much everything a girl could want. And he wanted Kayla. That made her feel good and she was beginning to think that this relationship, new though it was, might be exactly what she needed.

'Come back to my place tonight,' he whispered in her ear. 'We could get naked and drink Champagne to celebrate another of your triumphs.'

It was a very tempting idea. 'I shouldn't …'

'Come on. Let me pamper you. A bottle of the Dom somehow found its way to my fridge, and it's waiting just for you.'

Just as she was about to say yes, a door swung open and a kitchen hand appeared.

'Chef Henderson, you're needed. The sauce …'

'My sauce?' Lachie roared. 'Who has defiled my sauce?' He winked at Kayla as he followed the terrified kitchen hand back into his personal domain.

It was well after midnight when Kayla let herself into her flat. She was alone, having declined Lachie's offer because she was exhausted and just wanted a little peace and quiet. She'd call him tomorrow and arrange another night for the Dom. She dropped her bags at the entrance and kicked off her shoes. Her feet were killing her. She padded across the carpet to her small kitchen and reached into the cupboard for a shot glass. She had a bottle of eighteen-year-old single malt scotch in her bar, her reward on nights like this. One shot: that was all she allowed herself. But that one shot, and the ceremony surrounding it, was enough to unwind after a frantic day. She poured the shot into the glass and added water. Just a few drops; enough to awaken the aroma of the fine spirit. She started to carry it out onto her small balcony. Her view of the harbour was a mere glimpse, but it was enough because it was hers and hers alone.

Then she stopped.

The light on her answerphone was blinking. That was strange, she never used her landline for anything. She only had it because it had come as part of the package deal with her broadband and cable TV. Only a handful of people had that number. Actually, only two people had that number and Pascale never used it. Only one person ever called her on the landline. Kayla couldn't remember when the last call had been. A year? Two?

She didn't want to pick up the phone. She just wanted to go and sit on her balcony, relax and take a few minutes to herself. But that flashing light would still be there when she came back inside.

With a sigh, she walked over to the phone and hit a button.

'We need to talk. Please call me as soon as you can.'

Her sister was not one for long telephone calls. Or messages. Or long face-to-face conversations for that matter. At least not with Kayla. There had to be a very good reason for this call. Kayla glanced at her watch; it was too late to call now. Liz had always been an early-to-bed, early-to-rise sort of person. Waking her at this hour was not going to make whatever conversation they were about to have any easier.

She walked into the kitchen to pour her drink down the sink and headed for her bedroom.

The next call came at seven thirty, pulling Kayla out of a deep sleep. She was reaching for her mobile on the nightstand before she realised the ring tone wasn't right. Her landline was ringing. She dragged herself out of bed, but before she got to the phone the machine cut in. She heard her own voice and then a pause.

'It's me again. I really need to speak to you ...'

Kayla picked up the phone. 'Hello, Liz.'

There was a moment's silence before her sister answered. 'I guess I woke you.'

'Yes. I was working late last night. I didn't get to bed until the wee small hours.'

'Working?'

'Yes. Weddings happen on Saturdays. And they usually last until Sunday morning.' She sounded annoyed. She hadn't meant to, but she was tired and this was her sister. Those were the two things absolutely guaranteed to make her annoyed.

'Yes. Well, sorry. I guess.' Liz hesitated. 'I need you to come home.'

'I am home.'

'All right then, I need you to come to Willowbrook. We have things to talk about.'

'Can't we do that on the phone? Or on Skype? This is a busy time for me. Spring brides and all that. I can't get away.'

'Apollo is dead.'

The blunt words shocked Kayla. The news shouldn't be a surprise; the stallion must have been a million years old. He'd been at Willowbrook almost as long as she could remember. He'd been her father's horse, and so many of her memories of him also included Apollo. It was hard to think of them both gone.

'I'm sorry about Apollo, but why do you need me to come back there?'

'Because—'

Was Kayla imagining it, or did Liz's voice break?

'Is everything all right?' she asked.

'No. Not really. There's stuff we have to talk through. Decisions to make. When can you come?'

Kayla hesitated. The last thing she wanted was to go back to her childhood home. The last person she wanted to see was her sister. But something in Liz's voice disturbed her. It had to be more than just losing the stallion.

'I'll talk to Pascale—my boss—and see what I can do. I'll let you know.'

'It has to be soon.'

'I'll get there when I can.' Kayla hung up the phone before she could say anything she might later regret. She glanced at her watch and winced. There was no point going back to bed, she'd never sleep. She was far better off getting organised for a quick trip to Willowbrook. Liz would be back on the phone if she didn't—she had always been the impatient one.

CHAPTER
3

The sun has barely risen above the top of the hills when three people emerge from the stone house and start walking towards a cluster of outbuildings. The oldest girl skips ahead of her father, who is carrying her younger sister. She is dressed in jeans and riding boots and her hair is caught into a ponytail. She is ready to start her day. The younger girl is still wearing her pyjamas, and her hair is tousled from sleeping.

'What colour is he, Dad?'

'He's going to be a dark chestnut, Lizzie. Like his sire. With a small white star like his dam.'

The stables are not new, but they are well kept, the stalls clean and the laneways free of mess. The nearby yards are strong and in good order. The horses that are moving restlessly in the half-light are also well cared for. Generations of men and women have worked hard to build Willowbrook Stud. It is much loved.

'Slow down now, Lizzie,' Sam Lawson says. 'The foal is just a couple of hours old. His dam is nervous. You don't want to startle her.'

'I won't.' At twelve years of age it's hard to contain the excitement of such a momentous event, but Lizzie does. She's already good with horses. She has her father's skill and empathy for them.

Two faint lights illuminate the foaling boxes. Only one is inhabited and the father takes his daughters there. Lizzie is tall enough now to see over the stall door if she stands on tiptoes.

'Where is he, Dad? I can't see him.'

'Wait a minute, Lizzie. You will.'

Inside the box, the mare turns her head to stare at the intruders. Her ears flicker as she recognises the whispered voices. There is no threat here. She lowers her muzzle to nudge the dark shape at her feet. The foal lifts his head and senses the newcomers. He scrambles to rise on legs that are too long and too shaky and falls forward, almost onto his nose. His mother nickers her encouragement and gives him another gentle nudge. The colt somehow untangles his legs and has a second attempt. This time he makes it, despite a pronounced wobble in his knees. With his mother's gentle nudges to guide him, he finds his way to her side, where the scent of rich, creamy milk is all the encouragement he needs. He shoves his head under her belly and fastens his lips around a teat, drinking deeply.

'Look, Kayla.' The dad gently rouses his youngest daughter.

The little girl opens her eyes. Her face splits into a huge smile as she watches the tiny foal's tail wagging. She laughs, a light, gentle sound that causes the mare to flick her ears.

'Shh. We don't want to scare him,' Sam whispers.

'What's his name?' The five-year-old voice is soft, with a hint of a lisp.

'He hasn't got one yet. I told your sister she could name this foal. So, Lizzie, what is his name?'

Lizzie hasn't taken her eyes off the colt. She has been preparing for this moment ever since her father told her she could name their stud's most eagerly anticipated new arrival. All the Willowbrook horses have a connection to the sparkling night sky and are named after stars or planets. She has talked to her teachers and she has taken books out of the library. Now she has seen him, she knows who this foal is.

'Apollo,' she says confidently. 'He's a god. And it's also the name of the rocket that went to the moon.'

'Willowbrook Apollo.' Sam nods. 'That's a good name.'

'He's going to be a champion, Dad. I know he is.'

'I think you might be right.'

But at just a few hours old, the colt is not concerned about Lizzie's dreams for his future. His belly is full now. Carefully, he turns in a circle then starts to bend his legs. Halfway down, he loses control again and drops into the bed of straw. His mother nuzzles him again, but he is already falling asleep.

So is Kayla. Her father carries her back to the house while Lizzie stays behind. She climbs onto a stack of hay bales and settles herself where she can watch over the mare and foal.

CHAPTER
4

Liz didn't hurry her morning workouts. The horses needed her time, and Kayla would be late. Her little sister was always late for everything. It had driven Liz mad during those years when it was only the two of them. She always heaved a sigh of relief when Kayla headed back to boarding school or off to uni. No more waiting around, wasting time while Kayla got dressed or found her hairbrush or got off the phone. It was only after she was gone that Liz realised how big and quiet the house was without her. How lonely.

She had just finished lunging a horse in the covered round yard when she saw the flash of sunlight off a small red sports car coming up the drive. Leading the horse to the stables, she glanced at her watch. If that was Kayla, she was right on time. That was new. By the time Liz had hosed the horse and turned it back into the sand-covered yard for a roll, Kayla was walking from the house. If she hadn't been expecting her sister, Liz might not have recognised her.

Kayla looked like something out of one of those magazines Liz sometimes glanced at in the dentist's waiting room. Her younger sister had always been slim and a touch taller than Liz, but now she looked even taller. It must be her clothes. She was wearing a pair of black pants that hugged her like a second skin. Her shirt was made from some soft, silky material and her boots were purple. Unlike Liz's RM Williams riding boots, Kayla's boots had heels. Liz wasn't even sure she'd be able to walk in them. Not that she was ever likely to try. But the greatest change of all was in Kayla's face.

She was wearing make-up, her lipstick bright red. Her hair fell in gentle waves around her shoulders. When the sun hit it, it gleamed with a bright chestnut shine. Where had that come from? Kayla's hair used to be exactly the same shade of dark brown as Liz's. Kayla walked with an easy stride with her head held high. She looked well-off, confident and attractive. As their eyes met, Liz wondered what her sister was seeing. Where Kayla had curves, Liz was thin and muscular; almost masculine. Her face hadn't been touched by make-up in years. Her boots were workboots; her legs encased in faded and stained blue jeans. Liz was a worker, and that's exactly what she looked like. Where Kayla looked successful, Liz was worn down by years of hard work in all weather, and by worry.

When had they both changed so much? Liz tried to remember the last time she and her sister had been together. It couldn't have been a year ago, could it? Or was it longer?

'Four years and nothing has changed. The place looks the same.' Kayla's voice was like her face. Confident. There was no sign that she felt in any way awkward about this reunion.

'Has it really been that long?'

'The last time I was here was to sign the paperwork for selling that land on the other side of the creek. Is that why you wanted me to come back this time too?'

'Kind of. Let's go inside.'

Liz began to walk up the slope to the house. She turned towards the rear of the homestead. Kayla hesitated a second then followed her.

'You don't use the front door?'

'I'm usually wearing boots. I don't want to traipse mud and dung through the house. The back door is easiest.' Were they really talking about which door she used? Four years since Liz had last seen her sister. Four years since Kayla had set foot in the place where her family had lived for a hundred and fifty years, and she was talking about doors. Was that what an expensive education and living in the city had done to her?

Once they were inside the kitchen, Liz opened the fridge and reached for the jug of water. 'It's not that fancy bottled stuff,' she said a touch defensively, 'but it's cold and it's wet.'

'It'll be fine.' Kayla wandered around the room, her fingers touching the cupboards, the top of the table where they had eaten as kids. Then she vanished through the door into the hallway. For a moment Liz felt her hackles rise, then she shrugged. Technically Kayla owned half of Willowbrook. She had a right to go anywhere she wanted.

There was no sound from the front rooms as Liz poured two glasses of water and waited.

'Do you ever go into the front of the house?' Kayla asked as she returned to the kitchen.

'Not much,' Liz admitted. 'I use the office. And here.' Liz was reluctant to take Kayla through to her office. The room was tidy and well organised. She wasn't ashamed of it. But it was pretty obvious that she spent most of her time in there. She didn't really want her sister to comment on that, or to notice the sofa where she slept most nights.

'Where do you relax? You know, watch TV. Or read a book?'

Liz started to prickle at the implied criticism in Kayla's voice. 'I don't get much time to relax. Running this place on my own takes up all my time.'

'You could get help, you know. A jackaroo or a stable hand.'

'No. I can't. There isn't the money for a jackaroo. That's what I need to talk to you about.' She went into the office and returned with a folder of papers. She'd read and re-read these papers every day since the bank manager's visit. And every day she'd come to the same conclusion. She dropped into a chair and put the folder on the table in front of her.

Kayla ceased her restless moving and sat down opposite. 'So tell me what's going on.'

'I can't do this any more,' Liz said. The words didn't come easily. 'I can't keep running this place. The drought was hard, and I had to increase the loan to buy feed. There's not enough money to meet all the payments. And now that we've lost Apollo there'll be no stud fees and less agistment income.'

'Then get a new stallion.'

'I can't afford a new stallion.'

'What about one of the colts you've bred here? One of Apollo's sons? Continue the bloodline.'

'For the last few years, I've sold the best of them. I had to. There isn't a horse on the place that can replace Apollo.' Liz took a deep breath and said the hardest words of all. 'I need your help.'

'What do you expect me to do?'

Liz pushed the folder towards her. 'It's all in here. You're the smart one. The one who went to university. This place paid for your fancy business degree. Now I need you to put that degree to good use and come up with a way to save our father's legacy.'

Kayla looked at the folder. 'It's not that easy.'

'Do you think running this place all alone is easy?' Liz heard the tightness in her voice.

'You don't have to. You could always sell it.'

'Never!'

'You might not have that option.' Kayla pulled the folder towards her. 'I'll take this home with me and have a look. I'll come back next week.'

Liz felt a weight lift from her shoulders. 'All right. Do you want to stay for a while? I could make us some lunch. Nothing fancy. Maybe a sandwich but—'

'No. It'll take me four hours to get home. And I have to work tomorrow. It would be best if I headed back now.'

'If that's what you want.'

And Kayla was gone again. Just like that. It wasn't until Liz was standing in the drive, watching the last of the dust settle behind the departing car, that she realised two things.

Neither sister had asked the other how she was, far less anything about her life. And they had not touched—not so much as a handshake.

Liz could remember a time when she and her sister were insepa-rable. When hugging each other was as natural as breathing. But that was a very long time ago; a lot had changed since then, and the blame lay squarely on Liz's shoulders. She had broad shoulders. She could handle it.

She could handle anything except losing Willowbrook.

CHAPTER
5

Kayla dropped into her chair and deposited her take-away coffee—a latte with an extra shot—on the desk in front of her. She sighed deeply. After the unsettling trip to Willowbrook, it was good to be back at Elite Weddings. From the framed wedding photos on the pastel walls to the flowers at the reception desk and the worktable covered with sample books of fabrics and stationery, this was her world. She felt at home here; strong and in control.

'So, how did it go?' Pascale asked from her desk on the other side of the office.

'I don't think I was there long enough for it to "go" any way.'

Pascale raised one carefully groomed eyebrow. 'That doesn't sound good.'

Kayla shrugged and removed the lid from her latte.

'Hey! This is me, remember. Talk to me.'

So she did.

It had always been like this, since the two of them had met on Kayla's first day at uni. She'd been feeling totally lost and out of place, a lonely orphan girl with no self-confidence and a reluctant student in a business course she didn't want to take. A country hick in the big city. Pascale Bonet had walked into the room like she owned it. It wasn't just that she was tall and blonde and probably could have been a model. And it wasn't just her fabulous clothes. It was the way she held herself. Pascale had confidence dripping from every pore, and if some of the people in the room assumed she was a dumb blonde bimbo, she was happy to let them—right up to the moment she floored them with a brilliant essay, or aced her exams.

Pascale was everything that Kayla wanted to be, and somehow the two had become friends. While Kayla put her nose to the grindstone of accounting practices and legal courses, Pascale spent her final year at uni specialising in event management and hospitality and left with an honours degree to start a high-end wedding planning business with funding and contacts from her wealthy family. Three years later, the ink barely dry on her own honours degree, Kayla had joined her. Although Pascale was the owner of Elite Weddings, Kayla had never felt like her employee. They were partners, even if it wasn't official, with complementary skills that had helped make the business a success. Kayla understood the laws regarding the hiring of staff. Pascale knew how to design a sales brochure. And they were friends. Pascale was probably the only person in the world Kayla trusted completely.

'I spent last night going through the papers,' Kayla finished. 'My sister's right. The place can't survive without a new source of income.'

'I thought you owned half of it?'

'Technically, I do. But … I don't have anything to do with it.'

'You don't get any income from it?'

'No. Liz used to lecture me all the time that Willowbrook had paid for my education. Boarding school after our parents were killed and then uni. I was supposed to run the business side of things, but that was never going to work for me. When I graduated, I vowed I would never take another cent. And I haven't. Not that there's been much to take.' Kayla tapped the folder lying on the desk in front of her. 'The place is going bust.'

'Why doesn't she just sell it?'

Kayla shook her head. 'She'll never sell it. The bank will have to drag her out in handcuffs if they want to repossess that place. Come to think of it, that's probably exactly what they will do.'

Pascale frowned slightly. 'How come you've never talked about this with me before?'

Kayla brushed her hair back, at the same time lightly touching the place where a small white scar was hidden by make-up and hair. The scar that was a constant reminder of the car crash that killed her parents. A crash she had survived but could not remember.

'It's my old life. I didn't really think it would—should—have anything to do with me any more.'

'But she's your sister. And that's your family home.'

Kayla shrugged again, but deep down she didn't feel as nonchalant as she tried to appear.

'What's the name of the property?'

'Willowbrook.'

Pascale's fingers flashed across her keyboard. She said nothing for a few moments then let out a low whistle. 'Really? This is where you grew up?'

Mystified, Kayla went over to see what Pascale had found. Her screen showed a beautiful image of the homestead, with a horse standing proudly in front of it. Apollo. The photograph had been taken years ago, when the horse was in his prime. Although the stallion dominated the picture, Kayla guessed it was the homestead that had captured Pascale's attention. Gentle early morning light and the faintest hint of fog disguised the faded paint and stained stone, while highlighting the refined lines of the building and its sense of history. The homestead looked beautiful, almost ethereal.

'How did you find that?' Kayla asked.

'I assume it's your sister's website. It's all about breeding horses. But seriously. You own this?'

'Mostly the bank does. What's left is my sister's. I walked away a long time ago. I wouldn't have gone back this time, but she insisted.'

'So what are you going to do now?'

'I'll take another look at the papers, in case there's something I missed. Then I guess next week I'll drive up and give her the bad news.'

'I'd like to come with you.'

'Really?' Kayla blinked in surprise. 'Look, I appreciate the support, but I can do this alone.'

'I know you can. I'm just not sure if …' Pascale's voice dropped off and two small creases appeared between her perfectly shaped eyebrows. Kayla knew that sign. Pascale's razor-sharp mind was kicking into high gear.

'If you want to come, I'd appreciate the company on the drive. We won't be staying long.'

Kayla settled herself behind her desk. Before checking her emails she googled her way to the site Pascale had found. While the homestead had interested Pascale, Kayla couldn't take her eyes off the horse. He really was a beautiful creature. Had been. Apollo. The horse Liz had named and their father's pride and joy. Although she hadn't seen Apollo for years, Kayla felt a deep sadness at his loss. He was probably the last horse her father had trained, and now he was gone.

Kayla closed the website with a firm click and opened her emails. She had weddings to organise. Across the office, Pascale was staring at her computer. But she had raised her right hand and her fingers, with those long and perfectly manicured nails, were twitching, as if she were writing on a mental whiteboard. Pascale's mind was in overdrive, working on whatever idea had materialised in that light-bulb moment. She'd tell Kayla when she came up with something concrete. And if not … well, it couldn't do any harm to take Pascale with her on her next trip to the Hunter Valley. If she had to break bad news to Liz, it might be nice to have some support.

She wondered who Liz went to for support. Because even some-one as tough and unfeeling as her sister must need a shoulder to cry on sometimes.

CHAPTER
6

The mare was obviously distressed. She was standing with one front leg held off the ground. Her head was low and her sides were dark with sweat. The mare had the quality and elegance of all the Willowbrook horses, and she looked pregnant. She barely twitched her ears as Mitch rode along the other side of the fence on his big black gelding. He stopped a few metres away and swung out of the saddle then flicked his reins around a fence post and stroked the gelding's nose. All the while he studied the mare. He could see that her leg was caught in the wire fence, three strands cutting into flesh that was badly swollen. He wasn't sure how long she'd been there, but quite a while judging from the look of her. That probably wasn't surprising. This was the far corner of his land, and also the far corner of Willowbrook land. Liz probably hadn't been up this way in a day or two; maybe longer.

Mitch opened the saddlebag in which he always carried fencing pliers, a basic first aid kit and some light rope. Then he slipped through the fence.

'Hello, girl. You've got yourself in a bit of trouble there, haven't you?'

The mare slowly raised her head and looked at him with dull eyes. She must have been here for a day or two without water. It was a good thing he'd found her.

Mitch paused to give her a chance to get used to him. If he startled her, she might panic and pull back. If she did, that fencing wire would cut through skin and flesh pretty easily. He was here to help her, not make things worse.

'Okay, old girl, let's see what we can do about all this.' He was by her side now, and began stroking her neck. The mare didn't flinch as he twisted the rope into a halter and slipped it over her head. 'I've got you now. Let's see if we can get that leg free.'

He ran his hand gently but firmly down the mare's leg. She twitched and he could see the wound. There were flies buzzing around the dried blood. He wasn't going to be able to free her by simply lifting her leg through the wire.

He pulled the pliers from his back pocket and carefully cut the first wire. The taut wire snapped back, but he was ready for it, catching it and twisting it away from the horse. She flinched, but stayed still as he cut the remaining wires. At last she was free.

'Come on, old girl, put that foot down. Let's see how badly you're hurt.'

He tried to lead her forward. The mare hesitated and then tentatively put her injured leg on the ground. She took one cautious step. Then another. After a few more steps she was moving with just the smallest limp.

'That's good, old girl. Now let's do something about those cuts.'

The wounds weren't as deep as he'd feared and wouldn't need stitching. The flies were a concern, but there was an answer for that, and it was found in every stockman's first aid kit.

The mare jumped a little as Mitch directed the purple spray onto her wound. That was actually a good sign—it meant she was much more alert now. She needed water, but he was pretty sure that once she'd had a few minutes to rest, she would head off in the direction of the creek. He'd come this way tomorrow to check on her. Most likely she would have moved on to join her fellow brood mares.

Although the mare was a dark chestnut, the colour of the anti-septic spray was clearly visible. If Liz saw her mare in the next twenty-four hours, she'd know someone had given her horse first aid. It wouldn't take her long to figure out it was him. A part of him wished she would. She might come by to say thanks, because that was the sort of person Liz was.

Who was he kidding? She wouldn't come by to say thanks. Liz would be furious that he'd been on Willowbrook land. The creek and the fence that separated her land from his might as well be gaping chasms.

He still hadn't found a way to bridge that gap, and he was no longer certain he ever would.

He gave the mare a final pat and turned away. It was the work of just a few minutes to repair the wire he'd cut, then he slipped back to his side of the fence and returned his things to the saddlebag. He mounted the gelding and headed home, wishing that his and Liz's wounds could be healed with a simple bit of purple spray.

CHAPTER

7

'Come on, Kayla. Come with me!' Lizzie's voice is pleading, but Kayla shakes her head.

'Dad says I'm not allowed to go riding without him.'

'He's not here. He'll never know.'

'Mum's here.'

'She's working in the office. She won't see us if you're quiet. Come on.'

Kayla puts down her book and follows her sister out of the room. Lizzie is the adventurous one and Kayla is the one who follows.

The two girls creep carefully down the stairs and into the kitchen. The back door creaks ever so slightly as they open it but a second later they are running across the lawn to the stables.

Several of the stalls are occupied by yearlings being groomed and prepared for sale. They're mostly colts. The fillies will remain for a bit longer. So will Apollo. He is destined for great things, Lizzie stops by his stall for a moment and the colt immediately puts his head over the door. He's Lizzie's favourite, and knows that she's likely to be carrying a treat for him. Not today though. After kissing the end of his nose, Lizzie moves on.

A grey pony is waiting in the last stall. Lizzie goes into the tack room and emerges with a bridle. She slips into the grey's stall and reappears in a few seconds, leading the animal.

'Lizzie, I don't think we should do this,' Kayla says. 'Dad says I'm too small to ride on my own.'

'You're not on your own—I'm with you. Come on. Don't be a coward. Look, I'll help you with Ginger just as soon as I've done Tasha.'

Kayla nods. She always goes along with her sister's plans.

As soon as the grey is saddled, Lizzie collects a smaller chestnut pony from the next stall and in a trice Ginger is ready for his outing. Side by side, the sisters lead their ponies out of the stables and through the gate. Lizzie holds Ginger's head while her sister mounts, then effortlessly swings onto her mount.

'Let's go.'

She kicks Tasha into a brisk trot. Ginger follows on behind, and the two ponies break into a canter as they start to climb the hill. Kayla grabs the front of her saddle with one hand. She's only cantered once before. Ginger is a fast pony, and she's a little bit scared.

By the time they reach the top of the hill, both ponies are sweating. The girls pull up beside a tall tree, white flowers dotted amid its dark green leaves. Nearby, a wrought-iron fence surrounds a small collection of old headstones. From here they can see the whole of Willowbrook Station. They can see the whole world!

'Our family has lived here for more than a hundred years,' Lizzie says. 'See those graves? Those are all our family. And someday you and I will run Willowbrook together. We'll breed the best horses ever. Dad says they're starting to talk about exporting Australian Stock Horses to other parts of the world. Maybe one day we'll export horses. You and I can travel with them to all sorts of exciting places.'

'But we'll come home again, won't we?' Kayla's voice trembles.

'Of course we will. The Lawsons have always lived here and they always will. Come on, let's go to the creek.'

The girls turn their ponies down the slope towards the line of tall river gums that marks the watercourse. There's a crossing just shallow enough for their ponies. The girls laugh as their mounts slap at the water with their front hooves, sending droplets high into the air to glint in the sunlight like diamonds. On the far side of the creek the bank is steep, but both ponies bound easily to the top.

The girls kick the ponies into a trot and within a minute or two they are at the old wooden church.

'This is where Mum and Dad got married,' Kayla says, although she is well aware that Lizzie has heard the story as often as she has. 'Mum looks so pretty in all the photographs. Her dress is so beautiful.'

Lizzie agrees, although she really isn't interested in dresses. She runs an eye over the weatherboard building, noting how the paint is starting to fade. The church is closed now. It hasn't been used since her parents' wedding, which is a shame. Lizzie knows that her great-great-grandfather built this church, as he did all of Willowbrook. She doesn't like to think of it standing empty and unloved. She doesn't like to see any part of Willowbrook being neglected.

As they turn away, Lizzie notices movement on the other side of the creek. There's a car coming down the long gravel driveway that leads from the main road to the homestead.

'That's Dad's car. We'd better get back.'

Kayla is about to turn Ginger for home when the pony suddenly flings his head up and shies violently. Kayla falls. As she does, movement in the long grass catches Lizzie's eye. A huge brown snake slithers away. Lizzie flings herself off her pony and races to her sister. Both know how dangerous snakes are.

'There was a snake! Are you all right?'

Sniffing, Kayla shakes her head and starts to cry.

'Did it bite you?'

Kayla shakes her head again. 'My backside hurts.'

A sore backside isn't too bad. Lizzie checks Ginger, running her hands along the pony's legs, feeling for a bite. Ginger calmly nuzzles her hair.

Slowly, Kayla gets to her feet, rubbing her sore bottom. 'Is Ginger all right?'

'He's fine.'

Kayla's sobs subside. Her backside doesn't really hurt that much. And Lizzie is here. As long as she is with Lizzie, everything will be all right. Dad will probably be annoyed that they took the ponies out and her mum will worry when she sees the dirt on Kayla's jeans, but Lizzie will fix everything, because Lizzie always does.

CHAPTER

8

Liz didn't normally ride across the creek, although there was nothing preventing her. It wasn't trespassing if she had permission from the owner—but that was the problem. She didn't want to be reminded that she now needed permission to ride on land that had belonged to her family for more than one hundred and fifty years, until Lizzie let it go. She'd sold it to the one person in the world who should have understood what it meant. The one person who should have helped her to keep it, rather than take it away from her. Four years later, she felt the same anger and shame as strongly as she had the day she'd signed away a part of her heritage.

But young horses had to be trained and a stock horse that wouldn't cross a creek was no good to anyone. The best place to cross the creek just happened to be on what was now the boundary between her land and the land that was no longer hers. If that wasn't painful enough, Kayla was also coming today, with what Liz knew in her heart would not be good news. It seemed a reasonable time to head to the crossing. Nothing could make today worse than it was already destined to be.

'Come on. Let's see what you're made of.'

She turned the colt's head towards the creek. The old road was still visible. In times past, carriages had taken this route from the homestead to the crossing. The church was on the other side of the creek, and her Irish forebears had made the trip often. Even after the road bridge was built, her great-grandfather had taken his family to church across his own land. But as the nearby town of Scone had grown, services had moved. The priest stopped coming to Willowbrook and the family had, in Irish terms, lapsed.

The church was no longer a church. The wooden cross had been removed from the corrugated-iron roof, although the round stained glass window remained. The faded cream paint had been replaced by a crisp white, and outbuildings and yards had sprung up around it. The old weatherboard building looked lived in and loved, but it no longer belonged to the Lawson family. Liz rode this path only when she had to.

When they arrived at the creek, Liz nudged the young horse with her knees, expecting him to refuse or at least hesitate. To her surprise, he walked in without breaking stride, wading through the knee-deep water and out the other side.

'Good boy.' Liz bent over to vigorously rub his neck.

The horse suddenly lifted his head, staring up the bank. His body quivered as another horse appeared. It was a brown gelding with all the hallmarks of Willowbrook bloodlines somewhere in his breeding. Liz, however, could only see the man on its back. He sat the horse as if the two were one, his back straight, his body lean and fit. His face was hidden in the shadow of his broad-brimmed hat, but she didn't need to see his face. She knew only too well who this was: the man who owned this lost piece of Willowbrook.

It seemed the day could get worse after all.

He saw her and raised an arm in greeting. He began to turn his horse's head in her direction, but Liz didn't wait. She turned her mount towards the creek. This time the horse hesitated, and she forcefully pushed him forward as a feeling of near panic swept over her. He gave a small leap into the water, plunging through and out the other side. She urged him up the creek bank and into a canter, telling herself she was training her colt, not running away from a man and her memories.

Liz was still disturbed when she arrived at the homestead. She dismounted and gave the colt a really good rub down before putting him into the round yard. The horse trotted easily in a circle, tossing his head, his movements strong and smooth. He had the look of his sire, Apollo, when he was a young horse. That seemed such a long time ago. When she and the man from the other side of the creek were both young and no shadows lay between them. When the future seemed full of promise.

She heard the sound of a car engine. Now she was about to find out if the future still held any promise. If Liz had ever wanted to run and hide, this was the moment. But delaying the inevitable wasn't going to help.

She heard two car doors slam.

The woman who got out of the passenger seat was tall and blonde and beautiful, as out of place at a horse stud as Liz would have been in a nightclub. Her figure-hugging dress belonged in a fashion show, not in the bush, and her heels were even worse. Liz felt her hackles rising. What had Kayla been thinking, bringing a stranger to Willowbrook when they had serious decisions to make about the future?

The woman looked around. She paused as she took in the old fountain in front of the house, which hadn't worked in a decade.

What use was it to spend time repairing a fountain when there were horses to exercise and fences to fix? The woman's inspection continued, examining the front of the house, looking at the view across the valley, until finally her gaze came to rest on Liz.

Liz felt suddenly exposed, as if this well-groomed and beautiful woman could see every line on her face, every smear of dirt on her faded jeans and work shirt. More than that, she felt as if the woman could see the desperation in her heart and the terrible fear that she was about to lose everything she loved.

As always, feeling cornered brought out the fighter in her. As she had so many times in the past, Liz turned her anger on her sister.

'Kayla? I thought we were going to have a proper family discussion. Just the two of us.'

'Liz, this is Pascale Bonet—my friend and boss and business partner. Pascale, my sister, Liz.'

'It's good to meet you.'

When Liz reluctantly took the offered hand, she couldn't help but notice how coarse her skin looked next to Pascale's. How chipped and broken her nails were. Her hands looked like the hands of a workman. Pascale had the hands of a lady, and judging by the rings she wore, a rich lady.

'I know you weren't expecting me.' Pascale's voice was deep and rich and cultured. 'And I certainly don't wish to intrude. But I was interested to see the property where Kayla grew up. I hope you don't mind.'

'Come in.' Liz led the way to the back of the house, not pausing to see if either of her guests followed.

Once inside, she busied herself making tea without bothering to ask if they wanted any. She needed a few moments to get herself together. As she dropped tea bags into mugs, she was conscious of Kayla showing her companion through the disused rooms on the ground floor of the house. It had been months, maybe years, since Liz had used some of those rooms, and she hadn't cleaned them more than once or twice in the same period. She shuddered at the thought of Pascale's judgemental eyes on the faded curtains and unpolished wood and she silently cursed Kayla for bringing the woman here. Then she heard footsteps on the grand staircase leading to the upper floor. Those rooms, she knew, were in even worse condition. She should feel ashamed. She would, if she didn't prefer to feel angry at the intrusion.

When the two of them reappeared, Liz just wanted to get this visit over and done with.

'Kayla—shall we get down to it?'

'I'll excuse myself,' Pascale said. 'I'd like to wander around the outside, if that's all right.'

'Don't go to the stables or open any gates.' Liz didn't care if that sounded rude.

'Of course not. I only want to look around the outside of the homestead.'

The door had barely closed behind her when Liz rounded on her sister. 'You're trying to sell the place to her? Without even asking me? Well, you can stop wasting your time and hers. I am not selling.'

'Don't be stupid.' Kayla pulled out a chair, dropped her bag on the table and took out a familiar folder. 'Pascale wouldn't want this place. But selling it may be your only option.'

With the words finally spoken, Liz felt as if the ground had dropped out from beneath her. She sat opposite Kayla. 'Okay. Tell me everything.'

Everything was as bad as she had expected.

'There must be some cuts you can make,' Kayla said as they stared at the spreadsheet she had prepared. 'This column shows expenses that can't be reduced—loan payments, rates and so forth. What about the stud costs—vets, feed bills? Competition costs. Are there significant cuts you can make there?'

'I've already made all the cuts I can. The horses have to be fed. We've had three years of bad drought and hay has to be brought up from South Australia. It's expensive. Prices have more than doubled. And I have to get out there and show the horses. Those competitions are my marketing tool. If I'm not out there, I'm going to have trouble selling the young horses.'

'Can you reduce the number of horses?'

'I've only got ten mares left. That's really not enough as it is. And a couple of them are getting on. I don't know how many more seasons I'll get out of them.'

'Can you get more income from agistment?'

'Not without a stallion to attract breeding mares.'

'Then you need another stallion.'

'Do you think I don't know that?' Liz didn't even try to keep the frustration out of her voice. 'But I can't afford to buy one.'

'Is there one of Apollo's colts you can replace him with?'

'Maybe.' Liz sighed as anger gave way to resignation. 'I have one promising colt, but he's just a three-year-old. It'll be a couple of years before he can make a big enough name for himself to attract many outside mares.'

'Then you're going to have to sell land. Try to clear some of the loan and refinance it so payments are lower.'

'No. I can't. If I sell any more land, this place will be too small. It will never ever be successful again.'

'Then it's very likely the bank will take the place. You'll be left with nothing.'

Liz struggled to take the next breath. And the one after that. It wasn't as if this was a surprise; she'd figured it out herself weeks ago, even before the bank manager's visit. But somewhere deep inside she had clung to a tiny hope that her sister, with her expensive degree and her years of working in the city, might come up with a solution.

'I'm sorry, Liz. I don't know what else to suggest.'

'I do,' Pascale said as she walked back into the room.

Liz felt her hackles rise. 'This is a family matter. It's nothing to do with you.'

'You're right, of course. It isn't. I'll just go back to Sydney and when the bank takes this place away from you, you'll always wonder if my plan could have saved it.'

CHAPTER

9

'I'm sorry?' Liz turned to Pascale.

Kayla knew that tone and resisted the urge to slide her chair away from the table to duck Liz's anger. During the past few days, she'd watched Pascale staring at her computer and making notes. While she was sure Pascale was here to offer her moral support if she needed it, she was equally sure that her boss had other things on her mind. And she knew her sister well enough to know how she was likely to react. Kayla decided her best course was to say nothing and let her boss do what she did best.

'Please forgive me,' Pascale said as she sat on a spare chair and placed an iPad on the table. 'As you know, I own Elite Weddings. It's a high-end wedding planning business. Kayla and I work with top designers and caterers and photographers to provide very specific and exclusive services for people who want the very best and are wealthy enough to pay for it.'

Pascale paused to give Liz a chance to comment. When none was forthcoming, she continued as if there was no tension in the air.

'There's a growing demand for rural weddings. Not only from my Sydney clients, but also from overseas clients looking for a unique wedding experience. This area has most of the services we'd need. There are wineries and plenty of accommodation nearby. There's an airfield for private planes. This homestead is perfect. It needs a lot of work, of course, but the basics are all there.'

'This isn't a party venue. It's a working horse stud.'

'But it's not working any more, is it?'

Pascale's words seemed to echo around the room. Kayla waited for Liz to explode. But she didn't. Instead, her sister dropped her eyes and her shoulders slumped. That, more than any of the accounts sheets and bank statements, told Kayla just how bad things were. Part of her wanted to tell Pascale to stop, to leave Liz alone. But deep inside, she knew Pascale was right, and Liz needed to know that too.

The silence lengthened uncomfortably.

Pascale got to her feet. 'Let me show you what I mean.'

Without a word, Liz stood up. Kayla joined them as Pascale led them through the kitchen door into the main part of the house. She stopped in the entrance hall, a broad space that featured a lovely curved staircase.

'The downstairs will be the focus of the public area. The front veranda and this lovely entrance will provide all-weather areas for arrivals and drinks and canapés. This staircase to the upper floor is beautiful. Fabulous photo opportunity. This room …' Pascale swung a door open.

'Is my office,' Liz snapped.

'Which can be moved upstairs,' Pascale continued smoothly, 'leaving this as the groom's retreat. The room on the other side of the entrance will make a lovely bride's retreat. We'll set up one room upstairs as the bride's dressing room for those who want to make their grand entrance down the stairs. Those who can't manage that in heels will use the downstairs room.'

'Do I still get a room somewhere?'

Ignoring Liz, Pascale carried on. 'This ballroom was an unexpected bonus.'

Kayla watched as the door swung open to what had been the family room when she was growing up. She'd never thought of it as a ballroom, but it could easily be that. It was large enough, with a high, embossed ceiling and arched windows at the far end. The floor was covered with a thin layer of dust but Kayla could remember a time when the timbers glowed with a rich golden sheen.

Pascale continued to outline her vision as she led the way upstairs. Kayla hadn't climbed these stairs for years. Nor, it seemed, had Liz. As she focussed on the rooms that were at once familiar and yet so distant, Kayla began to see the neglect. A picture hanging at an angle. A pile of papers, the edges curling with age, sitting on the top of a bookshelf. The dull timber of the bookcases, which their mother had kept so beautifully polished. Dust had invaded every corner.

'Liz, do you ever come up here any more?'

'What do you mean? Of course I do.' As she'd followed Pascale through the house, Liz's back had become straighter and her face harder.

'When? You eat, work and sleep downstairs. Do you use the utility room shower as well?'

'I know it's a bit dusty, but after a full day's work outside I have to do office work as well. I don't have time to come up here and fuss. And I certainly don't have the money to pay someone else to.'

'That's no real problem.' Pascale stepped in. 'Now, I had imagined this to be the upstairs bride's room.'

She pushed the door open and Kayla's breath caught in her throat. This largest of the upstairs rooms had been their parents' bedroom. For a few moments she saw it through her memories, the lace curtains and hand-sewn quilt on the bed where she had taken shelter on stormy nights. She thought she caught a whiff of her mother's perfume and the pain came rushing back. But it lasted only a second as she saw the reality: a few pieces of bare furniture and dust motes dancing in the sunlight that streamed through a gap in the curtains, now grey with age. No visible trace remained of the people who had once lived and laughed and loved here.

Without a word, Liz spun on her heel and marched down the stairs. Kayla stood with Pascale and heard the back door open and then slam shut.

'Where has she gone?' Pascale asked.

'Where she always goes when she's upset: to the stables. She'll come back when she cools off.'

'I'm sorry. I didn't think she'd react that way. I thought she'd be pleased at the chance of saving the place.'

Kayla waved her concerns away. 'It's a shock to her, that's all. Come to think of it, it's a shock to me too. But I have a better idea of what you're talking about. I don't know if Liz has ever even been to a wedding.'

'How can someone in her thirties never have been to a wedding? There must have been school friends. Or relatives.'

'We don't have any close relatives. Of course there were friends. But after our parents died, Liz distanced herself ... from everyone. Including me.' Kayla heard the edge in her voice. Even after all these years. That was surprising, but it was also a place she didn't want to go right now. 'So, I get the picture. Are you able to talk details yet? Exactly what are you planning and how is it going to be financed?'

'Based on what you've told me, I'll finance the refurb. We will do it in phases. The first phase will allow us to run a couple of smaller events to test the water. Then we'll use the profit from that to do the next phase.'

'How is that going to help Liz's situation?'

'I'll take over the interest on the loan for a specified time, to be paid back from event profits. Once we're square with that, Liz will start taking a share of profits.'

Kayla was well acquainted with Pascale's business practices and knew those profits would be considerable. Although scrupulously honest, Pascale was a tough negotiator. Liz would do all right out of the deal. It might just be enough to save Willowbrook, and none of this would interfere with the horse stud. Liz could keep working to resurrect that.

'Hopefully Liz will see sense when we've had a chance to talk.'

'You own half the place. Don't you get a say?'

That was a question Kayla didn't want to answer. Technically, she did have a say, but Liz had considered Willowbrook hers for so long, Kayla didn't feel comfortable asserting her right of ownership. Liz wasn't going to give up control of the homestead easily. Not to Kayla and not even to save it.

CHAPTER
10

The night sky above Willowbrook is inky velvet; the stars bright embers that seem almost close enough to touch. Liz and Kayla are standing with their mother on the stone steps that sweep down from the front of the house to the curved driveway. In the grassy centre of the driveway is a fountain where three stone horses dance around a central pillar. In the stillness of the night, they can hear the splashing. Water is a precious commodity, and the fountain is seldom turned on, but this is a special occasion.

A blanket has been spread on the grass, ready for a late-night picnic. Liz is surprised to see candles. According to her father, fire is a dangerous thing in the bush, or around horses. She is about to say something when she sees that the little candles are all inside glass jars. That looks safe enough. Of course Kath Lawson would do the right thing.

Kayla walks carefully down the stairs, her eyes fixed on the plate she is carrying. There's a cake on the plate, chocolate, with the words 'Happy Birthday' written on the top in icing. The words are a bit wobbly, as if the hand that wrote them was young and not familiar with the art of writing—with icing or with anything else. It's the first cake Kayla has ever made. Her mother helped, but Kayla had carefully followed the handwritten instructions in Kath's recipe book. She's so very proud of the results.

Lizzie's hands are full too. She's carrying four plates with a pile of cutlery on top of them. Their mother is carrying the esky, into which she has placed Champagne for the adults and lemonade for the girls.

The three of them surround the blanket and place their burdens on the ground. There are presents already on the blanket, each gaily wrapped.

'Now, who wants to get your father?'

'Me!'

'Of course, Lizzie. You go and get your dad, while Kayla and I make sure everything is ready here.'

In a trice Lizzie is gone, running into the house to the office where Sam has been tactfully 'working' this evening.

'Mum, let's put the cake here, with candles around it.' Kayla starts laying out the picnic. 'Then you and Dad can sit here, and Lizzie and I will sit there. The presents should be here, next to the cake.'

'That's a lovely idea.'

Kayla beams. She loves hearing praise from her mother. When she grows up, she wants to be like Kath, who is beautiful and clever and makes wonderful cakes.

Lizzie and their father appear at the top of the stairs. Sam has a big smile on his face as he approaches the fountain.

'What a lovely surprise,' he says. 'Thank you, my three beautiful girls.'

He ruffles the hair on both his daughters' heads, then embraces his wife in a kiss that takes a little longer than most.

'Ugh!' Lizzie is old enough to be embarrassed by the show of affection. She looks at the stables, her mind bouncing back, as it always does, to her pony Tasha and where the two of them will venture together the next morning.

Kayla doesn't turn away. She thinks it's terribly romantic to see her parents kissing in the candlelight. Under the stars. In her books, the handsome prince always kisses the princess before they go off to live happily ever after. Kayla believes in happy ever after. One day her prince will appear and she will have a happy ever after too.

But first, there are presents to be unwrapped.

Sam reaches for the biggest box.

'That's mine,' says Kayla in a high-pitched, excited voice. 'I picked it myself and even wrapped it myself.'

Sam smiles and carefully removes the colourful bow before turning his attention to the rather inexpert gift wrapping. The object inside is encased in tissue. He folds that back to reveal the shape of a horse. Made of china and painted a reddish brown, it's the sort of thing a small girl would choose for herself. The horse's mane and tail are blowing in an imaginary wind as it stands with its front feet raised in a half-rear.

'It's beautiful, Kayla,' Sam says as he holds it high to examine it in the dim light. 'It even looks a bit like Apollo. See, he has the same white star on his face.'

Kayla giggles with delight. 'That's why I chose him.'

'I think I'll put him in my office.' Sam carefully rewraps the gift in its protective tissue. 'That way I will see it every day as I work.'

Kayla is glowing with pleasure.

'Open mine now, Dad,' Lizzie urges.

Her father is already reaching for the next present. This one has been wrapped by a steadier hand, but has no bow or protective tissue. He opens the wrapping to reveal a framed photograph and holds it up to catch the best light.

'That's me and Apollo,' he says. 'The day I first rode him.'

'I took the photo with Mum's camera,' Lizzie says, her voice dripping with pride. 'You didn't see me do it.'

'No. I didn't. It's a wonderful photograph. Thank you. Thank you both.' He enfolds his daughters in a hug. 'These can sit side by side in my office. And every time I look at them, I will think of the two of you. Even after you've both grown up and gone away.'

'I'll never go away from Willowbrook,' Lizzie whispers in his ear, and his arm tightens around her just a little bit more.

CHAPTER

11

Liz waited until it was almost dark before she returned to the homestead. She was too tired to be angry any more. She just wanted Kayla and that dreadful blonde woman with the ridiculous heels to be gone. She didn't want to think about money. Or Willowbrook. And she most especially didn't want to think about weddings. All she wanted was a shower and perhaps a beer. Then she had to face a task she had put off for far too long.

Approaching the house, she was annoyed to see there were lights in the windows and Kayla's car in the driveway. Her sister and that woman were still here. Damn them! Her long absence from the house should have given them the answer to their proposal, but obviously neither of them could take a hint. Her feet faltered. She really didn't want to go back into the house and that was wrong. A person shouldn't feel reluctant to enter their own home. Now she was going to have to face Kayla and her associate and say no to their faces.

There was no way she would allow Willowbrook to be turned into a wedding venue. She would not have women prancing around in absurd dresses and high heels. She did not want anything to do with anyone's wedding. Her life was lonely enough without frilly white frocks and mushy music bringing back the memories she had fought so hard to suppress. She would find a solution that did not re-awaken the past or cheapen her heritage.

She'd spent a long time leaning on a yard rail watching the colt she'd been riding earlier in the day, and had come up with a plan of her own. She didn't like the plan—but it might work. Willowbrook Deimos was the image of his sire. The three-year-old was just starting his career as a saddlehorse, but as he'd shown at the creek crossing, he had all the potential in the world. He might make a champion, and if he did she had her new stallion and her new source of income. But that wasn't going to happen overnight. It takes at least a couple of years to make a champion and to build the kind of reputation a stud horse needs. Until then, she had bills to pay and a loan to service.

So, much as she hated it, she'd sell some of her brood mares. They would bring a good price and those too closely related to Deimos couldn't be bred to him anyway. Reducing her breeding stock would reduce her costs. It would also give her time and space to take in horses on agistment. Her other idea was to offer her services as a trainer. She was good, very good. People would pay her to train their horses and maybe she could even train the riders too.

It wasn't what she wanted to do, but it might just keep her afloat for long enough to bring Deimos on. And if he proved as great as Apollo, she'd be all right. Willowbrook would be all right.

It wasn't a good plan. It wasn't guaranteed to succeed. But it was the only plan she had. And it was certainly a better idea than letting some stranger who wore too much make-up invade her life and change the home she loved.

Liz closed the last gate and leaned against it. In the soft gold of twilight, Willowbrook homestead looked lovely, with its wide verandas and elegant railings. The stone glowed, and even the fountain seemed to shine. She could almost imagine the water sparkling in the sun's last rays. But that fountain hadn't contained water for years now. The stone was stained. The upper floors of the house were always dark, the curtains drawn. Tilting her head, Liz suddenly saw Willowbrook through the eyes of a stranger. It was shabby, neglected and run down. The horses and the stables had been the sole focus of her attention for so long, the house was falling into decay. She was failing in her promise to her father. But the house could be revived without much money. All it needed was time. She would find that time. She had to.

If only she wasn't so deathly tired.

The first thing she had to do was send Kayla and that Pascale woman back to Sydney.

Filled with new determination, Liz marched up to the house.

When she entered the kitchen, Kayla was there alone. She was sitting at the kitchen table, a book open in front of her.

'Do you remember this?'

Liz knew the old schoolbook in an instant. And the handwriting. 'That's Mum's old recipe book.'

'Yes. The recipe for her chocolate cake is in here. That was the best chocolate cake ever. Remember that year I cooked it for Dad's birthday? It wasn't very good, but he ate it anyway.'

'Where has your friend gone?' Liz was in no mood for reminiscences. That was a world of pain she could well do without.

'I ran her into Scone. She's waiting there for me to pick her up. But I thought first you and I needed to talk.'

'There's nothing to talk about. I've thought about what she had to say and I've decided no. That's not the path I want to take.'

'I know it's not. But you really don't have any option. I've seen your bank statements, remember. It's not your fault, but Willowbrook is in real trouble. This is a way out.'

'It's not my way out. I can sell some of the breeding stock, take in horses on agistment and do outside training. And I have one of Apollo's colts out there who is the spitting image of his sire. He can be as good as Apollo. I only need to manage for another year or two, then there'll be stud fees coming in and I can start to rebuild.'

'You won't last a couple of years,' Kayla said. 'The bank will foreclose.'

'Then help me. You have that posh job. Surely you can lend me some money?'

'I don't have the sort of money you need to save this place.'

'Then I'll just have to work harder.'

'For God's sake, Liz.' Kayla stood up. 'How many hours a day do you work now? And still this place is falling apart around your ears. It's too much for one person. You've run Willowbrook single handed for fifteen years. You've done everything Dad could have asked and more. When are you going to let go?'

'Never!'

'Then I can't help you. If you change your mind, let me know.' Kayla picked up the recipe book and walked out.

A few seconds later, Liz heard the sound of a car engine moving away.

Silence fell on the house.

She took a cold beer from the fridge, walked through to her office and turned on her computer. As she waited for the aging machine to boot, she drank her beer while staring at a photograph on the desk in front of her. It was an old photograph of a man and a horse, printed from a negative in the pre-digital days. The colour had faded over the years, but in Liz's mind she saw the photograph as it had been when she placed it in that frame the day before her father's birthday. She looked up to the ornament pushed to the back of the top shelf of a tall bookcase. She could just make out the brown horse's head with its flowing mane. She had no idea why she'd kept that childish toy all these years. It was time she cleared out this office and threw away the old rubbish.

When the computer was ready, Liz went straight to the Willow-brook Stud website. She sat, staring at the image of the horse on her home page. At last she turned to the window. In the darkness, she couldn't see the place where she had buried Apollo. Nor could she see the dark shape of the hill with the graveyard at the summit. She didn't need to see it. She would never forget it was there.

She opened the website for editing, moving the small white arrow to the image of Apollo. After a second's hesitation, she hit the delete button.

CHAPTER

12

Ten bridesmaids. Who in their right mind has ten bridesmaids? Kayla kept her smile firmly locked in place as she watched the gaggle in the room. Ten maids, the bride, the mother of the bride and a slightly vague, grey-haired woman referred to as Auntie Anne by everyone. Add to that two hair stylists and three make-up artists and a harassed-looking waitress holding a tray of Champagne. The tension was almost physical.

'Where are our canapés?'

Kayla focussed on the bridesmaid standing in front of her. She searched her mind. Oh yes, one of the bride's sisters. For the life of her, Kayla couldn't remember the girl's name. The four sisters were all blonde, all beautiful and all spoiled by their wealthy parents.

'They will be here in a moment,' Kayla hastened to assure the girl. 'In fact, if you'll excuse me, I'll go and check right now.'

With relief, she slipped out of the door. The first thing she saw was a room service waitress pushing a food trolley.

'There you go.' Kayla held the door open for the woman to enter the suite. 'Good luck.' A chorus of squeals greeted the arrival and Kayla guessed it would be safe for her to take a few minutes to rest her ringing ears.

She leaned against the wall and closed her eyes. There were a million things she should be checking and double-checking, but she needed to stop and take a few deep breaths. Since her visit to Willowbrook three weeks ago, Kayla's mind hadn't been as on her job as it usually was. Not that she was making mistakes—she was too good for that—but neither was she enjoying the work. And that was wrong. She loved her job and deep down felt a nagging resentment with Liz for putting Willowbrook and its problems into her head. She didn't care about Willowbrook any more and she was not her sister's keeper.

Why, then, did she lie awake at night, remembering? She shouldn't be losing sleep remembering the good times. Nor should she be losing sleep trying to remember the day that changed everything— the one day she could not remember at all. She touched her hair to make sure the scar on her face was properly hidden.

'Hey, Kayla. You all right, my sweet?'

Kayla opened her eyes and pushed herself off the wall. She smiled at the tall man in front of her, one camera hanging from his neck, a second in his hands.

'Hi, Ken. I'm fine thanks. Just a bit tired. This lot have been hard work.'

'Thanks for the warning. Are they ready for me yet?'

'Pretty much. I hope you're ready for them. They are a bit much.'

'Not for me. Watch them swoon when they see my eyelashes.'

Ken Leighton was a brilliant photographer, much in demand not just for weddings, but also for high-end fashion shoots for glossy magazines. He'd dealt with his fair share of bridezillas and fashion divas. His rather spectacular good looks helped. As did the fact that he was gay. Women were generally putty in his hands.

'Are you busy?' Kayla asked casually as she prepared to re-enter the lion's den.

'As always. At the moment I'm location hunting for a fashion project. I've got to go up the bush, and you know how much I hate being more than five minutes from a good latte.'

Kayla chuckled as she pushed the door to the suite open, but any response she might have made was lost in the excited squeals that greeted Ken's appearance.

Ken's words came back to Kayla as she sat at her desk three days later. She re-read the email in front of her. A couple wanting a small rustic wedding somewhere in the Hunter Valley. This was the second such request they'd had since her visit to her sister. Either would have been perfect to launch Willowbrook as a wedding venue. And then there was Ken's fashion shoot. It seemed the gods were conspiring against her. Everywhere she looked there were opportunities that would be perfect for Willowbrook, opportunities that would make a significant profit. She could do this, but her damn sister was too stubborn to bend.

Well, that wasn't Kayla's problem any more, was it? She had long ago given up any interest in Willowbrook. If the place was sold, it would pay off all the loans. Then Liz would have to sort out her own life, the way Kayla had sorted out hers.

'Kayla?'

She looked up. 'Sorry, Pascale. My mind was wandering. What did you say?'

'Well, my original question had to do with the harp player you were booking for the Bailey-Clark wedding. But forget that. Instead, you could tell me what's bothering you. You're not here today.'

'Sorry. It's just there's another enquiry here for a rustic rural wedding. I'm starting to believe you're right. Willowbrook could be saved if my sister wasn't so stupid.'

'Liz is far from stupid and you know it. What's really going on?'

'I don't know. It seems a waste to just let it all go without trying to save it.'

'Kayla. You really don't want to let the old place go, do you?'

'Liz is the one who won't let go. I don't really care.'

'No?'

Kayla scowled and looked at her screen. Maybe she did care. A bit. When the phone rang, she was glad of the distraction.

'Kayla, I've got the proofs for the Chambers wedding. I was passing anyway so thought I'd drop them off.'

'Sure, Ken. I'm here whenever.'

'See you soon.'

One of the reasons Ken was so popular for society weddings was that he still did physical proof sheets. Better than proofs, really: he produced a folder of the best images from each wedding, and Kayla and Pascale would work with their clients to select the favourites for a glossy printed book. In a digital photographic world, that book was special. And it didn't come cheap.

'That's great work as always,' Kayla told him after she'd looked at the photos. Then she changed the subject. 'Have you found a location for your rural shoot yet?'

'Not yet.'

Before she could talk herself out of it, she reached for her laptop and tapped an address into her browser. 'Would this work?' While the page was loading, she turned the laptop towards Ken.

He frowned as he looked at the screen. 'My sweet, that's a horse. I don't photograph horses. Well, not unless there's a cowboy involved.' He waggled his eyebrows and grinned.

'Look behind it.'

'That's a tree.'

'What?'

She spun her machine back. He was right. The picture on the Willowbrook website was a bay mare standing in front of a tree. Of course! Apollo was dead. Liz had taken the stallion's image off her website. For the first time, Kayla felt a contraction in her gut. Willowbrook was changing and the threat to her heritage suddenly became very real.

'Just give me a second.'

Her fingers flew over the keyboard. People said that once you posted something on the internet, it never went away. Surely the original image would be somewhere?

'Try these.' Pascale handed Ken her tablet.

Kayla resisted the urge to look over Ken's shoulder as he slid image after image across the screen. Instead she watched his face for reaction.

'This isn't bad,' he said at last. 'Where is it?'

'Scone.'

'And it's available?'

'Yes.' Kayla spoke without hesitation.

'Okay. I'd need to go up and have a look. We are doing both video and stills in this shoot. But if it's as good as it looks—'

'Oh, it is.'

'Then I'll suggest it to my client.'

'You haven't asked how much.'

'I'm not too worried about that. As long as it's a reasonably standard rate then we won't have a problem. My client is prepared to pay for the very best. After all, they chose me!' Ken winked at her.

Kayla didn't know whether to be pleased or scared at the prospect of taking Ken to Willowbrook. If he liked the location, she still had to convince Liz to go along with the idea, and she wasn't entirely sure she could do that.

CHAPTER

13

Kids of all ages are leaping off the dusty school bus and pouring through the gates into the schoolyard. Most of them are in groups of three or four, but a few of the older kids are in couples, with linked hands. The noise is quite deafening, as it always is at the start of the school day. Just inside the gates, two girls are standing to one side. The little one is staring about with tear-filled eyes.

'Come on, Kayla. It's fine. And you have to go to school.'

The little girl shakes her head and stares with desperate longing at the road down which her mother's car has vanished after dropping them off a moment ago.

'It's been weeks since school started. You should be used to it by now.'

Kayla bites her lip and shakes her head. 'Never gonna get used to it.'

Lizzie sighs. It isn't a big school. About three hundred kids from the town and neighbouring properties. There's nothing scary about it. At least, not when you've been going there for a few years and have friends, like she does. Right now, she'd rather be with her friends than babysitting her tearful little sister.

'Come on, Kayla. I promised Mum I'd keep an eye on you. Do you want me to walk with you to your classroom?'

'I don't wanna go to my classroom.'

'You have to. Come on.'

Lizzie picks up the school bag lying at her sister's feet and takes her hand. She leads the reluctant girl across the playground to the first-grade classroom. Two other figures are heading for the same door. The boy is quite tall, with wavy brown hair and dark eyes. He moves with a kind of easy assurance, despite the fact that his uniform pants are just a little bit too short for him. His shirt isn't properly tucked in either. He has the air of someone who has thrown on his uniform and made a last-minute dash to the bus. He's holding the hand of a girl who is almost a reflection of Kayla, from the uniform to the tears in her eyes.

The boy and Lizzie draw near to each other and stop. She hasn't seen him before. He must be new.

'Hi.'

'Hi.'

The two of them stare at each other for what seems like a very long time.

'I'm Mitch.'

'I'm Lizzie.'

Kayla tugs on her sister's hand.

'Oh, yeah. This is Kayla, my little sister.'

'And this is my little sister, Jen. We're new here, and she's a bit scared of starting school.'

'My sister's scared too.'

Mitch hunkers down in front of Kayla. 'You're not scared, are you? You don't look scared. You look like the sort of brave girl who could help Jen settle in to class.'

Kayla's eyes grow even wider but there are no tears now.

'This is Jen. I think the two of you could become really good friends.'

Kayla looks at the girl standing in front of her. Jen has blue eyes and sandy brown hair. She's carrying a plastic lunchbox with a pretty pink pony on it.

'I have a real pony, you know. His name is Ginger.'

'A real pony? Wow. I want a pony so much. Can I come and see your pony?'

'I guess so.'

Mitch and Lizzie exchange relieved looks and a smile. They're both thinking the same thing: a disastrous scene has been avoided thanks to the universal appeal of ponies.

The first-grade teacher emerges from her classroom.

'Hello, girls.' Her voice is cheerful and friendly. 'The bell is about to go and it's time you were in class. Why don't you come with me? And you two—' she waggles a finger at Lizzie and Mitch, '—should be on your way to class. Go on now.'

Lizzie and Mitch walk obediently away.

'What class are you in?' he asks.

'Miss Simmons.'

'Me too.'

He smiles at Lizzie. She smiles back, suddenly aware that this boy is different from the others in her class. They're just ... boys. They're stupid. But Mitch isn't. He's kind. And good looking too. Especially when he smiles at her like that. She wishes she'd taken a bit longer brushing her hair that morning before coming to school.

CHAPTER
14

'You grew up here? Seriously?' Ken had been staring out the window since they left the city behind, growing ever more wide-eyed as the landscape grew browner and less civilised. He'd almost fainted when he saw the huge trucks powering past the collection of buildings that she had assured him really was all the shopping available in the tiny town of Aberdeen.

'I did.' Kayla took her eyes off the road long enough to look around. A coal train was passing on the railway line that ran parallel to the road. It had been passing for what seemed like a long time. Coal trains had become longer over the years she'd been away. But the mountains were the same blue they had always been. The paddocks were grazed by the same horses and cattle. Crops grew as they always had. She would probably remember what they were if she tried hard enough.

'So you were a country kid, I never knew that. Can you do all those country things?'

'What do you mean, "country things"?'

'You know. Ride horses and drive tractors. Rope steers. Did you wear an Akubra and RM Williams boots?'

Kayla smiled and flexed her toes inside her Salvatore Ferragamo ankle boots. 'I can. Horses and tractors. Not the steers though. My sister does that. And yes to the hat and boots. Although not so much these days.'

Ken shook his handsome and carefully groomed head. 'I don't suppose you've got any brothers out here, the sort with cowboy boots and tight jeans?'

She laughed. 'No, just my sister.'

'Is she anything like you?'

'No. Not really.'

She felt, rather than saw, Ken's sideward glance. He was good at picking up undercurrents and moods; it was one of the things that made him such a great photographer. She would really prefer he didn't do it to her.

'Kayla, you did tell her what this shoot would involve, didn't you? She's okay with what we are going to do? Assuming the location is as good as it looks.'

Damn his empathy. 'Not exactly.'

'Do go on.'

'She doesn't know anything about the shoot. She doesn't actually know you're coming. I told her I was coming up to talk about … family things.'

'Why am I starting to get a bad feeling about this? Do you and your sister have issues?'

That was putting it mildly, but she wasn't about to explain. Ken was a nice guy and she enjoyed working with him. They were friends—more or less. But not close enough for that sort of discussion.

They drove in silence for a couple of minutes, then Kayla let the car slow. She turned off the highway onto a smaller road.

'It's only a couple of kilometres now. When we get there, don't come on too strong. Let me talk to Liz before you start shooting. Okay?'

'If that's what it takes.'

Kayla could only hope that was all it was going to take.

When they pulled up in front of the homestead, Ken gave a whistle. 'Oh, yes! This could be just what I'm looking for.'

Kayla glanced at the house. It was the middle of the day, Liz wouldn't be there.

'Wait here,' Kayla told the photographer. 'Liz will be in the stables. Let me talk to her for a couple of minutes and break the idea gently.'

'All right.'

'And don't go poking your nose around just yet. My sister can be a bit … prickly.'

'Got it.'

As soon as she approached the stables, Kayla heard the hoof beats. She turned in the direction of the flat yard where generations of Lawsons had trained a succession of champions and paused in the shade of a tree to watch. Liz was working a dark chestnut colt. The horse was the spitting image of the one that had graced the Willowbrook website until a few days ago. He must be Apollo's son. Although Kayla had moved to the city, she was still a Lawson and the Lawsons knew good horseflesh when they saw it. She watched carefully, taking note of the colt's well-muscled frame. His legs were clean and his stride straight. His head was well shaped and intelligent. He had the potential to be something special.

And Liz was the right person to develop that potential.

Watching her sister ride was like watching their father again. Liz had a connection with her horses that Kayla had never mastered—and always envied. It was as if one mind controlled two bodies. She did it with just the subtlest movement of hand and heel. When the colt made a mistake as Liz turned him into a figure of eight, she didn't punish him. She simply and smoothly put him back into the turn and asked him to do it again. This time he did, although his tail flicked in protest. Liz made him do it again and this time he perfectly answered her. Liz knew what she was doing. She knew when to relax and give, and when to hold firm.

At least, she did when she was riding a horse. Kayla hoped she would be the same in the conversation they were about to have.

As Liz brought the horse to a walk and let him relax, Kayla stepped out of the shadows. Liz saw her at once, but she didn't come over. She walked the horse once around the enclosure, allowing him to stretch his neck and cool a little before turning him towards the gate. The horses always came first with Liz.

'I wasn't expecting you.'

'Hi. Have you got a minute to listen?'

Liz didn't bother to dismount. She looked at her sister with barely disguised impatience. 'I guess so. But I don't want to leave this guy standing around for too long.'

Kayla took a deep breath and all her carefully rehearsed arguments went out the window. 'I know you didn't like the idea of using this place for weddings. Wait—' She held up a hand as Liz opened her mouth to speak. 'I still think you're wrong on that, but I have someone here with me, a photographer who's looking for a location for a high-fashion shoot. Stills and video.'

'If I don't want weddings here, what the hell makes you think I'd want film people?'

'It's not film as such, it's a fashion shoot. And you want them because they pay, Liz. They pay well. You asked me to try to help you. You wanted me to come up with ideas. Well, here's one.'

'There is no way—' Whatever Liz had been going to say was interrupted by the appearance of Ken, climbing onto the yard railings.

'Kayla, my sweet. It's perfect.' He grasped the top rail and vaulted into the exercise ring with the ease of someone who spent long hours at the gym.

The colt shied violently away, leaping sideways as if to flee. Liz gathered up the reins and held him tightly, speaking to him in gentle tones, although her face was like thunder.

Kayla wished the ground would open up and swallow Ken.

Liz forced the colt to turn and face the approaching photographer, who seemed to have realised his mistake and was now moving slowly and quietly.

'Sorry, my darlings,' he whispered.

Liz looked at Ken then raised an eyebrow. 'Is he your boyfriend?'

'No, Liz. He has a boyfriend of his own. And so do I, if you actually want to know.' If Kayla had hoped to get any sort of reaction from Liz, she was disappointed. Her sister wasn't to be distracted that easily.

'I think you should probably get him out of the yards before he hurts himself.'

'It's perfect for my shoot,' Ken said in an exaggerated whisper that was equally as startling as his shouting. 'I can see it all. Faded glory to frame high-end fashion. The sleek and the shabby. The juxtaposition of the beautiful and the ugly.'

The expression on Liz's face darkened. She rounded on her sister. 'So that's what you think of this place, is it? That's how you want to help. By showing my failure to the world?'

'No, Liz. That's—'

'No. I won't have it. Get him the hell off my land.'

She jerked the colt's head around in a short, savage motion and urged him forward. The colt leaped away and bounded across the yard to stop at the far gate. Liz leaned over and swung it open, kicked the colt into a canter, and left the gate swinging open behind her.

Kayla had never seen Liz leave a gate open before. Not once. Even as kids.

Stunned by her sister's reaction, Kayla walked across the yard to shut and latch the gate.

'Is everything okay?' Ken caught up with her.

'Idiot,' she told him. 'I told you to stay put.'

'I couldn't help myself. I was intrigued. This place is perfect. Do you really own it?'

'The bank owns most of it.'

'Well, I have to tell you, if the rest of this place is as good as the bits I've seen, my client will want to do both stills and video here. It's their big campaign. They'll pay for the right place. A lot. And I haven't given up hope of a cowboy with fancy boots, although I might have to hire one and bring him up for the shoot.'

Watching the rapidly vanishing colt and his rider, Kayla shook her head. She wasn't sure who she was more annoyed with: Ken for making a difficult situation even worse or Liz for overreacting. Liz had asked for help but then, when it was offered, she not only refused but she was rude about it as well. But that was Liz all over. She never listened to anyone, especially not her sister. She'd ridden rough-shod over Kayla's wishes ever since their parents died.

Well, not any more. Strengthened by her growing anger, Kayla came to a decision. Technically she owned half of Willowbrook and had the right to make decisions about it. And she had the right to bring Ken or anyone else she wanted onto the property. To hell with Liz and her possessiveness and her need to control everything. She'd had things all her own way for too long.

'Come on, Ken.' She slapped her hand on the rail hard enough to sting. 'I'll show you around. Tell me the sort of things you're looking for.'

CHAPTER
15

The colt stumbled and almost fell to his knees. Liz cursed herself and as he recovered, she brought him to a trot and finally to a walk. He was blowing heavily, his neck streaked with sweat and foam. Liz loosened the reins and let him lower his head as he walked.

She knew better than this. She never rode a young horse when she was angry. That was how horses got ruined, and her future was dependent on this colt.

He halted gratefully at her command and she dismounted.

'Sorry, Deimos.' She rubbed behind his ear, that sweet spot that horses love. He turned his head and pushed her gently. She smiled at that, but it was a sad smile. 'Come on, let's cool down. Both of us.'

She loosened the saddle girth a little and started to walk, the horse at her side. Gradually his breathing started to slow, along with Liz's.

'Faded glory. Shabby. How dare he!' The horse flicked his ears as she muttered softly. 'Ugly. This place isn't ugly.' To her eyes Willowbrook was beautiful. In all honesty, though, she wasn't sure she could argue against the photographer's description.

She glanced over her shoulder to the lone tree growing on the top of the hill overlooking the homestead. She was too far away to see the two crosses in its shadow. Normally, when she was troubled, that's where she went. It made her feel close to her parents. To her father, especially. But right now if she climbed that hill she would be doing it to admit defeat and beg forgiveness. She wasn't ready to do that yet.

She kept walking, slowly heading towards the tree line and the creek beyond. By the time she reached it, Deimos would be cool enough to take a drink. Then she'd go back to the stables. Hopefully Kayla and that nosy photographer would be gone.

But as she approached the creek the glint of sun off metal caught her eye. The old work ute she used around the property was parked near the crossing. She could see two people moving about: Kayla and that photographer. As she drew closer, Liz realised that the man was taking photographs of the creek. Why would he be doing that? Hadn't she already made her feelings clear? If not, she would make sure he was left in no doubt this time. She was not going to allow a bunch of city strangers to take over Willowbrook ... not even for a day.

Kayla must have heard her approaching. She said a few words to the photographer and left him at the edge of the creek as she hurried to intercept Liz.

'I thought you would have figured out that I don't want to get involved in this photo business,' Liz said.

'I've decided to save you from your own stupidity.'

'What's that supposed to mean?'

'Liz, if they do decide to do the shoot here, it'll take about three days.'

'That's three days of disruption I could do without.'

'But it's three days of location fees you can't do without.'

'What's that? A couple of hundred dollars. That's not going to solve my problems.'

'They'll pay a lot more than that. Maybe three thousand or a bit more. You could argue for a wrangler's fee too if they want to use the horses.'

Liz blinked. That was a lot more than she had expected.

'If I went to your office now, how many unpaid bills would I find? Bills that could be paid with that money?'

Her sister was right. It wasn't the answer to her problems, but it would keep a few of the wolves from the door.

'Come on, Liz. It's only three days. You'll be here all the time to keep an eye on everything. I'll come up too if you want me to.'

'All right. I still think it's a bad idea, but I do need the money.'

'Great. Come and talk to Ken. He can tell you what he's planning.'

The photographer had his camera glued to his eye as they approached, and he was aiming his zoom lens across the creek. A horse and rider were silhouetted against the sky on top of the creek bank.

'Who's that over there on the horse?' Ken asked without lowering the camera.

Liz didn't have to look. There was only one person it could be.

'It that Mitch?' Kayla asked. 'Hey! Mitch!' Kayla waved wildly and the horseman turned his mount towards the creek. Without a moment's hesitation, the horse stepped into the water and calmly crossed.

'Mitch. It is so good to see you!'

'Kayla. It's been a while.' Mitch swung down from his horse and enveloped Kayla in a bear hug. He held her for several seconds before releasing her.

'Hello, Liz.'

'Mitch.'

'That settles it. I have definitely changed my mind!' Ken said as he hurried over.

'What? You don't want to use Willowbrook?' Kayla asked.

'Of course I do. It's perfect. But I've changed my mind about bringing up a couple of male models. I'm going to use him instead.' He waved a hand at Mitch, indicating his height, his lean, well-muscled body, his worn work clothes and the hat that now dangled from his right hand. 'You are just perfect, darling!'

He wasn't perfect, Liz thought. His face was lined from hard work under the harsh Australian sun. Like hers, his hands were rough. His hair had always had a mind of its own, sticking out at strange angles despite being damp with sweat and flattened by his hat. No. He was far from perfect. He might have been once, when he was younger—when they were both younger—but not any more. He had been responsible for too much pain and heartbreak. They both had … and her parents had died because of it.

Ken was still studying Mitch. He snapped a couple of photos and then looked at the images in the camera's view screen.

'Yes. Perfect.'

Mitch frowned. 'Liz? Kayla? What's this all about?'

'You have been discovered, you gorgeous man,' Ken enthused. 'A couple of months from now, every woman in this country will be in love with you. And half the men too.' He winked broadly.

That was more than Liz could take. She turned her attention to Deimos, who had been moving restlessly since Mitch and his horse had crossed the creek. She flung the reins over his head and mounted. As she slipped into the saddle, the colt squealed and rose in a half-rear. Liz tightened her legs around his ribs and pushed him back onto all fours before turning him towards home. As she forced the colt on, she heard Ken's even more excited voice.

'Oh, yes! That horse and this man. This shoot is going to be awesome!'

CHAPTER
16

The Tamworth Show is in full swing. The site is alive with colour and movement and noise. In sideshow alley, teenagers are eating Dagwood Dogs, the tomato sauce dripping from the hot battered sausages onto their fingers. They're holding hands as they scare themselves silly on gravity-defying rides and stealing kisses in the darkness. In the exhibition halls, everything from embroidery to woodwork and cooking is on display and the competitors are viewing the judges' decisions with a mixture of glee, disappointment and annoyance. But the heart of any agricultural show is the ring, where horses and cattle take centre stage. And in this place, the horse is king.

Judging of the junior riding events is almost over. Competition is fierce. After all, every little girl dreams of owning a pony. Every young boy wants to grow up to be a stockman or a jockey. This is a stepping stone to those dreams. Kayla is sitting still and straight on Ginger's back. She has been awake since before the sun came up, brushing the pony's long tail and shining coat. This year, she has done all the preparation herself, twisting the neat plaits along his neck, painting his hooves black. And all her hard work is about to be rewarded. This morning, Ginger won his pony hack class. Now he's in the running for champion pony hack.

When the judges call her forward, she straightens her back just a little more. In the crowd, her mum and dad and sister are watching. Mitch is here too. She has to do well.

She closes her legs firmly on Ginger's sides and sends him trotting in a figure eight. She has listened carefully to the judge's instructions, and now follows those instructions to the letter. Ginger is the perfect pony. He behaves beautifully and, a few minutes later, the purple Champion Pony ribbon is placed around his neck.

Kayla's heart is almost exploding with pride. She can't keep the huge smile from her face. But then, no one expects her to. Little girls are allowed to be proud of their beautiful ponies. She leads the other competitors in the victory lap of the horse ring. She hears her name, and Ginger's name too, announced over the speakers. It's a big ring, and it takes a long time to get to the gate, but that doesn't matter. People are clapping and a couple of times she hears a school friend shouting her name. It's nice to win. Everyone loves you when you win.

She slows Ginger to a walk as she nears the gate, her eyes scanning the crowd there. She sees her mother, waving and smiling. The steward opens the gate. She rides Ginger through then jumps off. She wraps her arms around the pony's neck and hugs him, her heart full of love for her very best friend. A moment later Kath is there, smiling and hugging her.

'You did so well, Kayla. That's wonderful. I'm so proud of you.'

'Thanks, Mum. Ginger was so good, wasn't he?'

'Yes, he was, darling. You were both very, very good.'

There are tears in her mother's eyes. But her youngest daughter is used to that. Mum always cries when her daughters do well at shows. Kayla looks around for the one person she really wanted to impress.

'Dad's at the other ring,' Kath says. 'The working hunter classes have started. He went to watch Liz. Come on, let's take Ginger back to the truck then we can go and watch too.'

It wasn't her father Kayla was looking for, but she can't tell her mother that. She hides her disappointment, but follows Kath to their truck. Her father has taught her that the horse's welfare must come first. Ginger's work is finished for the day, so she settles him in with a hay net and kisses him on the nose.

Her friend Jen appears, running.

'You won!' Jen cries. Ginger flings up his head in alarm as Jen grabs Kayla in a hug. 'I knew you could do it.'

Kayla allows herself a moment to enjoy the praise, then detaches herself from the hug to settle Ginger. Jen is her very, very best friend, but she knows nothing about horses, and she's not interested in them any more. She much prefers playing with clothes and dolls. Kayla likes clothes and dolls too, but if she had to choose, her pony would win.

'Let's go and find your father.' Kath leads them to the ringside where Sam is leaning on the top of the fence, watching the event. Mitch is standing beside him, holding a bucket with brushes and hoof black and a cleaning cloth.

Her dad takes his eyes off the ring and grabs her, swinging her high in the air and planting a kiss on her cheek. 'Well done, sweetie. I'm so proud of you.'

'Thanks, Dad.' She wriggles a bit and he puts her down. She loves that her dad is proud of her. But she wishes he would stop doing things like that, at least in front of people. It makes her look like a child. And she isn't. She is nearly nine years old.

Mitch drags his eyes away from the activity in the ring for a moment. 'Well done, Kayla.' He smiles and ruffles her hair.

Kayla feels her face starting to colour. She hates that she blushes so easily. She hates that Mitch ruffles her hair, too, but she loves it every time he does. She doesn't say anything, and when she finally looks up he has turned away and is looking at the competitor in the ring. Of course it's Lizzie. She's no longer riding her grey pony, she's graduated to one of the Willowbrook horses. The gelding is almost too big for her, but that doesn't matter to Lizzie, who has inherited their father's touch. And she has courage. She guides the animal through a perfect clear round.

Beside Kayla, her parents and Mitch break into applause.

Lizzie comes trotting over to the fence. 'I've made the jump-off.'

'Well done, Lizzie. Now walk him around while you wait. Don't let him cool down.'

'I know, Dad. I've got it.'

'Go, Lizzie!' A broad smile stretches across Mitch's face. Lizzie returns it.

When Lizzie rides her next round, Kayla isn't looking at the ring. Under her long lashes, she is surreptitiously watching Mitch. She sees the emotions on his face as Lizzie completes another clear round. There is admiration in his eyes as her sister collects her winner's ribbon. During her victory lap, she slows to wave at Mitch. He waves back.

Jen tugs at Kayla's hand. 'Come on. Let's go and get some fairy floss.'

Kayla doesn't want to go. Much as she loves her friend, she'd rather stay here. But then she looks up at Mitch. His eyes are fixed on Lizzie and the look on his face is one that Kayla never sees when he looks at her.

She goes in search of fairy floss with his sister.

CHAPTER
17

Why on earth had she let Kayla talk her into this?

Liz stroked Deimos's nose, speaking to him calmly as, all around them, chaos reigned. At least, it seemed like chaos to Liz. Since early this morning, her beloved Willowbrook had been overrun by strangers. A convoy of vans had deposited more people and equipment than she had ever imagined would be needed to take a few photos. Marquees had suddenly appeared to hold the racks of clothing. A team of hairdressers had set up shop in her outbuildings, helping themselves to both her power and her water. Three very tall, very thin girls were being fussed over by make-up artists and people whose jobs Liz could not even guess at. Ken was darting about with his camera, followed by two assistants draped with chairs and computers and other assorted paraphernalia. In the middle of all the chaos, the sister she barely recognised stood as a voice of calm reason.

Liz had insisted that Kayla be here for the shoot. She had decided that would be almost adequate punishment for daring to suggest it in the first place. But she hadn't been prepared for what she was seeing: Kayla was totally in her element. When the invaders had arrived, Kayla, dressed in jeans and brown boots that were certainly never meant to be worn while riding a horse, had looked more like a model than the tall, thin girls. She moved with assurance, and it was clear right from the start that she was the one people looked to for leadership.

As she approached, Liz suddenly felt like the lesser sister.

'We're going to do the outside shots first,' Kayla said. 'We'll do some around the stables and sheds. Then we'll move down by the creek crossing.'

'You're not taking all this down there?' Liz's voice dripped with disgust as she waved a hand to indicate the equipment and the marquees and the people.

'No,' Kayla said in the voice of a patient adult soothing a child. 'Just some of it.'

Ken joined them. 'Kayla, sweetie, I am going to need power over there, in that grimy corner near the muck heap. It's so delightfully awful. I love it.'

'Of course it's awful,' Liz snapped. 'It's a muck heap. What do you expect? Roses?'

'No. No.' Ken waved a hand. 'Roses would be all wrong. My vision here is for beauty in the midst of ugliness. The clothes are the only things that are beautiful. No roses. No. No.'

Liz wanted to hit him.

'There are extension cables and power boards in the van,' Kayla said. 'Liz, is there still power to the tack room?'

She nodded, not trusting herself to speak.

'There you go, Ken. Come on. I'll show you.' Kayla flashed Liz a look as she led the photographer away. 'We probably won't need any of the horses for a while. Come on over and watch the shoot if you like. You might find it interesting.'

Liz was tempted to decline. But after a few minutes of watching people cluster near her covered round yard, curiosity got the better of her. Ken was already shooting inside the yard where she had exercised Deimos earlier that morning. The sand was dark with use, the surface pitted with hoof prints. There was even a pile of manure that she had yet to clear away. The model was wearing something white and soft and totally out of place for the surroundings. Her shoes looked like instruments of torture and her hair and make-up were like something out of an old Hollywood movie but the girl herself lay in the sand, her body twisted in an awkward way. Under the harsh glare of the lights, she looked broken.

Nearby, Ken was perched on top of a stepladder held steady by his assistants. He was staring at the girl through the lens of his camera.

'Good, sweetie. That's good. Now move your leg. I want angles. Everything in angles. And look at the camera. Eyes! Give me more in the eyes …'

Liz watched with disbelief as the girl and her beautiful white dress became covered in sand and filth and sweat.

'What do you think?' Kayla said softly.

'I thought the idea was to make a nice picture. Make the dress look beautiful.'

'It all depends on your definition of beautiful,' Kayla replied. She moved away, signalling for Liz to follow.

Liz hadn't noticed the cables running from the camera to a desk with a computer. A middle-aged woman was seated there, her eyes fixed on the screen. The images from the camera were appearing there.

'Maggie, this is my sister, Liz.'

The woman didn't look up. She simply raised a hand in acknowledgement, her eyes glued to the screen. There, the somewhat ordinary-looking girl seemed fragile and doll-like in her exaggerated make-up. The coarse sand only emphasised the softness of the fabric that encased her form.

Unconsciously, Liz wiped her hands against the rough denim of her jeans. With her short hair, her work clothes and boots, she felt … ugly. Ugly and ungainly and unfeminine. Liz wasn't sure she could remember the last time she had worn a dress. Or make-up. Not that it mattered—that wasn't her life. Her life was hard work, sweat and the smell of leather. It was her job to make her horses beautiful when they entered the show ring and to protect her father's legacy.

Another photo flashed onto the screen in front of her. A second girl had joined the first, her outfit the soft yellow of a winter dawn. The two of them lay on the rough sand like discarded toys. Liz turned away. The photographer might think those images were beautiful, but to her, they were heartbreakingly sad, a reminder of how fragile life could be. As if she needed a reminder.

As she stepped out into the bright sunlight, she heard restless movement and thumping coming from the stables and raced inside to find two people waving around a huge flexible reflective fabric disc. The horses in the nearest stalls were wild eyed with fear, kicking the timber as they spun, looking for a way out.

'Stop that.'

'Us? Or the horses?'

'If you stop, they will.'

Liz stepped forward and took hold of the disc, forcing it towards the ground. The men struggled with her for a moment, then one of them grabbed the disc with both hands. He gave a twist of his wrists, seeming to almost magically fold the huge disc into something far smaller and less threatening. Liz glared at him and stepped past to calm the horses. When she looked up, the young men were standing outside the stables, looking in. She hoped they would stay there.

'Liz, is everything all right?' Kayla appeared outside the stable door.

'No, it is not. Tell them—' Liz jerked her head, '—to stay away from the horses. I told you, I am the only one who goes near them. No one comes into the stables unless I am here.'

'Of course not. They won't do it again. Will you?' Kayla shot the men a steely glare and they murmured their agreement. 'Right. So we're moving the shoot into the yard now. We need the colt, if you could bring him out, Liz.'

'You'll have to wait. These idiots have gotten him all stirred up. I'll need to settle him first.' She turned her back on Kayla and walked to the stallion stall. The horse wasn't at all disturbed when she reached him. He nuzzled her hand, looking for treats, as she rested her forehead against his glossy neck and fought to contain her anger. It wasn't really those idiots' fault, they were city types and didn't know any better. All this was Kayla's fault. She'd left Willowbrook and her sister behind years ago and had no right to come back and start ordering her about. With luck, when these few days were over, she'd just leave again and Liz's life could return to normal.

Except that normal wasn't working.

When she finally led Deimos through to the open-air arena, with its dark surface of shredded rubber, she found Ken atop his ladder. He was peering around, his brows creased in thought.

'Let's have the horse over here,' he said. 'I don't suppose you can get him to lie down?'

'Not with all this going on. Not a chance.'

'All right. Simone, love, over here.'

A model, teetering on high heels, answered his call, eyeing off the horse cautiously as she approached. 'You are going to keep hold of him, aren't you?' the girl asked hesitantly.

Liz looked more closely and realised that underneath the expensive clothes and the fancy hair and make-up the girl was probably no more than eighteen or nineteen. And she was terrified.

'Don't worry. I've got him. Here, come around to the front and let him see you. Good. Now stroke his nose.'

Deimos tossed his head as the girl reached out her hand, then sniffed first her hand then her hair. Maybe it was the hairspray or the perfume, or maybe it was just bad luck, but the horse snorted vigorously.

'Eww!' The model stepped away and raised her hand to wipe her face.

'No! Don't,' Ken said abruptly.

'You're kidding?' The girl's face was a mask of disgust.

'No. I like the muck on your face.' Ken was snapping as he spoke. 'Move back to the horse. Liz, make him turn slightly this way to catch the light.'

'Hang on. I'm not going to be in any photos.'

'Of course not,' the model whispered as she followed Ken's instructions. 'They'll just edit you out.'

By mid-afternoon, Liz was sick to death of the photo shoot. She had brought out three different horses to be in the photos. Apparently it was important to colour coordinate the horse with the clothes. She had watched in fury as the various assistants had thrown her tack around carelessly, broken open bales of hay and bags of feed and generally turned her neat and carefully tended yards and stables into something suitably messy for a fashion photo. She had stood over the same assistants as they repaired every bit of damage.

At last, Kayla set her free.

'We're going to the creek now,' she said. 'We don't need you or any of your horses.'

'Thank God. Just make sure they don't poison the water or do something equally stupid.'

'Don't worry. I'll keep an eye on them.'

As the convoy headed to the creek, Liz took a long deep breath. It had been a tough day, but if she was entirely honest, perhaps not as tough as she might have expected. There were two more days to go. She just had to keep thinking about the money, that was the point of this. It wasn't enough money to get Willowbrook out of trouble, but in her mind, she had already spent every cent of it.

She heard a deep whinny from the stables. After the morning of posing, Deimos deserved a bit of fun. And so did she.

Soon Liz and her horse were running across the gentle slopes of Willowbrook. The horse was eager to gallop and she was happy to let him. The feel of the wind in her face and the eager colt beneath her helped clear away the day's cobwebs. When they were both feeling more relaxed, she pulled him to a walk, and once again her curiosity got the better of her. She turned Deimos towards the creek and the cluster of people around the crossing.

The models were in the water, their expensive clothes floating around them. Also in the water was a black gelding. Mitch's horse. And Mitch was sitting on him.

Liz guided Deimos into the shade of a river gum, well away from the activity. She left him tied there and found herself a place where she could watch without being seen. Ken was in full swing, calling directions to the models. They moved as he instructed while Mitch remained aloof.

Voices floated her way. 'I can see why Ken wanted him rather than a professional model. He's just gorgeous and so rough.'

'Yeah. The way he looks on that horse … He's a natural too. So much more real than any model could be.'

'He could put those cowboy boots under my bed any day of the week.'

'Yeah. There's no way he's gay. It makes a nice change.'

'Ken will be disappointed.'

At the water's edge, Ken lowered the camera briefly. 'Now, girls, it's time. You want that gorgeous man. This shot is all about sex. Come up. Ramp it up.'

In the creek, the girls began to rise up out of the water. The wet clothes clinging to their bodies were virtually transparent. Their graceful arms reached up. Even from a distance, Liz could feel a crackling sensuality about the images that were being created.

Mitch was looking at the models, and although Liz couldn't see clearly, every line and angle of his face was already imprinted on her mind. She could imagine the light in his eyes. What man could resist such beautiful women as they looked up at him with raw sensuality? One of the girls placed a hand on his thigh, her slim fingers and bright red nails stark against the blue denim. Liz closed her eyes, but she could still see his handsome face. She could see it change as desire took him. She could see the light of passion in his eyes.

Once he had looked at her like that.

Enough. She turned to go, but Mitch must have caught the movement. He glanced in her direction and their eyes met.

Liz felt as if her breath had been torn out of her body. She hurried back to Deimos, threw herself into the saddle and headed to the homestead.

CHAPTER

18

The bar was crowded when Mitch walked in. It seemed all of the people from the photo shoot were there, all talking and drinking. With their city clothes and their loud voices and extravagant gestures, they stood out like a backyard dunny. No-one was ever going to mistake them for locals. Behind the bar, the harassed-looking barman saw Mitch and raised an eyebrow. Mitch didn't come in very often, but tonight he had a good reason for being here.

Ken appeared at his side. 'Mitchell, you gorgeous man. So glad you could make it. I'm not sure what this place has in the way of Champagne, but shall we have some? To celebrate your entrée into the modelling world.'

'I'm fine with a beer, thanks.'

'Oh, all right. Whatever you want. You deserve it.' Ken waved at the barman. 'You were wonderful today. Exactly what I needed.'

Mitch did his best to ignore the flirtatious look on the photographer's face. He glanced around the crowd, searching for the one person he'd come to see. Instead, he saw the models who had been draped over his horse earlier in the day. They waved and smiled in invitation.

'Go on, then,' Ken said. 'Go play with the girls. But seriously … you could have a modelling career if you wanted one. I could get you started. No strings of course.'

Mitch shook his head and reached past Ken to grab the beer being thrust at him by the barman. 'Thanks, but no thanks. Not my thing. Although I did enjoy today.'

'Fair enough. Talk to Kayla. She's organised this whole shoot. She'll see that you get a proper fee. And if you ever change your mind …' Ken winked broadly, 'Kayla also knows how to find me.'

'Sure thing, mate. Speaking of Kayla, do you know where she is?'

'She's here somewhere.' Ken waved a hand vaguely at the packed room.

'I'll go look for her. See you around.'

As Mitch made his way across the room, he found one of the models in his path. She looked up at him, blue eyes unnaturally big in her pale face.

'Well, hi,' she said, batting her eyelids in a far too obvious way. 'I was hoping you'd be here tonight.'

'Hi …' He searched for her name.

'I'm Loraine.'

'Of course. I'm sorry.'

'No need to apologise. How about you and I find somewhere quiet and have a drink?'

The invitation in her eyes was as clear as it was unappealing. He'd come here to see someone else. And even if he hadn't, he liked a woman with a bit of meat and muscle on her. A woman he could hold tightly without fearing she might snap. And he'd long ago given up one-night stands.

'I'm sorry, but I'm meeting someone.'

The full lips pouted. 'Lucky girl. If you change your mind, I'll be here for a little while yet.'

Mitch spotted the face he was looking for. She was standing in a relatively quiet corner, talking to one of the few locals in the pub tonight. He paused until he caught her eye, and then tilted his head to indicate the pub's rear door. She nodded. He stepped out of the noisy bar into the relative quiet of the empty beer garden and a few seconds later, Kayla joined him.

'I'm so glad you came,' she said, kissing him on the cheek. 'I was really hoping we'd get a chance to talk.'

Mitch took a step back and looked at the woman in front of him. It seemed just yesterday they had all been kids together: Mitch, Lizzie, Kayla and Jen.

'You look terrific, Kayla. It's been far too long.'

'Yes, it has.' Kayla took his hand and led him to a nearby table. 'Gosh, Mitch, it's hard to know where to start.'

'Let's start with you. I didn't realise you worked with models and … whatever that's all about.' He waved a hand at the bar and the people inside.

Kayla grinned. 'I don't really. Actually, I'm a wedding planner.'

'A what?'

'A wedding planner. Mostly for people with a lot of money and not much time. Not much taste either, sometimes.' Kayla grinned. 'I love it. I've just bought a flat in Sydney overlooking the harbour.'

It was hard to imagine Kayla owning a flat in the city. Before this week, she had remained a small girl with plaits and a short, fat pony.

'Well, it obviously suits you. You look terrific. I bet those blokes down in Sydney are queueing to ask you out.'

Her laugh was much as he remembered it. 'Well, I am seeing someone. He's a chef, which is probably not good for my waistline. Enough about me, what about you? I saw the models watching you today. Are you sure you want to waste your evening with me?'

'I'm sure.'

'All right then. Tell me everything. I was surprised when I saw you by the creek the other day. Where are you living now?'

'I renovated the old church …' He stopped speaking. Something wasn't quite right. 'Kayla, you do know that I bought the four hundred hectares that you and Liz sold off a few years ago? The old church and the river flats.'

The look on her face was all the answer he needed.

'Liz never told you that it was me.'

'No. I came up and signed the paperwork. At that time, things between Liz and I were … well, not good. I don't think I looked beyond the corporate name on the paperwork. She didn't say anything about who was buying it and that was the last time I was here before this all started.' Kayla frowned. 'Don't get me wrong, I am really glad it's you living there. It sort of keeps it in the family. But I don't understand why Liz didn't tell me.'

Mitch understood. At least, he thought he did. But it wasn't for him to explain that to Kayla. If Liz wanted to keep their past a secret, even after all these years, he would respect her wishes.

'That's something you'll have to ask Liz. Anyway, I turned the old church into a home. I added to the yards and stables. I'm training there. I take in outside horses and I breed a few of my own. And during the season, I work for some of the studs. Mostly as a breaker, but I help with the foaling too. Whatever they need. Whatever they'll pay me for.'

'That's great. I'm so pleased for you. I remember when we were kids, that was all you ever wanted.'

He shrugged. It wasn't quite all. There was something else he'd wanted even more. He'd come so close, and then it had been snatched away by one tragic mistake.

'So, what's this photography thing at Willowbrook? I would never have imagined Liz being involved in something like that.'

'She's not really. It was all my idea.' Kayla hesitated. 'Did you know that she had to get Apollo put down?'

'No. That's a shame. He was a great horse. But I guess he was getting on.'

'Losing Apollo and the money he brought in was the last straw, with the drought and everything. The place isn't doing well financially. Liz needs to find ways of making money. This opportunity came along and I took it.'

'You took it? I didn't think Liz let anyone make decisions about Willowbrook except for her.'

'I didn't give her the choice. I don't want to see the bank foreclose, and that's a very real possibility.'

'It's that bad? Losing the place would break her heart.'

'I know. This shoot is bringing in some money. Not a lot, but enough to cover a few bills. And I'll add my fee to her payment. She doesn't have to know that. It will keep her afloat for a while and give us a chance to try to figure out a long-term strategy.'

Mitch was struggling with the implications of Kayla's words. Lose Willowbrook? The property had been in the Lawson family for generations. Sam Lawson had hired Mitch as a young stable hand the day he left school. He'd taught him so much in just a couple of years. The thought of Liz walking away from Willowbrook was almost painful for him—and that was nothing to what it would feel like to her.

'I don't know what to say. I wish there was something I could do, but Liz and I ... well we don't see each other.'

Kayla shook her head. 'One of these days one of you will tell me what the hell happened between the two of you. But at this point, that's the least of my worries. I'm trying to find a way to help her, but you know what she's like. Totally stubborn.'

Mitch reached for the beer that had sat forgotten on the table. He took a long drink to give his mind a few minutes to absorb what he'd heard. Then he put the glass down with a solid thump.

'Just now, Ken told me I have a fee due for today. I didn't realise that. I guess it's not much, but can you add that to Liz's payment? Without her knowing.'

'I can ...' Kayla spoke slowly. 'But are you sure? It's the best part of eight hundred dollars. That's a lot of money to give away.'

Mitch was sure. 'What else can I do to help?'

'Can you stop her being so pig-headed? Can you get her to listen to reason? And maybe even accept that I might have an idea worth considering?'

'Of all the people in the world, I am probably the last person she will listen to.' It was a hard admission to make. It was even harder to see the sadness and sympathy in Kayla's eyes.

'I know. I'm really sorry. I always thought the two of you ...'

He looked down as she laid her hand on his. 'So did I, Kayla. So did I.'

CHAPTER
19

Kayla wondered if she had gone too far with Mitch.

The two of them had sat at the pub late into the night, and she'd told him exactly how things were for her sister and Willowbrook. It didn't feel like betraying a confidence. Mitch was family—or as good as. Kayla knew why she and her sister had drifted apart, but she had no idea why Liz and Mitch were not together. She could sense a deep sadness in him when he talked about Liz, but he'd never been one to let his emotions show. Or to betray someone he cared about. Or to reveal a secret.

Mitch was, however, a smart man and he knew the horse industry. Kayla had decided to get his opinion on the problems that beset Willowbrook. When he agreed that there was no easy way out, she had felt her heart sink a little more. Near midnight, when they had finally parted with promises to stay in closer touch, only one thing had changed. Kayla had begun to think that she cared more about Willowbrook than she liked to admit.

Now, standing in the dawn light on the last day of the photo shoot, she looked up at the house and felt tears prick her eyes. In the soft yellow glow, the homestead's faded glory was masked and the place was quite simply beautiful. Or maybe it was her memory that was repainting the faded timbers and cleaning the mould-stained stone. All she saw was the elegance of the structure. The graceful lace of the cast-iron balcony railings. The humour in the stone animal faces peering through the carved vines on the edges of the fountain.

She felt warmth and heard the laughter of childish voices. Her own and Lizzie's. Now she could only wonder when Liz had last laughed, or been happy. So much love. So much loss. She blinked away the tears.

'Let's go, girls and boys.' Ken's voice was a welcome return to reality. 'We are shooting inside the house today. Now, I don't want anyone wandering around. There's a layer of dust in those rooms and I don't want it disturbed by any of your great clodhopper feet. It's pristine and decayed and lost and beautiful and that's how it's going to stay until I say otherwise.'

As Ken hurried past, followed by his entourage, Kayla saw Liz standing at the gate leading to the horse yards. The day had barely started, and already she looked angry. Cursing Ken's lack of tact, Kayla walked over to her.

'Good morning,' she said brightly. 'The old place really does look lovely in this light, doesn't it?'

'I was going to ask you to keep them out of my office, but I guess I don't have to. Those rooms probably aren't dirty enough or sad enough to be beautiful.'

'Liz. He didn't mean it like that.'

'Didn't he? So you're saying I've got no reason to be ashamed that he thinks my home is dirty and sad and lost. Maybe you think I am too.'

Kayla opened her mouth to deny it, but stopped. There was some truth in what Liz said. Kayla really did believe her sister was unhappy. Lost? Maybe that too.

'I'm just saying—'

'No. I don't care. I've got work to do. Horses need feeding and exercising. While I'm working, make sure that lot don't damage anything. And if they're gone when I get back, so much the better.'

Liz stormed away. Kayla didn't bother trying to call her back. She'd cool off. In the meantime, the best thing Kayla could do for all of them was make sure this final day went well.

Kayla found Ken and his models on the main staircase. From there they moved upstairs. The hallway was dark and when Kayla hit the light switch, nothing happened.

'Sorry. I'll see if I can find a new bulb.'

'Don't worry. I like it like this. I can spotlight that place where the timber is cracked. Now, girls, see the broken line of that crack? I want the same broken line in your bodies.'

Kayla left them to it. She walked to a door halfway down the hall and hesitated, her hand hovering over the door knob. How many years had it been since she was last in this room? She took a deep breath and turned the handle. The door swung open to reveal a shockingly empty room. She stepped inside. The posters were gone. The bright yellow walls had faded and dulled and the curtains were grey with dust. The bed remained, pushed into a corner and covered with a dust sheet. Kayla remembered that bed. She had come home from her last year at boarding school and found it already in place. She'd grown too tall for the child's bed she'd previously slept in and Liz had replaced it. That was about the same time her parents' double bed had disappeared from their room. Kayla had always had a sneaking suspicion that one had been sacrificed to buy the other, but she had never asked.

Two dust-covered cardboard boxes sat on the floor next to the bed. Kayla opened the first. Inside, a few books lay on top of a bundle of cloth. She picked up the top book and opened it.

Happy Birthday, Kayla, with love from Mum.

The book was *My Friend Flicka*. This copy had been Kath's and she had passed it on to her youngest daughter. And just like her mother, Kayla had loved this book. Kayla and her mother had been so alike. They both loved reading and nice things, cooking too. Kayla had been learning the recipes from Kath's handwritten book when everything changed. Well, she had the book now, and her boyfriend was a chef, so maybe she could pick up where her cooking lessons had so abruptly ended.

She removed the other books without bothering to look inside. She remembered each and every one of them. They had all been gifts from her parents. Underneath the books she found strips of once brightly coloured felt. She lifted a couple out. They were the show ribbons she'd won as a child. As she tried to straighten the ribbons, the aging fabric tore under her fingers. Looking at it closely, she saw moth holes and frayed cotton where the gold braid was coming away. She dropped the ribbons and books back in the box and left the room, wondering why Liz had kept these things when she'd removed all other traces of her sister from the room.

Another door beckoned at the end of the hallway. How many times as a child had she run down that hallway and flung open the door? When a thunderstorm scared her at night, her parents were always there to make her feel better. On Christmas morning and on birthdays they were always ready with a smile and a present. Standing alone in the middle of the room, she felt the loss of her parents as keenly as she had all those years ago.

A dark timber wardrobe stood in one corner, and alongside it the antique dressing table with its big mirror was ready to catch the light that would stream through the window in the morning, if only the window was not darkened with dust and cobwebs. Kayla crossed to her mother's dressing table. The top was bare, but when she slid open a drawer she saw a familiar carved wooden box. She lifted it out and opened it. Lying on the velvet interior, her mother's rings had lost their shine. The gold was dull and the stones barely reflected any light.

Kayla began to cry. She wondered if Liz ever came up to this room. If she ever stood here surrounded by memories and cried.

'Kayla, sweetie ...' Ken burst through the door.

Kayla dashed away the tears. 'Yeah?'

'What's wrong?' Ken frowned. 'Are you all right?'

'Yeah. It's just sad memories, that's all.'

'Sorry to disturb you, but I wanted to ask ... that hill I can see from the window, with the single tree on top? I was wondering if it's worth going up there. It should be a nice view of the homestead.'

Kayla put her hands into the pocket of her jeans so Ken wouldn't see that they were shaking. 'I don't think so. It's not that good.'

'Okay. Well, I'm moving down to the old dining room now.'

'Sure. Right behind you.'

After Ken left, Kayla brushed a few of the cobwebs from the window and looked towards the hill. She couldn't see the old graveyard and the two newer crosses, but she didn't have to. She knew they were there.

She took three deep breaths as she brought her emotions under control. And as she did, she made a decision. Willowbrook wasn't the only thing in danger of being lost. Everything about the place suggested Liz was pretty lost too. And despite everything, she loved her sister even more than she loved her childhood home.

Kayla didn't see Liz again until the end of the day. The convoy of vehicles had just set off along the gravel road to the highway when Liz appeared from the direction of the stables.

The two of them stood by the silent old fountain as the last dust from the convoy of vehicles settled. Silence returned to Willowbrook. There was the occasional noise from the direction of the stables, where the horses were already bedded down for the night. One by one, the early evening stars began to appear in the darkening velvet sky. Kayla recognised what she was feeling. Peace and a sense of belonging. A sense of home.

'You'll receive payment in a few days,' she said at last. 'If you have any questions, drop me an email.'

'All right.'

'How do you feel now about the idea of using Willowbrook as a venue?'

'Kayla, this has helped, I'm not going to deny it. But this is my home and I don't want this sort of disruption every bloody weekend. I will find another way.'

'But look around you. Everything is as you wanted it to be. Nothing has changed except you'll be able to pay a couple of bills. Maybe feed the horses for another month. Surely you can see now that this is the way out of the hole you're in? Wedding venues make money. And Pascale's investment will refurbish the place before it starts to fall apart around your ears.'

'No. I don't want interference in my home and my business.'

Kayla didn't even pause to think about the next step. She didn't want to do it, but she had no choice. She started speaking, before her courage failed her. 'Liz, this is not just your decision to make. These last couple of days have made me realise I want to save Willowbrook too. And I will. Are you going to help me? If not, will you at least not get in my way?'

'You can't do that.'

'I can. This is my home too. I legally own half of it. The only way you can stop me is to take me to court, and you haven't got the money to do that. But I don't want it to be like that. I want us to work together. Please, Liz. Can't you see it's the best thing for Willowbrook?'

Kayla watched the emotions flicker across her sister's face. Then Liz seemed to harden.

'Do what you want. You always have,' she said through gritted teeth.

The injustice of the comment was like a steel blade in her guts. 'No, I haven't. I've never done what I wanted. It was all about you, Liz, after they died. You sent me away to boarding school and I went. You told me I had to study at university—learn how to run a business—so I did. And not once did you stop to think what I wanted. What I needed.'

'This place paid for that school and it paid for that university education. Look at you, in your fancy clothes and your expensive shoes. Willowbrook money made you what you are today, with your arty friends and your fancy car. Don't you ever forget that.'

'Oh, Liz. I will never forget what you did to me.'

Kayla couldn't bear to look at her sister for one second longer. She spun on her heel, got into her car and started the engine.

As she drove away, she could see Liz staring after her through the long twilight. She wondered if her sister even realised that it wasn't just Willowbrook that needed help.

CHAPTER
20

There was something not quite right about the house. Liz wasn't exactly sure what it was, but she certainly knew who to blame: that photographer and the crew and the models who had invaded her space and changed things. She blamed Kayla too. Kayla had assured her that the house would not be affected in any way and the crew would put everything back exactly the same after the shoot. They'd all been gone for two days, but Willowbrook still didn't feel right. Something had changed, and she just couldn't put her finger on it.

Restlessly she left the kitchen and walked into the formal dining room. The room hadn't been used in years, not since her parents last used it. Liz stepped close to the beautiful mahogany table and ran her fingers along the polished surface.

The polished surface?

Now she knew what had changed. She left the dining room and walked through the house, taking careful note of the state of every room. The photo crew had indeed cleaned up after themselves. They had cleaned the house better than it had been cleaned in …

forever. She should be angry, but she wasn't. She was embarrassed and ashamed. Was this how people now saw her father's legacy? Was this how Kayla saw her sister—a lonely woman living in a dusty and unkempt reminder of the past?

This wasn't her. At least, it hadn't been her. She'd always been the one full of energy. The one who had wanted everything done immediately and properly and taken pride in everything she did. What would her parents say if they saw her now? If they saw the home they had all loved in such a sad state?

Liz returned to the kitchen and the pile of mail she had collected from the mailbox out by the road earlier that day. When the horses were all safely bedded down, she spent her evenings reading the mail and keeping the stud records and accounts. It filled the hours before she fell asleep in the bed on the other side of her office. She carried the mail into her office and flicked through the envelopes, pulling out the bills and setting them to one side. After a moment's indecision, she turned her computer on. Tempting as it was to put off dealing with her bills, it wouldn't help. An alert prompted her to open her email, where she found a message from Kayla with an attachment titled 'Willowbrook Account'. The top of the document featured an orange blossom surrounded by the words Elite Weddings. The logo suited Kayla perfectly. Liz glanced at the number at the bottom of the page. She blinked in shock and read the document carefully, wondering if there was a mistake. It appeared not. When she'd agreed to the photo shoot, she'd hoped for one, maybe two, thousand dollars in payment. Enough to take care of the most pressing bills. This was a lot more. The accompanying email said the money would be in her account within a week.

Still feeling a little stunned, Liz found her most pressing bills, the ones that were printed in red. Then she set aside a payment for the bank. It felt so good to say yes, that bill is covered. But that feeling came to an end far too soon when the money ran out.

Liz sat back in her chair and looked at the screen in front of her. The accounts looked so much better than they had just a week ago, but she wasn't out of the woods. Not by a long shot. At best the photo shoot had kept her afloat for maybe two months. She was still going to have to sell some stock. She was still going to have to train outside horses while she also worked to make Deimos a profitable stud stallion. And even then, there was only the slimmest possibility she could make it work. Not to mention the years it would take to put Willowbrook back on a sound footing.

She dropped her head into her hands and allowed the reality of her position to sink in. She was in trouble and there was no way out.

Unless …

She reached for the phone. Kayla answered on the third ring.

'I got your statement for the photo shoot today,' Liz said with no preamble. 'It was a lot more money than I expected.'

'That's good.'

'Yeah. It's taken some of the pressure off. Thank you.'

'I was glad to help out. Willowbrook is my childhood home too. I don't want it lost any more than you do.'

Liz heard criticism and anger in every word.

'Have you thought any more about Pascale's proposal?' Kayla asked.

Liz took a deep breath. It was too late now to back out. 'Yes. I have. I want to see just what is involved and understand it all better before I commit to anything.'

There was a moment of silence. Liz could imagine the shocked look on Kayla's face.

'Sure. That's great. Why don't you come to one of our weddings and have a look? We can talk through what we would want to do. Then Pascale and you can sort out the contractual and commercial details.'

'You want me to come to Sydney?' Liz hadn't considered that.

'You can stay with me, so you won't have to worry about a hotel or getting about or whatever.'

'But I can't be away for more than a day. The horses—'

'Liz.' Kayla spoke slowly as if talking to a child. 'There isn't any other way for you to really see everything you need to see. Surely you can find someone to take care of Willowbrook for a day and a night? Ask Mitch. He'd be more than happy to help.'

Asking Mitch was possibly the only thing Liz wanted to do even less than she wanted to go to Sydney.

'This weekend won't work, but we have the perfect wedding for you to see next Saturday,' Kayla continued. 'It's an outdoor wedding in the grounds of a historic home, almost exactly the sort of thing we would look at doing at Willowbrook. Why don't you come down for that?'

'All right.' There, she'd said it. She was committed now.

'Great. I'll talk to Pascale in the morning. Give her a chance to think about the financials for Willowbrook. I'll give you a call in a couple of days.'

'All right. And Kayla … thanks. I mean it.'

'I know you do.' With a click her sister was gone.

Liz got to her feet and left the office. There would be no more work for her tonight. She slid on her boots and set off for the hill overlooking the house. The bright moon lit the landscape around her, but her feet knew the way; she'd taken this path many, many times before. When she reached the top of the hill, she sought out her usual position, sitting almost between the two crosses. From there she could reach out and touch them or, when she was really struggling to cope, as she was now, she could lean against the hard stone of the cross that bore her father's name. It wasn't the same as leaning into his warm, strong chest when she was a child but it was all she had now.

She stared out across the valley and caught a glimmer of light from across the creek. The old church where her parents had married, and where Mitch now lived. Was he alone too? She didn't spend much time socialising, there wasn't enough time in her life for that. But Scone was a small place and the horse community was even smaller. At shows and sales and events, she sometimes heard the women talking about Mitch, about how attractive he was. How nice. About dating him. Which was fine. Really. She had no claim on Mitch any more. Nor he on her.

'I'm going to have to ask Mitch for help,' she said to the night air. 'I don't know why you felt the way you did, Dad. I always thought you liked him. I know you thought he was a good horseman. I don't understand why you didn't want us ...' Her voice trailed off as the crushing guilt swept over her. Even after so many years, it hurt too much to say the words.

'I'm sorry for what happened that day, Dad. More sorry than you will ever know. But I do have to ask him for help. I can't do this alone, and there isn't anyone else.'

That thought hurt too.

Liz closed her eyes and leaned against the cold stone. She gave herself up to her memories, as all around her the night wrapped Willowbrook in its gentle caress.

CHAPTER
21

The girl is running across the showground, a winner's ribbon clutched in her hand. She's looking for her best friend, to tell him all about the hunter class she's just won. She's a little surprised and maybe even annoyed that he wasn't there to watch her and cheer her on. But the show is always a busy time for everyone. She's sure he has a good excuse.

Lizzie slows to a walk as she approaches a long line of stables, filled with horses from the biggest Australian Stock Horse stud in the area. The heads looking over the doors are handsome and refined. Almost every one is a champion. She takes great pride in knowing that none of them has ever beaten her father and Apollo. They never will, either, she's sure of it. Mitch's father works on the stud as a trainer and Mitch rides the young horses in competitions. His youth and light weight work to the stud's advantage. In return, Mitch gets to ride some of the best horses in the country. He'll be with the young gelding he's been riding for a year now. They've done well in this show, and she knows they have one event still to come today. She's so proud of Mitch and now that her events are all done, she'll definitely be there to watch him compete.

Raised voices reach her long before she gets to the right stall. She stops, frowning. She recognises one of the voices. She's never known Mitch to raise his voice around a horse before. People don't normally fight around the horses, especially during competitions, because loud voices and sudden movements disturb them. The other voice is familiar too—it's his father's. Mitch and his father usually get along almost as well as Lizzie and her dad. Something is very wrong.

She walks silently along the row of stalls. The voices are coming from the gelding's stall.

'Come on, Dad. He's doing great now. Look at his performance yesterday. Give me another year with him. Please!'

'Mitch, I can't. The boss is choosing horses for the next sale. Baz is ready to be sold. There's no point in keeping him and he'll bring a good price. Sure, we'd get a bit more for him next year, but not enough to cover a year's costs.'

'But in another year, I'll make him a champion. I know I will.'

'You could, Mitch. But that doesn't change anything. He's not your horse. Or mine. If the boss decides to sell him, then he's going to be sold and there's nothing you can do. Or me either, for that matter.'

'Then I'll buy him. If you lend me the money, I'll pay you back. Honestly. I'll find work and pay you back every cent.'

'I'm sorry, Mitch. If I could afford to buy him for you, I would. But I can't. There'll be other colts for you to train. Better ones.'

'It's not fair!'

Lizzie can hear the break in Mitch's voice. She steps forward, wanting to help him, or perhaps comfort him. The stable door opens and Mitch stumbles out. He doesn't see her and pushes his way through the crowd. Lizzie follows. Mitch leaves the showground and crosses the road into the cemetery. Just inside the gates, there's a small brick building, which Mitch ducks behind, hiding from the road and the showgrounds and Lizzie. She starts to run and when she gets there, she sees him sitting on the grass, leaning against the brick wall, his face in his hands. It's obvious that he's crying. Lizzie is shocked. She's never seen Mitch cry before. She drops to the ground beside him, instinctively wrapping an arm around him.

'Did you hear?'

She nods.

'How can he do that? Just take Baz away from me like that.'

She doesn't answer. She knows nothing she can say will take the hurt away. Instead, she tightens her arm around his shoulders, pulling him closer to her.

'He's the first horse I ever trained. He was mine right from the first time he had a saddle on his back. No one but me has ever ridden him. And now they're going to sell him. They won't care who buys him or how they're going to treat him. All they care about is the money.'

She holds him tightly, wishing she could take away some of the pain.

'I'll never forget him,' Mitch vows.

Lizzie knows exactly how he feels. You never forget the first horse that touches your heart. She still has Tasha, the grey pony she outgrew years ago. Tasha is old now, but Lizzie visits her every day and takes her a treat.

Mitch looks at Lizzie. The tears have stopped now, but his dark brown eyes shine with the trace of them. Or perhaps with something else. His shoulders cease shaking, and his arm wraps around her. Without thinking, Lizzie leans forward and kisses him on the cheek. It is an automatic action, fuelled only by her love for him.

Mitch touches the place where she kissed him and the anger and pain in his eyes melts away. He reaches out to stroke her face, and then he kisses her. On the lips. She is fifteen and she has never been kissed by a boy before.

You never forget the first person to touch your heart.

CHAPTER
22

Mitch hefted the rail into place and held it with one hand as he pulled the fencing pliers out of his back pocket. His new stallion yard was almost finished. It had taken a lot of work, but it was worth it. He'd just been offered the chance to train one of the best bred two-year-olds in the valley. The colt was destined to stand at a top stud, but first he had to prove himself in competition, and the owner thought Mitch was the man to make that happen. The deal included a chance to put a mare to the stallion when he was ready. Mitch was already on the lookout for the right mare, because nothing short of disaster was going to stop Mitch turning the colt into a champion. Training a horse of this quality, with the resources the owner was prepared to invest, was a chance for Mitch to really make his mark.

He made a last twist on the wire and stepped back, pushing his hat up and wiping the sweat from his forehead. As he took a moment's well-earned rest, he ran his eyes around his place. *His place*. Those words meant so much. Unlike Liz and Kayla, he hadn't been born into land. His dad was a competent horse trainer and never out of a job, but he'd always been a hired hand, moving around the country, following the work. He was currently working at a racing stable in Queensland. Two or three years was the longest the family had ever stayed anywhere until they came to the Hunter. For teenage Mitch, the Hunter Valley had been everything he'd ever dreamed about. Horses were his world, and this valley was a world of horses. They had stayed here long enough for Mitch to fall in love—and not just with the valley.

A flash of movement caught his eye. A horse and rider were approaching from the direction of the creek crossing. The horse was obviously Willowbrook bred, and he didn't need to see the rider's face to recognise her.

Liz hadn't come near the old church since he'd moved in. The creek had become an impassable barrier the day he had bought this block of Willowbrook land. He could still remember the look on her face. Those four hundred hectares had been the fulfilment of his dream, but had meant far more than that, because Willowbrook had been more his home than the many houses he'd lived in with his parents and sister. Hearing that part of it was for sale had shocked him to the core and his decision to buy the property was, in part, to stop it being sold to a stranger. Willowbrook was a family's heritage, and in Mitch's eyes, when he bought the land, he was keeping it in the family.

But that wasn't how Liz had seen it. Her eyes as she'd relinquished the land had been filled with something very like hatred. When Mitch bought part of Willowbrook, he had hammered a final nail into the coffin of their dreams ... dreams that had died on a slippery road on a frosty winter's morning when they were still kids, and still in love.

His head knew that. But as he watched Liz approach the home he had made for himself, his heart skipped a beat as it had all those years ago.

Mitch put down his tools and waited. Liz pulled her horse to a halt a few yards away. She hesitated, as if she was reluctant to relinquish her means of a speedy escape, then she dismounted and tied the horse to a railing.

'Hi, Liz.'

'Mitch.' Her face was hard and impossible to read.

'I only just heard about Apollo. I'm really sorry. He was a great horse.'

'Thanks.' The barest flicker of emotion crossed her face. It closed down after a second, but not before Mitch had caught a glimpse of her pain. Losing her father's horse had hit her far harder than he had expected.

'How did the photo shoot go in the end?' If he could get her talking about something, anything at all really, it might chip away at the barrier between them.

'Fine.'

'Have you seen any of the photos yet?'

'No.'

An uncomfortable silence settled, broken only by the occasional movement of Liz's horse.

'Mitch, I need a favour.'

'Anything. You know that.'

'I have to go to Sydney for a couple of days. Next weekend. I need someone to look after Willowbrook.'

Mitch hid his surprise. Even after these years of separation, he knew Liz better than anyone. Going to Sydney would be her idea of going to hell. Whatever was taking her there, it must be important. 'No worries. I can do that. Let me know what needs doing.'

'Thanks. I'll be leaving Saturday mid-morning and be home on Sunday afternoon. If you could check them Saturday evening and Sunday morning that would be really helpful.'

Mitch didn't say anything. He was waiting to see if she would tell him what this was all about. She didn't, of course. He had lost the right to know that sort of detail about her life a long time ago.

'Whatever you need, it's fine. If there is ever anything at all I can do to help, you know you only have to ask.'

'Thank you.' Liz turned away to untie her horse.

'Liz …' He stepped forward and put a hand on her arm.

His touch seemed to turn her to stone. She didn't move. He wasn't even sure if she was breathing.

'Don't touch me.'

He let his hand drop.

She kept her face averted. Without another word, she swung into her saddle and turned her horse to the creek, pushing into a trot and then into a swift canter. She didn't look back.

Mitch watched her go. She hadn't asked him for help since the day she buried her parents in the graveyard on the hill above Willowbrook homestead. The situation must be even worse than Kayla had told him.

That night, he powered up his computer and sat staring at the card Kayla had given him, along with her promise to keep in touch. He could just email her and ask why Liz was going to Sydney, but that seemed too much like spying on her or betraying a confidence. He would never do that.

Instead, he opened an email from Sue, the woman he'd been dating for a few months, suggesting a weekend visit. He liked her a lot, but the relationship wasn't serious—at least not to him. Sue was intelligent and attractive and easy to be with and he always enjoyed their time together, but right now he was relieved to have an honest reason to say no. As he was trying to compose an answer, another email pinged into his inbox.

Kayla's message was brief: *I thought you might like to see these.*

There was a link and a password. He clicked through to a download site. The password gave him access to a gallery of images from the photo shoot.

Mitch had never been a vain man, but curiosity compelled him to click on the pictures taken by the creek. Images appeared of him with the models draped all over him. It was so strange to look at himself like that. He looked ... different. Not like himself. Some of the images were overtly sexual. Others were just a bit weird. But even those were ... interesting. Although he was alone, Mitch felt himself blushing.

A few more clicks took him to the photos taken inside the homestead. He hadn't been inside the building for years. As he flicked through, he was shocked at the dust and the cobwebs and the signs of neglect in the beautiful old home. That wasn't Liz. She cared too much about Willowbrook to let it get like that. Unless she had no choice.

Obviously things were worse than he'd ever imagined, and his heart went out to her. He wished she would open up to him. Or if not him, someone, anyone, who could help. She shouldn't be facing this alone. At least she was seeing more of Kayla; if she could heal the rift with her sister, that would be a start.

Then maybe one day there might be a place for Mitch in her life. Perhaps not the place he had always imagined, but there must be some way they could at least repair their friendship. Until then, he would be here to help if—or when—she called on him.

He returned to his email to Sue, to explain why it wouldn't be possible for him to spend the weekend in Tamworth.

CHAPTER
23

Liz looked uncomfortable and totally out of place as she stood alone in the garden, almost hidden in the darkness, as far from the lights and the party and the people as she could get. Kayla wasn't sure whether to feel sorry for her sister or angry at her. Apart from a brief exchange with Pascale on arrival, it appeared that she hadn't said a single word to anyone other than Kayla. This was supposed to be her chance to understand what Willowbrook could become. Instead she had retreated. What was wrong with her?

Kayla glanced around. The wedding was in full swing and nobody seemed to need her for a few minutes. She started to walk in Liz's direction.

'There you are!' The mother of the bride appeared from nowhere. 'I don't know what is going on in the kitchen. There was supposed to be proper caviar in the canapés but I swear it's not. It's a cheap substitute.'

Kayla bit back an exasperated sigh. 'I'm quite certain everything is as specified. I know the caterer very well. He serves nothing but the best.'

'I insist that you double-check. I'm not paying for second-rate caviar.'

'I will. Immediately.' Anything to get away from the woman. Kayla was used to dealing with anxious and difficult brides, but even the worst bridezilla had nothing on this mumzilla. Much as Kayla loved her job, some events—or rather, some people—made her want to commit murder.

She did go into the kitchen to check how things were progressing, but she didn't even mention the caviar. Even if it was wrong, which she doubted, the food had all been prepared off site and brought in by Lachie and his team. The mother of the bride was just going to have to live with the caviar she had.

As she made her way back to the gardens, Kayla paused to tick one more item off her long list. The sun was sinking over the extensive gardens of this heritage home on the Upper North Shore. She slipped through the staff entrance to the office, where the venue technician was waiting. At her nod, he began flicking switches. Kayla heard the murmurs of approval before she even made it into the gardens. Fairy lights glowed brightly in the trees, and soft lights in subtle colours of mauve and pink surrounded the dance floor where the bride and her father were dancing. The band was playing a slow song, and Kayla felt a prick of moisture in her eyes. She loved this part of her job, but sometimes it just served to remind her that she would never dance in her father's arms at her own wedding. Her mother would never send some poor caterer crazy asking about caviar. Not that Kath would have done that. Kayla took a deep breath. She had long since given up wondering if a time would come when thoughts of her parents did not make her slightly teary.

Liz was standing in the shadows also watching the father and daughter dance. Kayla couldn't help but wonder if Liz was having the same thoughts. Liz had always been closer to their father. Did she ever get teary? Not in public. Liz would never show weakness in public. But did Liz ever cry in the long, dark nights she spent alone at Willowbrook, where the memories would be harder to deny?

Kayla spotted the mumzilla working her way through the crowd in her general direction. She ducked down a path hidden among the bushes, not just to avoid the annoying woman—she also wanted a few minutes with her sister. She angled her way through the gardens towards Liz. But before she could get there, a hand grabbed her and pulled her into the shadows.

'At last!' Strong arms went around her and she was being kissed thoroughly and with great expertise. For a moment she fought, but then she gave up. She could not resist those arms or those lips and the delicious scent of chocolate that always seemed to accompany them.

'Ah, Kayla. You know you look incredibly sexy in that tight black skirt and those heels. I want to—'

Kayla gently pounded her fists on his broad chest as Lachie finally let her come up for air.

'You fool,' she gasped. 'I'm supposed to be working. And so are you.'

'Pah.' He waved a hand dismissively. 'My work is done. And it was a triumph as usual.'

Kayla shook her head. On any other man that would be boasting, but Lachie Henderson was without a doubt the best event chef and caterer in the city. Possibly in the country. She'd say that even if she wasn't dating him.

'The mother of the bride is not impressed with the caviar,' she couldn't resist teasing. 'She thinks you've used a cheap substitute.'

'The mother of the bride is a Philistine. She wouldn't know real caviar if it bit her. She obviously doesn't appreciate or deserve me.'

'Do you know your modesty is one of your most charming features?'

'I know. Why don't we meet up after this lot have all gone home? Your place … or mine?'

'Sorry, I can't. My sister is in town and staying with me.'

'Your sister? I didn't even know you had one.'

She hadn't told him because they'd only been dating for four months, and were still discovering their relationship; it was too early yet for family, or to delve into the past.

'I do. She pretty much raised me after our parents were killed in a car crash, but we don't really get on. She lives on the family farm up the Hunter Valley. This is the first time she's come to Sydney in … well, ever I think. She didn't even come to my graduation.' Kayla heard her voice tighten. She hadn't realised she still carried so much bitterness about that event.

'So is this some kind of reconciliation?'

That was a good question to which Kayla had no real answer. 'I've got to get back in a minute,' she said instead. 'Mumzilla is sure to have found something else worth complaining about.'

'Okay. Give me a call when your sister's gone. Or even if she's still here. You can always come and hide at my place.'

'Thanks, Lachie. You're an angel.'

He kissed her briefly on the lips and melted into the shadows.

Liz was watching her as she approached.

'Who was that?'

'Lachlan Henderson. He's a chef. He owns the catering company that we work with a lot.'

'Do you kiss all the caterers?'

Kayla bristled. 'He's my boyfriend.' She hated how defensive she sounded.

She waited for a derisive comment, but there was none.

'I think I've seen all I need to see.'

'It's early, Liz. The party will go until midnight.'

'There's no need for me to stay.'

Kayla's heart sank. If Liz was being this dismissive, it didn't bode well for her plans for Willowbrook.

'So what do you think now you've seen the sort of thing we do?'

'It seems to me to be a lot of palaver and a lot of wasted money.'

'It's a wedding. That's what weddings are supposed to be. When we were little, we used to dream about our wedding days. Remember, we'd talk about long white dresses and being married in the old church where Mum and Dad were married.'

As soon as the words were out of her mouth, Kayla wished she could take them back. She watched Liz shut down even further.

'If we did, it's too late now.' Her voice was as cold and hard as the ice keeping the Champagne chilled. 'Dad is never going to walk either of us down the aisle, is he? And that church doesn't belong to Willowbrook any longer. It's not even a church now.'

'No, Liz, he's not. But he and Mum would want us to have the sort of wedding we dreamed of.'

'So you're going to marry the chef?'

'No! That's not what I meant.'

'I'm leaving now. I can get a taxi to your place.'

Kayla sighed. 'Don't worry about the taxi.' She pulled her phone from her pocket and tapped in a text message. The reply pinged immediately. 'One of the drivers out the front will take you back. Take my keys to let yourself in.'

Kayla handed over the keys and, without another word, Liz turned to go.

'Liz ...'

Her sister stopped walking.

'Do you think about it? Getting married, I mean. Having a family. I always thought that you and Mitch would ... well. You know.'

Liz didn't answer. She just walked away.

Kayla stifled the urge to run after her sister and shake her until her teeth rattled. Until she came to her senses and recognised that there was more to life than a piece of land, no matter how precious it was.

'One of these days,' she muttered as she started thinking about work again.

CHAPTER
24

As soon as she stepped inside Kayla's flat, Liz kicked off the shoes that had been tormenting her all evening. She glared at the heels, then wriggled her toes and sighed. How on earth did Kayla manage to walk in those things? The next step was to get out of the borrowed skirt and jacket. She carried the shoes through to the bedroom, catching a glimpse of herself in the mirror as she did so. She looked like a fool.

She'd arrived at Kayla's place in the early afternoon as instructed. The journey down the motorway to Sydney had been nothing, but she had hated every minute of weaving her way through the city traffic. Liz had never been to Kayla's flat before and although she didn't say it, she was impressed by the smart building and the glass doors opening onto a balcony with a view of Sydney Harbour.

Kayla had been much less impressed with Liz's outfit, describing the slacks and blouse as better suited to a horse sale. She hadn't been far off the mark, but Liz wasn't going to admit it was the best outfit she owned. Luckily the two sisters were much the same size, and Kayla had pushed Liz into wearing something of hers for the evening. Liz's place at the wedding was supposedly as one of Kayla's staff and Kayla was going to make sure she looked the part. Liz had wondered if that was for her benefit or Kayla's.

Liz looked at her work worn hands as they unfastened the chic pearl buttons of a fine cream silk blouse. They almost looked like a man's hands, with short, ragged nails and the tiny white scars of many small scratches from fencing wire and raw timber. She remembered a time when they were softer; a young girl's hands, one slender finger adorned by a gold ring. The sort of ring a teenage boy would give to the girl he loved. As she slipped off the skirt and placed it carefully on the hanger, Liz allowed the embarrassment and shame she had felt earlier full rein. Was this what she had come to? Borrowing her sister's clothes so she was fit to be seen in public? It was true that she didn't go out much, but that was because she worked all hours of the day. The few places she did socialise were mostly horse shows and sales. And anyway, she wasn't a girly girl. Never had been.

That's not strictly true, said a voice deep in the back of her mind.

Liz pushed away memories of fussing with her hair and clothes. Of wearing a pretty ring and even nail polish. That was another time and place; the world had moved on since then. She changed into the jeans and cotton shirt she had brought with her for the journey home, then feeling restless, she opened the glass doors onto the balcony and stepped out into the night. The city lights were spread out in front of her like jewels. They were beautiful, but they were also distant. She was on the twelfth floor, but the sound of car horns and the occasional police or ambulance siren floated up to her. There was nothing of nature here. Not even a whisper of breeze. Liz felt no connection with her surroundings. It wasn't like

Willowbrook, where the very feel of the ground beneath her feet gave her energy and strength. In the city, she had nothing. She was nothing. But that was fine. She didn't belong here. Willowbrook was her home and she knew it always would be.

But what if you have to give it up? The voice in her head just wouldn't leave her alone.

Inexplicably irritated, Liz walked back into the flat, firmly closing the door behind her. She pulled the curtains closed to keep out both the lights and the noise of the city. Then she looked around. Kayla must have some sort of bar. Liz opened the doors of the living room's pure white cabinets and found glasses and bottles. She studied them. Liz seldom drank more than the occasional beer at home or at a show or sale while talking and doing deals with other breeders. But tonight she wanted something a bit stronger.

She rejected the spirits and pulled out a bottle of wine. A glance at the label showed it to be from the Hunter Valley. How apt. Kayla didn't have screw-top bottles, but it didn't take Liz long to find a corkscrew. The wine made satisfying glugging noises as it flowed into her glass.

She sat on one of the sofas in the centre of the room and aimlessly picked up a magazine from the glass coffee table. It was, of course, a wedding magazine. She flipped through the pages. Cakes and gowns and shoes and something called bomboniere leaped off the pages at her. It all seemed such a waste of money and effort. She took a sip of her wine and reached for another magazine. This one had a feature on what it called 'rustic weddings'. These seemed to involve restored sheds, vineyards and, yes, properties not that dissimilar to Willowbrook. But those places had beautiful gardens and their timber floors shone with a golden glow, the sort of glow her mother had managed through much polishing. These 'rustic' properties were old, but they weren't like Willowbrook.

'It's shabby and neglected. And no matter how hard I work, I can't fix it.'

There. She had spoken the words out loud. She couldn't ignore them any longer.

The magazine had a series of advertisements for wedding venues. Liz studied them carefully. There were lots of things she didn't really get, but the figures—those she did understand. One article on the cost of a big wedding suggested people would pay $10,000 or even more for the venue. That couldn't be right. It must include food and drink as well, surely? No one was going to pay that sort of money just for a place to stand and say 'I do'.

But it didn't matter if you were spending thousands of dollars on a dress and lights and fancy food, or standing in a little wooden church with just a priest and his wife as witnesses. The feeling was what mattered—the place, the way you chose to be married, didn't matter at all.

Unless the cost of the time and place was beyond bearing. Unless that cost was measured in lives and tears and heartbreak.

Liz dropped the magazine on the table and stood up. She had to get out of the city. She couldn't think clearly here amid the people and the noise and the lights. She couldn't find herself in this stylish apartment where the stranger who was her sister lived. She poured her barely touched glass of wine down the sink and collected her overnight bag from the bedroom. She was looking for a pen and paper to leave a note when she heard the sound of a key in the door.

'I wasn't sure if you would still be up,' Kayla said as she walked in, looking as cool and stylish as she had all those hours ago when they'd set out for the wedding. 'Lachie has a key so I borrowed his to let myself in.'

She looked at the open bottle of wine and raised an eyebrow. Then she poured herself a glass and dropped onto the sofa. She slipped her shoes off, but without the grimace of pain that Liz had made.

'So, Liz, what did you think?'

'Think?'

'About the wedding.'

'It seemed an awful lot of mucking about.'

'Okay, the mother of the bride was a bit of a bitch, but the bride herself was lovely. This was a bit upmarket, but it can't have been much different from any other wedding you've ever seen.'

Liz didn't answer.

'Liz,' Kayla said slowly. 'You have been to other weddings, haven't you? Everyone's been to at least a couple.'

Liz's mind flashed to a place a long way from this smart city flat. To a time when she was much younger. A time when it was all right to defy her parents—because they were still alive. She remembered a small country church with sun-faded paint. There had been no Champagne, no music and no crowd of well-wishers. The only flowers had been a small bouquet carried by the young bride as she stood in front of a priest with a kind face. The policeman's face was kind too, but the words he'd said had robbed her of almost everything she loved. All she had left was Willowbrook, and the sister who was now looking at her with something approaching pity on her face.

'What do you want me to say? That I've never been to a wedding? What does it matter if I've been to a wedding or not? You've been to enough for both of us.'

She ignored Kayla's startled reaction and reached for her bag. 'I'm heading back now. It'll be much easier driving at this time of night.'

'It's late. You must be tired. And you've been drinking.'

'I didn't drink the wine. Sorry to waste it. I hope it wasn't expensive.'

'But it's such a long drive. You don't want …'

An uncomfortable silence settled on the room as both sisters' thoughts returned to another day and another hurried journey.

'It's not the time of day or the distance that matters, is it?' Liz said softly. 'I'll be fine. Don't worry about me.'

'Liz, you've got to stop it.'

'Stop what?'

'Stop running away. You've been running away since the day of that crash. And you weren't even in the car. I was, and I've got the scars to prove it. I've come to terms with it. It's time you did too.'

Liz paused. 'You don't understand, Kayla. You never will.'

'I can try, Liz. For God's sake, just this once, talk to me. We used to tell each other everything. What the hell is it you've been holding inside all these years? Whatever it is, I'm your sister. You can tell me.'

Liz shook her head. 'No. I can't.'

She picked up her bag and walked out the door.

CHAPTER
25

There's nothing better when you're sixteen than starting work at your first job. Especially when that job is your dream job. It's even better when the two people you want most in the world to impress are there.

Better, but scary.

Mitch's hands aren't shaking, but that's only because he's got a tight rein on himself. He isn't going to mess this up. And besides, his hands never shake when he's handling horses. That comes as naturally to him as breathing.

'When you're ready, Mitch.'

'Okay, Mr Lawson.'

Mitch gathers the reins in his left hand and places his foot in the stirrup. His boss is holding the filly's head. She's never been ridden before, but Mitch isn't afraid. He and Sam Lawson have been working with her for several days. She's shown herself to be smart and good tempered and she's ready. Mitch has always dreamed of training young horses, and this holiday job on Willowbrook is his chance. He's not going to mess it up.

Mitch lifts himself onto the horse's back in one fluid movement. As he lowers himself gently into the saddle, he can feel her stiffen beneath him.

'Let her get used to your weight,' Sam says in a steady voice. 'There's no rush.'

Mitch loosens his hand on the reins a little and forces himself to relax his body. 'I've got her, sir. I think we're fine.'

Sam nods. 'I think so too.' He releases his hold on the filly's bridle and backs away.

It's all up to Mitch now.

He does nothing for several long heartbeats. He knows how to be patient. He doesn't want to frighten the filly.

'What do you think?' His voice is soft and the young horse flicks her ears as she listens to him. 'I know it feels funny to have me up here. The weight is all wrong, isn't it? But that's fine. You'll soon get used to me. Do you want to take a couple of steps forward? Go on. It won't hurt.'

He gently squeezes his legs against the filly's sides until she hesitantly moves forward. His hands are rock steady on the reins. His legs keep a solid pressure, with no signs of jerking or kicking, and he never stops talking in that soothing voice.

Leaning against the wooden rails of the fence, Sam nods slightly. The boy is good. Very good. Mitch gently urges the filly forward another few steps. Then a few more. The filly is walking easily now, her muscles starting to relax. Her breathing returns to normal and she is no longer wild eyed and frightened.

Lizzie and Kayla are beside Sam, also watching Mitch and the horse.

Kayla is too little to look over the rails, but she peers between them, her face shining with admiration. She's spending more time watching Mitch than the horse. Her heart clenches with fear when the filly suddenly stops and humps her back, as if to throw Mitch off. But he's ready for this and urges her gently on. The moment passes, and Kayla sighs with relief. She couldn't bear it if Mitch was hurt.

Lizzie is standing on the bottom rail and leaning on the top of the fence. She too is watching Mitch, thinking how very good he is, but she is also watching the horse. Sam has promised her that she can ride this filly in competitions when they're both ready. She's thrilled at the thought that she and Mitch can compete together. They'll make a great team.

'I think that's enough for this first session,' Sam says. He steps into the yard, ready to take the filly's head while Mitch dismounts.

'I've got her, sir,' Mitch says.

Sam hesitates, then steps away. He trusts the boy's judgement.

Mitch brings his mount to a stop in the centre of the yard. He sits for a minute, stroking her neck and talking to her quietly. Then he swings down off her back. The filly tenses, but begins to relax again as Mitch strokes her neck.

In an instant, Lizzie is over the fence. She knows better than to run and approaches boy and horse quite slowly. She joins Mitch in stroking the filly's face. 'That was so good,' she says.

Mitch isn't sure if she means him or the horse, but either is fine by him.

'When can I ride her, Dad?'

'Let's give her a few more days,' Sam says, smiling. 'Once Mitch has her responding well, you can have some time with her.'

'Okay.'

'For now, why don't both of you take her to the stables and give her a good rub down? It will be good for her to have the handling.'

'All right.' They speak in unison and set out, chatting happily about their plans for the filly.

At the fence, Kayla watches them walk away. From where she stands, it looks like they could be holding hands. She goes to follow them, but her father puts his hand on her shoulder.

'Kayla, do you want to get Ginger? We could take a short ride together and check the fences along the river flat.'

What she really wants is to go up to the stables with Mitch … and Lizzie. But then her father smiles at her. She goes with him to fetch her pony.

CHAPTER
26

Once again, Mitch guided his mount across the creek and up the steep bank onto Willowbrook land. He was very aware that he'd spent more time here in the last twelve hours than in the past fifteen years since Liz, standing next to her parents' graves, had pushed him away and told him she never wanted to see him again.

He glanced at the hilltop, and without thinking too much about it, turned his horse's head in that direction. At the top of the hill he dismounted and stood beside the stone crosses. There were no weeds around the graves. Liz obviously spent a lot of time here; perhaps more time than was good for her. It was a beautiful spot, with a view across Willowbrook. Mitch could see his place and wondered if Liz ever thought about him when she was here. Did she ever regret sending him away?

She had been little more than a kid, trying to cope with unimaginable grief and a burden of guilt she did not deserve. He'd been a kid too, and much as he'd wanted to help, he was too young to know how. Deep in his heart, he'd always believed she'd change her mind in a week or a month or a year. But she never had. She'd straightened her shoulders and carried on alone, sending Kayla away, first to boarding school and then to university. Not once had she asked anyone for help as she took on running a property that was too much for one man, far less a girl who had just turned eighteen.

Mitch still hadn't known how to help her. Each time he tried she had pushed him away. He'd hated her for that. He'd hated himself too. Then finally he'd left because it hurt too much to stay. He'd joined his family in Queensland and tried to bury his dreams in hard work and hard drinking. Women too.

'I came back, sir.' Mitch gently ran his fingers across the top of his mentor's grave marker. 'I should never have left her like that, but I did find my way back. I couldn't let her sell the church and the river flats to a stranger.'

He'd used every cent of his savings and tied himself into a bank loan he could barely afford to buy that piece of Willowbrook. The land was exactly the sort of property he'd always wanted. But this purchase wasn't just for himself. It was for Liz too, and the hope that one day his land and hers might be reunited. Instead, he'd found himself faced with more of her anger. Anger he didn't understand.

'It's good to be back here,' he said, 'and Liz is talking to me again. That's something.'

But it wasn't all good, because Liz was in trouble. She would never have asked for his help otherwise.

'Sir, you know how I've always felt about her. I've been patient all these years. I'm not going to wait any longer. I hope you understand.'

Hope is a hard thing to kill; almost as hard as love. But if it's left too long, it will wither and die. Mitch knew that now.

He turned away from the graves and swung onto his horse, pointing its head down the hill, towards Liz's stables. He wasn't sure when Liz would return, but he wanted to make sure the work was done before she got here. She would probably be happier if he was gone too.

He put his horse into an empty yard and walked to the stables, stopping by the feed room. Liz had left pre-mixed buckets of feed for each of the stabled horses, not trusting Mitch to do it. When it came to her horses, Liz liked to make sure everything was done just right. He picked up two buckets. Like last night, the first horse he'd encountered was Liz's much loved old gelding Zeke. He'd been her competition horse when they were teenagers and she would no doubt care for him to the end of his days. That was the sort of loyalty Liz could show.

Mitch stroked the old guy's greying muzzle as he opened the stall door. When he stepped inside, he saw Liz, curled up asleep on a pile of straw in a corner of the stall. She had done this so often when she was a kid. She would come to the stables late at night when she was troubled. The horses were her great love, and being around them calmed her, so this wasn't the first time Mitch had found Liz asleep in the stables near her favourite horse. He was pretty sure there had been many, many other times when there was no one here to find her.

A strong push on his arm reminded him he was here for a purpose. He tipped the feed into Zeke's bin and then walked over to where Liz lay. Her face was totally relaxed, her lips parted as the breath came slowly and softly between them. She looked so young, almost as young as the first time he'd seen her like this. Until you looked at her hands and the lines starting to form around her eyes. A lot had happened in those intervening years.

In his mind's eye, Mitch saw his teenage self lying on the straw beside her. They would lie there waiting for the sun to rise, whispering their hopes and dreams. Making plans for their future. Making promises that they were certain they would keep.

Liz sighed and moved slightly in her sleep and Mitch looked away. He no longer had the right to watch her sleep but maybe he could take a little bit of the weight off her shoulders, even if just for one day.

It didn't take long for him to finish feeding the horses in the stables, taking care all the while not to disturb their owner. He thought about taking the colt to the round yard for exercise, but decided against it. Liz would want to do that herself. Instead, he turned his attention to the horses in the yards—or, more specifically, the yards themselves. The Willowbrook yards were old. The posts and rails were timber, rather than the metal more commonly used these days. Personally, Mitch liked the look and feel of the wooden rails. They were a nod to tradition and history and the days when you didn't simply place an order and have something delivered the next day.

He ran his hands over the timber. These rails had been cut by hand and the yards built by hand. By people who cared for the land; people like Liz's father and Liz herself. Mitch had done his share of work on them too, back in the day. He looked along the fence line and noticed a place where the wire needed tightening. The gate latch was loose too, and he'd already spotted that a couple of nails had come loose from the corrugated iron around the muck heap, making it bend away from the frame. They were little things that could be fixed by anyone in just a few minutes. But it seemed Liz never had a few minutes, whereas he was here and could get them done before she woke. He even knew where the tools were kept.

CHAPTER
27

When Liz opened her eyes, the first thing she saw was Zeke. The horse had settled into the straw next to her and if she reached out her hand, she could stroke him on the nose. How many times in the last few years had she woken like this, when the house had been too full of ghosts for her to stay? The house's creaking timber and the wind whispering through the eaves seemed to condemn her; to judge her and find her wanting. The memories in the stables were easier to bear.

Rubbing her eyes, Liz sat up and stretched. The drive back last night had been long and tiring, but Willowbrook hadn't brought the comfort she sought. So here she was in the stables with Zeke. The old gelding was a symbol to her—of pride in her achievements, and of unconditional acceptance and love. The things she was lacking right now.

Liz sat in the straw for another couple of minutes, absently stroking Zeke's face. For the first time in a very long time, her mind wasn't full of what needed doing today. A part of her just wanted to sit in the quiet with her old horse and remember the good times together when she had been a child. She didn't want to face the day ahead and the decision she was about to make.

Shaking her head, she forced herself to her feet. Sitting in the stables moping was not going to change anything. She had work to do.

As she let herself out of Zeke's box, she ran her eyes around the stalls. The horses had all been fed and watered and the boxes had been mucked out. Mitch had been here while she was sleeping. Of course Mitch had been here. She'd asked him to look after the horses and no matter what else had gone wrong with her life and their relationship, Mitch would never go back on a promise.

He must have seen her sleeping in Zeke's box.

There had been times when opening her eyes to find Mitch watching her sleep had been a joy. Now, she wasn't sure how she felt. She had spent so many years building her defences it was disconcerting to be seen at her most vulnerable now.

Still trying to sort out her feelings, Liz walked out of the stables. The first thing she saw was a figure down by the foaling yards. Mitch. He was working on the fence, his shoulders and head bent to the task. She'd forgotten the way he did that, giving everything he did his total focus. Whether it was building a fence, cleaning the stable or patiently teaching a young and frightened horse, Mitch never gave less than his total concentration. Never less than his total effort. Or his total love.

Liz ran her fingers through her sleep-tousled hair, brushing away the last few bits of straw. A few hours at a wedding had turned her all soppy and she had to snap out of it. She didn't have the luxury of giving in to her feelings.

'Mitch.'

He straightened and smiled at her. That smile was unguarded and so familiar it made her heart lurch. He held up a hand, asking her to wait as he finished what he was doing. That was something else she remembered about Mitch. He hated to leave something unfinished. And he rarely did. Only when he wasn't given a choice.

She watched him as he finished up and collected his tools.

'Thank you for doing that, but you didn't have to.'

'It was nothing. I was here and I saw it needed fixing.'

'Thank you for looking after the horses.'

Mitch held her gaze for a long moment. 'You know I'm here anytime you need me, don't you?'

Liz stiffened. He wasn't talking about feeding horses or fixing fences.

Before she could speak, a rumbling noise disturbed the silence that had settled between them. Mitch's face broke into a smile.

'Sorry about that. I haven't had any breakfast.'

'Well, then, I won't keep you any longer.' She turned to leave, hating herself for the coldness of it but hating the nearness of Mitch even more.

'Liz … I know about your situation.'

She froze. 'What do you mean, "my situation"?'

'Your financial problems. Kayla told me.'

'She had no right to do that.'

'I have eyes too, Liz. I know how much you love this place. You wouldn't let it get like this if you had an option. If you could afford to hire someone to help, you would have.'

She kept her back to him, terribly afraid that if she saw sympathy on his face, she would lose her fragile control on her emotions.

'And losing Apollo must be a blow. You'll lose stud fees and agistment for the mares as well.'

'Some of the mares have already gone,' she admitted.

'I'm sorry, Liz.'

'Does the whole valley know?'

He didn't answer, which told her everything.

'Why didn't you ask me for help?' he said instead, softly. 'I would have been happy to pitch in. I still am. If there's anything I can do …'

'Anything you can do?' The words were almost a scream as her pent-up pain exploded into fury. 'Haven't you done enough?'

She could face him now. The shocked look on his face was no threat to her.

'Liz—'

'No. It's our fault. If we hadn't done what we did, they would still be alive. It's too late for them. And for us. I can't even look at you without thinking about what happened. The only thing you can do now is just … stay away from me.'

His face was a mask of disbelief and pain. He half lifted a hand as if to touch her, and that was more than Liz could take. She almost ran back to the safety of the homestead.

She was breathing heavily as she slammed the kitchen door and leaned against it, as if to remove any chance that someone—Mitch—might walk in to confront her.

It took a long time for her calm to return. When it did and her hands were no longer shaking, she acknowledged the decision that she had been avoiding for days. She walked through the empty rooms and climbed the stairs to the top floor that was so rarely used. She opened the door and stared into her parents' old room. Then, with a feeling of grim determination, she went downstairs into the office and picked up the phone.

As she listened to the ringing at the other end, she stared at the framed photograph on her desk and hoped her father would understand.

There was a click at the other end of the line. 'Hello?' Kayla sounded a bit fuzzy. She must have just woken up.

Liz wondered just how late her sister had been up last night. She also wondered if the decision she was about to make would give her many late nights—or maybe sleepless nights. But it was too late now to change her mind.

'All right. I'll do it.' Liz put down the phone before she could take the words back.

CHAPTER
28

Kayla arrived at the office early on Monday morning, but Pascale was already there, checking the society and gossip websites.

'Some nice shots from Saturday up on social media,' she said. 'Well done, as always.'

'Thanks.' Kayla stopped by the coffee machine and made herself a latte. 'I got a call from my sister on Sunday morning.'

'And?'

'She said yes.'

'Excellent.' Pascale's face broke into a wide smile, the kind she only had when she was excited about a new challenge.

'I wonder what changed her mind.'

'Maybe she enjoyed coming to the wedding.'

Kayla gave a derisive snort. 'It certainly wasn't that. She hated every bit of it. It's really strange that she's never been to a wedding before. I thought everyone went to weddings. She must have school friends who are married … someone to invite her.'

'Maybe she always said no. Too busy working on the property.'

'Maybe.' Kayla wasn't so sure. She was beginning to realise how little she really knew her sister. And how terribly alone Liz seemed to be. If Liz had pushed even Mitch away, she probably had no one left.

'We need to start making plans.' Pascale left her desk and took a seat at the table in the middle of their shared office. This was the one place where Pascale's natural neatness went out the window and its surface was littered with notebooks and sketchpads and drawing tools. There were books of fabric swatches and menus and photo catalogues. She pushed a few things aside and pulled a drawing pad towards her then reached for a box of coloured pencils and highlighters.

'I've been mulling this over,' she said as she swiftly began to sketch. 'If we get started now and work pretty fast, we can have the place ready for the last few weeks of the season. I think we have plenty of potential markets—the Japanese wedding tours and anyone who wants a rustic ceremony. There's an airport at Scone, right?'

Kayla nodded. 'No scheduled flights—private only, I think.'

'That's fine. It makes high-end transport easy. We can promote this as a very private venue too. Maybe do a celebrity wedding or two. Then there's the horsey set. They'll love it.'

As she talked, Pascale's hand moved over the drawing paper. Kayla had seen her do this before. She let Pascale get on with it undisturbed.

'What do you think?'

Pascale spun the pad and Kayla saw Willowbrook. It was roughly sketched, but was beautiful. The fountain where she and her family had held their birthday picnics looked more elegant than it had ever been in real life, as water cascaded across the stone. Lines around the edges gave the look and feel of flowers, and two wedding rings gleamed at the top of the page, where the words 'Willowbrook Weddings' had been written in cursive script.

'Wow.'

'I think this is going to work,' Pascale said. 'For us and for your sister.'

'I was thinking,' Kayla began hesitantly. 'About this project. I'd like to be involved. Closely. I mean, I do sort of own half the place. And Liz can be awkward. No one knows that better than I do. And—'

'Of course,' Pascale interrupted her. 'Someone needs to spend a lot of time up there. I certainly couldn't bear being that far from a good nail salon for more than a few days. I want you to manage the renovations. And the venue too, when we get that far.'

Kayla decided not to mention that Scone had several nail salons. 'Thanks. I won't let you down.'

'I know you won't. Mind you, you're going to have to work your tail off. There are a couple of good candidates to take some of your load during the week, but I'll still want you back here on weekends for the weddings themselves, until you start having events at Willowbrook.'

'Of course ...'

'Okay, first things first. I'll talk to the lawyers and get them to draw up an agreement. While they're doing that, you should get started thinking about contractors and such. You know the area, so that'll help.'

'You'll be doing the design?'

'Who else?'

Two weeks later, Kayla was on her way to Willowbrook. On the seat beside her lay her laptop, a brown envelope and a folder full of sketches. In the boot of her car was a small suitcase. Traffic out of the city was light and the journey took far less time than she'd expected. When she arrived at the homestead it was mid-afternoon, and there was no sign of Liz. Kayla left her suitcase in the car, but carried the rest of her stuff through to the kitchen, fighting back the feeling of being a stranger in the place she had once called home.

Leaving her things on the table, she walked through the house, pausing in each room, trying to see in her mind the place as it would be when Pascale's design ideas were put in place. She tried to imagine white flower arrangements on an antique table in the entranceway. Or a gold-framed mirror reflecting a beautiful bride in a long white dress. But each time she thought she had captured Pascale's vision, the image faded, pushed aside by a memory of a vase filled with the wildflowers her mother had picked in their garden. Or a table covered with scraps of fabric as her mother made costumes for Kayla and Liz to wear at the horse festival.

That was how Willowbrook was supposed to be. Their family should have had more time to be together. Kath would weep if she saw the dust on the banisters and the faded curtains. She would weep if she saw her oldest daughter's loneliness. Would she be proud of Kayla's success in her job, or would she be disappointed at the estrangement between the sisters?

She would never know.

Kayla was settled at the kitchen table, working on her computer, when she heard footsteps outside.

'Sorry I wasn't here,' Liz said as she washed her hands. 'There was a bit of a storm last night. A tree branch fell across a fence. I've been fixing it.'

'That's fine. I was earlier than I expected anyway.'

Liz slid into the seat opposite her. 'So?'

'It's all here.' Kayla pushed the envelope to her. 'This is the contract drawn up by Pascale's lawyers.'

Liz looked at the envelope but made no move to open it. 'You've read it?'

'Yes. I'm happy with it. I will sign as co-owner.'

'All right then.'

'Liz—you are going to read it before you sign it?'

'I'll look at it tomorrow. We may have had our differences, but in this I trust you, Kayla. If you think it's a fair deal for Willowbrook then I'll sign it.' Liz waved a hand at the papers spread all over the table. 'What else?'

Kayla wasn't sure whether to be flattered that Liz trusted her, or concerned that she was showing so little interest in the legalities. Kayla pushed the folder across the table. 'I thought you might like to see these.'

Liz opened it and flicked through the pages. Kayla had spent hours looking at those drawings. Something about them reminded her of the Willowbrook of her childhood. Not because they looked similar, but because of the hint of the warmth and joy that her mother had brought to the same rooms. Based on the photos she'd taken, Pascale had sketched the key rooms at Willowbrook. Her innate sense of design and flair had given the old mansion new colours and shapes—new life.

Liz skipped fairly quickly through the interiors, but gave careful scrutiny to the outside of the house and the gardens.

'I won't have that,' she said in a clipped voice as she tapped one of the drawings. 'That will interfere with the access to the stables for feed trucks and floats.'

'Fine.' Kayla wasn't going to argue any of the details at this point. 'Remember, these are just initial plans. We can modify them as we go along.'

'We?' Liz finally looked at her.

'I will be handling all the renovations and decorating.'

'Long distance? From Sydney?'

'Of course not. I'll be spending a lot of time up here. I'll be in Sydney too. Maybe split my time fifty-fifty. For now.' Kayla tried to read Liz's face, but it was like trying to read a stone.

After a few moments, her sister got up from the table. 'I guess you'll be staying here then. I sleep downstairs, so you can have my old room. It's a bit dusty—or at least it was before your photo shoot people cleaned it. The bed is still there and should be fine.'

'But you'll be needing that room soon—when you move your office upstairs.'

'Fine. You can sleep on the floor for all I care.' Liz walked out.

Kayla sat quietly for a few moments, trying not to feel angry. She heard banging and scraping upstairs. What the hell was Liz doing? It sounded like she was dragging heavy furniture about. Kayla's curiosity got the better of her and she headed upstairs to find Liz trying to push a chest of drawers through the doorway to Kayla's old bedroom.

'What the hell are you doing?'

With a grunt, Liz pushed the chest through the door and slid it into the centre of the room. The dust cover had been dragged off the bed, and sheets tossed onto the mattress.

'There you go. I guess you can consider this your room again.' She stormed off down the stairs, and Kayla heard the back door slam. Liz heading to the stables.

By the time Kayla had fetched her bag from the car and put the room to rights, the sun was well down on the horizon. Liz had obviously finished her chores, because she was in the kitchen, a cold drink in one hand, the unopened brown envelope on the table in front of her. She looked up as Kayla entered.

'I normally don't spend too much time cooking,' she said. 'I can rustle up some steak. Maybe vegetables.' It wasn't exactly effusive, but it was a start.

'Why don't we go into Scone for dinner?' At least in town there was less chance of open warfare at the table.

'I don't have the money for eating out. You know that.'

'But I do. Let me shout you dinner. Maybe a glass of wine to mark the start of this venture.'

'Well, we could go to the pub,' Liz said slowly. 'I'm not getting dressed up to go anywhere better than that. I don't have the time or energy.'

And probably not the clothes either. Kayla mentally chided herself. She had to stop being so judgemental. This might be her last chance to rebuild her relationship with her sister and she had to at least give it a try.

'The pub it is,' she said.

CHAPTER
29

Liz hesitated at the entrance to the pub. How long was it since she had last been here? A year? Maybe more? She usually came by the pub after shows and sales. After the King of the Ranges event and the Scone Horse Festival. The whole town turned up, or at least the horsey part of the town, and that was most of it. But recently she had been too conscious of her financial status to spend time there. People would buy her a drink and she'd have to buy one back, that was the way it worked. One night at the pub could cost a hundred dollars, and Willowbrook didn't have the money to spare.

Come to think of it, she had given the pub a miss last year as well. And the year before? She wasn't going to let her mind go there—it made her sound too much like a hermit, sad and lonely. That wasn't who she was.

Was it?

Extremely conscious of how little cash she had in her wallet, Liz took a deep breath and followed her sister into the pub.

It was busy but not particularly crowded. Liz immediately spotted some familiar faces: horse breeders and trainers. One or two of them raised an eyebrow on seeing her, and then smiled to cover their surprise. She nodded her greetings and raised a hand, trying not to show that their reactions made her feel awkward. Surprisingly, a few people greeted Kayla too. In fact, her sister seemed more familiar to the locals than she did. But of course, Kayla must have come here during the photo shoot with her big city friends. They would have had plenty of money to toss around and anyone with money was always welcome in the pub. Even as she thought that, Liz admitted to herself it was unkind and uncalled for. The people of Scone were a friendly bunch; she was the one who wasn't.

'How about we grab that table in the corner?' She pointed to the table furthest from the bar. 'It'll be quiet.'

'Good idea. Then we can talk about my plans for Willowbrook.'

That wasn't what Liz had been hoping. She wanted to avoid thinking about that as much as possible. Was it really the only thing she and Kayla had to talk about?

You get the table, I'll get us a drink,' Kayla said. 'Beer?' Without waiting for an answer, she went to the bar.

Beer wasn't the only thing her sister brought back. Liz's heart sank as she watched Mitch follow Kayla across the room, two glasses in his hands.

'Look who I found,' Kayla said cheerfully.

'Hi, Liz.'

She didn't respond, didn't look at him. She couldn't look at him.

'I should leave the two of you to catch up.' Mitch began to step away.

'No. Stay,' Kayla insisted. 'We've got plenty of time.'

Liz could feel Mitch looking at her. Those deep brown eyes of his would be looking into her heart, as they always had. He'd know how she felt.

'No. I think it's better if I go now.' He put the glasses on the table and returned to the crowded front bar.

'What the hell was that?' Kayla dropped into a chair.

'What was what?'

'You know what I mean. You were so rude to Mitch.'

Liz reached for her beer and took a swig. 'Shall we order some food?'

'Don't change the subject.'

'I don't have to explain myself to you, Kayla.'

'In this case you do.'

'Just because you had a crush on Mitch when you were little ...'

'Yes, I did, but that's got nothing to do with it. I'm his friend. He doesn't deserve to be treated like that. Especially not by you.'

'It's none of your business.' The words came out just a little too loud. Heads turned their way.

'He loved you, Liz.' Kayla's voice dropped to a whisper. 'I think he might still love you.'

'No.'

'What happened? It's something to do with that day—the crash. You know I can't remember it. Why won't you tell me?'

Liz sat in silence. She and Kayla had been close once. As girls, they had talked about everything. If there was anyone she could talk to about this, it should be Kayla. But she had never talked about this, not with anyone. And she couldn't talk to Kayla about it either, because if her sister knew what had really happened that day, she would walk out the door and never come back. Despite their estrangement, Kayla was all Liz had left, and she didn't want to lose her.

'Hello, Liz!'

She looked up. The face smiling down at her belonged to one of the local stockmen. They'd met a few times at the show and other work events.

'Hi, Jack.'

He swayed slightly. He'd obviously been at the pub quite a while. 'I just wanted to say what a shame it is about Apollo. That was a good horse. I've been riding one of his offspring during the mustering. A bloody fine bit of horseflesh.'

'Thanks,' Liz muttered, not wanting to encourage him.

'I remember watching your dad on that colt, years ago. Now he was a horseman, your dad. He and that colt were destined for great things—'

'Jack.' Mitch appeared at the man's side. 'I've been looking for you. I wanted to talk to you about the King of the Ranges. Are you entering this year?'

'Yeah, think I might.'

'Come on, let me buy you a round and we can talk about it.'

'All right then.'

He led the drunk stockman away.

'See? That's what I'm talking about,' Kayla said. 'Mitch is still looking out for you, and you treat him like dirt. There has to be a reason. Why don't you just tell me?'

Liz stared at her glass until she couldn't stand it a moment longer. 'I'm not hungry any more.'

Without a glance at either her sister or Mitch, she walked out of the pub. She got as far as the car park before her stomach started to churn and she gasped for breath and leaned against Kayla's car until she felt as if she could stand on her own two feet again. It was a long walk home, but that seemed to be her only option.

She'd reached the main road when she heard the sound of an engine behind her. Kayla pulled the little red sports car up next to her and waited until she got in. The two sat in silence for the rest of the drive to Willowbrook, the tension between them thick. As they turned down the drive to the homestead, the car's headlights picked out the shape of the house against the dark blue velvet of the sky.

'When you look at it like this, it's almost like it used to be,' Kayla said softly.

'But that's just an illusion,' Liz said. 'Nothing is like it used to be.'

Kayla pulled up in front of the house and the sisters got out. She hit the switch on the key fob, and with a flash and a beep, the car locked.

'You've become a city person,' Liz said. 'I never lock the cars out here.'

'Some habits are hard to break.' Kayla headed inside..

Liz watched her departing back then walked to the kitchen. The brown envelope lay on the table where she'd left it. She stared at it for a few minutes, and then opened it. Without reading a word of the contract, she reached for a pen.

If she was ever going to start trusting people again, she had to begin with her sister. And besides, when it came to saving Willowbrook she didn't have any choice. If this didn't work Willowbrook was lost, and so was she.

Liz scrawled her name on the bottom of the contract, then got to her feet and walked out the door and along the path leading to the stables, seeking the comfort she always found there. She stopped at Zeke's stall and stroked his greying muzzle. He nudged her gently, just in case she had a treat for him.

'Sorry, old friend, no treats tonight.'

She stepped into his stall and buried her face in his neck, soaking in the warm, earthy smell of him. This was the point at which she would so often settle into the straw to sleep. But not tonight.

Her mind was too filled with pictures of Mitch. Not so long ago, he'd been in this stall, feeding Zeke. He'd probably groomed him too, with those strong, gentle hands of his. And he'd certainly seen Liz sleeping in the straw. What had he been thinking as he watched her? Did the memories haunt him too? How did he seem so unmoved by everything? Did he ever lie awake at night, thinking of her and the what they had once meant to each other? Had he forgotten their dreams?

Liz patted Zeke on the nose, trying not to remember all the times she and the horse had ridden next to Mitch, matching stride for stride over the hills and plains of Willowbrook.

There was no rest for her here tonight. She left the stables and walked back to the house, very aware that her sister was sleeping there. Much as she loved this land, and Willowbrook Stud and growing up here, there were times she wished the memories would fade.

CHAPTER
30

The moon is full for the Show Society dance. The old wooden hall is looking particularly cheerful, decorated with balloons and coloured streamers. The people inside are cheerful too. It hasn't been an easy year, the summer has been hot and dry and the region has been plagued by bushfires. But it rained last week, and now green is beginning to show through the brown. There will be winter feed and that is cause for celebration. Everyone is ready to let their hair down.

Kayla nervously brushes her hands over her new dress. The dress is a copy of one from a magazine. Kayla and her mum made it together. The dress in the magazine was black, but Kayla doesn't like black, so her dress is in pretty pastel shades. Kayla's taken extra care with her appearance tonight. She has painted her nails in pretty pink sparkles. Her mother has helped with her hair, and has even allowed her to wear light eye shadow and pale lip gloss. She's eleven and this is the first time she has ever worn make-up.

'You look so pretty,' Kath tells her, as if sensing her nervousness.

Kayla feels her heart beat a little faster as they walk into the hall. Lizzie immediately vanishes into a crowd of her friends. Kayla doesn't think Lizzie looks pretty tonight. She is wearing a dress, which is unusual for her, but it's a plain blue denim dress and not at all pretty. At least, not to Kayla.

'Oh, Kayla, you look really terrific.' Her best friend Jen appears.

'So do you,' Kayla says as she detaches from her parents.

'We're going to have fun tonight,' declares Jen as she leads the way to the section of the bar where they're serving soft drink. Jen is no longer the frightened little mouse Kayla met on her first day at school. She's older than Kayla, and having turned twelve a few weeks ago, she now considers herself almost a teenager. Jen is basically a kind-hearted girl, but she's always up to something and there are times she drives her parents and teachers to despair. Although the two girls are very different, the friendship forged on that first day has never faltered. Not even Kayla's crush on Mitch is going to spoil her friendship with his sister.

Taking glasses of orange cordial from the table, the two girls head for the open side door of the hall. Outside, there are traces of light in the evening sky. People are milling about under the lights strung between the trees. Kayla looks around, searching for one particular face. He's not there. She can't see Lizzie either.

Jen and Kayla walk around for a little while, talking softly about important things like dresses and boys, but Kayla never stops looking for the only person she wants to see tonight.

'I have to wee,' Jen says. 'Be back in a minute.' She vanishes in the direction of the brick toilet block behind the hall. Kayla ignores her friend's departure, because she's just spotted Mitch ducking between the trees on the edge of the party area. He seems to be heading to the stables, and he's carrying something.

Without a second thought, she starts to follow him.

'Here she is.' Her father's voice intrudes and his hand falls on her shoulder. 'Kayla, this is Mr Walker. He works at the bank.'

'Hello, Mr Walker,' Kayla says. She doesn't want to talk to this man. She wants to find Mitch, but her mother has taught her not to be rude.

'Hello, Kayla. My, don't you look pretty.'

'Thank you.'

'Kayla likes her nice things,' Sam says. 'Not like her sister. You practically have to drag Lizzie out of the stables. But not Kayla. She's the smart one too. Liz is never going to leave Willowbrook, but Kayla has a different future. University, I think, and a business degree. I think she and her sister will balance each other very nicely. Liz will run the stud while Kayla keeps an eye on the business side of things. The place will be in safe hands for the next generation. You'd like that, Kayla, wouldn't you?'

'Yes, Daddy.' She is barely listening to him. She thinks she has seen someone in the moonlight at the far end of the stables. It has to be Mitch.

'Well, that's a fine thing. Education is important,' says Mr Walker. He doesn't pat her on the head, but it feels as if he has.

'Glad you feel that way, I'll probably be coming to you for a loan to pay those university fees.' Her father claps his hand on his companion's shoulder.

'I'll do my best.'

Kayla wriggles slightly in her impatience to be gone.

'I guess you don't want to stand here with us old people,' Sam says. 'Off you go now and have fun.'

Kayla smiles and nods and walks away very fast. It takes her a couple of minutes to wind her way through the crowd of party-goers, too many of whom seem determined to speak to her. At last she steps between the trees and her way is clear. There's no sign of

Mitch, but she has a good idea where to look. She runs between two buildings until the end of the stable block is in sight. There is a security light and it shows an open door. Kayla stops running and stands still for a few minutes until she is breathing normally again. Her heart is racing, but even at her age she knows that is nothing to do with running. It's because Mitch is there.

Carefully, she straightens her dress and finger combs her hair. She presses her lips together the way her mum showed her. She wants to look her best. She wants Mitch to say she looks pretty. If he does, she can tell him that she loves him. Then he'll kiss her, the way the people kiss in the movies that her mum watches. It will be her first kiss and that's perfect, because she never wants to kiss anyone except Mitch. Well, she will probably still kiss her mum and dad, but that's different kissing.

At last she's ready. Trying to calm the butterflies in her stomach, Kayla steps through the door. It takes a minute for her eyes to adjust to the darkness. She looks around but there's no sign of anyone. Then she hears noises from one of the stalls. The stall door is open. That's not right. Stall doors are always closed. That must mean Mitch is in there. Waiting for her.

She steps forward, her eyes lowered to make sure she doesn't step on any horse dung in her lovely new sandals. Then she looks into the stall.

Mitch is there. He is lying on a horse blanket that covers a bed of straw. And Lizzie is with him. As Kayla watches, Mitch takes Lizzie into his arms and kisses her. Like they do in the movies. Like people do when they are in love. And Lizzie is kissing him back. Her hands are around his shoulders and their bodies are pressed close together.

How can Mitch love Lizzie? She is usually dirty and smells of horses. And she wears jeans and looks like a boy most of the time. Mitch and Lizzie are friends. They ride together and compete against each other at shows. But that isn't what being in love is about. Being in love is about holding hands and kissing. And that isn't what Lizzie and Mitch do.

Except, of course, it is. It is what they are doing right now. Mitch shouldn't be kissing Lizzie. He should be kissing Kayla.

She backs away. They must not see her or the tears that are now streaming down her face. As she gets close to the open stable door, she starts to run. She doesn't go to the hall. She doesn't want anyone to see her, certain they all know what a fool she is. Instead she runs to the car park and sits next to her parents' car, wishing she was old enough to drive so she could go home. She never wants to see Mitch again. Or Lizzie. She hates both of them.

CHAPTER
31

The noise woke Kayla. Strange that after all these years in the inner city it should be the bush that was noisy. Her Sydney flat was well insulated and air conditioned and high. She seldom heard any of the city's noise, and when she did it was familiar and muted. But sleeping in her old room with the windows open to let in the fresh air was a different matter. She heard the birds welcome the dawn, and she heard the horses, too, nickering. She guessed that they were looking for their breakfast. It was all so familiar and yet so strange.

At last she got up. After a quick shower, she dressed for the day. Her jeans were designer and her shirt was too. She guessed she would have to buy some work clothes soon. Well, she was in the right place for it. After brushing her hair, her hand reached automatically for her make-up kit. Then she stopped. Make-up? Out here? What was she thinking? She ran her finger over the small scar above her left eye. Without make-up, she could see it quite clearly. It was a souvenir of the day that had changed all their lives. A day that had started with her waking up in this very room. She didn't remember anything at all about it, or much about the days that followed. She'd been told she was in the car when it crashed. She recalled being in hospital for what seemed a long time. And she had the scar on her temple. The doctors had told her that the memory of that day might never return, or that something might unexpectedly bring it all back. There were times she wished she could remember that last morning with her parents, but a small part of her brain kept telling her not to even try to remember the crash and what she must have seen and heard in that car.

She caught her hair into a ponytail and left the room.

The house was deserted. A cup and plate sat in the drainer by the sink, but they were quite dry. Kayla glanced at her watch. It was only eight thirty. Liz must have left very early this morning. The brown envelope lay on the kitchen table, the contract on top of it. There was a pen there too. Kayla put the kettle on and found a mug and the tea bags. While the kettle boiled, she sat and flipped to the last page of the contract and looked at Liz's signature. There was no going back now.

She sent a text to Pascale then opened her laptop. There was a lot to do. She needed to find workmen who could start right away: painters, carpenters, gardeners. Then she needed to source all the things the events themselves would need. Wine for a start. She knew of a few nearby wineries that might do a deal in exchange for a chance to have their wines served at high-end weddings. As for food, there would be local caterers she could call on. Or maybe Lachie would agree to do some of the catering. Strangely though, the thought of Lachie at Willowbrook didn't feel right. She hadn't felt that way about Ken coming up—there was no issue letting him see the part of her past that she so seldom talked about—but she wasn't dating Ken. Lachie would hate Willowbrook. He would dismiss Scone as a one-horse town and go home to the city as fast as his sports car could take him. He wasn't going to like her spending so much time up here on this project. But she'd deal with that problem later.

First, breakfast.

She opened the fridge again and peered inside. It was almost empty. The kitchen cupboards held tinned food, and the freezer was full of what looked like steak and frozen vegetables. Steak was all very well, but there was a limit. If she was going to live here, she was going to have to buy her own groceries. She found a loaf of frozen bread and made herself toast as she consulted Google about local tradesmen. It didn't take long to fill her afternoon with meetings. She closed the laptop with a feeling of satisfaction, and went to fetch Pascale's sketches from her room. Before the tradesmen arrived, she needed to check the plans against reality. Some modifications would be needed, she was sure, but Pascale's eye was good, and they wouldn't be major.

Kayla decided to look at the outside first. With the sketches under her arm and a notebook to hand, she began at the front of the house, where the gravel driveway curved around the old fountain. This was one of the items on her 'must do first' list. Water was a valuable commodity, and the fountain had been a luxury when installed by her great-great-grandfather. During Kayla's lifetime, it had run only on special occasions: birthdays and at Christmas. The bowl at the statue's feet contained a small amount of dark and stagnant water left by a recent rainfall. The stone was stained and even cracked in a couple of places, but the fountain itself was elegant and whimsical. Ken had chosen it as a backdrop for his fashion shoot and she had no doubt that cleaned and glistening with water and light, it would be an equally suitable spot for bridal photos. A little smile found its way onto her face. Her mother had always loved this fountain and it would be nice to see it running again.

As she walked around the garden making notes about the work that was needed, her mother was never far from her thoughts. Kath Lawson had been the gardener. Kayla and she had spent hours together planting and trimming and weeding. Not just flowers, but also home-grown vegetables, but the vegetable patch was now just grass. Kayla stopped at the gate to the laneway and the stables. That part of the homestead was not going to be changed—she just needed to think about a nicer fence and shrubs to hide the machinery shed. She didn't want to block the view across the paddocks down to the river flats; that was part of what made Willowbrook so unique. Nor did she want to block the view of the hills leading away from the homestead into the mountains in the distance.

Her eyes came to rest at the top of the nearest hill, where a single tree was highlighted against the blue sky. Her parents were buried there, but she had never climbed the gentle slope to their graves. After she woke in the hospital, they told her that her parents were already buried in the family graveyard—she had been too hurt to attend. And at only eleven years old, possibly too young as well. To this day, she wasn't sure if that was a good or a bad thing.

But it was time—well past time—that she climbed that hill.

She paused long enough to drop her notes back in the house, and then set off.

CHAPTER
32

It looked like Kayla was making her way to their parents' graves. Liz pulled her mount to a halt and watched. She couldn't remember her ever doing that before. Kayla might have gone there when her sister wasn't around, but Liz didn't think so. She hesitated. Should she let Kayla do this alone, as she had so obviously set out to do, or should she join her? They had never really talked about the past. Perhaps it was time they did.

When she reached the gravesite, Kayla was already there, sitting on the log that Liz had placed in the shade of the tree. Liz tied her horse to the tree and took a seat beside her sister. For a long time, they said nothing.

Kayla broke the silence. 'I wish I could remember that day.'

'Are you sure you want to?'

'Yes … No … I don't know. I want to understand what happened. I feel as if I've lost something important—those last few hours with them. The first thing I remember is waking up in hospital and being told they were gone.'

Liz was silent. This was another piece of the guilt she carried.

'Why didn't you tell me, Liz? Why did I have to find out from someone else?'

'You know why—I wasn't there. I'd gone to the other hospital with Dad.'

'I know now. But back then, all I knew was that you weren't with me when my whole world was ripped apart. I was eleven years old. I was frightened and I was hurt and I had no one. And then I wasn't even allowed to come to the funeral. You took that away from me as well.'

'I thought that after everything you'd been through ... And you were in hospital. I just wanted to spare you one more trauma. I'm sorry if I was wrong.'

'When I came home, I saw the new crosses up here, and I sat in my room and cried. I remember crying until I thought I was going to die. But I never saw you cry.'

'Not then. No. I did my crying the day we laid them both here.'

Silence settled again, broken only by the sound of the horse stamping his feet against the flies.

'Dad would have been proud of the way you've worked to save this place,' Kayla said.

Liz shook her head. 'But I haven't saved it. If it's going to be saved, you'll be the one to do it. He always said you were the smart one.'

'But you've kept it running for the past fifteen years. All alone.'

'When I was really small he told me that whatever happened I must never sell the land. I promised him I wouldn't. I broke that promise.'

They looked across the river to the church and the outbuildings that surrounded it.

'Why didn't you tell me that it was Mitch who bought the church and the river flats?'

It was a good question, and Liz didn't have an answer. At least, not an answer she was prepared to give. That would open a can of worms she would much rather avoid.

'I guess I forgot. It wasn't a good time. We were suffering from drought, and we had that Hendra virus scare. The horses were quarantined. Everybody here was holding their breaths waiting for the worst to happen. And I was so ashamed.'

'Of what?'

'Of letting Dad down.'

'Are you ever going to tell me what happened with you and Mitch?'

That question again. Kayla wasn't going to let it go, but Liz couldn't tell her. To tell her that would be to reveal fifteen years of lies and deceit.

'What do you mean? We were kids. We grew out of it.'

'Don't play innocent with me. You and Mitch had something more than a teenage crush. I remember walking in on the two of you in the stables at the showground.'

'When?'

'That year.'

'Oh.'

'Given the size of the crush I had on him, you were lucky I didn't tell Mum and Dad just to get you in trouble.'

'Yeah, but that would have got Mitch in trouble too.'

'It must have been a real pain having your little sister moping around behind you like that.'

Liz smiled at the memory. 'It was a bit.'

'So, are you going to answer my question? What happened to you and Mitch?'

'He went away.'

'I know. That surprised me. I thought he would have stayed on Willowbrook to help you. He already practically lived here.'

'But he didn't live here. He was Dad's employee. That's all he was. Okay, I might have had a thing for him as a teenager, we both did. But so what? We were all kids. When his dad got work in Queensland, he went with his family.'

Kayla was frowning and her piercing blue eyes seemed to look past Liz's words into the truth that she was hiding.

'But he came back.'

Liz hadn't known he was coming back. She'd been struggling financially then too. The bank had threatened foreclosure unless she raised money the only way she could—by selling off a parcel of land. She had barely glanced at the papers as she signed them. It wouldn't have told her anything anyway, because Mitch had hidden his identity behind a company name. It was only after it was done that she had found out who now owned a piece of her heritage. She had seen it as a betrayal. Even now, she winced when she remembered the things she'd said to Mitch when he came to tell her he was her new neighbour. She had made the most terrible accusations. She knew that she had deliberately created a rift between them because his return from Queensland terrified her—the only way she could stand to have him so close was to hate him.

If she told herself enough times that she hated him, maybe one day she really would.

'I didn't have time for—'

'Oh, for God's sake, Liz. Okay, you were busy. But that doesn't mean you cut yourself off. And Mitch would have helped.'

'Busy?' Liz gave her emotions full rein. It was so easy to get angry. Far easier than facing the truth. 'Busy? Kayla, I don't think you have any idea how hard it was for me. Dad wanted you to have every chance for the future you wanted. I gave up so much so that you could get an education.'

'I never wanted any of that. I was still a child, Liz. I'd just lost my parents in horrible circumstances that I couldn't even remember. And you sent me away. Have you even the slightest idea how much that hurt? How much I hated you for that? How much, sometimes, I still hate you for that?'

Liz leaped to her feet. Anger had always been her defence. 'And I was only eighteen. I was too young to care for a property and a child. I did the best I could for you. If that wasn't good enough—'

'I'm not saying that.'

'Yes, you are. I failed you and now I've failed Dad as well ... I had to sell the river flats and now Willowbrook is being turned into some sort of party place. And someone else is paying for that too.'

The words were too harsh in her ears. Liz felt shame and anger and self-loathing close an icy fist around her heart. She crossed swiftly to where her horse stood and swung into the saddle.

'I've got horses to exercise and repairs to do. I'll be late this evening.'

CHAPTER
33

Mitch braked as a kangaroo appeared out of the twilight and bounded across the road. Where there was one there would be more, and he was travelling too fast for safety. He'd seen what hitting a roo could do to a car and its driver, not to mention the poor animal. He flexed his fingers on the steering wheel and forced himself to concentrate. He was on his way to meet Sue for the first time since before the Willowbrook photo shoot. She'd been pleased when he'd rung that morning to suggest they meet up at their favourite pizza place in Tamworth. Up till now they had pretty much taken turns making the hour and a half drive between Tamworth and Scone, but he was more than willing to volunteer this time. He was feeling a bit guilty about neglecting her.

And he was feeling even more guilty about Liz.

Not that there was anything to feel guilty about. He'd seen more of Liz in the past two weeks than in the last couple of years, but nothing had happened between them and it never would. He and

Liz were in the past. She'd made it clear more times than he could count that there was no place in her life for him.

He accepted that.

He got to the restaurant and noticed that Sue's Toyota was already in the car park. He saw her the moment he walked through the doorway, head down, checking something on her mobile phone, her blonde hair falling forward and hiding her face. He watched for a few moments as her fingers, long and tipped with red, danced over the phone. They looked delicate, but Sue was in no way delicate. She would never run a property alone, but she had a different kind of strength. Everything about her was different from Liz, from the flash of red on those nails to her pretty amber eyes and the way she welcomed people into her life. Especially the way she welcomed him.

Sue looked up and saw him and immediately put the phone away. That was something he really liked about her. People first. Always.

He walked up to her and bent to kiss her. Just a swift kiss on the cheek.

She smiled at him as he sat opposite her. 'It's good to see you,' she said.

'Sorry about the last few weeks,' he said. 'I've been caught up in stuff happening.'

'I was worried.' She grinned. 'When you emailed about that fashion photo thing, I thought one of those models might have whisked you away from me.'

'Not likely. But the photographer did suggest ...' Mitch raised his eyebrows in a suggestive manner.

'Oh, really? I thought you said the photographer was a guy.'

'He was.'

Her laughter was like the rest of her, straightforward and without artifice.

She plied him with questions about the photo shoot as they ordered pizza and wine. Then she started talking about a case that had come into their clinic this week. Sue was a vet nurse. They met when she was volunteering at a local campdraft, and she had the kindest heart and soul he had ever known.

'... shooting native birds is illegal. That poor cockatoo. We've saved him, but we won't be able to release him back into the wild with that wing.'

He watched her face as she talked. He liked being around Sue. Her love for life cheered him when he was down and he laughed a lot when he was with her. He liked her heart and her mind and her body. He liked her very much, and that was the problem. He liked her, but he wasn't in love with her. He should be—he wanted to be. There were worse things in life than waking up in bed next to a beautiful, loving woman.

And one of those worse things was being dishonest to a beautiful and loving woman.

Their conversation faltered as they ate and didn't pick up again afterwards.

Finally, Sue leaned back in her chair. 'What's wrong?'

Time to confess. 'Sue. I think—I mean, you're special. To me. But I think, maybe, this isn't right for us.'

She closed her eyes for a very long time. When she opened them again, there were no tears. He was thankful for that, but it was more than he felt he deserved.

'This doesn't really come as a surprise,' she said softly. 'It was three weeks ... I guessed there was a reason.'

'It's not—'

'Uh-uh.' Sue shook her head. 'No explanations and definitely no clichés.'

He stopped talking. He didn't know what to say next. Sue folded her napkin and placed it on the table beside her empty plate. She lifted the wine glass and took one small sip. Mitch thought her hands were shaking a little, but he wasn't sure.

'Is there anything I can say?'

Sue shook her head and smiled a sweet, sad smile. 'No. I think I always knew this wasn't long term. I hope she knows how lucky she is.'

Mitch frowned. 'What?'

'This girl you're carrying a torch for. She must be pretty special.'

Mitch lowered his eyes to look at his clasped hands.

Sue got to her feet. 'Well, I wish you luck, Mitch. See you around.' She kissed him on the cheek and walked out of the restaurant without looking back.

Through the window, Mitch watched her cross the car park, get in her car and drive away. He dug in his pocket for his wallet and left a pile of money on the table. As he walked to his car, he told himself he'd done the right thing; Sue deserved someone who loved her, and he wasn't that someone. It didn't make him feel any better.

He drove out of town, the white lines on the road shining in his headlights. He thought about those years in Queensland. The years after Liz's parents died and she sent him away. He'd been angry and hurt, and he'd chatted up every pretty girl he came across. He realised now how badly he'd treated some of them. He was sorry and ashamed. He'd been very young, but that was no excuse. Even then, he'd known better. He was trying to do the right thing by Sue, but a small voice at the back of his mind was asking him if he hadn't just made a mistake in giving her up for a dream that was long gone.

CHAPTER
34

It is very cold for July and the frost crackles under Mitch's feet as he sprints through the grass. It's after midnight on a moonless night. He doesn't want to risk bringing his car too close to the house. Mr or Mrs Lawson might see him. He has to talk to Lizzie. It has to be just the two of them ... and it has to be tonight.

He slows as he approaches the house and ducks around the back. Lizzie's room is on the top floor, but that's okay, he has a good throwing arm. He picks up a couple of small stones and carefully pitches one at Lizzie's window. Then another. The window slides up and she peers out before he throws the third. He can barely see her, but the light above the door is always on. That's enough to see her wave before she vanishes. Mitch backs away from the house in case her parents are still awake, but he doubts it. Like everyone else on the land, the Lawsons get up with the sun, work hard and go to bed early.

The door opens silently and Lizzie slips out. She has pulled jeans on over her pyjamas and grabbed her father's warm coat from the peg beside the door. She's not a fool though, and is wearing thick socks and boots. She hurries over to Mitch. He puts his arms around her and kisses her, a long, passionate kiss that leaves both of them gasping.

'Come on.' He takes her hand and they fade into the shadow of the trees then start running in the direction of the stables.

The feed room is warmer than outdoors, but their breath comes in white clouds.

'What's wrong?' Lizzie asks. She's shivering.

'My dad has got a job in Queensland and he wants to take us all with him.'

'No! You can't leave. Why would he leave? He's got a job here.' Lizzie doesn't believe what Mitch is saying. It's not true because it can't be true. Mitch can't leave her.

'He says this is better. It's as assistant trainer at a racing stable.'

'When?'

'In about two months. I said fine, I'll stay. I've got a good job here. I'll find somewhere to live. I'm almost eighteen. I'm not a kid any more.'

'And what did he say?'

'He said no way. That I was going with them.'

'You can't go.' It is a cry from the very depths of her young heart.

'And I won't.' He kisses her again. 'Lizzie, I love you. I never want to be without you. Let's get married.'

Lizzie stops breathing. 'Married?'

'Yes. Of course. We love each other. Why should we wait?'

She flings her arms around his neck and kisses him again and he knows he has the answer he wanted. The kissing continues for a few minutes before she gently pushes him away.

'But our parents won't let us.' Her face falls. 'They'll say we're too young. That we don't know what real love is.'

'They're wrong. I know what real love is, Lizzie, and I think you do too.'

She nods, and this time a tear springs from the corner of one eye. He wipes it away gently.

'You're eighteen, Lizzie. I will be too in a couple of weeks. Then they can't stop us.'

Lizzie isn't like other girls. She doesn't have dreams of a big wedding with a cake and flowers and a fancy white frock. Lizzie thinks it might be nice to have her father walk her down the aisle. But even that seems unimportant against the threat of Mitch leaving.

'Yes. Let's do it!'

Mitch picks her up and spins around, his face a picture of joy. He starts kissing her again even before her feet are on the ground.

'How do we do this?' she asks when at last they break apart.

'I don't know. I guess we'll have to find out.' Mitch pauses. 'You don't mind doing it like this, do you? With just us.'

'No, silly.' She slaps his arms none too gently. 'And anyway, we won't be alone. There have to be witnesses. I know that much.'

'All right. It might not be in a church.'

Lizzie thinks about this for a few moments. She has always assumed they would be married in the church across the creek, like her parents. But if it comes to a choice between a church and losing Mitch, there is no choice.

'A church would be nice, but I really don't care. As long as we are married.'

'I'll see if I can find a church, but we've got to keep this a secret. If either of our parents find out, they'll stop us.'

'Once we're both eighteen they can't.'

'Are you sure you're okay with this? I mean, doing it in secret. Without all the fuss and the presents and things.'

'I'm sure. I'm not that sort of a girl.'

He smiles. 'But if you wanted to be …'

'I don't.'

'My parents will be disappointed. Yours too. I'm sure your dad would want to walk you down the aisle. Isn't that what all dads want?'

'He'll get over it. He can walk Kayla down the aisle. I know Mum and Dad like you. They must realise that we want to be together forever. It'll be fine.'

But deep inside she's not so sure. She's pretty certain her mum and dad would say they were too young and expect them to wait a year or two, or even more. Kayla will definitely be upset at not being a bridesmaid.

But then Mitch takes her hand. He drops onto one knee in the straw. 'I don't have a ring, but I will get you one just as soon as I can,' he says. 'But—I want to do this right. Lizzie, will you marry me?'

She wants to do it right too. 'Yes. I will marry you, Mitch.'

He leaps back to his feet and they come together in a kiss that lasts a very long time. It is a better kiss than all the kisses that have gone before, because it's the beginning of their future.

When finally they part, both are breathing heavily. Lizzie slides Mitch's jacket over his shoulders and begins to tug at his shirt. This is not new to either of them. Mitch pulls his shirt over his head, and Lizzie's hands stroke the firm, warm skin of his chest and shoulders. Then she throws off her heavy coat. Her pyjama top is old and well worn. It's made of flannel to protect against the chill, but there's no chill in the tack room as Mitch slips it off her body. His hands and lips on her smooth skin are keeping her warm.

Mitch takes his hands from her just long enough to pull a horse blanket onto the floor. They drop to their knees and Lizzie falls onto the blanket, pulling him after her.

'Ow.' She flinches.

'What?' Mitch pulls himself upright.

'Buckle,' Lizzie says, pointing to the mark left by the leather and metal on the tender skin of her side.

'Oh, sorry. Is it all right?'

'You could kiss it better,' she teases, loving the look in his eyes, and he gently runs a finger over the red mark. Then his lips touch the same place, and she is lost. She reaches for his hips, fingers tugging at the belt that holds his jeans.

'Lizzie. Wait.' He pulls away. To her it feels like a part of herself has been taken away.

'Mitch?'

'We said we would wait. Until we were older. Until we were married.'

'I don't want to wait. I love you, Mitch. And I want to. We're engaged. That's almost married.'

Mitch shakes his head. He isn't sure. It seems more honourable— more respectful—of Lizzie to wait.

'Don't you want to?'

How can she ask such a thing, when his whole body is trembling with the desire—no, the *need*—to be with her? 'Yes.' That one word is all he can manage.

'Please.'

He cannot deny her. Slowly, he removes her clothes. They laugh together at her woolly socks, but he removes them despite the cold. He will have all of her.

She marvels at the beauty of his naked body, and the strength of him. She wraps her arms and legs around him as if to never let him go and gasps with awe and joy as she feels him move inside her.

He is gentle, because he will never hurt her.

It never occurs to him that he could be the one hurt.

CHAPTER
35

'I need to get Deimos to this competition but I can't ask Mitch to look after the place again. So … would you be able to feed the horses for me, just for the weekend?'

Kayla looked up from her plate. For dinner, she and Liz were sharing a chicken pie, which Kayla had made from their mother's old recipe book. Maybe the familiar taste had taken them back to another time, when conversations weren't always so difficult.

'I guess I can. But I haven't been around horses for a very long time. Are you sure it's safe to leave me in charge?' She had meant it as a joke, but it hadn't come out quite that way.

'Of course. I'll mix all the feeds before I go. You just have to put them out Saturday night and Sunday morning.'

'And muck out the stables too, I suppose.'

'Well, yes. If you're willing to.'

Kayla groaned. She'd asked for that. 'All right.'

'There'll only be one or two horses in. And you can't have forgotten how to shovel manure.'

'Like riding a bike, is it?'

This time they both laughed a little.

Kayla slept late on the appointed morning and stretched as she slowly came awake. In the distance she heard a kookaburra laugh, and smiled. The morning noises of the bush no longer woke her. This bed no longer felt strange and she had just had a deep and restful sleep. A glance at the clock on her bedside table told her she'd best get moving. There was a tradesman due in an hour.

She crossed the hall to the bathroom, which had taken on the delightful scent of her favourite rose soap. After her shower, she pulled on a pair of jeans, T-shirt and trainers from the growing collection in the chest of drawers and the wardrobe she had recently added to the room. Her laptop was charging on the dressing table, but she didn't need that this morning. Everything she needed to know was in her head.

The only sign of Liz's departure was a glass sitting upside down next to the sink. It was a long drive to Coonabarabran, and the competition would start early. She would have fed all the horses before she left at the crack of dawn, so there was no need for Kayla to visit the stables until later this evening. She made herself coffee and toast and checked her emails on her phone as she waited for the sound of a workman's van making its way down the driveway.

When the van arrived, she left the house by the front door, not the kitchen, taking her coffee with her. She liked looking from the wide veranda onto the front lawn, which was beginning to take shape. Trees and bushes had been trimmed where necessary, and flower beds planted. It was a real pleasure to see the new, bright green shoots and buds. There were roses among the native plants, and any day now she expected to see bright flashes of colour. Lawn was the next step, but only after all the construction work was finished. She was going to cover the old gravel driveway with a wide swathe of green, which meant the vans would have limited access to the house. Not the stables, of course. She'd made sure Liz would have nothing to complain about in that regard.

The man studying the old stone fountain looked up when he heard her approaching.

'G'day.' He tipped his hat. Kayla loved it when men did that. 'I'm Jake Ellis.'

He was middle aged and unshaven with work-worn hands. Everything about him said he was a man of the bush. Everything about him said that whatever the job was, he'd get it done. Kayla didn't meet too many people like that in the city.

'Pleased to meet you. We spoke on the phone. I'm Kayla Lawson.'

'This is the fountain you were talking about.'

'Yes.'

'Well, let's have a good look at her then.'

He ran his hands over the carved horses that danced around the central pillar and looked at the spouts where water had once leaped into the air to fall with a musical tinkle into the bowl below. As he crawled around the base to inspect the plumbing, Kayla found her mind drifting to the late-night birthday picnics that had been held here when her parents were alive.

Jake scrambled to his feet. 'She needs a fair bit of work.'

'Can you do it?'

'I'll have to replace some of the plumbing. I guess it's attached to the house water supply.'

'I really don't know.'

'No problems. I'll figure it out. The stone needs cleaning. There's a few chips and cracks here and there. I'll mend some. Others will just add character.'

'When can you start?'

Jake patted the head of the nearest stone horse. 'Well, this is a bit of a challenge for me. Never done nothing like it before. I'm working on the showgrounds right now, but I could do this on the weekends.'

'And how long will it take?'

'Dunno. A bit depends on what I find when I get a look at those pipes.'

'And now the big one. What's it going to cost me?'

Jake pulled back his hat and scratched his head. 'I can't rightly say. I'll have to price the parts. And then there's my time. Not sure how long it'll take. But I'm sure we can figure something out.'

If she was in her office in Sydney, Kayla would have thrown him out by now. She expected her contractors to be precise and professional about everything, especially price. But this was the bush and things were different here.

'When can you start?'

'Right away. If you're happy, I'll have a bit of a poke about now so I can see what parts I need to get in. Then next weekend, I'll get stuck into it.'

'Fine.'

Kayla left him to it. She was about to start checking the work on the inside of the house when she heard noises coming from the stables. If anything happened to the horses in her absence, Liz would kill her. She left her coffee cup on the veranda and walked to the stables.

By the time she got there, whatever disturbance she'd heard was over. Only one head was looking over a stall door: Zeke. Liz's much loved gelding was alone in the stable block.

'Are you a bit lonely, Zeke?' Kayla rubbed the old horse on the cheek. In response he stretched out his neck and turned his head.

'Oh, you want your ear scratched.' Kayla obliged.

She spotted a grooming brush on an upturned bucket next to the stall door. Picking up the brush, she stepped into the stall and began grooming Zeke's shiny coat. Her arms fell into a rhythm that lingered deep in her memory. How long was it since she'd last groomed a horse? She had forgotten how satisfying it was. How soothing, not just for the animal, but also for the person doing it.

Her hand paused and Zeke looked at her.

'Want do you think, should we go for a ride?'

Zeke blinked at her.

'I'll take that as a yes. I hope I can remember how.'

Before she could think better of it, Kayla darted to the house and found her oldest pair of jeans. Boots were a problem, until she remembered the cupboard in the laundry, where she found several pairs of boots in various states of disrepair. Liz never threw anything away that might prove useful. One pair of those boots fitted Kayla well enough. It was surprising how comfortable she felt. She wondered what Pascale or Lachie would say if they could see her now. She smiled and headed back to the stables, jamming a battered old Akubra onto her head as she did.

The same memories that guided her hands when she was grooming Zeke helped her again as she found a saddle and bridle for him. As she led him out of the stable, common sense told her she should spend a little time in the safety of the big exercise yard. She hadn't ridden a horse for more years than she liked to admit, and Zeke hadn't been ridden by anyone other than Liz for even longer than that. But this wasn't a morning for common sense. She led Zeke through the gate to the home paddock.

'We'll be all right, won't we?' She stroked the horse's nose, then slipped the reins over his neck. 'You'll look after me.'

She checked the girth one more time. It was tight. She slipped one booted foot into the stirrup and lifted herself into the saddle.

Zeke stood stock still as she settled herself into the embrace of the old but well cared for leather.

'Okay.'

She nudged Zeke gently with her heels and the horse started moving at a walk. He didn't need much guiding as they made their way along the fence line.

'What do you think, could we step it up a bit?'

Kayla nudged the horse again and he broke into a trot. She struggled for a few minutes to find her rhythm, but not for long. This really was just like riding a bike—she hadn't forgotten. Zeke tossed his head, looking at the open country ahead of him and Kayla didn't try to stop him as he broke into a canter. She knew she would pay for this tomorrow, when long unused muscles complained, but for now, she didn't care. She loved the feel of the wind in her face and the horse running beneath her.

It felt like coming home.

CHAPTER
36

'Listen up, riders—next up will be seventy-eight, and I want one-fifteen, thirty-seven and eighty-three ready when I call them.'

One-fifteen. That was her. Liz stroked the dark glossy neck of her mount. 'Okay, Deimos. You're doing fine so far. This next bit is the part that really counts. Stay with me, boy.'

Deimos shook his head in what Liz hoped wasn't disagreement. She gathered up the reins and turned the horse towards the steward and the gate leading to the competition ring.

The steward looked up as she approached and smiled in recognition. 'Hi, Liz.' The man was a regular at competitions, both as a steward and a competitor. He'd competed against her, and against her father before that. He ran his eyes over Deimos with more than just a steward's interest. 'Is that one of Apollo's? He has the look.'

'He is. I'm thinking I might stand him to a few mares next season.'

'If he performs as well as his sire, I might be interested. You can go through now to the warm-up area.'

Liz nodded as the steward opened the gate. She guided Deimos to the far corner of the warm-up ring, walking him in a small circle to keep him alert and loose as she waited to enter the main ring. A couple more competitors entered the ring. They acknowledged each other with a nod, but nothing more—all were focussed totally on the job at hand. There was a small jump along one fence. Liz tightened her reins and urged Deimos into a trot. He stepped forward eagerly, bending to her hands as she turned him in a tight circle. She lengthened his stride as they moved along the fence, still at a trot. Deimos saw the jump and his ears twitched. Without breaking stride he leaped easily over the red-and-white-striped rails.

He was ready, and so was she. This competition was a novice event and not a regular part of the main show circuit. It was designed specifically to give young horses their first outing and there would be a lot of very critical eyes out there. If she had any hope of Deimos replacing his sire, he had to impress even at this early stage of his career.

The previous rider left the competition ring, and the steward waved her forward.

The speakers around the arena crackled into life. 'The working stock horse class continues with competitor one-fifteen—Elizabeth Lawson riding Willowbrook Deimos.'

Liz took a deep breath and walked Deimos towards the judge. Her hands were steady. To win this class, Deimos had to show himself to be balanced and obedient. Responsive to his rider's every command. She asked Deimos to halt and he stood rock still as she saluted the judge with a nod. She closed her eyes for half a second, picturing in her mind the workout pattern she had memorised and practised.

Deimos responded instantly when she closed her legs against his side. She turned him in a smart half-circle at a walk, then pushed him into a trot. His ears pricked as his strong, even stride carried them in a half-circle around the ring. His transition into a canter was everything Liz could have hoped for.

As they curved into a figure of eight, Liz felt the moment when Deimos seemed to hover in the air for a heartbeat as his legs flashed with a flying change of lead. Her heart soared with him. The colt effortlessly stretched his legs into a hand gallop along the far side of the ring. She closed her legs hard against his side and called for a halt. Deimos tucked his hind legs beneath him, flung his head up and slid to a stop. A twitch of the reins and he was galloping in the opposite direction.

The last test came as Liz pulled him to a halt once more. She was breathing heavily, but Deimos hadn't even raised a sweat. At her command he stepped smartly backwards. One ... two ... three ... Liz counted the six steps in her head and told him to stop. She let out her reins, allowing the horse to stretch his neck and relax. As she pushed him into a walk towards the judge, Liz put the reins into her left hand as with her right she shook out the stock whip she had carried all through the workout. She raised the handle and swung the whip. A loud crack echoed across the ring, and another and another. Deimos kept up his steady walk, a slight twitch of one ear his only reaction to the movement and the noise.

The judge was nodding in approval as Liz stopped to salute at the end of her round.

As she left the ring, she was greeted with similar nods from the stewards, other competitors and people who had just been watching. She smiled in return, but mostly she just wanted to find a quiet corner to await the results. Once there, she slid out of the saddle and wrapped her arms around Deimos's neck.

'That was wonderful. You were perfect,' she told him as she buried her face in his mane and breathed deep while her heart seemed ready to burst with pride.

Liz loved horses. Being with them, training them, riding them and competing with them. She always had and she always would. But as she heard the judge call her and Deimos back into the ring for the awarding of ribbons, she realised that she hadn't taken this much joy in her life and work for a very long time.

CHAPTER
37

Kayla stood back and viewed the statue with a critical eye. Jake Ellis had finished his work and he'd done an exceptional job. New life had been breathed into the stained old fountain. Water flowed again, the sound of it cascading into the stone basin an almost bell-like counterpoint to the stillness of the afternoon. It would be a perfect place for bridal photographs.

The phone in the pocket of her jeans buzzed. She pulled it out and saw a message from Pascale.

How is it going? I have a potential client.

Already? Kayla shook her head. Pascale had never been one to take things slowly. Kayla inspected the work that had been done. Now that the fountain was ready, the grounds were almost complete. More work was needed on defining a car parking area, but depending on the kind of wedding it was going to be, that might not be an insurmountable problem.

She looked up at the homestead. The painters had finished yesterday. The wrought iron on the upper balcony gleamed faintly, the brickwork had been cleaned and the grand staircase to the front door once more looked well-kept and stylish. Kayla smiled faintly. Her mother would have been pleased to see it looking like this. The wide, shady veranda offered a refuge from the afternoon sun, and the beautiful dark-wood doors glowed softly with much polishing.

Kayla walked inside to be greeted by a cacophony of sound and the smell of fresh paint. The two main rooms on the ground floor were almost finished. The bride's retreat featured carefully lit make-up mirrors. There was a gilt-edged full-length mirror for the inspection of bridal outfits, and her own special touch: a gold and cream brocade-covered chaise longue that she had found at a nearby antiques shop. Well, second-hand furniture and junk more than antiques, but now that it was re-upholstered the chaise looked wonderful and, at this moment, particularly inviting.

She was exhausted after four weeks of running to Sydney and back, working her normal weddings as well as supervising the refurbishment at Willowbrook. Living with Liz hadn't exactly been easy either, but there had been good moments too. They had celebrated Deimos's first competition win together. The celebration had featured beer, not Champagne, but they had done it together. That meant something.

Leaving the bride's retreat, Kayla walked down the hall to the ballroom. There was no furniture there yet since the newly polished floor was drying. But in a day or two, a couple of rugs and some leather armchairs in a colonial style would complete the room. The kitchen and dining facilities were another matter. Just this morning Kayla had run through a status with the workmen there, and there was quite a bit more to be done. All the food would be prepared off site, but commercial heating and refrigeration units would need to be installed to preserve the food once it was delivered. Initially the crockery and cutlery and glassware would be hired in, but in the future she might need storage cupboards for those. And the kitchen still had to function as a domestic kitchen for Liz.

As always, her laptop was sitting open on the kitchen table. She found the expected email from Pascale. A Japanese wedding tour operator had been let down by his venue. He was looking to give his six couples and about thirty guests a true outback wedding experience three weeks from now. Pascale was known for pulling rabbits out of hats when it came to weddings at short notice. If they could get the tour operator out of trouble by offering Willowbrook, it might lead to more bookings from the same company.

Kayla was about to send an email telling her partner that Willowbrook wasn't ready yet because of the catering, but as her hands hovered over the keyboard her brain spun into high gear. If the wedding was to be a true outback experience, they could probably do it. It would just take a bit of lateral thinking. She tapped words into her search engine and, after carefully perusing the results, made a phone call. Then another. Fifteen minutes later, she hit reply on the email.

She was engrossed in her plans when a voice disturbed her.

'When can we clear the next room?'

It took a moment for the full impact of the decorator's words to hit home and it was a good thing Liz was out with the horses somewhere. Kayla followed her decorator into Liz's office, the inner sanctum from which everyone had been banned, including her. Until now.

The decorator stepped into the centre of the room and looked around with something very like a curled lip. Kayla didn't need to be a mind reader to know what he was thinking. This room was supposed to become the groom's retreat, but it was still piled high with Liz's paperwork and horse magazines and stud books. And, of course, her bed. Liz had so far resisted all Kayla's efforts to move upstairs into what was to become the private part of the house. With Pascale's request foremost in her thoughts, Kayla knew she had run out of time.

'I'll get this cleaned out today or tomorrow,' she said, trying to sound certain.

'Good. We've got to get this mess sorted. I really don't know why anyone would live like this. How they could live like this.' The decorator didn't shudder, but it was a near thing.

There was a noise from the doorway. Kayla flinched as she saw Liz standing there, her face like thunder.

'What do you think—'

'Liz, I have good news.' Kayla cut her sister off before she could go any further. 'Thanks, Peter. I'll talk to you tomorrow.' Kayla dismissed the decorator, who sidled out of the room without making eye contact with Liz.

Liz folded her arms and waited for Kayla to continue.

'I think we have our first wedding.'

'But I thought the place was a long way from ready.'

'Not really. This wedding will be small, and quite special. In the garden. It's an overseas tour group who want an Australian outback experience. We can have a barbecue and roast a pig or some such. They'll love it.'

Liz was silent.

'Liz. Come on. You agreed to all this. You need the money. I've got enough to do and I don't want to have to fight you as well.'

'I know, it's just ...'

'Just what?' Kayla's voice softened. Maybe this time she and Liz could talk things through without a blazing row.

'Forget it. Everything's fine.'

Kayla knew that it really wasn't, but she was going to take whatever small steps she could.

'As you say, I agreed and I've taken the money, so it's too late to stop it now. If you'll just get out of my office, I'll start clearing it for you to do what needs to be done.'

'It doesn't have to be right this minute.'

Liz ignored her. She walked over to her desk and reached for a pile of books and magazines on the shelf above it. As she did, the pile toppled sideways and started a near avalanche of the contents of the shelves. Instinctively, Kayla darted forward to stop the calamity. Her fingers closed around a china ornament as it teetered on the very brink of disaster.

As Liz fought with the piles of paper, Kayla looked at the object in her hands. The horse she'd given her father all those years ago. Memories came rushing at her, of visiting Sam in this office when she was small and being so proud that he had her gift on display. She turned it over in her hands. It was a cheap thing, old fashioned and dusty, but to her, it had its own special beauty.

'I can't believe you've kept this all these years,' she said softly.

Liz had dragged a box from beneath her bed. It was half full of old papers and, without a word, she lifted it onto a chair and started throwing more papers into it.

'Liz. Slow down. We never did clear out the office after Mum and Dad died. Perhaps we should do this together.'

'You've got the weddings. This is all stud business. It's my responsibility.' Liz picked up her heavy box and pushed past Kayla, who stepped back. Her foot connected with the bed. As she tried to regain her balance, the china horse slipped from her fingers. The sisters watched as, almost in slow motion, the horse fell onto the hardwood floor and shattered.

After a few moments of shocked silence, Kayla walked away. She went to the kitchen and stared at her laptop, pretending to work while she fought tears. Breaking the horse had been an accident. She knew that. But breaking the relationship between two sisters … that was different. No one could say that was an accident. And it looked to her that it might prove the hardest to fix.

She heard a series of loud noises from the office then footsteps stomping up and down the stairs. Liz must be struggling with those heavy loads, but Kayla was not going to offer to help. Not again.

'There. It's done.' Liz walked through the kitchen to the door.

'Liz—wait.'

Her sister didn't break stride.

'You know, one of these days you're going to have to stop running away.'

But the words fell into the empty space. Liz was gone.

Kayla walked into the office. It was just an empty room, the dust settling once more. Liz had swept everything away, even the pieces of broken china. Kayla wondered if the remains of her father's horse had been thrown out, or if they had been preserved: a hundred pieces of something precious with only a faint hope of repair.

CHAPTER
38

Mitch saw her as he walked out of the saddlers carrying two new halters. Liz was driving through the centre of Scone much faster than safety, or the law, allowed. That wasn't like Liz. She was the most cautious driver he knew. It was contrary to her nature, but after what had happened to her parents, he understood perfectly why she drove as she did. She never drove fast or dangerously. Something was very wrong. Then she jumped a red light.

Mitch sprinted for his car. He tossed his purchases onto the passenger seat of his ute and started the engine. He caught up with Liz, who was now on the highway out of town and still speeding. Mitch hung back. He didn't want to push her to greater speed, but he was careful to keep her well in view. It took about thirty minutes to reach Murrurundi, where she slowed and turned off the highway. Mitch eased off. He knew where she was going and he wanted to give her a few minutes to calm down before he arrived. He had a pretty good idea she wouldn't be very welcoming.

When he reached the Rosedale Equine Complex, he saw her car parked under a tree. He parked next to it, got out and looked around. Instinct led him to the grassy bank that overlooked the horse area and the mountains beyond. She was sitting on the slope, her knees pulled up tight to her chest, her head resting on her arms. And if he didn't know her better, Mitch would have sworn she was crying.

But she couldn't be. Liz never cried.

He approached her, making just enough noise that she would be aware of his arrival. He dropped to the ground beside her, close but not quite touching. He could feel the tension in her body and wanted nothing more than to put his arms around her and pull her close. But he didn't.

'Why did you follow me?' she eventually asked.

'I saw the way you were driving. You never drive like that. I figured something was wrong.'

'And now you're going to ask me what it is.'

'No. Now I'm going to sit here and be your friend. If you want to tell me, you can. But if you don't, I won't ask you.'

The silence that followed was strained. He could hear her short, jagged breaths. A couple of horses wandered into sight in the paddock. A kookaburra laughed in a nearby tree as the wind gently shook the branches. Liz's breathing gradually returned to normal.

'Kayla has had people working at Willowbrook. Turning it into a wedding venue.'

'I know. It's a small town. People talk.'

'She says it will make money. And I really need the money.'

Mitch didn't say anything.

'It's a horse stud. It's my home, but these past few weeks it's been full of strangers, changing everything. I don't want strangers wandering around. And I don't like weddings.'

There it was. The one thing they could not talk about. But he had to say something.

'When is the first one?'

'Not that far off. The place isn't ready yet, but she says it'll be some outdoor touristy Australiana thing. It sounds awful.'

Mitch chuckled. 'It does a bit. You know, if you want to get away from the wedding, you can always come over to my place.'

Liz froze, then he heard her breathe again. 'I don't think so,' she said quietly, then continued in a firm voice, 'Anyway, I don't want to leave them alone. Without me there goodness only knows what they'll get up to. I have to make sure the horses aren't disturbed.'

'I'm sure Kayla has thought of that.'

'She has. She's thought of everything. She's controlling everything now. I don't feel like it's my place any more. I've lost it.'

'No, you haven't. Willowbrook is a part of you, Liz. Even if you left, which I don't imagine you will ever do, you will not lose Willowbrook. Ever.'

They sat in silence for a while. The tension in her body seemed to have faded a little.

'You know, Dad was part of the organising committee that planned the very first King of the Ranges,' Liz said thoughtfully. 'He was the one who convinced the council that it would be a good idea. Tourist money and all that.'

'I know.' Mitch was surprised by the turn of the conversation. Liz never talked about her father and the accident. The changes at Willowbrook must have rattled her more than he'd thought.

'And he never got to compete. That seems so unfair.'

'I think he and Apollo would have won hands down.'

'Are you entering next year?' Liz asked.

'Yep. I guess you are too.'

'Yeah. That colt, Deimos, has all the potential in the world, but I don't want to rush him. We've done a couple of small shows and he did all right. He's not a champion yet, but maybe one day he will be. I have to get him out more. He's a bit green for the King of the Ranges, but we've got some time. If he puts up a good showing, he might attract a few mares.'

'I might be interested in sending a mare to him.'

'Don't. I don't want your pity.' Her voice hardened.

'It's not pity. It's business. I wanted to send a mare to Apollo, but Deimos carries his bloodline.'

The silence that settled over them now was peaceful. The long twilight was falling and the heat of the day had dissipated.

At last Liz got to her feet. Mitch did too and they walked to their cars. Mitch didn't try to open her door, he knew her better than that.

She stood with one hand on the door and for the first time looked him squarely in the face. 'Thank you.'

'What for?'

'This. For being my friend … despite everything.'

'I am here any time you need me, Liz.' He wanted to say so much more. That he would be more than a friend to her if she would let him. But this was not the time. Such a declaration would scare her away just when she was taking the first tentative steps back to him.

Mitch was a patient man.

CHAPTER
39

'Come on,' Lizzie whispers as she leads the way through the trees. It's almost six o'clock, and the first dawn light is beginning to appear. Her breath steams in the freezing air. Mitch is dressed in his best clothes. He's warm inside his sheepskin coat, but shivering with anticipation. Or maybe nerves.

'Let's take a shortcut through here,' Lizzie suggests, reaching for the gate to one of the foaling paddocks.

'But the grass is wet. It'll be a bit muddy too. What about your dress?'

Lizzie looks down. She's not used to thinking about clothes and shoes. The hem of a dress peeps out from under her long coat. She's wearing her riding boots, but she's carrying another pair of shoes in a bag. Those are certainly not for riding. Her heart thumps a little. She hopes Mitch will like what she has chosen to wear today. She doesn't want her dress to get messy either. After all, today is special.

'Okay. We'll go the long way.'

It only takes a few more minutes to reach the road, where Mitch has left his car. It's a pretty old car and, like most farm cars, a bit beaten around the edges. But when she opens the door, Lizzie sees a soft blanket covering the tattered old seat cover. There's a bunch of flowers lying on the blanket. Red roses.

'Oh. They're so pretty.' She can't help herself. She has to pick them up and bury her face among the soft petals, breathing in the delicate scent.

'I thought you should have a bouquet.' Mitch looks a little embarrassed.

Lizzie flings an arm around his neck and kisses him. A short fervent kiss that tells him all he needs to know.

'Let's get going.'

They leap into the car. They have a bit of a drive ahead of them because they didn't dare risk arranging a local wedding; word would have gotten back to their parents. But there's a small church at Merriwa about sixty kilometres away. It has taken a bit of work to convince the priest that he should marry two teenagers, but they are old enough by law, and he has finally agreed. His wife and daughter will act as witnesses.

'They're expecting us at nine,' Mitch says. 'With the fog, it'll take a bit over an hour, I think, in this old car. But we'll still be very early.'

'That doesn't matter.' Lizzie's eyes are shining. 'It'll take that long, or even longer, for them to even realise we're gone. They won't think to look in Merriwa. And even if they do, it'll be too late for them to stop us.'

Mitch hesitates before starting the engine. 'Are you really sure?'

'I am more sure about this than anything in my life.'

'All right then.'

The car engine has cooled. Mitch turns the key and the engine turns over slowly, making a loud grinding sound. He pumps the accelerator a couple of times. This time the car responds and he slips it into gear and flicks on the lights. They are on their way.

In the house, Kayla stirs. The sound of the engine has disturbed her. She rolls over and sees a flash of light through the window. Puzzled, she gets out of bed to look and sees a set of headlights in the distance on the road. She shrugs it off and goes back to bed. But for some reason, she can't sleep. Instead she heads for the bathroom. That's when she notices that Lizzie's door is shut. That's strange. Lizzie usually sleeps with the door open just a crack. Kayla hesitates, but finally decides to open the door.

She peeps inside. The bed is empty. Puzzled, she pushes the door open. Lizzie's pyjamas are lying in a heap on the floor. Kayla's first thought is that Lizzie is already at the stables, but her jeans are also lying on the floor. The wardrobe door is open and Kayla frowns. That's unusual. Lizzie's wardrobe isn't like Kayla's. Where Kayla has everything neatly organised, Lizzie's is a mess. But something is different: all the clothes have been pushed to one side to get at something that must have been hidden in the far corner.

Kayla rushes to her parents' room and pushes the door open. Her mother and father are fast asleep. She hurries to Kath's side of the bed.

'Mum.' When there is no response, she gently shakes her mother's shoulder. 'Mum.'

At last Kath's eyes open. 'What's wrong, Kayla?'

'It's Lizzie. She's gone.'

'Honey, she's probably just gone down the stables to sleep with Zeke. You know she does that sometimes.'

'Not when it's this cold. And besides, her pretty shoes are gone too. And her birthday party dress. The one she hardly ever wears.'

Kath shakes her head to clear it a little and raises herself on one elbow. 'What?'

'Lizzie's gone. And so is her party dress. And her good shoes.'

Of course Kayla would notice that. Kath frowns. She slides out of bed and follows her younger daughter to Lizzie's room. The bed is unmade. Lizzie never makes her bed and Kath has given up trying to force her. The wardrobe door is open, and Kath sees that Kayla is right. Lizzie lives in jeans and riding boots. She hates dresses and Kath can think of no reason she would wear one at home.

Unless she's not at home.

Kath's eyes widen and she hurries back to her husband.

'Sam. Wake up.'

'What?'

'Sam, I think Lizzie has run away. With Mitch.'

CHAPTER
40

'What do you think?' Kayla held her breath. She was as nervous as she had been the first time she'd planned an event for Elite Weddings.

'You've done a great job.' Pascale turned slowly, taking time to examine the water trickling over the fountain, the neatly cut green lawn and the rich heritage colours on the freshly painted sections of the homestead. A large white marquee filled one side of the garden. Inside were tables and a bar. 'It's just as I imagined it would be. Except for the bower. That's a very nice touch.'

Kayla beamed. The bower had been all her idea. Between two tall gum trees, a white wire frame had been erected. Bunches of bright yellow wattle and red bottlebrush blooms covered the frame, entwined with the orange of the banksia flowers and delicate white of blue gum blossom. Baskets of red and green kangaroo paw and waratah defined the area in front of the bower, where the ceremony would take place.

'I think the native flowers have given the whole setting an extra Australian feel,' she said proudly.

'They are going to love it. If it goes well, this guy might become a regular. Apparently there is a real appetite in Japan for Australian weddings at all levels from cheap and cheerful to totally upscale. This could be a good money spinner.'

How like Pascale to be thinking of the money while Kayla was too busy checking and double-checking everything to make sure it was absolutely perfect.

'So, my lovelies, what time does this all kick off?' Ken appeared from the direction of the house, a camera in his hand.

Kayla glanced at her watch. 'The first bus should be here in about an hour ... and that,' she nodded at two vans making their way up the driveway, 'should be the caterers.'

'I don't suppose that gorgeous cowboy is going to appear at any time?'

'No, Ken, he's not.'

The photographer pulled a face. 'Ah, well.'

'Have you found the right places for the photos?' Kayla said to distract him as she saw Liz approaching. The last thing she needed today was for Liz and Ken to clash again. This first wedding had to be perfect.

'I have. I think I prefer it as it was, that broken and ruined feel it had was fabulous. Still, I guess that's not what this lot will want. I like the bower, by the way. Can I just move a couple of things?'

'Yes. Whatever you like. Can you do a few extra shots of the bower for us? For the website.' She shooed Ken away. 'Ignore him,' she said to her sister. 'He's an artist. He sees things differently from the way we see them.'

Liz pulled a face that was far more eloquent of her disbelief than any words might be.

Any further conversation was interrupted by the caterer, who was starting to unload and needed instructions on what and where and how everything was to be served.

'You should set up over there.' Kayla pointed.

'Wouldn't it be better if they set up closer to the house?' Liz suggested. 'There's water there in case there's an accident with the fire.'

'It'll be fine where it is, Liz.' Kayla nodded for the caterers to continue.

'Where do you want these?' The florist was indicating two white arrangements.

'In the marquee. Top table.'

'They could sit over there, blocking the view of the stable gate,' Liz offered.

The florist raised an eyebrow at Kayla then scurried off in the direction of the marquee.

After fifteen minutes of Liz's 'help', Kayla couldn't stand it any more.

'Are you planning to spend the whole day doing this?'

'Doing what?'

'This! Wandering around, criticising. Getting in the way.'

Liz bristled. 'I was only trying to help. You wanted me to go along with your plan. That's what I'm doing.'

'I know.' Kayla sighed. 'And I appreciate that. I really do. But you're the one who knows about horses. I'm the one who does weddings. It would be better if you just let me do my job!'

Liz stared at her for a long moment and blinked, a slightly stunned expression spreading over her face. 'Sorry, little sister. I guess I just—'

Kayla's phone beeped. She glanced down. 'Oh, damn it!' The first bus, carrying the brides and their mothers and maids, was just a few moments away. The grooms would be following twenty minutes later. 'Sorry, Liz, but they'll be here soon. I've got to—'

'I know. I'm sorry I got underfoot. I'll go hide.'

'No. I didn't mean that. Honestly.'

Liz gave her a sort of sad half-smile, then walked away. Kayla would have gone after her, but the first bus was pulling up in the designated parking area. Kayla turned her attention to welcoming the women who alighted, their faces bright with laughter and anticipation. It was easy to pick the six brides: their faces and hair were already done. All they had to do was slip into the dresses now being unloaded in their protective garment bags and they would be ready.

To Kayla they all looked so very young.

She led the brides and their bridesmaids and mothers up the front stairs and into the bride's room. It was a bit crowded with so many, but the girls didn't seem to mind. They chattered among themselves and oohed and aahed at the dresses as they were revealed. A waitress came in with a tray of Champagne, and Kayla withdrew. Back at the bus, she collected a cardboard box, which she carried to the bower and opened. Inside were dozens—hundreds—of origami paper cranes, joined into long garlands. Kayla examined a particularly lovely garland with birds made all of red and gold paper. These, she knew, were an important symbol of good fortune ahead. She added them to the bower.

The men arrived soon after, already resplendent in their tuxedos. They were accompanied by a priest. Although the groom's room was available, the men stayed outside, looking at the gum trees and the homestead and taking photographs with everything from a phone to a camera almost as impressive as Ken's. Just as Kayla was beginning to think it was time to get things started, someone rang a bell. The grooms took their places in the bower.

They turned as their brides appeared at the top of the front stairs. With their parents by their sides, the veiled girls walked towards their husbands. As they did, a kookaburra laughed, loud and long. Kayla frowned, but then noticed the smiles that lit the faces of the wedding parties. Obviously they thought this was a good omen.

She wondered briefly if there was a way to ensure the bird performed at every Willowbrook wedding.

CHAPTER
41

Liz was surprised to see the brides wearing traditional white dresses. Very frilly and sparkly bridal dresses at that, with huge skirts that barely fitted through the doorways. She'd expected the group to wear traditional Japanese wedding costumes. Not that she had any idea what those traditional costumes might be, but she was pretty sure they didn't involve that much tulle and lace. It would appear tradition didn't mean that much to the young people now gathered on her front lawn.

She turned away from the window.

Traditional or not, a wedding was a wedding. Weddings were definitely not something Liz felt comfortable around. Weddings were not for her; she knew that as certainly as she knew the sun would set over the hills. She crossed the room, trying hard not to acknowledge the memories that were following close behind.

This room on the top floor at the front of the house was her new office. While she had happily had a bedroom and office in one space on the ground floor, nothing would entice her to set up her bed in the room that had been her parents' bedroom. She'd vetoed suggestions for a bride's room here. It seemed right to use it as the Willowbrook office, while she slept in her old room. Kayla also had her childhood room, which she used whenever she needed to sleep over and supervise the renovation. Her visits had become more frequent and now that the business was actually started, Liz guessed Kayla would spend even more time here. Probably a couple of days for each wedding. That was good, wasn't it? She and her sister had been apart too long. When they were kids, they had been as close as two sisters could possibly be. But then everything changed. And since then they had drifted apart.

No. Not drifted. They had deliberately gone their separate ways after many arguments and recriminations and pain.

Liz left the room and headed downstairs. She was almost at the bottom of the grand staircase when she came face to face with a young couple. The bride looked up, startled. Then she and her groom recovered enough to bow.

'Right there on the stairs ...' Ken appeared behind them, clutching his camera. 'Oh. Hi, Liz.'

Liz stared at the bride. Her dress shimmered in the late evening sunlight streaming through the front door. The girl's eyes shone with happiness as she clasped her new husband's hand. She was so young and so beautiful and so very, very happy. A lump formed in Liz's throat. That had been her once. A lifetime ago.

She nodded to both the photographer and the bridal couple before slipping through the kitchen to the back door. She was acutely aware that, with her jeans and faded old work shirt, she was totally out of place here. At the door, she slipped her riding boots on, but didn't even think of going to the stables, which would once again put her in danger of intruding on the wedding. She had settled the horses safely in their stables and fed them before the wedding started; the mares and foals she had moved to a slightly more distant paddock. She hadn't been at all sure how this wedding would unfold, but she wasn't taking any chances with her precious horses. They were fine and safe.

She wasn't so sure about herself.

Liz walked quickly through the home paddock towards the creek. She hadn't been this way in quite a while. She and Kayla—Mitch too—had worn a path between the house and the swimming hole over many hot summer days but the path was long gone, lost in the long grass. Liz didn't need a path to show her the way to the spot where a fallen gum had created a bridge over the creek. Once it had united two parts of Willowbrook. Now it simply served to highlight that those parts were connected by only the finest thread. She stepped onto the log and walked to the centre where she sat, dangling her feet over the clear water. She noticed water primrose growing on the far side of the creek. The little yellow flowers were pretty, but the weed could be a nuisance. It was just one more thing she needed to attend to. One more thing she really didn't have enough time for.

She pulled a piece of rotting bark from the tree trunk and began to shred it between her fingers. Her head was spinning with the memories this place held: long summer evenings when she and Kayla and their parents had cooled off here after a hard day's work; the times she and her sister had slipped away early in the morning to come and watch the kingfishers diving for their breakfast. They had sat side by side and shared their secret hopes and dreams.

It looked as if Kayla's dreams had come true—or were heading that way. She spent her days surrounded by the beautiful things she had always loved. She was successful and living the life she wanted in Sydney. But none of Liz's dreams had come true. She had never seen her father's face light up with pride as she won the King of the

Ranges competition. She had never developed her own bloodlines at the stud. She had never …

What was the point of these kinds of memories? They only hurt. She had never expected her life to be easy; she'd never wanted it to be easy. She liked to work and see the results of her work. But, oh, she had never expected it to be this hard. Or for it to hurt this much. She had never expected to fail.

A breeze wafting from the homestead brought with it a trace of music and laughter. The music was strange to her ears. Perhaps it was Japanese. Whatever it was, it simply reinforced her feelings that she no longer belonged in her own home.

She let her eyes follow the rise of the bank on the other side of the creek. It was almost fully dark now, but she could still see the outline of the old church. Of course, it wasn't a church any more. It was a home, and there was a light shining in the window like a beacon. And another reminder of her failures. Mitch belonged to this lovely spot by the creek even more than Kayla. Her strongest memories were of the two of them, kids just finding out what love is all about. Even after all these years and everything that had happened, the magic and the aching beauty of those first kisses and that one night together almost broke her heart.

As she stared at the water, a shadow detached itself from the trees on the far bank. At first she thought it was a memory come to haunt her. But the man who stepped easily along the fallen tree and sat beside her was very real.

CHAPTER
42

Mitch didn't say anything. Part of him believed Liz would try to send him away. Or get up and leave him there alone. This place was so very personal to both of them, but it had been a lifetime since they'd been here together. Mitch had avoided this spot since his return, not wanting to give himself up too much to the past when he had no hope for the future. But tonight, the draw of this place and the memories it held had been too strong to fight. He hadn't really believed she might be here, but here she was.

For a long time they both just sat there. Mitch was acutely aware of her hand on the tree trunk, so close to his. More than anything, he wanted to reach out and touch her skin. But he didn't dare. Instead, he stayed silent, listening to the night sounds of the bush and the sound of Liz breathing.

When the silence was finally disturbed, it was by the sound of an engine roaring into life. They both looked at the homestead. A shaft of bright light began to move down the long driveway, followed by another.

'So, Willowbrook's first wedding is over.' Liz sounded tired more than anything else.

'And how did it go?'

'I'm not sure. Kayla is the expert. And her boss Pascale came up to help. I suppose it went all right. I can't see Pascale letting it be anything else but perfect. Kayla too, for that matter. She seemed to be very good at whatever it is they actually do for these things.'

'So, now that the first one has happened, how do you feel about it?'

When Liz finally spoke, her voice was hesitant and maybe a little afraid. 'I don't feel like it's my home any more.'

His beautiful, brilliant, brave Lizzie had been brought to this? He wanted to take her in his arms and hold her tightly until all the pain went away. He knew some of the blame was his, but mostly it was because Lizzie had lost her way. He also knew that no one would be able to do anything to help her until she was ready to accept that help.

'Lizzie—'

'Please don't call me that.'

'All right. Liz, is this really what you want to do?'

'Yes, it is.' She bristled slightly and he got a flash of the girl he used to know. 'This can save Willowbrook. At least, Kayla and Pascale think it can, and I have no other option. I can't lose this place. I promised Dad—' Her voice broke.

'I know. You promised him you would never sell Willowbrook. But he had no right to ask that of you. You were just a teenager. No one has any right to expect a teenager to shoulder all the responsibilities you did.'

'He had every right! What happened was my fault. *Our* fault, Mitch. I have to atone for that.'

He heard the sorrow in her voice. She wasn't entirely wrong. But she wasn't right, either. Yes, the two of them did hold some of the blame for what happened that day, but maybe Sam did too. They would never really know. Mitch had tried to tell Liz that fifteen years ago. She hadn't listened to him then and she wouldn't listen to him now, but he could still try to convince her to take her life back.

'Tell me something, Liz. When did you last do something for yourself? Not for Willowbrook. Not because you promised your father. Not for Kayla. Just because you wanted to do it.'

He sat for a long time, waiting, then realised she would never give him an answer, even if she could.

When she spoke again, it was to turn his question on him.

'And what about you, Mitch? Tell me something. You were gone for a long time. Why did you come back?'

'Because this is where I belong. You pushed me away so often, I got angry. I went away. I found a new job. New friends. It was the only way to stop the hurt. And yes, I found new women. There was a lot of beer and there were a lot of women. The problem was, none of them was you.'

He turned to look at her but she wouldn't meet his gaze. She kept her eyes firmly fixed on the water, which was now glinting in the light of the full moon above them.

'Why did you buy the river flats and the old church? It was hard enough for me to have to sell that land. But when I realised it was you … Why, Mitch? Was it pity? Did you think I would forgive you? Forgive us?'

'I bought it because this is where I want to be. It always has been and it always will be.'

'I felt as if you had betrayed me by taking part of Willowbrook away.'

'No, Liz. Never that. I was trying to stop it being taken from you by a stranger.'

She looked at him then.

She was so close. He reached a hand out to touch her cheek. His hand was toughened through years of hard work and burned dark by the sun. Her eyes had lines around them, but they were the most beautiful eyes he had ever seen. He leaned forward to kiss her and their lips touched. It was only the briefest moment, but it brought a flood of memories. The taste and the feel of her lips were as much a part of him as his own heartbeat.

'No!'

She pushed his chest so hard he almost toppled off the tree into the water, and he thought he saw the shine of tears in her eyes.

'I can't do this, Mitch. I really can't. Not again. The memories are too much. I can't bear it.'

'Your dad would hate to see you like this,' Mitch said as something close to desperation filled him. 'He'd want to see you happy. And he knew we were good together. He would want to see us—'

'No!' It sounded like the cry of a wounded animal. 'Don't you see? He didn't want us to be together. Why do you think he was following us that day? He was trying to stop us. That's why he's dead. Why they're both dead.'

'No, Liz. You're wrong. He knew we—'

'He told me. They were the last words he ever said to me. I will never forget them.'

'No. That can't be right.' Mitch felt as if the old log was about to topple into the creek. He gripped it so hard it felt like his fingers might tear through the weathered wood. 'I mean, I didn't ask him or anything. But I always assumed they were on their way to celebrate with us.'

But he looked again at her face and knew she wasn't lying. The pain of that day rose out of his memory to wrap itself around his heart. He was almost gasping for breath as he stood. He didn't look where he was going, but his feet knew the way as they carried him off the log and away from the lonely figure sitting in the deepening shadows above the creek.

CHAPTER

43

The young couple are standing on the steps of the church as the police car pulls up. The officer turns the engine off and takes a deep breath. Even if dispatch hadn't told him, he would know what they are here to do. It is written in every line of their bodies and the happiness surrounds them like a glow.

There are times he really hates his job, and this is one of them.

He picks up his hat from the seat beside him and gets out of the car. The couple have seen him now. They hold hands tightly as they watch him approach. He knows what they're thinking. They expect him to interfere with their plans, to try to stop them. The boy, for he is little more than a boy in the officer's eyes, steps slightly in front of his girl, instinctively trying to protect her. The officer admires the youth for trying, but he can't protect her from what is coming. No one can.

The priest appears in the doorway behind them. He and the officer share a look. It is the kind of look professionals share when they know what lies ahead. Someone has called him already.

'What's going on?' the boy asks.

The officer can see now they both are teenagers. For years he's hardened his heart, ready for moments like this, but when they come, nothing makes them easier.

'I'm looking for Elizabeth Lawson?'

The girl takes half a step forward. 'That's me.' Her tone is defensive.

The officer makes sure his voice is unemotional. Official.

'I'm very sorry, Miss Lawson, but I have bad news for you. There has been an accident. Your parents and your sister—'

'What? Where? Are they all right?' Lizzie glances up at Mitch as if looking for courage. Then she looks at the officer. Perhaps she reads something in his look, because her face begins to crumple.

'Their car ran off the road at Owens Gap a little over an hour ago. We've been looking for you.'

'We were at the café having breakfast,' Mitch says in a tone that shows he knows such things are unimportant right now.

The officer has rehearsed the next words. 'Your sister is in an ambulance on her way to Tamworth Hospital. She has head injuries but they're not too serious. The Westpac rescue helicopter is taking your father to Newcastle. His injuries are severe. He needs the facilities at the bigger hospital there.'

'No!' Tears are streaming down Lizzie's face now. Mitch puts his arms around her. Without his support, Lizzie would have fallen to the ground. 'No. It can't—' Lizzie suddenly stops speaking.

The officer knows what is coming next.

'My mother?' The words are almost a whisper.

'I am so sorry. She was trapped in the car. They are still trying to free her.'

'How badly hurt is she?' This time Mitch asks. Lizzie has her hands over her mouth and is unable to speak.

'I'm sorry. She was dead when the ambulance arrived.'

The sound that escapes Lizzie is like the cry of a wounded animal. Her knees give way and Mitch holds her as she sinks to the wooden steps.

'Lizzie. I'm here,' he says as she sobs in his arms. 'I'm here.'

The priest steps forward as if to offer comfort, but Mitch waves him away. He holds Lizzie while she cries.

After a few minutes, he looks up at the officer.

'Lizzie needs to get to the hospital to see her father.'

'Of course. Can you take her, or do you need help?'

'I'll take her,' Mitch says in a voice strong beyond his years. 'Lizzie. Do you want to go to your father?'

Numbly, Lizzie nods.

'Come on.' Mitch helps her to her feet.

Lizzie reaches somewhere deep inside herself and finds the power to speak. 'But what about Kayla? She's in a different hospital.'

'That's right,' says the officer. 'She's getting good care. There is a female officer with her. Her injuries are not life threatening.'

They understand what the officer is not saying.

'Can you get in touch with my parents?' Mitch says. 'They know Kayla. My little sister is her best friend. They can go to the hospital to be with Kayla while we go to Newcastle.'

'I will.'

'Mitch. Please. Take me to Dad.'

'Come on.' Mitch puts his arms around her shoulders and guides her to his car. A few moments later, the pair drive away.

The priest and the officer watch them go.

'That poor child,' says the priest.

CHAPTER

44

Her job was finished. Or at least the first phase was finished.

Kayla ran her fingers along the top of the kitchen table; the table she had eaten at every day for so many years. The refurbished kitchen looked modern and clean and practical—because it was. It was perfect for everyday use, but at the same time the commercial warmers and coolers that had been installed in an unused pantry were ready for the next wedding. It was just the right balance of both purposes.

'What do you think, Mum?' The words are barely a whisper. 'I think we'd have enjoyed cooking here together. Well, I guess Lachie will get to use it more than me. But he'll love it.'

But she wasn't so sure he would. The kitchen was great, but Lachie wasn't a country boy. She hadn't even been able to get him to visit her up here. And strangely enough, she hadn't missed him at all. He wouldn't really fit in at Willowbrook anyway. Well, she was about to head back to Sydney. She'd see him soon.

She walked through to the homestead's entrance hall. The staircase looked wonderful. She'd seen Ken's photos of the Japanese couples on those stairs, and it was exactly as she'd imagined it. She opened the doors into the bride's room. It was bright and pretty and the realisation of every little girl's bridal dreams. The groom's room across the hall was a masculine haven. When she walked out onto the veranda, the heritage green paint blended beautifully into the colours of the lawn and the gum tress, with the native flowers growing in the renewed garden beds giving a splash of brightness. And the fountain looked lovely.

This was how Willowbrook was supposed to look. It was all perfect, just as she had imagined it when she started this project all those weeks ago. And there was more she could do. Although Willowbrook's church was out of her reach, she had plans to build a permanent wedding pavilion, an all-weather place for ceremonies to be held. It would be nice to add an antique touch too—perhaps an old Cobb & Co coach if she could find one. She suddenly thought of old wine barrels. Why hadn't she considered that before? They would add the flavour of the Hunter Valley in more ways than one. But that would have to wait. For now, she was done and it was time to go home to Sydney, at least until the next Willowbrook wedding.

Kayla picked up the overnight bag that she'd left by the entrance and closed the door behind her. She carried it to her car and looked at the stables. Liz had been gone when she woke that morning. Probably out somewhere training a horse on the hills and flats of Willowbrook. She knew Kayla was leaving, but Liz had never been one for long goodbyes. Kayla got into the car and started the engine. As she watched Willowbrook recede in the rear-view mirror, she wasn't sure when she would be back, and felt an unexpected twinge of sadness.

A little over three hours later she pulled her car into her designated spot outside the Elite Weddings office. Leaving her travel bag, she picked up her laptop and headed inside. She had work to do.

'Hi, Pascale.'

'Welcome back.' Pascale raised one perfectly manicured eyebrow.

'What?' Kayla dropped her things on her desk.

'This is a new look for you.'

Kayla looked down at herself. She was wearing a short-sleeved shirt tucked into cream chinos. Her boots were new and comfortable, but bore little resemblance to the high-heeled fashion statements that normally adorned her feet. And it occurred to her she wasn't wearing make-up. Apart from the day of the wedding, she couldn't remember when she last sat in front of a mirror perfecting her appearance. She'd been too busy fixing Willowbrook.

'Sorry. I came straight in after the drive down. We don't have any meetings today, do we?'

'No. It's fine. Don't worry about it. I was just thinking you're a lot more relaxed since you've been spending time back home.'

'It's not really my home any more. My home is here in Sydney.'

'Are you sure?'

'Yes, I'm sure. I'm also sure I need coffee. You want one?'

As she made the coffee, Kayla thought about Pascale's words. She thought about them even more when she checked her email. Top of her inbox was a message from Lachie.

> *Hi babe.*
>
> *It's been a while. I know you've been busy but I miss you. When can we get together? You can wash off all that country dust and let me take you somewhere nice for dinner … or better still, let me wash it off and we can stay home and I'll cook you dinner.*

It couldn't be that long. She'd seen Lachie … she checked her diary. Three weeks ago. That was a long time. She replied, proposing dinner and whatever bathing Lachie liked, but not until Friday night. She'd been away so much she had a mountain of work to catch up on and she needed to get herself and her flat in order. But even as she hit the send button, it occurred to her that if she hadn't seen her boyfriend for so long, she should want to see him tonight. Maybe Pascale was right. Maybe she was changing.

She shook her head. There was no time to think about that now. She scrolled through her emails. There was never a quiet time in the bridal business. Love happened. So did unexpected babies. There were a couple of rush weddings needing her attention. But first she needed to finalise the account for the Japanese tour weddings. She wanted to get Liz's share of the profit to her as soon as possible not just because her sister needed it, but because when she saw some actual money, Liz might feel better about the decision she had been forced to make.

Kayla stopped at an email Pascale had forwarded to her with a single word in the subject line: *Willowbrook?* Kayla scanned it.

Another couple were seeking a rural setting for their ceremony. Yes, this would be perfect for Willowbrook. If she went up there this week, she might have time to find some old wine barrels to decorate the garden. Then she remembered—she had a date with Lachie. And there was a wedding in Sydney this weekend as well.

She ignored the twinge of disappointment. She had plenty of time to get up to Willowbrook and look for barrels. Her life was here in Sydney. Her work was here, as was Lachie. Willowbrook was fine for a visit but it wasn't her home any more.

Was it?

CHAPTER
45

Liz reached into the fridge and pulled out a can of beer. It wasn't exactly Champagne, but that didn't matter. She pulled the tab and raised the can to her mouth to suck at the overflowing foam. Turning to the white sheet of paper lying in the middle of the kitchen table she raised the can in salute before taking a long drink. For once, the letter from the bank was not a cause for despair. Signed by the same Mr Richard Walker who had caused her so much distress after his last visit, the letter congratulated her on making headway on her loan repayments, and wished her continued success in her new business venture. Some payments had been made by Pascale as part of their business deal, but Liz was proud to note that part of the money had come from her account.

She wasn't out of trouble yet, but the plan might be working.

Liz took the letter and her beer and headed for her office. As she passed through the newly renovated rooms and up the staircase, she experienced a deep sense of pleasure. Not only was her bank statement looking better, so too was the home she loved. Not that the credit was hers. This was all Kayla's work. She'd expected to resent the fact that Kayla was succeeding where she had failed, but she didn't. In her own way, Kayla worked as hard as Liz and if Willowbrook benefited from that, Liz would be grateful. Liz wished her sister was here to celebrate with her. Maybe tomorrow morning she might sleep late for once, then ring Kayla to tell her the good news and thank her. She deserved that.

A strident sound woke Liz from a deep slumber. She leaped out of bed. Dragging on her clothes, she glanced at the clock by her bed. Three o'clock. This could be a false alarm, but she didn't think so. The darkest hours were the best time for a foal to enter the world.

She made her way very quietly to the foaling box. In the dim glow of the night lights, Liz could see that the mare was lying down. That's what had triggered the alarm on her foaling collar. She was sweating lightly. As Liz watched, the mare lifted her head and started to roll, as if trying to get to her feet. She sat for a moment, breathing deeply, then rolled back on her side. Liz leaned on the door to the box. It wouldn't be long. The mare was one of her best and an old hand at this. She'd birthed eight live foals, the youngest of which was even now roaming the yearling paddock growing more and more like his sire every day. Unless something went wrong, she was best left just to get on with it.

Liz took a long drink from her water bottle. She wasn't usually one for bottled water—that was Kayla's doing. But she had to admit it was handy. This was her favourite part of her world. Around her, the other horses moved restlessly in their stalls. They knew what was happening. She heard a loud bang from Deimos's stall. She walked down the laneway to where the colt's head was hanging over his stable door.

'Hey, settle down.' She stroked his nose. 'Everything is not about you. Tonight, it's all about Cassie and her foal. So you need to stay quiet and not cause a fuss. All right?'

The colt nuzzled her face and blew gently through his nose.

'That's better. Now, behave yourself and let Cassie have her baby in peace.' She gave the colt a final pat and made her way back to the foaling box.

Of course she had missed the birth. In the two minutes she had been away, Cassie's foal had slipped into the world. It was lying in the deep straw, not moving. Cassie lifted her head to look at the tiny shape. She struggled to sit then began pushing the foal with her nose. Lizzie held her breath. Then the foal kicked and tried to lift its head. Cassie shoved it gently with her nose and began licking it clean.

Lizzie sighed with relief. This was a good start. She leaned on the stall door in anticipation. She always enjoyed the next bit.

After a little while, Cassie got to her feet, nudging the foal to follow suit. The little one lifted a long, ungainly leg and planted its hoof firmly in the straw. It tucked its back legs under itself and gave an almighty push. The little creature rose from the straw and fell forward, almost onto its nose. Liz grinned. It didn't matter how many times she watched this, each time was different. And each time was wondrous.

Not to be deterred, the new arrival tried again. It somehow got control of its too-long legs and managed to rise to its knees. Cassie nickered anxiously as the foal gave another enormous heave, and promptly fell down again. Liz would swear the look on its face was one of determination as once again it tried to get to its feet—and this time succeeded. The thin legs were shaking slightly as the newborn filly tried to accustom herself to this new state of affairs. Cassie nudged the baby gently in the right direction and the filly caught an enticing scent. She lifted her nose and began nudging her dam's side, seeking … Cassie moved her body and the foal found what she sought. She latched onto her mother's udder and began to drink. Her short fluffy tail began to wag.

Lizzie nodded as she watched. All foals were pretty, but this one seemed especially so. She had one white stocking and a smudge of white on her forehead. Although it was a bit early to say for sure, her coat seemed dark like her sire's. The youngster was strong, too, just like him.

'So, what's your name, little one?'

Cassie's ears caught the softly spoken words and she turned her head towards the stable door.

'Well done, Mum,' Liz said. 'You have a beautiful baby. She's going to need a name though. Let me see. Her sire is Apollo. He is the sun. But you, little one, will need a star name like all your brothers and sisters. We have a big astronomy book that my grandfather used for finding star names. We're up to V now—so you will be Vega. Willowbrook Vega. How does that sound?'

The foal, tired now and full of warm nourishing milk, didn't seem to care at all about the momentous act of being named. Her knees buckled and she flopped into the straw. In a moment she was fast asleep, her mother standing guard over her.

'Vega,' Liz whispered again. 'We're going to run out of star names soon.'

That's when it hit her. This was Apollo's last foal. This scrap of life, sleeping so soundly on the deep bed of straw, was the end of an era for Willowbrook.

Older stallions can service fewer mares. And last season, out of respect for Apollo's age, Liz had restricted the number of mares sent to him. Because she needed the money his service fees generated, she'd taken almost entirely outside mares. She'd done deals to breed her mares to outside stallions, and only three went to Apollo. Two had already dropped fine colts. Cassie was the last to foal. And Vega was Apollo's last daughter.

The filly twitched in her sleep, and Cassie lowered her head to sniff her.

'You take good care of that little girl.' Liz's voice broke a little as she whispered. Some of the joy had gone out of the moment for her. Certain mother and daughter were going to be fine, she left the foaling box. She paused by Deimos's stall. The colt was dozing. Liz knew that when the time came she would breed Cassie to Deimos. It was time for him to take Apollo's place at Willowbrook. He couldn't attract the same stud fees as his sire, though. At least not yet. He had to earn that.

The King of the Ranges was three months away. Deimos was developing well and she was hopeful he'd make a good showing there. If she could get him to a few shows, he might attract a few outside mares next season. But that was almost a year in the future, and competing took money. She had been fooling herself to think her father's heritage was safe. There was a good chance she might save the homestead, but saving Willowbrook Stud and the bloodlines Sam Lawson had worked so hard to establish—that was another matter.

Weddings took a long time to plan, and Kayla's emails had all been about weddings next year. That was a bit late. As Liz made her way to the house, she thought about the horses she had. There was a sale coming up. She had a couple of youngsters she was just starting to train that could bring a reasonable price at the sale, if they were going well. She had hoped to keep them longer, but needs must. She'd have to go in as a late entry, but there should be time.

The sun was still below the horizon as Liz slipped up the stairs to her bedroom and threw herself on top of the bed, where she dozed fitfully for an hour or more before the sunrise came to call her to work.

CHAPTER
46

'Five thousand, five hundred dollars. I have five-five. Do I hear six? Come on, ladies and gentlemen, this fine three-year-old gelding by a champion sire. He'll be a champion too. He's beautifully brought on and ready for competition right now. Do I hear six?'

Mitch decided it was time for his next move. He pulled the gelding from a gentle hand canter to a stop and reined back six paces. Then he walked the horse forward while he cracked his stock whip three times. The gelding did not flinch. Mitch set the horse cantering once more around the sale ring, then pulled him to a halt, dismounted and removed the saddle. Holding the reins, Mitch stood the horse with his feet square and his head extended. Then he turned him and stood him again, showing off the animal's fine conformation.

'Look at that, ladies and gentlemen. That's as fine an example of an Australian Stock Horse as you will find anywhere. Now, who will give me six?'

'Five-seven-five!' a man's voice called from somewhere in the grandstand.

'All right. I have five-seven-five. Five-seven-five ...' The auctioneer's voice droned on.

In one fluid movement, Mitch swung onto the horse's bare back. He tightened his legs around its body and pushed it straight from a standstill into a hand canter. He circled the far end of the sales ring, then steered the animal at a low jump that had been set up in the ring for this very purpose, although Mitch supposed it was intended that the horse should be saddled. The gelding cleared the jump with inches to spare, and Mitch heard the auctioneer declare a bid of six thousand dollars.

The gelding sold for six thousand, seven hundred dollars.

Mitch slid to the ground. He threw his saddle onto the animal's back and tightened the girth. Then he led the gelding from the ring. The horse's breeder was waiting for him, a wide grin on his face.

'Well done,' he said, clapping Mitch on the shoulder. 'That's a bit more than I had hoped for. Thank you.'

'He's worth it,' Mitch said, patting the gelding's neck. 'He's a good horse and was a pleasure to train.'

'Well, you earned your money, that's for sure. I could never have brought him on that well in that amount of time. I do have a couple of other youngsters I want to talk to you about.'

'Great.' Mitch tried to hide his satisfaction. That was good news indeed.

As he took the horse to its stall to await a visit from the new owner, he was greeted by a few friends, breeders and trainers all. It had taken some time after his return from Queensland, but he'd earned his place. People were starting to notice the higher prices brought by Mitch Saunders–trained horses. With luck there'd be a few calls in the next couple of weeks from people wanting to place their horses with him. And then in February, when he took the stallion he was training into the King of the Ranges contest, his reputation would be made.

Although he had a couple of mares, Mitch wasn't really a horse breeder. He had little interest in bloodlines and breeding programs. He was a trainer. When faced with a good young horse, all he wanted was to bring out its potential—that was his skill and his joy. Each new horse was a new challenge. He'd come a long way from the boy who had cried when he said goodbye to the first horse he ever trained. There were still some horses he hated to see leave— horses that were special—but there was always another horse that needed his skill and his patience.

The gelding's new owner appeared only minutes after Mitch had settled the horse. A tall man who walked like he'd spent his whole life in the saddle, accompanied by a young woman who had eyes only for the animal she now owned.

'He's beautiful. I am so thrilled.'

'He's a good horse,' Mitch told her when introductions had been made. 'What are you planning for him?'

'I need an event horse. Cross country. Jumping and a bit of dressage.' The young woman ran a knowledgeable eye over her new purchase. Then she scratched him behind the ear. The gelding angled his head towards her, and Mitch knew that two hearts had just been won.

'Well, you've got the right horse here for that,' Mitch assured her, pleased that his charge had so obviously found a good home.

Once arrangements for the gelding's transport were set, Mitch was free. He set out for the bar to treat himself to a cold beer in celebration of the successful sale. More importantly, the bar was the gathering place for owners and breeders and trainers. It was the place Mitch would be sure to meet the people who might send a horse to him. Or buy one from him in the future. He made his way through the busy sale grounds, pausing here and there to chat. He was almost at the bar when the auctioneer's voice caught his attention.

'... Willowbrook filly. She is one of two late additions to your catalogue. It's not often we get Willowbrook stock in the sale ring. This two-year-old filly is by Willowbrook Apollo. As many of you know, the stallion was lost earlier this year, so there won't be many more chances like this. Who will start the bidding? Do I hear four thousand dollars?'

Mitch pushed his way through the crowd to a place on the rails where he could see what was going on. Sure enough, Liz was in the ring, leading a filly to each grandstand, positioning her so potential buyers could get a good look at her.

'As you can see, ladies and gentlemen, the filly is well handled but not yet broken. She is ready though. Her dam is the well regarded ...'

Mitch tuned the auctioneer's voice out as he looked at Liz. Her face was a mask. Whatever she was feeling, he saw no signs of it. What was she doing selling an unbroken filly? Even newly broken with the most basic of training, the filly would bring a much better price.

Liz led the horse forward at a walk, then urged her into a trot. She began to feed out the lead rein in her hand and the filly was soon circling her, falling into an easy canter. She had a lovely easy gait and Mitch heard a couple more bids from the stands, but the price wasn't good. It wasn't what a Willowbrook horse should bring. He was tempted to make a bid. Not to buy the horse—he couldn't afford that—but just to run the price up. To help Liz.

Down in the ring, the auctioneer caught Liz's eye and raised an eyebrow. She hesitated for a moment. He knew why. The bid must be below the reserve she had placed on the filly. Then Liz nodded.

'This horse is for sale. She is on the market, ladies and gentlemen. She will be sold today. So—take another look at her. A fine filly with an impeccable bloodline. She will make a fine brood mare. Dig deep in those pockets, ladies and gentlemen. You'll regret it if you miss this chance. So, my bid is five thousand even. Do I hear five-five?'

Come on, Mitch mentally urged the crowds in the stands. But it was the end of the day. Most had made their purchases and were ready to go home. The filly sold for five thousand, two hundred and fifty. Not a bad price, but not a good one either.

Mitch pushed his way to the gate as Liz led the filly out. She handed the lead rein to someone waiting there, and took the reins of another young horse. This one was saddled. Mitch recognised it. He'd seen Liz riding him in the distance. He was a good young gelding, but needed more work before he was sale ready. Mitch could help with that.

'Liz.' He stepped forward and put a hand on her arm. 'Don't sell him. A few more weeks' work and he'll bring a much better price. Don't let him go now. I'll help you if you're too busy.'

She shrugged his hand off and swung into the saddle.

'Liz, this isn't going to save Willowbrook. You have to know that.'

As she looked at him, her blue eyes were icy and he saw something close to desperation there. She opened her mouth as if to speak, then shook her head and rode the horse into the sale ring.

For the first time in his life, Mitch cursed his mentor. What kind of father laid such a burden on his daughter?

CHAPTER
47

No one likes the way hospitals smell. They smell cold and clinical. They smell of chemicals and despair. Lizzie's knees are shaking as she walks through the hospital doors. She is alone. Mitch has dropped her off and gone to find somewhere to park the car. He will come back and be there for her, but for now, she is alone and frightened.

Signs on every wall point to places with unknown and terrifying names. Places like Nephrology, Oncology and Haematology. She has no idea where to go, but her father is here somewhere in this massive hospital. She will find him. Someone brushes past her. He is wearing a pyjama-looking outfit in blue, and has a stethoscope draped around his neck. A doctor.

'Excuse me ...'

The words are only a whisper and the doctor keeps walking, in a hurry. Lizzie looks around. There are people everywhere, but no one seems to have noticed her. No one has time for a girl who is desperate to find her father. A nurse appears from behind a door with a sign saying *No Admittance*. Before Lizzie can cross the room to talk to her, she disappears back through the door.

Then Lizzie sees a sign pointing to an information desk. The women at the desk are dressed like normal people. She hurries over. Maybe they'll help her.

'I need to find my father. He was in an accident. They brought him in on the rescue helicopter. His name is Lawson. Sam Lawson.'

A look of sympathy crosses the woman's face. 'You need to go to the Emergency Ward. Go down that corridor. At the end, turn left and keep going all the way. There are double doors there. The sign will say Emergency. If you go in there, someone can help you.'

'Thank you.'

When Lizzie opens the double doors, it is the noise, rather than the smell, that hits her. Doctors are issuing orders in curt voices. Nurses are calling for orderlies. In the middle is a desk, where people are queueing, talking loudly and occasionally waving their arms at the two nurses working there. Lizzie doesn't want to go into the emergency area. Going in there will make her one of those poor frantic people searching for their loved ones.

She walks through the doors and takes her place in the queue. She wishes Mitch was with her but he'll find her as soon as he can, she knows that. Right now, the most important thing is to get to her father.

'Nurse, I've been waiting now for more than an hour ...' An angry man pushes in front of Lizzie. 'I want to see a doctor. I need to see a doctor right now!'

'Yes, sir. I understand. But as you can see, we are very busy. If you'll just take a seat.'

'I've been sitting there for an hour!' The man is shouting now. Lizzie wishes he would stop.

'Sir. Please.' The nurse comes out from behind the desk and leads him away, attempting to calm him as she does.

'What can I do for you?'

Lizzie realises the other nurse is talking to her. 'Please. My dad ...'

'What's his name?'

'Sam Lawson. He was brought in by the helicopter. After a road accident. Up near Scone.'

The woman is nodding and consulting the computer on her desk. 'Lawson ... Lawson. Oh, yes. I see. Your father was taken into surgery and then up to intensive care. Go back through those doors and take the lift to the third floor. When you come out of the lift, turn left and follow the signs to ICU.'

'Thank you.'

It is the slowest lift Lizzie has ever been in. When at last she steps out on the third floor, it takes her a moment to find the signs. The ICU is at the end of another very long corridor. This time, when she steps through the doors, she is struck by the calm around her. The silence is broken only by the occasional beep of a machine. The nurse at the desk sees her.

'My name is Liz—Elizabeth Lawson,' she says. 'My dad ...'

'Of course. Come with me.'

The nurse leads her to an empty waiting room. 'Please wait here. I'll let the doctor know you're here.'

Feeling as if her legs won't support her any more, Lizzie sinks into a chair. Her head is spinning slightly and she closes her eyes.

She doesn't hear the door open, and is startled when the doctor speaks to her.

'Miss Lawson. I'm Doctor Wilson.'

Lizzie gets to her feet. She opens her mouth to ask about her father, but the words won't come.

'Your father was very badly hurt in the crash,' the doctor continues. 'He's just come from surgery. He has some serious internal injuries. We have stopped the bleeding. It's up to him now.'

'He's going to be all right, though. Isn't he?'

'I hope so, Miss Lawson. But, I have to be honest. It's touch and go.'

The words are so terrible, Lizzie lets them wash past her as if by ignoring them she can pretend they were never spoken. 'Can I see him? I have to see him. Please.' If she can just hold her dad's hand, everything will be all right. She knows it will.

'Of course. Come with me. He's still unconscious at the moment, but you can sit with him.'

That man on the bed can't be her father. Lizzie barely recognises him. His face is swollen and livid with bruising. A heavy bandage covers the top of his head. His chest is bandaged too. She sees a dark patch where the blood has seeped through. There are tubes running to both his arms, and another directing oxygen into his nose.

'His face? You didn't tell me he'd hurt his head.'

'The head injury is not severe,' the doctor tells her as he checks the monitors by her father's bed. 'It's a nasty wound, but not life threatening.'

He doesn't say it, but Lizzie's mind finishes the sentence: the head wound isn't life threatening, but his other injuries are. She steps to the bedside and reaches for his hand. Her fingers stop a hair's breadth from actually touching him.

'It's all right,' the doctor says. 'Be careful of the lines, but you can hold his hand. Talk to him too. A familiar voice will comfort him.'

'He can hear me?'

'Maybe. It certainly can't hurt for you to talk to him.'

Lizzie takes her father's hand. 'Dad. It's me. Lizzie. I'm here, Dad.' The tears are running down her face now, and she makes no effort to wipe them away. 'Dad, I'm here. I am so sorry. I never meant for this to happen, Dad. Please forgive me.'

She doesn't see the doctor leave. Her eyes never leave Sam's face. The words continue to flow, but Lizzie has no idea what she's saying. She doesn't dare stop talking. Because if she does, she might lose him.

Lizzie doesn't know how long she stays there talking to him. Time doesn't matter. But at last his eyes flicker.

'Dad. Dad? It's Lizzie. Can you hear me, Dad?'

On the bed, her father's head moves a little. Then his eyes flicker again. They open, but it seems to Lizzie a very long time before he's able to look at her.

'Lizzie …' His voice is rough and so weak she can hardly hear him. But it is the best sound she has ever heard.

'Dad. I'm here.'

Does she feel his fingers move? She holds his hand even more tightly.

'What—'

'Shh. Don't try to talk. There was an accident, Dad. You're in hospital.'

'Kayla? Your mother?'

What can she say? She knows her mother is gone, even if the fact of it hasn't really struck home yet. But she can't tell her father that. Not now.

'They're being looked after, Dad. You mustn't worry. Just lie still. I'll call the doctor.'

'Lizzie … I had to get to you. I didn't want you to …' Sam's eyes widen as one of the bedside monitors shrieks a loud alarm.

'Dad—*Dad*!'

Suddenly a nurse appears, then another. Lizzie is physically pulled out of the room as more medical staff enter.

'Dad!' She fights to get back into the room, but a nurse restrains her.

'He's in good hands. Please wait here. Let us do our jobs.' The nurse guides Lizzie to the waiting area and pushes her unresisting body into a chair.

Confused and more frightened than ever, Lizzie stares at the door to her father's room. All the walls and doors in ICU are glass, and while this might help the medical staff monitor their patients, it's not helping Lizzie. She can see the urgent movements of the team around Sam's bed. She can see them place the paddles on his chest and step back. She can see the jerk of her father's body as the current hits him. She can see the nurse shake her head.

'Lizzie. Lizzie.'

Mitch is there. She turns to him as he sits beside her and reaches for her hands.

'I'm sorry. It took so long to find you. How is your dad? Have you heard?'

He stops speaking as the doctor approaches. Lizzie stands up, eyes glued to the doctor's face. She shrugs off Mitch's hand and squares her shoulders for what she knows is coming.

'Miss Lawson … I am so very sorry.'

CHAPTER
48

The noise level was astonishing. Almost painful. Kayla winced as Lachie yelled something from the other side of the buffet table. She didn't catch more than a word or two. She smiled and shrugged. He nodded his head in the direction of the terrace and the two of them fought their way through the crowd. The terrace was only marginally less noisy and crowded than the ballroom, but it was an improvement.

Lachie put his arms around Kayla's waist and guided her to the far end of the terrace, where the view opened to show the Harbour Bridge, with all its lights shining. He glanced at his watch.

'I'm done. What about you?'

'I am so done!' Kayla checked her phone again. There were no messages. No missed calls. No emergencies she had to deal with. 'Who gets married on Christmas Eve? Really? A totally stupid idea.'

'I've got an idea that's not totally stupid.' Lachie took Kayla by the shoulders and pulled her close. 'How about you and I take off?'

he whispered in her ear. 'We can start our Christmas break a bit early. I've got a surprise for you.'

'Oh—I love a surprise.' Kayla couldn't help but smile. 'What is it?'

'Ah, that would be telling. Are we on?'

'Yes, we are. Just let me text Pascale.'

'No. No. The minute you text her, she'll have some reason for you to stay. Come on. Don't be so noble. Remember what I said—a surprise.'

Kayla resisted for all of ten seconds while her conscience told her she was technically still on duty. But her work was all done and it was Christmas Eve … almost Christmas Day. It wouldn't hurt to give in to temptation this once. And Lachie was so tempting with that wicked grin and blue eyes. With all the time she'd spent at Willowbrook, she's neglected him. Not to mention that right now, she could use a bit of Lachie's magical TLC. She pulled out her phone one last time and with a flourish, turned it off.

'That's my girl.' Lachie kissed her. 'Let's blow this popsicle stand.'

They headed for the lift. Several wedding guests shared the ride to the ground floor with them and then there was the inevitable wait for a taxi. By the time they pulled up outside her building, Kayla was tired. Still, once she and Lachie were alone, she was pretty sure that feeling would go away pretty fast.

'Wait here. This won't take long,' Lachie told the driver as he opened the taxi door.

Kayla frowned. 'What do you mean? Aren't you staying here tonight?'

'No. And neither are you. We've just come to grab your things.'

'What things?'

'No questions. It's a surprise, remember.'

Once they reached her apartment, Lachie relented enough to tell her what to pack: a bikini, shorts and sunscreen, sunglasses and a hat. Based on that, Kayla packed an overnight bag with everything a girl would need for a weekend at the beach and a night or two in a fancy hotel with her man.

'I'm ready.'

'One last thing.' Lachie held out his hand. 'Phone.'

'What?'

'No phones. Here's mine.' He pulled it out of his pocket and put it on her coffee table. 'Now yours.'

'But—'

'No buts. You work too hard. We both work too hard. When did you last properly relax and enjoy yourself? Well, for the next two days, we are both unavailable. Not for work. Not for our family and friends either. These two days are just for us.'

It sounded a lot like heaven, but still Kayla hesitated. It was Christmas and there would be people calling her. Liz might even phone, now they were talking again. What if there was a last-minute glitch at the wedding party they'd just left? Or—

'Come on. It's Christmas Day in about three minutes. Take a day off. Take two of them. The world won't come to an end, you know.'

He was right. She was a wedding planner not a brain surgeon. No one was going to die if she wasn't on call. Kayla firmly placed the phone on her table next to his.

'Let's go.'

'Great!'

Lachie took her hand and they left the apartment. The taxi was waiting as requested. Lachie gave the driver instructions so quietly that Kayla didn't hear. They continued to hold hands for the short drive to the nearby marina.

'What are we—'

'Come on.' Lachie paid the driver and grabbed Kayla's bag out of the boot. He took her hand and let her into the marina. Kayla looked around, pleased she had changed out of her work wear into slacks and flat shoes. Quite a few of the moorings were empty. Lights were on in one or two of the boats. Lachie led her to a graceful white cruiser. He leaped on board, then held his hand out to her.

'Welcome aboard,' he said.

He went to the pilot's chair and flicked some switches. Lights came on and Kayla almost gasped as she looked through the sliding glass doors into the boat's luxurious cabin. She slid the doors open and walked inside. At the far end of the cabin, steps led down to what appeared to be a beautifully equipped kitchen. And beyond that, no doubt, an equally impressive bedroom. It was a toy. A beautiful expensive toy.

'This is lovely, Lachie.'

'Isn't it, though? And it's fully stocked with Champagne and caviar. Everything we might need. I thought a couple of days cruising around the harbour, or if the weather is good, we could head up to the Hawkesbury. Just the two of us.'

'What a wonderful idea. But whose boat is it? Did you rent it?'

'No. I bought it.' He beamed at her with that cheeky, proud-little-boy grin.

'You bought it? But I thought you were going to buy an apartment.'

'I was. But then I saw her.' Lachie ran a hand lovingly over the polished wood of the bar. 'And I fell in love. You know me, I can be totally crazy when I'm in love. She's my Christmas present to myself.'

Lachie disappeared behind the bar to emerge with a bottle of his favourite Champagne and two glasses. As she drank with him,

Kayla's thoughts wandered to her sister. She wondered what Liz would be doing. This adventure with Lachie had put paid to her plan to call Liz to wish her a merry Christmas. It shouldn't matter too much. She and Liz hadn't exchanged gifts or even cards for the past few years. But things had changed and they were closer now than they had been. Kayla could have, should have, done something. It was too late now. This one time, she was not going to do the right thing. And she wasn't going to let herself think too much about the fact that the Champagne she was drinking probably cost more than whatever Christmas dinner Liz might have planned for herself.

Lachie pulled her into his arms and kissed her, and Kayla forgot all about her sister.

'Right. Let's get underway.'

Lachie seemed to know what he was doing. He darted around the boat, smiling and singing under his breath, while handling ropes with a knowledgeable air. Then he started the engine and the elegant craft pulled away from its mooring. He wasn't in a hurry. The engine sound was a low hum as they cruised around the dark headland and out into the harbour.

Kayla relaxed on the soft upholstery, Champagne in her hand as they passed under the brightly lit arch of the Harbour Bridge. In the distance, the graceful curves of the Opera House glowed red and green and gold with a special Christmas light show. Behind the wheel, Lachie looked handsome and happy and when he glanced at her, his eyes glowed with the promise of a wonderful time ahead. Kayla took another sip and gazed up at the inky sky. The stars glistened like diamonds on fine velvet. It was perfect.

Almost.

Kayla knew it was a trick of the ambient light of a city, but she couldn't help thinking that the stars shone just a little bit more brightly above Willowbrook Station.

CHAPTER
49

Christmas Day was not a day for lingering in bed. Liz leaped up as soon as she opened her eyes. The past tended to come flooding back when she lay in bed. A lot of memories were hard to take, but none more so than Christmas memories. So Liz pretended today was like any other day and got up at her usual time. She didn't turn on the radio in the kitchen as she normally did. It would be nothing but Christmas carols and Christmas stories and she didn't want to hear them. But as she was making breakfast, she had a change of heart. This Christmas was a little bit different. She and Kayla were mending bridges. Maybe it wouldn't hurt to call her sister and wish her a merry Christmas. After all, they were family, and family really was important.

Mug of tea in hand, Liz dialled Kayla's number. She leaned against the kitchen bench and listened to Kayla's phone ring ... and ring. Then she heard her sister's voice.

'Sorry, I'm not able to take your call right now. Please leave a message after the beep and I'll get back to you.'

Liz didn't leave a message. Feeling strangely disappointed, she didn't bother washing her dishes but headed straight to the stables. The horses knew nothing about Christmas. They would be her best companions today.

She distributed the morning feeds and then allowed herself to take a little time to lean on the fence of the mare's paddock. Little Vega was feeling particularly fine this morning. The filly skittered about the yard, tossing her head and kicking up her heels. Although she was the youngest, she was the leader of the gang and her five older siblings followed behind.

Six foals were not enough to support a stud. She needed outside mares to generate stud fees and to bring in agistment fees. Her paddocks held only her horses now, and they looked very empty. The next stud season was eight months away; that's how long Deimos had to prove himself. How long she had to prove him. Getting herself in debt with Pascale might have restored the homestead, but it hadn't really improved her financial position. The photo shoot and the wedding had kept the bank from her door, but only just. It had helped pay her feed bill, but there was a lot more to running a horse stud than simply feeding the few horses she had left.

The King of the Ranges competition was two months away. That was going to be her turning point. She and Deimos had to win. The competition was more about the rider than the horse, but if she won, people would notice Deimos. By then hopefully another wedding or two would give her the money to start taking the stallion around some shows. People needed to see him. And he needed to start winning both as a led horse and under saddle.

She returned to Deimos, who had finished his breakfast and was looking out over the top of his stall, eager for his morning ride.

'Not today, boy. Today you get a day off.' The horses could have a holiday. But not her. There was too much to do.

She turned Deimos into the round yard to stretch his legs before heading to the machinery shed. She loaded tools and wire and a chainsaw into the back of her old four-wheel-drive ute and set out across the paddock. She found a suitable-looking spot and stopped. If Deimos was going to start winning, she needed to push him a little harder. She lifted the chainsaw from the tray of the ute and approached a dead gum tree that was still standing, its bleached white branches stark against the blue sky. This would be her starting point. She pulled the starter on the saw. The engine roared into the quiet of the day as the chain bit into the timber.

Liz didn't stop for lunch. By the time the sun was starting to move lower in the sky, she had built three good-sized jumps from timber she had felled. She stood looking at the last one. This was the most difficult. It was on a slope and could be approached either uphill or down. It barely reached her waist, but it was almost as broad as it was high. Deimos wasn't quite ready for it yet, but he soon would be.

Liz wiped the sweat from her face and took a long drink from her almost empty water bottle. Her muscles ached and she was tired. But it was a good tiredness. It was born of honest hard work, not of sleepless nights or stress. She put her tools in the ute and returned to the homestead and her evening chores.

By the time the horses were bedded down for the night, her feet were dragging. She wanted nothing more than a refreshing shower and a chance to relax. Despite missing lunch, she was too exhausted to think about food. There must be some bread she could toast; that would do. And afterwards, maybe she would fall asleep … and perhaps even sleep the whole night through.

As she approached the house, she saw something by the back door: a parcel wrapped in shiny red paper to remind her of what she had been trying to forget all day. Who on earth would leave a Christmas present on her doorstep?

Her first thought was her sister. Had Kayla driven all the way from Sydney? There was no sign of her car, and she wouldn't have come all this way just to leave a gift and then go. Liz hadn't been that far from the homestead. Kayla would have found her if she'd looked.

If not Kayla then who?

She picked the box up and looked for a card. There was none. She took it inside and placed it on the kitchen table. She started to unwrap it, trying hard not to think how long it was since she had last unwrapped a Christmas present. As she opened the bright paper, Liz exposed another layer, this time of bubble wrap. So, whatever it was, this gift was breakable. She picked at the tape holding the bubble wrap in place, biting her lip in frustration because her short nails weren't able to lift it. She found a pair of scissors in a drawer and carried on with her task.

She hesitated before revealing the contents, which she now saw was something rectangular and flat. It wasn't thick enough to be a book. As she folded the last of the wrap back, she realised what it was: a photo frame. It lay on the table in front of her, face down so she couldn't see the image. Her hand trembled ever so slightly as she turned it over and looked at her father's face.

She remembered the day this had been taken so clearly. It was the Tamworth Show, the year of her sixteenth birthday. She and Mitch had ridden two Willowbrook horses in the pair of hunters class. The two matched browns had taken each obstacle as if it was nothing, and resoundingly earned their blue first-place ribbons. Mitch's parents had been there too and his mother had taken a photograph. This photograph. It showed the two teenagers still mounted, their faces glowing with the excitement of their win. Standing between the two horses, holding their heads, Sam Lawson was alight with pride. She remembered that look. He was proud of his horses. But he was even more proud of his daughter and his protégé.

Liz slid onto a chair and closed her eyes as the memories played like a film in the darkness. She heard the laughter, felt the heat of the sun and smelled the sweat on the horses' necks. But most of all she saw the way they looked at her, Mitch and her father. She didn't know who was the proudest—or who loved her the most. Nor did she know which of them she loved more.

She sat there not moving for a very long time. Now she knew who the gift was from.

At last she got to her feet. She carried the photo in its plain silver frame upstairs and placed it on the desk in the room that had once been her parents' bedroom. It looked good on the desk, right next to the old framed photograph of her father and Apollo. The photos had not been taken that far apart but the state of the older print told her how much time had passed since then. She stared from one to the other, and came to a decision. But before anything else, she needed to shower and change out of her filthy work clothes.

On the way to the bathroom she had to pass the door to Kayla's bedroom. She paused and went inside. Kayla had accidentally left behind a dress, nothing flash, just a simple cotton summer dress, but it had probably cost far more than Liz spent on clothes in a year. Liz had washed it carefully and put it away for Kayla to collect on her next visit.

Now she opened the wardrobe and looked at the dress. It really was very pretty. How long had it been since she had last worn a pretty dress? She reached into the wardrobe and took it out. She ran the fabric between her fingers. Like Kayla herself, it was soft and feminine and classy. All Liz's clothes had been designed for work, but this existed for the sheer pleasure of looking good. Of making the person who was wearing it look and feel pretty.

No. This wasn't right. She went to put the dress back, but paused. What harm could come of this? After all, it was Christmas.

In the bathroom, she used Kayla's rose-scented soap and tried the expensive beauty creams she'd left behind too. They smelled good, but it was going to take more than a dollop of cream to take away the lines that years of hardship and hard work had left on Liz's face and hands.

When she put the dress on, she almost changed her mind. The woman looking out of the mirror didn't look like her. Her lean, straight body seemed awkward in a dress that was designed for curves. Her short hair was clean and brushed, but looked almost masculine against the soft yellow and cream fabric.

This was silly … yet, when she looked again, there was something in the mirror that reminded her of the girl she had once been. Kayla had left make-up behind in the bathroom, but Liz thought that might be a step too far. She hadn't worn make-up for fifteen years. She had always meant to ask her mother to show her how, but then it was too late.

She dismissed the make-up idea and instead picked up the light sandals in the bottom of Kayla's wardrobe and hurried down the stairs. She paused briefly in the kitchen, then got into her car and started the engine before she had time for second—or third—thoughts.

CHAPTER
50

'Goodbye, Uncle Mitch. Merry Christmas.'

'Merry Christmas to you too, sweetie.' Mitch blew a kiss at the dark-haired girl on his computer screen. 'Now put Grandma back on.'

'Okay.'

His five-year-old niece disappeared, replaced by his mother. 'It's really a shame you couldn't get here at least for a couple of days,' she said wistfully.

'You know what it's like, Mum. Horses need looking after. I can't leave them.'

'Oh, I know. I haven't been married to your father for all these years without knowing that the horses come first.'

Mitch could hear the affection in his mother's voice. A second face appeared on the screen as his father sat on the sofa in front of their laptop.

'Speaking of which, how is that colt turning out?'

Mitch started to answer, then stopped. He could hear the sound of a car approaching down his driveway.

'Mum, Dad. I've got to go. There's someone here.'

'Who is it?' his mother asked. 'Is it that nice girl you're seeing? Sue?'

'Mum …'

'I know. I want you to be happy, that's all. Get married. Have babies. Like your sister.'

'I know, Mum. I'd better say goodbye, now, and see who's here.'

'And I like being a grandmother, remember. I'm good at it too. There's plenty of room for another grandchild or two.'

'Pay no attention to your mother,' his dad cut in. 'Goodnight, son. Go see your visitor. And merry Christmas.'

'Merry Christmas to you both too.' Mitch clicked end on the Skype session just as a sweep of light across the window told him his visitor had parked in front of his house.

It wasn't Sue, of course, and he wondered for a moment why he hadn't told his mother he'd ended that relationship. Maybe it was because he was having second thoughts. Maybe he should give up on Liz and call Sue again, because only a fool would keep waiting when there was no hope at all.

He heard light footsteps on his wooden porch. Those certainly weren't riding boots. That meant it wasn't Liz. Who else could it be? Could it be Sue after all? If he was getting a second chance with her, maybe he should take it.

He opened the door and for a moment he almost didn't recognise the woman standing there.

It wasn't Liz … but it was almost the Lizzie he had lost all those years ago. She was wearing a dress. And sandals. The faint breeze lifted her hair, which shone under the porch light. She was holding a bottle of wine in her hands.

'Hello, Mitch.' Her voice had a soft shyness he had never heard in it before.

'Lizzie—Liz. I wasn't expecting—'

'I came to say thank you. For the photo. It's … well, thank you. I don't really do Christmas, but I brought you this.' She held out the wine.

He took it. 'Come in, Liz.'

'No, really. I just …'

He stepped back, holding the door open. She hesitated. He knew how hard it must have been for her to cross the invisible barrier she had constructed between them. It was like a wall along the top of the creek bank. She stood silently for what seemed a very long time, not meeting his gaze. He thought she was going to leave, but finally, slowly, she stepped over the threshold.

Mitch stayed where he was until she'd walked into the centre of the room, then he gently shut the door. Liz was silent as she turned in a circle, studying the place he called home. He'd done a lot of work on the deconsecrated church since he'd bought it. The main body of the church was an open living space with a high roof and large windows. There was a fire at one end to warm it on freezing winter nights. The sofas facing the fireplace were generous and comfortable. At the other end of the building, he'd constructed a kitchen with a breakfast bar. In fact, the only internal walls surrounded the bathroom at the far end, behind the kitchen.

'What's that?' Liz indicated the mezzanine floor, with stairs leading up to it from near the bathroom.

'That's my bedroom.'

To give her a minute's breathing space, Mitch took the wine into the kitchen.

'It was left behind by Kayla's team after a wedding,' Liz said, following him. 'I hope it's all right.'

'Let's find out, shall we?' He reached into a drawer for a corkscrew.

'No. I mean, I'm not staying. I have to get back.'

She was like a frightened young horse, poised to run at the first sign of danger. He wasn't going to force her to do anything. 'All right, if you have to. But first, just share a glass of wine with me. It is Christmas, after all.'

She didn't say no. That was good enough for him. He poured the wine and carried both glasses to the lounge area. He put them on the low coffee table, and sat at one end of the sofa. As he expected, Liz chose the armchair opposite him. That was fine. She was here, and that was all that really mattered.

He raised the glass in a silent toast and took a sip of the crisp white wine. 'Nice.'

Liz followed suit. 'I am more of a beer girl myself, but it's not bad.'

'An unexpected bonus from the wedding business. How is it going?'

'All right, I guess. We've only had one wedding so far, a bus load of Japanese visitors. Five or six couples all getting married at the same time.'

'That's different.'

'According to Kayla, it may become a regular thing. They like the outback experience. And that's fine by me. I made some money out of it and that came in handy.'

'And what about the renovations on the homestead?'

'They're finished ... or at least what Kayla calls the first stage is finished. She's done a good job. The place looks great. Except the bride's room is all a bit girly for my tastes, but she says that's what it has to be like.'

Liz fidgeted with the stem of her wine glass. Mitch almost reached over to take it out of her hands before she spilled the contents, or broke the glass and hurt herself. But he didn't. He was as aware as she was that their conversation had brought back memories that they had never discussed and maybe never would.

'So, how is your family?' Liz asked a little too quickly.

'Good. They're up in Queensland. Mum loves it there. Dad keeps talking about retiring, but of course he won't.'

'And Jen?'

'She's married now. Got one daughter and another on the way. He's a teacher; a good guy. They're really happy together and you know Mum loves being a grandmother.'

That was too much. He could see it on her face. She put the wine glass down and stood up.

'I really have to go.'

He wanted her to stay. He wanted to listen to her talk about … anything at all really. He really wanted to hear the sound of her voice in this lonely place he called home. He wanted to take her in his arms. He wanted to make up for all the lost time. But tonight was not the night.

He led the way to the door and opened it.

'It was nice to see you,' he said. He didn't say, 'Let's do it again.' Or 'Come over any time.' He stepped back.

She hesitated. It was just a fraction of a second, but it was enough to make his heart leap.

'Merry Christmas.' She stood on tiptoes and brushed her lips across his cheek. It was the briefest touch—like the caress of a butterfly's wings—but it was the best gift he'd been given for a very long time.

CHAPTER
51

Lizzie wonders how long the grass will take to grow on the freshly turned soil. Out of habit, she looks up at the sky. There are a few clouds near the horizon, but nothing to indicate rain.

'Lizzie, I am so sorry.'

She looks at the person speaking. It's Mitch's dad. He helped arrange for these graves to be dug in the old family graveyard on top of the hill overlooking Willowbrook. There are only a few people here for the burial. Lizzie's glad of that. The huge crowd at the church had nearly overwhelmed her. They were people who had known and respected her parents, but Lizzie didn't really know them. Their presence had been just a noisy blur on the edge of her grief. Mrs Saunders is here at the graveside too, but not Jen. She's at the hospital with Kayla today. The doctor suggested Kayla shouldn't come to the funeral. Lizzie agreed, but she's glad her sister isn't alone this afternoon. Not like her. Despite all these people, Lizzie has never felt so utterly alone in her entire life.

'Kayla still hasn't remembered anything of the accident?' This time it's Mitch's mum speaking. She knows the answer. Everyone knows that Kayla can't remember the accident at all. The question is simply an attempt to fill the terrible silence.

'No.'

Kayla doesn't remember, but Lizzie knows exactly what happened. Her parents were coming to stop the wedding when the car crashed. Her father must have been speeding on the icy road, determined that she and Mitch would not be married. That's how they died and it's all her fault.

'It's a shame she wasn't here. It was a lovely service. And this is a beautiful place for your parents to rest.'

Deep inside Lizzie a voice is screaming. No! It wasn't a beautiful service. It was horrible. The most horrible thing she has ever known. And the gravesite isn't beautiful. It's sad … terribly, terribly sad. This hilltop overlooking Willowbrook should be a place for her parents to have a picnic. Or to go for a walk. Or … just be alive.

Someone reaches for her hand, strong steady fingers closing around hers to stop them shaking. It's Mitch. He senses what she's thinking and feeling. He always has. But this time, there is no comfort he can give her. She pulls her hand away.

'Lizzie …'

'Thank you for coming,' she says to the Saunders family.

They know she is asking them to leave, but they hesitate. She looks so young and so lost.

'Are you sure you'll be all right?' Mrs Saunders' face is sympathetic and concerned. 'You're very welcome to come to our house. There's always room for you. You know that.'

'No. Thank you. This is my home. This is where I belong.'

'Then at least let me stay with you,' Mitch offers earnestly. 'Lizzie, you shouldn't be alone tonight.'

Maybe she shouldn't. But Mitch is the one person she absolutely cannot be with. She can't even bear to look at him. She shakes her head and turns to speak to the funeral director. She doesn't want to talk to this sombre man in the black suit—or anyone really—but she hopes this will make Mitch and his parents leave.

It does. The funeral director says something that Lizzie doesn't bother listening to, and then he too departs.

At last she is alone.

For a long time she sits by the graves, crying. She cries until she has no tears left, then she stands up.

'I'm sorry.' The words are a whisper. 'I promise you that I will look after Kayla. And Willowbrook. I won't let anything take them away from me. I won't let you down again.'

She wipes the tears from her face and walks down the hill.

She goes to the stables. She hasn't been there since the day of the accident. She knows that Mitch has been looking after the horses. They're fine, but Apollo needs exercise. Her father used to ride him every day and the horse is restless now, listening for a familiar voice he will never hear again. It's the work of just a few minutes to get the stallion saddled then they leave the stables at a brisk trot. Lizzie has no real destination in mind, she just needs to escape. She spends hours with her father's horse, trying to tire herself out so she will sleep properly.

That night, Lizzie stays in the stables. The house is too empty and too quiet. She lies awake, waiting, and stares into the darkness. In the stables there is faint noise and movement. There is life around her. She doesn't sleep well, but she does get a few blissful moments of forgetting.

In the early morning she hears the sound of a car. She knows immediately who it is. Mitch has come to help her. She gets up from the bed of straw where she has lain and, rubbing her hands over her face, goes to meet him.

Mitch doesn't go to the house. He thinks—hopes—that Lizzie is there, sleeping. He knows she is exhausted by her grief. He is grieving too, but he is also desperate to find a way to help her. Looking after her horses is not enough, but it's better than nothing.

Before he reaches the gate leading to the stables, Lizzie appears, her face puffy with sleep and tears. She is first to reach the gate. She walks through into the house yard and closes the gate firmly behind her.

'Thanks for coming, Mitch,' she says before he can speak. 'I really appreciate all that you have done for me over the last couple of days. But I'm fine now. I don't need your help any more.'

Her words are hard, but he knows that's just her grief. 'I want to help you, Lizzie. That's what you do for people you love. Whatever you need, I'm here for you. You know that.'

'I don't need your help.'

'You can't do this all by yourself. And you don't have to. We said we'd be together forever. This is what we meant. Helping each other through the bad times.'

'No, Mitch. Don't you understand? It's our fault that they're dead. My fault. And yours. If we hadn't sneaked away, they would never have been on that road. They wouldn't have died!'

She is almost screaming and that frightens Mitch. He reaches for her, but she slaps his hand away.

'Don't touch me. You can't help me. I have to live with what I did—what we did—for the rest of my life.'

'No! It's not your fault. It was a terrible accident, but you're not to blame. Neither am I.'

She shakes her head. 'Please go away, Mitch. I can't see you. I can't be with you. Not now. Not any more.'

He goes, because he knows that to stay will only make matters worse, but he will come back. He'll come back every day until she changes her mind. In a few weeks his family is moving to Queensland, and if she hasn't relented he'll have to go with them. But it won't be forever. He won't let her give up on them.

Lizzie watches him leave, fighting all the while not to call him back.

At last she is on her own. She takes a deep breath. She has done the hardest thing. Now she can face the rest of what has to be done.

She finishes the morning chores and goes to the house. Her first call is to the hospital to check on Kayla. Her sister will be allowed home in a couple of days. She'll need to recuperate for a few weeks, but then she will be fine.

Her second call is to her father's lawyer and then she calls the bank. These are not easy calls to make, but the meetings that will follow them will be even harder.

Her final call is to a number she has found through directory assistance. It's answered immediately by an efficient sounding woman.

She doesn't know how she will explain this to Kayla. How do you tell an eleven-year-old suffering the physical effects of an accident that she must leave her home and go somewhere to be surrounded by strangers? It won't be easy, but there is no choice. One eighteen-year-old girl cannot run a horse stud and care for her young sister at the same time.

'Hello,' she says to the woman on the phone. 'I want to make enquiries about a boarding school place for my younger sister. My name is Lizzie—Elizabeth Lawson.'

CHAPTER
52

'Kayla, you're going to have to drop everything else and sort this out. Sorry.' Pascale grimaced.

'I'll fix it. Don't worry.'

Kayla looked at her screen. The gossip website had almost got it right. 'Soap Star's Secret Wedding Plans' it screamed in a font far too large and far too red for comfort. The site then went on to detail plans for the celebrity wedding of the year between a famous soap star and her musician boyfriend. They had the right date and the right location and promised 'exclusive insider details' of the ceremony plans, including the dress designer. Much of it was rubbish, but that didn't matter. The date and place were the important things when it came to celebrity weddings. Now the secret was out, the venue would be besieged by paparazzi, and probably a crowd of onlookers. That was exactly what Elite Weddings was being paid to prevent.

Someone was likely to lose their job over the leak. Kayla would have to find out where it came from. It was the first time something like this had happened and she was not going to risk a second. But any investigation would have to wait. She had a wedding to move.

Changing the venue was the only option she had now, and there wasn't much time. It was a big wedding with a couple of hundred guests. Many of them were TV stars or pop stars and almost all of them were movers and shakers in the entertainment industry. If she got this wrong, it wouldn't be good for business. If she got it right, it would probably lead to a number of lucrative commissions. So right it had to be.

The problem was that there weren't many large, high-end venues to be had at short notice. Not many? Who was she kidding? There were none at all.

The first thing she had to do was talk to her client. The bride-to-be was, according to her assistant, on set. She would call back as soon as she was able. Everything in the assistant's manner suggested that neither she nor her employer had seen the article. But Kayla knew that it wouldn't be long before someone pointed it out to them. In the meantime, she needed to get to work.

Kayla worked the phone and all her contacts for an hour and came up with nothing. There were venues, but none that were big enough, good enough or provided enough security. She was almost at her wits' end when her phone rang.

'It's Beth Richards here.'

'Thanks for calling, Beth. I'm afraid I have some bad news.'

'I've seen it,' the actress replied in a remarkably calm tone.

'I don't know where the leak came from. Not from my office, I can assure you. I will track it down though.'

'I do know. It turns out our photographer told his assistant who told someone—and you know how that works. Can you find a trustworthy photographer for me? Someone good?'

'I have the perfect person in mind—I'll call him as soon as we're done.'

'Great. My publicist has already talked to the website—but that's not going to change anything.'

'No. It's not. My best advice would be to change venue—and date too if you can. I've already started looking at new venues, but it is short notice.'

'And there's no way we can keep the plans as they were?'

'We can—but it's highly likely there will be some sort of disruption. There will be paps there. And the less honourable news outlets will already be trying to bribe staff to take secret photos and it's impossible to keep all the staff's mobile phones out of the venue.'

'All we ever wanted was a quiet, private wedding. And now look at the mess we're in.' Now Beth sounded on the verge of tears, reminding Kayla that while she was a huge star, she was only twenty-two years old.

An idea sprang into her mind. Maybe ...

'Beth, do you still want a quiet, private wedding? I can give you that with total security. No paps. No crowds. Just the two of you and a few key guests. You can have that private moment. Then we can change the plans for the second and make it a big party, rather than the wedding itself. If the paps do turn up, they'll be on the edge of the party—but not disrupting your special day.'

Kayla crossed her fingers during the long silence that followed.

'I'm not sure ... exactly what were you thinking?'

'I know of a venue in the Hunter Valley. A lovely historic home-stead. It's a new venue so the paps have never been there. There's a beautiful dining room that will seat fifteen to twenty. Or you can have forty or fifty people if you only want outdoor drinks and canapés under a marquee. There's overnight accommodation locally if you want, or there's an airport and you can just fly in for the ceremony and back again in a day.'

'That's not many people.'

'How many of the people on your guest list are really that important to you? Personally important.'

'I guess …'

'Let me send you a photo of the venue right now.'

With a silent blessing to the god of technology, Kayla sent Beth one of Ken's photos of Willowbrook. It showed the homestead in the glow of dawn. She waited, saying nothing.

'That is pretty,' Beth said at last. 'And it might be nice to have a small wedding like we originally wanted to.'

Kayla could breathe again. 'Of course. Then the party can be just as spectacular as you want. With as many people as you want.'

'It's my publicist who wants the big party.'

'That's fine. She can even invite a few more people if it's not the wedding as such.'

'I'm starting to like the idea. Let me talk to Vince and get back to you.'

'Do that. I would suggest sooner rather than later. The longer you wait, the greater the risk that someone will find out. This is probably the most secret venue I can get for you, but you know how hard it is to keep things quiet once preparations have started.'

Kayla hung up.

'You're thinking of moving them to Willowbrook?' Pascale had obviously been listening.

'Yes.'

'Good idea, but is it ready for something this high end?'

'It will be. Trust me.'

'Oh, I do.'

Certain Beth would go along with her idea, Kayla started making plans and doing costings. Last-minute arrangements didn't come cheap, but her clients had plenty of money and they would be willing to pay for privacy. She needed flowers, catering, transport. She was pretty sure she could get Ken to do the photos. But none of them needed to know who this wedding was for. Nor did most of them need to know the venue until the actual day.

Her plans were already taking shape when the phone rang again.

'All right,' Beth said. 'Let's do it.'

'You won't regret it.' Kayla's brain switched into high gear, while her heart took a little leap at the thought of going … home?

CHAPTER

53

There was someone walking around on the other side of the creek, which was strange. Even more strange was the way they were moving, as if searching for something or hiding from someone. Mitch didn't like the look of it. He turned his horse's head towards the figure just vanishing among the trees. A minute later, he pulled up on the bank of the creek. He peered across the water at Willowbrook and caught a flash of movement. It wasn't a horse and it wasn't Liz.

Mitch trotted along the creek to the crossing. He sent his horse plunging through the water and out the other side, where he urged it into a canter. He saw movement ahead of him, and in a few moments caught up with a man who was on foot. The man spun and then backed away from the horse as Mitch swung himself from the saddle.

'What are you doing here?'

'I wasn't doing any harm.'

'That's not what I asked. Who are you?' Mitch noticed the bag on the man's shoulder. 'What's in there?'

'It's my camera. I'm a photographer. A local stringer for the news websites.'

'But what are you doing here?'

'I know a guy at the airport. He calls me when private planes land. He recognised some celebrity chef with boxes of stuff. I followed him here. I know this place is used for weddings, so I thought it might be someone, you know, famous. I could sell a photo and make a few bucks.'

'This is private land. You've got no right to be here.'

'Hey, mate. I'm just doing my job.'

'Well, you can do it somewhere else, all right?'

'Who the hell are you to order me about?'

'I'm the man who is going to knock you down if you don't leave right now.'

The photographer took a step away. Mitch followed, his anger rising. How dare this man trespass on Liz's land? How dare he spy on her and her home? Mitch had never hit anyone in his life, but if he was ever going to, this could well be the time.

Something of his feeling must have been visible in his face, because the photographer continued to back away, raising his hands.

'Okay. No problem. There's no need to get heavy. I'm leaving. It was probably a bad tip anyway. There's no way anyone famous would get married in a dump like this.' He began making his way to the fence and the road.

Mitch swung himself into the saddle and followed. The photographer moved quickly, occasionally glancing over his shoulder. When they reached the fence line, Mitch saw a car parked off the road, half hidden among the trees. The photographer vaulted over the fence and made for the car. Mitch stayed where he was, watching, until the man started the engine and drove away. The photographer drove straight past the Willowbrook driveway and kept on going. Mitch nodded in satisfaction, but he wasn't about to leave it there. He turned towards the homestead.

He dismounted at the stables but found no sign of Liz. There was movement at the house, so leaving his mount in an empty stall, he walked in the direction of the noise. He paused at the gate. There seemed to be a lot of people around and he didn't want to walk into the middle of something. Then he saw Kayla. She was carrying a tablet and looked the very image of efficiency as she directed people carrying flowers and chairs. Clearly they were preparing for a wedding that hadn't started yet. He opened the gate.

'Hi, Mitch. Um—I don't want to be anti-social, but we've got a wedding today.'

'I know. I just disturbed a photographer down by the creek.'

'Dammit! Where is he?'

'Gone. I chased him off. He said something about this place not being good enough for the sort of wedding he was looking for.'

Kayla grimaced. 'Not very flattering, but if he really has gone, I'll take it.'

'What's not very flattering?' Liz appeared beside Kayla.

While Kayla told Liz about the photographer, Mitch took the time to look around. Granted he didn't have much experience when it came to weddings, but there did seem to be rather a lot of fuss involved. There were people walking around with armloads of flowers and cardboard boxes with contents he couldn't even guess at. A car pulled up and someone got out carrying a huge garment bag. And something white in a box. It was all a bit much for him.

'Look, I don't want to get under your feet,' he said. 'I guess I'll head home now.'

Kayla laid a hand on his arm. 'Mitch, can you do me a favour? We have security at the front gates, but they're no use if word has gotten out and the paps start coming cross country. The couple's plane is due to land any minute. Would you—and you, Liz—be able to ride the boundary for the next few hours? Just in case there are more photographers out there? The ceremony will be over by one. Then everyone goes inside for a meal. They'll be gone by four at the latest. We need to keep the paparazzi and sightseers out until then. You'll get paid. I've got budget for security.'

Mitch waved aside the thought of payment. 'Happy to help out,' he said. 'But if we're going to stay out that long, I'll need to change horses. The colt I'm riding isn't up for that yet.'

'Do you have a horse he could ride?' Kayla asked her sister.

Mitch could sense the hesitation in Liz, but it didn't last long. She nodded. 'Sure.'

'Kayla, when do these guests arrive?' A man dressed as a chef stormed up to them. 'My smoked trout mousse can't be left just sitting there. If I'm going to be expected to provide edible food out here in the back of beyond, people need to be on time!'

'It's fine, Lachie. They're almost here. Come on. Let's head back and check the tables are ready.' Kayla flashed a smile at Mitch and Liz as she led the irate chef away.

'This wedding business appears to be pretty stressful,' Mitch observed.

He was rewarded with one of Liz's rare smiles. 'And would you believe that's Kayla's boyfriend?'

'Oh. Is it serious?'

'I really don't know. I haven't asked. Come on. We better get started if we're going to be the border patrol.'

CHAPTER
54

While Mitch took care of his colt, Liz set about catching two new horses.

When Mitch joined her, he carried his heavy stock saddle in one hand as if it weighed nothing.

'Why don't you take Deimos?'

Mitch frowned. 'Deimos? Are you sure?'

She understood his surprise. She was prepping Deimos for competition and most people didn't like strangers riding their competition horses. But Mitch wasn't a stranger.

'Of course. It will be interesting for me to watch him work. And to hear what you think of him.'

'If you're sure, I'd love to.'

Liz stood back and let Mitch do his thing with Deimos. He was gentle and gave Deimos time to think about him. But when Deimos showed signs of objecting to a strange saddle, Mitch was just firm enough. He led the colt into the working arena and swung into the saddle, then he gently guided the animal in a series of circles and figure eights at a trot and a canter. They were a joy to watch. Seeing him like this, Liz began to realise that Deimos really was a worthy son of his sire. Like Apollo, he moved with strength and grace, and he was quite beautiful.

And Mitch—he was beautiful too, in his own way. He wasn't just a good rider, his patience and empathy with the horse made him seem one with it. His body was lean and strong and totally under control. He guided Deimos with the smallest movements of legs and hand. And with his voice. Liz couldn't hear him, but she knew how his voice would sound: gentle and low, but firm and encouraging. She could have watched Mitch ride for hours.

Seeing him like this, it was almost as if the last fifteen years hadn't happened. As if they were teenagers again, preparing for a competition. Working together had always felt so good. No, that was wrong. Being together had always felt so good.

He looked up and saw her watching and smiled. This time, she didn't try to hide from him.

By the time Liz had saddled her horse and was ready to go, Mitch and Deimos were waiting for her, apparently already settled into a partnership.

'Let's split up,' she suggested. 'I'll do a loop from here out to the crossing then work my way back along the creek and up to the front gate. Why don't you head up to the hilltop and see if you can spot any cars where they shouldn't be? Then you can loop the other way to the front gate.' She didn't need to give him any more directions than that. Mitch knew Willowbrook almost as well as she did.

It wasn't until she was halfway to the creek that she realised she had sent Mitch to the graveyard. She halted her horse and watched as he and Deimos reached the top of the hill. They stopped near the lone tree and sat there for a short time. It was the first time Mitch had been there since the day of the funeral. Was he looking at the graves and thinking about that terrible day? It occurred to her that perhaps that day, and the guilt they shared, haunted Mitch as much as it haunted her. He had lost a mentor he cared deeply about and a woman who regarded him almost as a son. Except neither of them had wanted him as a son—nor wanted him to marry their daughter.

On the hilltop, Mitch pushed Deimos forward and the pair dropped out of view down the other side of the rise. It was time for Liz to move on too. There might not be any more photographers hanging around, but if there were, it was in her best interests to find them. Kayla wasn't the only one who would suffer if this wedding went wrong. Liz was beginning to understand how important this venture was becoming to her, financially. She would fight just as hard for it as she did for every other part of Willowbrook.

Liz patrolled the fence line for the next couple of hours. On each loop, she and Mitch would meet near the gates of Willowbrook where two of Kayla's hired security men reported no issues. There was never a lot of traffic on this road, and the cars that had appeared today had simply passed by. Liz was beginning to think it was time to call it a day, when she noticed cars starting to leave the homestead. She was near to the driveway, so paused to watch them go. The front car carried the bride and groom. A young woman all in white looked out the window and saw Liz on her horse. She waved, her face a picture of excitement and happiness. Liz waved back, silently wishing the girl more happiness than she had found on her own wedding day. Had she looked like that on the morning she and Mitch had set out to be married?

She saw Mitch on the far side of the driveway. He too was watching the newlyweds drive away. Were his thoughts the same as hers? From this distance, she couldn't read his face, hidden as it was in the shadow of his broad-brimmed hat. They rode to the homestead at the same time, but not together. They were separated by a stretch of graded gravel, and their memories.

When they reached the house, the clean-up was well underway. Chairs were being packed into vans, crockery and glasses and flowers too. And, as always, Kayla was at the centre of it all, like a policeman directing traffic. She looked over when she noticed Mitch and Liz and gave a thumbs up. Liz nodded and turned her horse towards the stables.

In thoughtful silence she and Mitch bedded their horses down, then came the moment they finally had to speak.

'Deimos has all the potential in the world,' Mitch said. 'You'll do well with him. But be careful, he seems to be developing a tendency to pull to the off side.'

'Yeah. I'd noticed that too,' Liz said.

Mitch hesitated. 'I guess I should head home now.'

'Why don't you come back to the house? We've been out for hours. I don't know about you, but I'm hungry. I could go a cold drink too.'

If he was surprised by the offer, he didn't show it. 'Thanks.'

By the time the two of them had walked to the homestead, the clearing up was almost done and Kayla was bidding farewell to her helpers. The chef was the only one not racing away. He leaned on his car, obviously waiting for Kayla.

'Well, that went really well,' Kayla said as they approached. 'Sorry you didn't get to meet Beth and Vince.'

'Who?'

Kayla laughed at Mitch's puzzled face. 'Our celebrity bride and groom. You'll see the official pictures in a magazine soon. Thanks to you, there won't be any unofficial pictures.'

'Glad to help out.'

'Well, I'm off. Lachie and I are spending the night in Scone. I'll be back tomorrow for a final check of everything before I head back to Sydney. There was a bit of food left over. It's in the kitchen. You two should eat it tonight. It's some of Lachie's finest and it would be a shame to see it go to waste.'

'Okay.' Liz waved her sister and Lachie off.

As their car vanished, a slightly awkward silence settled over Liz and Mitch.

Liz was the first to move. 'Let's see what they've left for us. Kayla's boyfriend is a pretty good cook.'

Kayla's crew was good at their jobs and not a trace remained of the wedding, except for what was in the new refrigerator.

'Well, it seems we have wine as well as food,' Liz said as she studied its interior.

'Just cold water will be fine for me,' Mitch said. 'I have to ride home and feed up.'

'Come on, one glass won't hurt. And you have to taste this food. It looks wonderful.'

She placed plates on the table, along with a chilled bottle of white wine. It didn't take long to find two wine glasses—Kayla had installed a small stock of them. Standing at the table, Liz poured the wine and pulled the covers off the food.

'These look really good.' She picked up a small piece of what looked like toast, with something yellow and green on it. She popped it in her mouth. 'Oh, that was really nice. Try one. Or have one of these things with—is that raw beef?'

Mitch shrugged, ate one and then nodded. 'Yep. Raw beef. Tasty though.'

Liz laughed and took a mouthful of wine. She was aware she was acting strangely. And she was aware that Mitch was watching her, his brow furrowed in confusion. She drank another mouthful of wine. She had to, because she just realised what they were doing. She and Mitch were eating a wedding breakfast together. Something they had not had the chance to do all those years ago.

It had been a mistake to ask Mitch to come inside, but she didn't know how to ask him to leave. Or if she really wanted to. Suddenly, it was all a bit much for her, and she found the nearest chair and sank into it.

'Are you all right?'

She nodded dumbly.

'You stay here. I'll make sure your animals are bedded down for the night. And then I'll head home.' He walked to the door. 'Bye.'

'Thanks for today.'

'My pleasure.'

'It was my pleasure too,' she said, too softly for him to hear. The door closed behind him and she was alone again.

CHAPTER
55

The school is a collection of red brick buildings set in neatly groomed grounds. Liz has no idea exactly how old they are, but they exude an aura of stability and history. She likes that—it's what Kayla needs right now. Liz parks her car in the designated visitors' spot.

'It looks nice, doesn't it?'

Her sister doesn't reply. With a sigh, Liz gets out of the car. A sign points to the school office. She sets off in that direction, but after a few steps, she stops. Kayla is still sitting in the car. Liz turns around.

'Come on, Kayla. We need to go and check you in.'

'Why do I have to come here?' Kayla's voice quivers. She's close to tears. 'I don't want to! I want to stay at my old school.'

Liz sighs. 'Kayla, we've talked about this. You can't stay at home. I have to look after Willowbrook all on my own now. I can't look after you at the same time.'

'I don't need looking after. I'm almost twelve.'

Liz has to bite her tongue. She knows how capable Kayla is. She doesn't want her sister to leave Willowbrook, but she also knows that no one, least of all the authorities, will accept that an eighteen-year-old is her best possible guardian. Liz is determined that Kayla will not be taken away from her. She made a promise and she intends to keep it. If that means boarding school then they'll just have to cope. Both of them.

'It'll be much more fun here.' Liz hopes the brightness in her voice doesn't sound as forced to Kayla as it does to her. 'There'll be new friends to meet. Here in the city there'll be all sorts of outings that we could never have in Scone. Museums and shows and art galleries and so on. You'll love all that.'

'Ginger will miss me.'

'I'll take good care of him, I promise. And in the holidays you and I can go riding together.'

Kayla shakes her head and Liz sees the glint of tears in her eyes.

'Come on!' She sounds far more brusque than she intended, but she too is fighting to keep the tears at bay. She's doing that a lot these days, and she's only winning the fight because she can't afford not to.

Kayla gets out of the car and the sisters walk up the stairs to the imposing entrance. The school administrator who greets them is kind and motherly. There is sympathy in her smile for these two orphaned girls. Liz hates that sympathy. So does Kayla. She pulls a lock of her hair over the scar on her temple. The scar will fade in time, but right now it is still as raw as the loss in her heart.

'I know you'll be happy here,' the administrator tells Kayla.

Kayla doesn't respond.

'Shall we go and get your things?' Liz suggests.

At the car, they remove two suitcases from the boot. The larger case is full of the new uniforms and books and sports gear from the list sent by the school. They were expensive. The school is expensive too, but their father left an insurance policy. It will be enough. Just.

The second case is smaller and contains a few cherished possessions from home. The school doesn't allow too many personal items, believing they only encourage homesickness.

Following the teacher's instructions, Liz and Kayla take the bags to the boarding house. Kayla will share a dormitory with three other girls. The girls aren't there now, but their beds are neatly made with identical covers. Each of them has a small cubicle for their personal possessions, and a desk. Kayla's is bare.

'You'll soon feel at home here,' Liz says as Kayla unpacks. 'And you'll make new friends. I bet you won't even want to come back to Willowbrook for the holidays. You'll probably be off with your friends visiting the beach or something …'

Kayla's face remains stony; her misery is palpable.

When the unpacking is complete, they make their way to the main building and Liz's car. As they walk along the pathway, several girls come past all wearing their school uniforms. They barely glance at Liz, instead inspecting Kayla as one would look at a lizard that had crawled out from under a rock. They note every aspect of her clothes and her hair.

'You'll fit right in, once you're in uniform,' Liz says, with a hint of desperation in her voice.

Still Kayla doesn't speak.

They reach the car and stand in awkward silence.

'Please, Lizzie. I don't want this. Can't I come home with you? Please don't send me away.' It is a plea from the very depths of Kayla's unhappiness and it breaks Liz's heart.

'I'm sorry, Kayla, but this is how it has to be.'

Liz bends to give her little sister a quick hug, then opens the car door and gets inside. She starts the engine and backs out of the parking spot, leaving Kayla standing alone. Liz waves with a brightness she does not feel and drives to the school's impressive gates. In the rear-view mirror she sees a little girl struggling with the loss of her parents and now abandoned by her sister. How she wishes it didn't have to be like this.

Kayla watches the car disappear, tears streaming down her face. 'I hate you,' she whispers.

CHAPTER
56

Liz arrived at the Rosedale Horse Complex in Murrurundi mid-afternoon on the day before the King of the Ranges event. She parked her truck and set up the portable yards that would hold her horses for the next four days. Deimos pranced down the ramp from the back of the truck. He lifted his head and neighed, receiving answers from some of the other horses already at the complex.

'Settle down.' She stroked the colt's nose as she shut him into his yard. 'You've got a big job ahead of you. Don't waste your energy showing off.' He didn't pay any attention and she really didn't blame him. She knew pretty much how he was feeling.

She installed Zeke into the yard next to Deimos. He was an old hand at this sort of thing and would be a calming influence on Deimos. Now all she needed was something to exert a similar calming influence on her.

It didn't take her long to get her camp ready for the weekend. She would have to leave once each day to drive back to Willowbrook and care for the rest of her horses. It was a burden, but she'd handle it because she had to. She couldn't afford to hire someone to look after the place for the four days, and there was no one she could just ask.

There's Mitch.

She ignored the small voice at the back of her mind. Mitch was competing himself and didn't need the added burden of helping her.

But if you shared the work of both properties it'd be so much easier ... for both of you.

'Hi, Liz.' A passing breeder tipped his hat at her, dragging her treacherous mind away from a path she did not want to take.

'Jack.'

'Groups and timings have been posted,' the man informed her. 'You're in my group. Vet check at four thirty.'

'Thanks. Good luck.'

'You too.'

As the man disappeared into the crowd, Liz set out for the stewards' tent to check in. There, notice boards displayed all the groups and their starting times. Liz was handed a bright orange vest to designate her group. She slipped it over her head, tied the tapes at her side and went to check the board. Mitch was also in the orange group. That meant she'd be seeing a lot of him this weekend as the competitors assembled for each event. She wasn't sure how she felt about that. When they were young, she and Mitch often competed against each other, but they'd been friends back then. It was true that they were spending more time together now, but whatever he was to her these days, he wasn't the friend he used to be. And this competition was too important for her to be distracted by wondering just what he was.

The complex was starting to fill with people and horses. Liz found Mitch's truck and campsite, but he wasn't there. She was walking to the stewards' tent when she saw him. He was standing near the bar, talking to a woman.

Liz's steps faltered.

The woman was blonde and pretty. On her, jeans and a T-shirt looked feminine and flirty. She was even wearing make-up and the sunlight caught a glint of silver dangling from her ears. Make-up? Here? And dangly earrings? The woman obviously had no idea. What the hell was Mitch doing talking to a woman like that? She wasn't even wearing riding boots.

The woman laughed. It was a light, joyful sound and it made Mitch smile. Then he kissed her.

Liz wanted the earth to open up and swallow her. The kiss was just a peck on the cheek, but that didn't matter. She felt as if her heart was being torn from her body.

A snatch of their conversation reached her ears.

'... missed you.'

'... you can always just call me.' The woman touched Mitch's arm, her body language making her meaning clear even to Liz. Mitch's eyes followed her as she walked away.

Somewhere deep inside, Liz wanted to go after her and tell her to leave Mitch alone. Mitch wasn't free to kiss anyone's cheek. He was—

He was what?

He was approaching her, frowning at the emotion he could no doubt read on her face.

'Liz ...'

'Who was that?' She'd wanted the words to sound light and uncaring. That's not how they came out.

'What do you mean?'

'I've never seen her around here, but you're good friends, obviously.' How horrible she sounded, but she couldn't stop herself.

'Sue is a friend.'

No, she's not. Liz wanted to shout the words. *I'm your friend but you don't look at me the way you looked at her.*

Not any more.

'She looked like she was more than a friend.' The words were out before Liz could stop them. She watched with something close to horror as Mitch's expression hardened.

'That's none of your business, Liz.' His body was taut and she could see a darkness in his face that rattled her. She'd seen him angry before, but not like this. This wasn't anger. It was as if he had totally closed himself off from her. A blank wall had risen between them. A wall that she was suddenly afraid would never come down.

'Did you forget what we did all those years ago? What we were to each other and the promises we made.' She wanted to shout, but the words came out as a whisper.

'No. I've never forgotten. But you seemed to. You pushed me away, Liz. When you decided that your guilt was more important than your future—than *our* future. A horrible, horrible thing happened that day, but it's not going to ruin my whole life. I deserve some happiness. Maybe I've moved on, Liz. You should think about trying it.'

'I can't just forget what happened. What I did—we did.'

'No. But I do think it's well past time you stopped punishing yourself. And me. I've had enough, Liz.'

This time it was Mitch who walked away.

As he disappeared into the crowd, Liz felt as if her whole world had suddenly fallen out from beneath her feet. Her hands were shaking as Mitch's words echoed in her head. *I've had enough.* Suddenly the people around her and the noise and the commotion of the event were all too much. A wave threatening to engulf her.

She had to get away and find somewhere she could clear her head. Somewhere Mitch's words would not overwhelm her. Somewhere she could hide while she fought the tears.

She pushed her way through the throng with no idea of where she was going, until she found herself standing on the edge of the arena, staring out over the empty paddocks of the cross-country course. She would walk the course. She'd be alone out there and maybe she could force her mind away from Mitch and the words that were echoing through her mind. Work was her answer and her shelter. It always had been. Nothing mattered except for Deimos and this weekend's competition.

Stop punishing yourself.

Was she really punishing herself? Mitch too?

The long grass brushed against her legs as she walked, but she didn't feel it. She didn't feel the cracks in the dry earth or the heat of the sun on her skin.

You pushed me away.

An obstacle loomed in front of her: several tree trunks stacked to form a cross-country jump. Without conscious thought, Liz climbed the logs and sat facing away from the busy arena and campground and Mitch.

He was right. About so many things. And now it was too late.

I've had enough.

When he was with that woman, the pretty one—Sue—he looked happy. He'd laughed and smiled. He'd looked relaxed. He'd been like that with Liz once. They had been like that with each other. And over these past few weeks, she had found herself wishing they could be again. Damn Kayla and her weddings, making all the memories return. The bad memories, and some of the good ones too. How wonderful it had felt when Mitch looked at her like that, and laughed with her, and kissed her. The realisation struck her with an almost physical blow. She was jealous of Mitch for moving on. And of Sue for being the one he had chosen to do that with.

She still loved Mitch. She always had and she always would.

Liz felt as if someone had snapped the chains that were holding her in the past.

It wasn't too late. She had started to mend the rift with Kayla. It was time she finished that, told Kayla all that she couldn't remember about that day. She should do that with Mitch too. If she went to him and told him everything, told him about the nightmares and her desperate need for him, a need she had to deny while her father's last words haunted her, maybe she could undo the mistakes she'd made. She had to.

Her heart was racing as she gathered her legs under her to climb off the obstacle. In the corner of her eye she caught movement between the logs. Instinctively she jerked away, but she wasn't fast enough. The pain in her leg lasted only a moment then she lost her balance and fell. Her head smashed against the hard dry timber and blackness claimed her.

CHAPTER
57

Mitch's anger dissipated as quickly as it had come. He hadn't seen Liz since the night of that wedding at Willowbrook, but he'd thought about her a lot. He had thought—hoped—that she was softening towards him. But he was obviously wrong, and his disappointment was overshadowed by his anger at how she had responded to seeing him with Sue. All he'd done was kiss Sue's cheek, as he would any friend. He'd ended their relationship, but Sue had taken it like the good-natured adult she was. Sue was still his friend. But Liz—Liz was quite a different proposition. And he was beginning to think he'd been a fool for hanging around all these years.

I've had enough. He'd spoken the words in anger and without thought, but maybe they were truer than he'd suspected. He'd told Liz that he had moved on. But had he really?

He was as much to blame for this mess as Liz was. Moving back to the Hunter Valley hadn't helped either of them. It might be time for each of them to make some tough decisions.

But first there was the King of the Ranges.

They each needed to win their classes, and for reasons that weren't that dissimilar. He and Liz had always been alike. That, at least, had never changed.

Still thinking about Liz, he decided to walk the cross-country course. On Saturday, he was going to have to guide his young horse over two kilometres and twenty obstacles. He wanted to get it right.

The course started behind one of the camping areas and it was easy to follow the flattened grass path created by other riders. He was glad to be walking alone. He wanted to clear his head of the turmoil Liz created every time she came near him, so he forced himself to focus on the course, on the jumps and the best way to approach them. How to guide his young horse to a good result. But try as he might, his thoughts never strayed all that far from Liz.

He was thinking about Liz and Deimos as he approached a wide jump on a slight downhill slope. It was a tough test, but he knew they were up for it—although he wasn't so sure about his mount. Instead of climbing over the fence, he walked around and turned to look at the landing. At that moment, he heard a rustle in the long grass and caught a glimpse of an orange vest.

A few long strides brought him close enough to see the figure lying face down on the ground. He dropped to one knee and gently rolled the person over.

'Liz!'

Her face was pale, except for the dark blood covering her forehead. Blood also stained both her clothes and the grass where she had been lying. There was a deep gash at her temple and her eyes were closed.

'Liz?' He gently touched her cheek. Her chest rose and fell with slow, laboured breaths.

He stood up and looked around. There was no one else to be seen. He automatically reached for his pocket, but then stopped. He didn't carry a mobile phone most of the time when he was riding, and hadn't thought to grab it before he left the campsite. It was quite likely there'd be no signal here anyway. He dropped back to his knees beside Liz.

Blood was seeping from her head wound. She must have hit her head as she fell, but that didn't account for the state she was in. A terrible thought struck Mitch. Careful not to move her, he pushed her jeans up her legs as far as they would go.

There it was. The small red wounds might have been mistaken for scratches, but Mitch knew better. He'd seen a snake bite before. Liz's leg had several livid red marks surrounded by a smear of drying blood. The snake had bitten her more than once. Only king brown snakes were that aggressive, and if it was a brown then that was a lot of venom. If help didn't come soon, a bite from a king brown would be fatal.

Mitch heard voices and leaped to his feet. Two people were approaching the jump.

'Hey!' He waved an arm to attract their attention. 'Have either of you got a phone?'

One of the men reached into his pocket. He looked at the phone for a few seconds and shook his head. 'No signal.'

Damn! On the ground, Liz stirred. Mitch crouched beside her, holding her leg steady. She mustn't move it.

'Jesus! What happened?' The two men had reached them.

'Snake,' Mitch said.

'You need a tourniquet. And a knife.'

Mitch knew better than that. He shook his head. 'No way. I need one of you to go get help. And I need to immobilise this leg. I need a couple of branches to make a splint and a pressure bandage.' He glanced up. 'You—that T-shirt will help. I need it now.'

'Sure.' The man removed the shirt while his companion set off at a run.

Mitch folded the T-shirt into a thick pad, which he placed gently over the bites, then began pushing down firmly. He had no way of knowing how long it was since Liz had been bitten, but every moment counted.

Liz moved her head and moaned softly.

'Liz, hang in there. Help's on the way. Stay with me, Lizzie.' He would have held her in his arms if he could, but he had to keep her leg steady and keep pressure on the wound.

'Will these do?' His helper had found two reasonably straight branches.

'Good.' Mitch removed his shirt. 'Now tear my shirt into strips so we can tie this on.'

They were just finishing the makeshift splint when they saw a four-wheel-drive ute making its way across the paddock. An ambulance officer leaped out and raced over. He took one look at Liz and grabbed a radio at his belt.

'Woman, age about thirty. Left leg. Multiple snake bites in the calf. I'm bringing her in now. Alert the hospital.' He turned to Mitch. 'You did the splint?'

'Yes.'

'Good job. Did you see what sort of snake it was?'

'No. It was gone before I got here. But from the look of the bites I'd guess a king brown.'

'Okay. Let's get her in the back. Carefully now. We need to keep her as immobile as possible.'

Mitch could not have been more gentle had Liz been made of eggshells. The other men dropped the tailgate of the ute and Mitch gently laid Liz flat on the edge of the tray. The ambulance officer leaped into the back of the ute and took her shoulders, gently pulling her further in as Mitch guided the splinted leg onto the hard metal surface. The ambulance driver laid Liz down, and then banged his hand on the roof of the cab. The ute drove away, leaving Mitch standing alone in the middle of the paddock.

CHAPTER
58

'Now what?'

Kayla put down her coffee and reached for the phone. It had been a hectic day and she desperately needed a moment of peace and quiet. But it appeared that the brides of Sydney could not manage so much as fifteen minutes without calling on her for something critically important, like querying the colour of the napkins they had chosen or to ask again if 2016 was really the best year for the Hunter Valley cabernet sauvignon. At this moment, she longed for the peace and quiet of Willowbrook.

'Hello. Elite Weddings.' She sounded annoyed, but that was nothing compared to the way some of her bridezillas sounded at times.

'Kayla? Is that you?'

'Mitch?'

'Yeah. Look, I'm sorry to do it like this—'

'Do what? Mitch, what's wrong?'

'It's Liz. She's been bitten by a snake.'

Kayla's hand clenched around the phone, and her heart began to beat a little faster. 'Is she …?'

'She's in an ambulance now, on her way to Tamworth Hospital.'

'What happened?'

Kayla listened as Mitch relayed what he knew. She had been so caught up in her work, she had forgotten that this weekend was the King of the Ranges competition.

'People recover from snake bites all the time. She is going to be all right, Mitch, isn't she?'

There was a silence at the other end of the line.

'Mitch?'

'To be honest, Kayla, I don't know. I think she had been out there a while before I found her.'

Kayla knew what that meant.

'And she must have hit her head on the jump as she fell. It didn't look good.'

'All right. I'm on my way. Where are you?'

'I'm still in Murrurundi. At the showgrounds.'

'I'm on my way,' Kayla said.

'Don't worry about Willowbrook, or the horses. I'll take care of all of that. You just go straight to the hospital.'

'Thanks, Mitch.'

'And when you see her, tell her …'

Kayla waited for him to continue. But he didn't. For the thousandth time she wondered what had happened to tear Mitch and Liz apart. It was obvious they still cared deeply for each other.

'I will. I'll see you soon.' She hung up.

Across the room, Pascale was looking at her, concern evident in her face. 'What's wrong?'

Kayla struggled to tell her, as if it wasn't real until she spoke the words out loud.

'Go,' Pascale said, coming out from behind her desk. 'I've got everything at this end. Just go.'

Kayla gave her a brief hug and then hurried from the office.

She didn't bother going back to her flat. She had everything she needed for a couple of days stored at Willowbrook. And she would only be there a couple of days. Because after that, Liz would be home.

She would be all right.

During the past few months, Kayla had become accustomed to driving from Sydney to Scone. Once she got out of the city traffic, she quite enjoyed the drive. It gave her time to think. But today the last thing she needed was time to think.

Every child growing up in the bush knows about snakes. As far back as she could remember, her father had taught her to be careful. Her mind filled with images of scaly creatures slithering through the long grass or emerging from the feed shed. She remembered watching one of her father's dogs confront a brown snake. Far from trying to escape the dog, the snake had struck at it again and again. She remembered the dog's pain-filled cries and the fear in Kath's voice as she had yelled at her daughters to stay away. Kayla now knew that killing the snake was illegal, but she was glad Sam had done it. Watching the poor dog die had haunted her. For weeks afterwards she had woken in the middle of the night, her heart hammering in fear, tears on her cheeks.

Living in the city, she hadn't even seen a snake for years, but today those memories were very, very real.

And today the drive to Scone took forever.

As she continued north along the New England Highway, she thought briefly about stopping at Murrurundi to find Mitch, but she had no idea if he was even there. He'd probably taken Liz's horses home. It was more important for her to get to the hospital. She kept driving.

Tamworth Hospital was a sprawling collection of buildings and in the dim light of the early evening, Kayla found it difficult to read the directions on the signs. After a couple of minutes of frustration, she simply parked and dashed into the nearest building.

'I'm looking for Elizabeth Lawson,' Kayla said to the woman at the reception desk. 'She was brought in by ambulance this afternoon. Snake bite.'

'Just one moment.'

The woman started tapping on the computer in front of her. She seemed to take an age, and a couple of times paused and frowned at the screen as if she was struggling with the technology. Kayla wanted to scream with frustration and go behind the desk and look herself.

'And you are?'

'I'm her sister, Kayla Lawson.'

'I see. Well, I think you need to go to the emergency ward, they can help you.'

'How do I get there?'

The woman in the emergency ward reception wasn't more helpful.

'Please take a seat in the family room.' She indicated a door. 'The doctor will be with you shortly.'

As she paced the small, pale green room that smelled strongly of disinfectant, Kayla began to wonder about the definition of 'shortly'.

At last a doctor appeared. 'Miss Lawson?'

'Yes.'

'I'm Doctor Marsh. I've been treating your sister since she arrived this afternoon.'

Those words brought a rush of relief. At least her sister was still alive.

'How is she?'

'She was bitten three times by an eastern brown snake. There was a lot of venom. It also appears she suffered a fall. She has a nasty head wound, although we are more concerned about the snake attack.'

'But you've given her anti-venom?'

'We have, but it was quite a long time before she got to us. We need to keep a close eye on her for at least another day or two.'

'She's going to be fine, right?'

'I hope so. It's rare for people to die of snake bite. She was very lucky. Whoever found her didn't try anything stupid like opening the wound or a tourniquet. They did just the right thing and may even have saved her life.'

Thank you, Mitch. 'Can I see her?'

'She's sedated now and sleeping, but I'll take you to her.'

Kayla felt like she was looking at a stranger as she stood beside the bed where her sister lay. Liz had always been the strong one; she had always glowed with life and energy. Even when they had been fighting, Kayla had admired her sister's courage and determination. Her big sister was her hero.

The woman lying on those starched white sheets looked tired and frail. She looked like a shadow of the sister Kayla had always loved and, to some extent, envied. Her face was almost as white as the sheets and a large dressing covered part of her forehead. Her hands lay still as a tube dripped into the vein on her arm. She looked helpless and hopeless and defeated. Kayla wanted to cry, seeing her like that.

Instead she pulled a chair to the side of the bed and carefully laid her hand over Liz's.

'Liz?'

There was no sign that her sister had heard her.

'I'm here, Liz. I'll look after you.' She paused. If Liz could hear her, there was something else she needed to know.

'Mitch is looking after the horses. He's taking care of Willow-brook too. And he sends his love.'

CHAPTER
59

The movement at the campsite started before it was fully light. Mitch hauled himself out of his sleeping bag and rubbed his face as he reached for his phone. The screen glowed, empty of any message. He wasn't sure if that was a good sign or a bad one. Reception here was a bit hit and miss. Maybe Kayla didn't have his phone number. But he knew she did. He typed a message and hit send, half in hope of the reply and half in dread.

He stretched his cramped muscles. He was beyond tired and he didn't want to be here. More than anything, he wanted to be at the hospital in Tamworth, but that wasn't where Liz needed him to be. Last night he had driven to Scone to check the horses at Willowbrook. For a long time he had considered just driving all the way to the hospital, but in the end he'd returned to the competition grounds and made his camp. Liz wasn't alone. And after the things he'd said to her yesterday, she was better off without him.

The campsite was getting busier as competitors went in search of breakfast and coffee. Horses were fed and so were their riders.

Mitch took care of his horses before going to Liz's campsite. Deimos was standing in his portable yard, Zeke dozing next to him. Mitch collected feed for both horses and refilled their water buckets. He stood next to Deimos, rubbing his neck as he checked his phone for a reply from Kayla.

Still nothing.

'That's Liz Lawson's horse, isn't it?' One of the other competitors paused as he walked past. Mitch knew him a little. He was a breeder from Victoria who competed in all the big events.

'Yes.'

'I heard she was hurt yesterday. Snake bite.'

Mitch hid the fear that was lurking inside of him. 'Yeah.'

'She okay?'

'I'm just waiting to hear.'

The man nodded. 'She's had a rough time of it. I heard that the old stallion died. He was a good horse. I was thinking of sending a couple of mares to him next season.'

'This is his son,' Mitch said. 'I think Liz is planning to stand him next season. Top bloodline. You could do a lot worse.' As he spoke, Mitch unbuckled the rug covering Deimos and pulled it off to give his companion a good look at the horse.

The man studied him for a bit.

'Good-looking colt,' he said. 'It's a shame he won't be in the field today. I'd like to see him under saddle.' The man wandered off.

Mitch ran his hand over the horse's back. 'Damn it,' he muttered as he stroked the animal. 'Liz needs this.'

Deimos started as Mitch's phone beeped. He pulled it out and read the message.

Dr more confident. She's still asleep. Haven't talked to her. Will let you know when I have news.

Not the news he had feared, but also not what he had hoped for. Liz was in the best place she could be, getting the treatment she needed. There was nothing he could do to help her.

He began idly combing Deimos's mane with his fingers. Competitions like King of the Ranges took months of training. Horse and rider had to understand each other, to work together almost without effort. It was crazy to even contemplate competing on a horse you didn't know. A horse that didn't know you. But he and Liz had been taught their horsemanship by the same man—Sam Lawson. They had ridden and trained together for years before the accident. And Mitch had ridden Deimos. Only once for a couple of hours, but it was better than nothing.

The colt lifted his nose from the now empty feed bucket and nudged Mitch gently.

'What do you think?' Mitch asked, rubbing the horse's ear thoughtfully.

Of course, there was the problem of the young horse eating its breakfast on the other side of the campsite. Mitch was being paid to ride that horse in this competition. Its owner was a good customer, but he wouldn't be pleased. He might take the horse back, but that was a risk Mitch was prepared to take. That left just one question. Did the rules allow a change on the morning of the competition? There was only one way to find out.

Decision made, Mitch set off in the direction of the stewards' tent.

The group of competitors clustered near the tent parted to make way for him.

'How's Liz doing?'

'Sorry to hear about what happened, mate.'

They looked at him with sympathy. Strange that even after all this time, the people of their town, their friends and fellow horsemen and women still linked Mitch and Liz, as if those intervening years had never happened.

The head steward nodded at him as he entered the tent. 'Any news?'

'Her sister Kayla came up from Sydney. She's with her now.'

There was nothing more to say. The steward shuffled through the papers in front of him and pulled out the list of competitors. Even upside down, Mitch could see Liz's name on the sheet. The man took a pen and drew a line through her name. That seemed so very final.

'While you're there, I need you to make another change,' Mitch said. 'My horse. Scratch Farwell Commander, owner Jack Tate, and replace with Willowbrook Deimos, owner Elizabeth Lawson.'

The steward raised an eyebrow. 'I'm not sure that's—'

'Just do it. Please.'

After a moment of hesitation, the steward drew another line on his paper, and wrote the name of Mitch's new mount above it.

'Good luck.'

CHAPTER
60

Liz woke slowly. She ached all over and didn't know why. She tried to move, but her limbs didn't want to respond. Slowly, she opened her eyes. The light was far too bright and she closed them again.

'Liz?'

That was her sister's voice. What was Kayla doing here? Was there going to be another wedding?

She tried opening her eyes again, and this time the light didn't hurt quite so much. She also saw the figure next to her bed.

'Kayla?' Her voice came out cracked and harsh.

'Liz. You're awake.'

Was it her imagination, or was her sister close to tears? 'What …'

'It's all right. You're in Tamworth Hospital. You were bitten by a snake and hit your head. But the doctors say you're going to be all right.'

As Kayla spoke, Liz's eyes began to focus on the room around her: the off-white walls and the machinery. Everything was unfamiliar and a little frightening, except for Kayla. She struggled to remember what had happened. The last thing she could remember clearly was arriving at Murrurundi for the King of the Ranges. She had no idea what had happened next. But she did remember one thing—Mitch. His face and his voice were the only real thing in the fog of her memory. They'd fought. She remembered that.

'Mitch was …'

'That's right. He found you and called for help. Don't worry about the horses, he's looking after them.'

Liz was relieved to hear that, but strangely enough, she hadn't been thinking about her horses. Only about Mitch.

She tried to sit up and managed on her second attempt, with Kayla's help. Her left leg was enclosed in a splint. Her head hurt and when she went to touch it, she felt a bandage.

'My head hurts.'

'You hit it on something when you were bitten yesterday.'

'Yesterday? But—'

That's when the nurse arrived, followed a few moments later by a doctor, and for a short time Liz had to suffer the indignities of being a hospital patient. Apparently her temperature and blood pressure and eyes were all looking good. The pain in her head would no doubt fade when the painkillers arrived. The leg was to remain in a splint for now, but the general consensus seemed to be that she was going to be fine in a few days.

When she was alone with Kayla again, Liz was feeling more alert and able to think.

'Exactly what happened?' she asked.

'Don't you remember? Any of it?'

She thought very hard and began to remember, but not clearly. And not all of it.

'It was a king brown, I think?'

Kayla nodded. 'That's what the doctor told me. They ran some test on the bites.'

'Bites?'

'Yes. Apparently it bit you three or four times. There was a lot of venom. You're lucky Mitch found you.'

'I was walking the cross-country course.'

'That's what he said. Do you remember how you hurt your head?'

She thought very hard, but no memory came.

'Don't worry, it doesn't matter. The doctor says you probably hit it when you fell. There were splinters.' There was a sound from a bag sitting on the table next to the bed. Kayla fished her phone from its depths and read the message.

'From Pascale,' she said. 'Asking how you're doing. I'll go and let her know you're okay. Back in a minute.'

During what seemed like a very long minute, Liz began to wonder just how close she had come to dying. Snake bites were not rare, but deaths from snake bite were rare enough to make the news. Anti-venom worked, but only if it was given promptly. If Mitch hadn't found her when he did …

'Pascale sends her best.' Kayla had her phone in her hand as she walked into the room. 'I texted Mitch as well to tell him you're awake. I'm a bit surprised he's not here. I thought he'd come after he'd seen to the horses.'

Those words forced Liz to face an uncomfortable truth. 'He won't come. The King of the Ranges started this morning and he's got to compete. It's important to him. Besides, he knows I don't want to see him. We had a fight yesterday.'

Kayla sat down. The no-nonsense look on her face was becoming familiar. Liz knew what was coming.

'I don't get it. You and Mitch were so close. A blind man could see he still cares for you and I know you still have feelings for him.'

'He's seeing someone,' Liz whispered.

Kayla snorted. 'Well, I wouldn't blame him. Not after the way you've been treating him all these years. What the hell happened? Everyone was so sure the two of you would get married someday.'

'We did.'

She hadn't intended to say that but the words just slipped out and as they did, Liz felt as if the Sydney Harbour Bridge had been lifted off her shoulders. It was time to stop hiding.

'You what?' The shock on Kayla's face was almost comical. But Liz wasn't in a laughing mood.

'We got married.' It was a little harder to say it the second time, because this time it was deliberate. But the words cracked some of the ice around her heart.

'When?'

This wasn't going to be easy, but it was well past time Kayla knew the truth. 'The day after his birthday. 2002.'

Liz watched Kayla's face as she made the connection. 'But ... that's the day ...'

'Yes. That's the day of the accident. Dad and Mum—and you too—were coming after us when the crash happened.'

'I—no. I don't understand. Why were we coming after you? And why don't I know anything about that? I know I lost my memory of the crash, but why don't I remember anything about a wedding?'

'Because you never knew anything about it. We were running away. Mitch's parents were moving north and he didn't want to go. I knew Mum would say we were too young to be married. And I know Dad didn't want us to. So we ran away. We'd arranged for a priest in Merriwa to marry us. Somehow Mum and Dad found out and they were on their way to stop us when the car crashed. It might have been a roo on the road. Or Dad might have been driving too fast. It was foggy and there could have been ice. We'll never know exactly what happened, but it's my fault Mum and Dad died.'

'And I was in the car with them.'

'Yes. Kayla, I am so sorry. I will never forgive myself for what happened.'

'No. That can't be …' Kayla's shock was evident on her face as she raised her hand to touch the small scar under her fringe.

Seeing that unconscious movement brought home to Liz how much her head wound was hurting, but the pounding there and the ache in her leg were nothing to the pain in her heart as she watched the horror spread over her sister's face. It was too late for regrets now. And it was too late to stop. Now that she had started, she had to finish.

'A policeman found us just as the ceremony ended and told us about the crash. You were hurt pretty badly. You were taken to … well, here, I guess. You know Mum died in the crash. Dad was really badly hurt and flown to Newcastle. He was …' This was so hard. She could hardly bear to say the next words. 'He was alive when I got there, but the doctors didn't have much hope. I saw him. He was—' She swallowed and forced herself to continue. 'He was conscious. He told me he was trying to stop me. He didn't want me to marry Mitch. Then he died.'

'You saw him before he died? Why didn't you ever tell me any of this?'

'You were so young. When it became clear you didn't remember anything at all, I decided it was better not to tell you why you were all in the car that morning. Then, when you were older, it was too late.'

'No-one else knew?'

'Mitch and his parents—but they moved away, so it was easier just to pretend it never happened.'

'But it did happen, Liz—and it happened to me. I was the one in that car—not you. I lost my parents that day just like you did. And all because of …'

Kayla's voice trailed off. She shook her head as she got to her feet and left the room.

Liz watched her go, forcing her eyes to stay open, because she didn't want to see the images that, for all these years, had seemed burned into her eyelids. She could not stand to watch her father die one more time.

CHAPTER
61

Kayla didn't know where she was going, she just knew she had to get away from Liz.

Liz was to blame for their parents' deaths.

The very words seemed impossible, but she did believe Liz had finally told her the truth about that terrible day.

Liz and Mitch were married? In all these years, Liz had never so much as hinted at it.

Her shocked mind tried to link the two facts. The echo of her footsteps in the hospital's empty corridors added to her feeling of detachment and disbelief. If only she could remember what had happened that day …

Her first memories were of waking up in this hospital, her leg in a cast and a bandage around her head. Just eleven years old and in pain and alone. She had cried for her parents, but they never came. Only Mitch's parents were there for her, and she had learned that she was an orphan from Mrs Saunders, not Lizzie. Her sister had been too busy to spend time with a terrified child. Strangers had comforted her when she woke screaming in the middle of the night. Kayla hadn't even attended her parents' funeral. It had all been done by the time she was released from hospital. And then Liz told her she was going away to boarding school.

Force of habit directed Kayla's fingers to trace the small white scar on her forehead. It really wasn't a big deal, and she'd always kept it hidden by hair or make-up. Now it was Liz lying in bed with her head swathed in bandages. Kayla hadn't seen the actual wound, but a small part of her, the part she hated, wanted the scar forming under those bandages to be too big and too ugly to hide. Liz deserved it.

Kayla kept walking along the corridor and went through a door. She barely noticed the steps down to another level and yet another long corridor. Her head was spinning wildly, and her knees suddenly began to shake. She dropped into a nearby chair and buried her face in her hands. When she finally raised her eyes, she looked across the room to see a huge, colourful mural covering most of the wall, too bright to be ignored. The painting was a vista of rolling hills dotted with deep green trees. The blue skies were filled with colourful birds, while ponies frolicked in the grass. Brilliant butterflies flitted through flower gardens, and black swans floated serenely on a pond.

She had seen that mural before.

She sat there and stared at the mass of colour, while in her head images began to form: a kaleidoscope tumbling so fast she could barely breathe.

'Excuse me, miss. Are you all right? Do you need to see a doctor?'

Kayla looked up into the concerned face of an elderly nurse, but struggled to focus on the woman. 'No. Thank you. I'm just a bit upset. There was an accident.'

'I'm sorry, dear. Do you need help finding anyone here at the hospital?'

'No. No, thank you.'

'All right. I hope everything turns out all right.' The nurse started to walk away.

'Wait!'

The woman turned back.

'I'm sorry, but I have to ask. That mural … it's been here a long time?'

'Yes, it has. This is part of the old hospital. The children's ward was here. The mural was for the kiddies, you see. When they redeveloped the hospital they were going to paint it out, but so many people argued against it, they decided to keep it. It's rather fun for the kids. It helps them when they are sick or frightened.'

'Yes, it does. Thank you,' Kayla whispered.

'Are you sure you're all right?'

Kayla nodded and the woman walked away.

Closing her eyes against the colours that suddenly seemed almost too bright, Kayla shivered. A darkness seemed to engulf her and her hands gripped the chair tightly. Then there was a light in the darkness behind her eyes. The hospital smells around her became more and more intense, and she remembered lying on her back, calling for her mother. A woman, a nurse, was holding her hand as she was wheeled along a corridor past a mural … a large, colourful mural of ponies running wild in green fields.

Kayla opened her eyes, but she couldn't stand to look at the mural any more. She wanted nothing more than to walk—no—to run out of this hospital and get in her car and drive to the safety of the city. The city had no memories to haunt her.

The wheels of her sports car spun in the gravel as she roared away. That sound too was terrifyingly familiar. She was driving on autopilot, her eyes and hands and feet kept the car on the road, but her mind was absent. The car raced south, past Murrurundi, where

Kayla didn't even glance at the horse arena. Without giving any real thought to what she was doing, Kayla turned right just before Scone, flashing past the sign that pointed to Merriwa. As the road began to climb, she suddenly pulled over and got out.

This was the place. She hadn't driven this road since the accident, but she knew in her heart that this was the place.

Her knees felt weak as she leaned against the bonnet of her car and looked around. There was nothing to see. No mark remained from the morning that had changed her life. Changed many lives. She gave up the fight against the images swirling at the edges of her mind, closed her eyes and let herself remember.

CHAPTER

62

'Get dressed, Kayla,' Kath says. 'Wear something pretty.'

'Mum?'

'Not now, sweetie. I'll explain everything later. Just go and get dressed.'

This is something to do with Lizzie being gone, but Kayla doesn't know what. She has no idea where her sister might be, nor why she has taken her prettiest dress. But she does know it has something to do with Mitch. Everything Lizzie does these days is about Mitch.

She comes downstairs wearing a dress like her mother said, and a coat, because it's cold and foggy outside, with frost on the grass. She hears her father's voice from the kitchen.

'I think they've gone to Merriwa.'

'How do you know?' Her mother is in the kitchen too.

'The rectory in Scone says Father Michael left a while ago for an early wedding. That has to be them.'

'Have you called the church there?'

'There's no answer. Mitch's dad is going to keep trying. I just want to get on the road.'

They all get in the car and set off. Sam Lawson is in such a hurry to get away that he revs the cold engine too hard. The car tyres spin, sending gravel flying across the driveway. His wife mutters a protest, but not too forcefully. Kayla peers out the window at the thick fog. It's daylight, but she can barely see the trees on the other side of the road.

'Where are we going?' Kayla asks her mother.

'We're going to Merriwa to meet up with Lizzie and Mitch.'

'Why?'

The older Lawsons share a glance. Sam nods.

'Mitch and Lizzie want to get married,' Kath says.

'We all know that.' Kayla's voice is petulant. 'But why do we have to go out today? It's cold.'

'I know it is, honey, but your dad has turned the heater on. The car will warm up soon.'

Just outside of Scone, the car suddenly swerves violently. Kayla hasn't put her seatbelt on, and is flung across the back seat, bruising her arm against the door.

'Shit!' Sam rarely swears, and his vehemence adds to Kayla's distress. 'Put your seatbelt on, Kayla. You know better.'

'It's all right, honey.' Kath turns to her daughter. 'It was only a roo. Your dad's a great driver. Everything is fine, but you really have to put your seatbelt on.'

Despite the reassuring words, Kayla is shaken, as much by the fierce look Kath flashes at her husband as by the near miss.

'Where are Lizzie and Mitch?' she asks as they reach the outskirts of Scone.

'They've gone to Merriwa. To get married.'

'Are you going to stop them?'

Once more Kath and Sam share a look as Sam brakes and turns onto the Merriwa road. The road goes over the hills, and is shrouded in fog. The car's headlights are on, but visibility isn't good.

'No, Kayla, we're not. They are very young, and we'd like them to wait for a while, but if they are determined, we just want to be there with them.'

'Can I be bridesmaid?'

'I'm sure Lizzie would love that.'

Something moves on the side of the road, then another shape leaps out from between the trees into the path of the swiftly moving car. Her father swears as he turns the wheel—too late to avoid the kangaroo, which flies into the air and lands on the bonnet of the car with a horrible crash.

Kath screams as the car starts to slide on the icy road. Her daughter screams too. Both voices are lost in the sound of tearing metal as the car rolls over and over again, before smashing into a tree. The engine splutters for a few seconds then there is silence, broken only by the sounds of a dying kangaroo thrashing in the long grass.

Soon that stops too.

Kayla opens her eyes. She is cold. So very cold. One of her shoes is lying in the grass near her face. It's one of her very best shoes. The ones with the gold straps, which she loves more than anything. Except there is something staining the shoe. Something dark and red. Now she can't wear it at Lizzie and Mitch's wedding.

She hears her father calling her name. She tries to call back to him, but the words won't come. Something wet and sticky is on her face and her head hurts. Her leg hurts too.

'Mummy? Daddy?'

She tries to move and screams. Then the pain and the noise and the fear fade to darkness and silence.

CHAPTER
63

There were lights in the kitchen of Willowbrook as Mitch pulled into the driveway. His heart leaped. Was Liz home from the hospital? But even as the thought formed, he knew he was wrong. If she'd been released, Liz would have gone straight to the King of the Ranges to check on her horses. The horses were always her first thought. He'd never really minded that. Mitch cared about his horses too, although they'd been relegated to second place in his heart after he and Lizzie had shared that first kiss in the cemetery. They'd laughed together about that later. What a place for a first kiss. As for their last kiss ... that had been standing in front of the altar at an old wooden church in Merriwa. Their first kiss as husband and wife. And their last.

He pulled up to the house and parked his car next to the red one that was already there. He was tired. After a full day of competition, the drive here to care for Liz's horses was tough. A neighbour was checking Mitch's horses, but he would trust no-one with the Willowbrook animals. He owed Liz that.

But first, he had to know how Liz was doing.

He knocked on the kitchen door. There was no answer. Kayla must be at the stables. There was a light on in the feed shed as he approached. The door was open, but the room was empty. Puzzled, he walked into the stables and found Kayla leaning on the door of Deimos's empty stall. She was crying silently, her face a mask of grief.

Mitch's heart stopped beating. 'Kayla? Is it Liz? Is she …?'

Kayla looked up at him, her brow wrinkling as if she was trying to remember who he was. 'Oh! No, Mitch. She's fine. She's going to be fine.'

He placed one hand on the wall of the stables until his mind and body absorbed what she had just said. 'That's—well, thank God.'

'Yeah. Look, Mitch, I'm sorry but I'm really not up to talking right now.'

'What's wrong? If it's not Liz.'

'Oh, it's Liz. It's always Liz.' The bitterness in Kayla's voice was shocking.

'What?'

She gathered herself up and seemed to focus on him for the first time. 'I'm sorry, Mitch. I can't. Not tonight.'

He didn't want to hear that. Something had happened between the sisters, and he needed to know what. He was no longer going to just stand back and wait, but the look on her face told him tonight was not the right time to push.

'All right. I just came to check Liz's horses.'

'I already did that.'

Mitch tried to hide his surprise.

'I'll look after them until Liz is out of hospital,' Kayla continued. 'After all, Willowbrook is my legacy too.'

'If you're sure …'

'I'm sure. It'll save you driving back and forth each day. You've got enough on your plate with the competition, without this as well. But I can't come and get Deimos. I don't have a licence for the truck.'

Mitch could have told Kayla then that he had just completed the first day of competition on Deimos. He could have told her the colt had done well and she could reassure Liz that her dream was still alive. But he didn't. It was clear she didn't want to hear that.

'It's all right, I'll look after Deimos and Zeke. But if you need any help, just call me. About anything.'

'Thanks, Mitch, but right now I need to be alone.'

He left. As he drove away, Mitch realised that everything was about to change. In many ways, he was glad. Things between the three of them couldn't continue as they had been. He hoped that the change would be for the better, but he wasn't certain.

CHAPTER

64

Liz lay in the hospital bed, watching the shadows move across the ceiling. Her head hurt under the bandage. Her leg hurt where the snake had bitten her. Her back hurt from a night spent in an unfamiliar bed. But most of all her heart hurt, and none of the painkillers the nurses brought would fix that. For most of the night, she had lain sleepless, counting the mistakes she had made in her life, starting with that day fifteen years ago. By the time the morning sun slipped softly into the room, she had a very long list.

It was no wonder Kayla had left.

No wonder Mitch had found someone new.

She had driven them away because every time she looked at them, the guilt threatened to break her. She had punished them for her guilt. And herself too. And look where it had left her: estranged from her sister, estranged from the man she had loved and married, and lying in a hospital bed while her chance to save the Willowbrook legacy slipped through her fingers.

'I'm sorry, Dad,' she whispered.

'Maybe you owe me an apology as well.'

Liz hadn't expected to see Kayla again, at least not so quickly. She struggled into a sitting position as her sister walked into the hospital room. She was tired and in pain, but she was ready for a confrontation. She deserved everything Kayla was about to say to her. She would lie there and take it.

'I do. And I'm so sorry, Kayla. Sorry for everything. I've been lying here all night thinking and wishing I had done things differently.'

'It's too late for that.'

Liz couldn't meet her sister's eyes. She stared at her work-roughened hands lying on the pristine white sheet. 'I know.'

'But it's not too late to fix things. Between us. And with Mitch. Because you've been wrong about something all these years.'

'I've been wrong about a lot of things.'

'True—but I think they all trace back to something that's been haunting you about that day.'

'You know we never meant you to follow us. The priest had agreed to marry us at eight o'clock. We would have called you all after that. I really thought no-one would miss me until then. Or they'd think I was down at the stables or something. I never thought you'd follow us. I still don't know how you found out.'

'I guess that part is my fault.'

'Your fault? How?'

Kayla slid into the chair beside the bed. 'Liz … I've remembered.'

After all these years, Kayla's unemotional declaration was almost like a physical blow. How could she be so calm? Liz struggled to find something to say, but there were no words.

'I've remembered everything. I guess from the shock of your being hurt and then being back here. Last night I drove out to the crash site. It's the first time I've been there since … it was strange. There's no sign of the crash after all these years, not that I thought there would be. But while I was there, something happened. I remembered everything about that day.'

Liz opened her mouth to speak, but she didn't know what to say. Kayla held her hand up before she could even try to find the words she needed.

'Let me finish. I'm the one who woke early that day and realised you were gone. I told them. If you are to blame, then so am I.'

'No.'

'Yes. I saw that your party dress was missing and told Mum. When they figured out where you were, all Dad wanted was to catch you.'

Liz shook her head. 'We thought we were being so clever. We were idiots.'

'I remember there was fog, and there were roos on the road. Dad was driving a bit too fast, but it was an accident, Liz. A horrible accident. You can't keep blaming yourself.'

'But if I hadn't—'

'Stop it, Liz. I could say the same thing. If I hadn't opened your wardrobe and seen that the dress was gone. If there hadn't been a fog. Or if there weren't roos on the road. Or if Dad was driving slower. There are so many ifs. After all these years, Liz, you have to let it go. Mum and Dad would want you to get on with your life. They'd want you to be happy, not punishing yourself for something that wasn't your fault.'

Liz blinked. 'That's easy for you to say.'

'It's not really. Don't forget, I lost my parents too. Then the only person I still loved—you—sent me away.'

'I had to. I couldn't run Willowbrook and look after you too. If I'd tried they would have taken you away from me.'

'I know that now. But at the time, all I knew was that my sister had sent me away. I lost all of my family … and my home. At least you were sleeping in your own bed.'

A sharp pain sliced through Liz. Another layer of guilt to shoulder. 'I never thought about it like that. I am so sorry. Can you ever forgive me?'

'I can understand. An eighteen-year-old should never have been asked to shoulder that sort of responsibility.'

'Thank you.' It was more than she deserved, but Liz was profoundly grateful to her sister. 'I really am so sorry. And if it helps, I missed you too. So many times I wanted to drive down to that school and bring you back home, but I was struggling and I didn't think I could care for you too.'

'Thank you. And yes, it does help.' Kayla walked over to the bed and, ever so carefully, hugged her despite the bandages and the splint and the drip. It was a short hug, but it meant more than Liz could say.

'Liz, I have to ask. What about Mitch? Why did you leave him?'

'How could I not?' Liz felt her heart breaking all over again. 'My parents were dead, and it was my fault. It was our fault. Dad told me, before he died, that he didn't want me to marry Mitch. He died trying to stop me. How could I be with Mitch after that?'

To her utter surprise, Kayla laughed.

Liz stared at her in astonishment. 'How dare you—'

'You're wrong,' Kayla said quickly. 'Liz, you are so wrong. He wasn't trying to stop you. He wanted to be there to walk you down the aisle.'

Liz blinked, trying to understand. No. That was wrong. It had to be. Her father's words came back to her: *I had to get to you. I didn't want you to …*

She shook her head. 'Kayla, he told me. There, in the hospital. He was—he was dying. He could barely speak, and the only thing he wanted to tell me was that he didn't want me to marry Mitch.'

'What did he say? Exactly.'

'He said he didn't want us to get married.'

'Are you sure? Really sure?'

Liz opened her mouth to say yes, she was sure. She hadn't given up all her dreams over something she wasn't sure about. Then she stopped.

'He said he didn't want me to do it. He was so weak he could barely speak. And then ... he died without saying anything else.'

'That wasn't what he was trying to say. He didn't want you to get married without him and Mum and me being there.'

'You can't know that.'

'Yes, I can. I was in the car that morning. I heard him and Mum talk. And I remember it now. All of it. They loved Mitch like a son, you know that. Maybe they would have liked you to wait a bit, but they always knew the two of you were right for each other. They weren't against you marrying Mitch. They just wanted to be there when you did.'

Liz closed her eyes, almost in pain as Kayla's words filled her brain, along with the echoes of their father's voice. The room seemed to spin as she struggled with conflicting beliefs. But when she opened her eyes again, it was suddenly very clear to her. Kayla was right.

'All these years ...'

'You idiot,' Kayla said, but Liz could hear the love in her voice. 'You divorced Mitch for no reason.'

'Well, actually ...' Liz hesitated.

'What?'

'We're not divorced.' The words came out almost as a whisper.

'What! Seriously?'

Liz nodded. 'For a while he stayed here, trying to get me to take him back, but I drove him away. Finally, he went up to Queensland. I didn't see him again until he bought the river flats and the chapel four years ago.'

'And why didn't you do something about it then?'

'I hated him for buying the place. More than that, I hated myself for selling it. It made me feel like a failure.'

'And—sorry, but I have to ask—in all that time, have you…?'

Unable to speak, Liz simply shook her head.

'No!' Kayla's shock was almost funny.

'We never had a wedding night.'

'But before you were married?'

Liz smiled faintly. 'Once. Just once. The night we decided to run away together. But after that … well, Mitch said we'd be married in a couple of weeks. He wanted to wait. Damn him for being so honourable.'

Kayla was still shaking her head. 'And I guess you're going to say that nothing has happened these past four years, when he's been living across the creek from you.'

'At first I was so angry that he'd bought the land. I saw it as betrayal and, yes, I know.' She waved Kayla's protests away. 'I know he was actually helping me. But I was so ashamed of my failure that I couldn't deal with that. And then it was too late, the rift between us was too deep. If your photographer hadn't made him join that first photo shoot, we probably would still barely be on speaking terms. All my fault too.'

'But you love him, don't you?'

Liz didn't even have to think about that one. She nodded.

'Then don't you think it's time you did something about it?'

'It's too late. We fought yesterday and he told me—he said he's had enough of waiting around for me.'

'And you said you didn't want to be with him? I think you were both lying—to each other and, more importantly, to yourselves.'

Kayla was right. How did her little sister ever get to be so wise?

Liz looked around excitedly. 'Let's get out of here. Mitch will be at Murrurundi, competing. I want to see him. We need to talk.' She pushed herself upright and made as if to get off the bed, but the splint enclosing her leg held her back. A twinge of pain in her arm reminded her she was on a drip. 'Kayla, I need a nurse to get this thing off my leg and ...' The room started to spin. She fell against the pillows.

Within seconds a nurse appeared. 'What do you think you're doing?' She checked the drip in Liz's arm and repositioned her leg into a more comfortable place.

'I need to go ...'

'Oh, no, you don't.' The nurse put her hands on her hips and gave Liz a stare that had no doubt terrified hundreds of patients before her. 'You're not going anywhere until the doctor says you can.'

'But—'

The nurse pursed her lips. She began tucking in Liz's bedding, as if to imprison her by bedclothes alone, then she glared at both sisters, before leaving the room with a warning sniff.

'Damn!'

'She's right, you know.' Kayla was trying not to laugh. 'You've waited this long. One more day won't kill you. And besides, just what do you think you're going to achieve with one leg in a splint?' She raised a suggestive eyebrow and Liz smiled.

It felt good to laugh with Kayla again, to talk like they used to. Liz was certain they'd butt heads again, but that's how sisters were. She knew there was a lot of healing to do, but they were on their way.

CHAPTER

65

Mitch was exhausted and beginning to wonder if he would be able to finish what he had started. He was caring for both his and Liz's horses at the Murrurundi competition grounds and he was competing in a gruelling competition, riding a horse he didn't know very well.

But that was nothing compared to the second-by-second fight against the overwhelming need to just drive to Tamworth Hospital to see for himself that Liz was all right.

He pulled his phone from his pocket and checked his messages again. Still nothing. He'd had no news since he'd found Kayla crying in the stables two nights ago. She'd said Liz was going to be all right, but Mitch needed more. He wouldn't be reassured until he saw her. Talked to her. Touched her.

Every time he closed his eyes, he saw her face as the paramedics had carried her away. She had been so still and so pale. If she was out of danger, was she still in hospital? If not, why hadn't she come here? Her first instinct would be to check on her horses. If she wasn't here, she must be in hospital. That wasn't a good sign.

And then there were Kayla's tears when he'd found her in the Willowbrook stables. He'd been so glad to see the sisters, if not exactly friends again, at least talking. Had that gone wrong? He wasn't sure either of them would get over another estrangement.

'Good luck in the cross country, mate. See you at the finish line.'

'You too.' Mitch raised his hand as a fellow competitor rode past.

It was time he got ready. During all his training for this important event, he'd never even suspected how intensely personal it would become. He had come to believe that his whole future happiness rested on winning. And it had very little to do with training horses.

He pushed back from the arena rail where he had been leaning and headed to his campsite. As he approached, the horse in the yard beside his float turned to look at him.

'Well, Deimos. What do you think?' Mitch stroked the animal's neck. 'Do you think we can do this one more time?'

The horse's only answer was to nuzzle into his chest.

Mitch reached for his saddle. It was foolish to believe he and Deimos had any chance of making the final round. No-one entered a competition like this on a horse they barely knew. The stewards had certainly raised eyebrows when he'd suggested it. They understood that Liz would not be competing, but for Mitch to substitute Deimos for his own horse in the open competition was, they said, unprecedented. But, after putting their collective heads together for a good fifteen minutes, they'd decided that, foolish as it was, it wasn't against the rules. If he wanted to virtually throw away his chances of winning, it was his choice to make.

Against all odds, he and Deimos had done all right so far. They'd been lucky in the order of his events. The first event was shoeing, which was all about him and did not rely on Deimos to work with him at all. That had given Mitch a little time before the next event to ride the horse in the exercise ring and for them to come to a better understanding of each other. As a second event, the whip crack had also been perfect. It was literally a test of Mitch's skill with a whip. Pretty much all the horse had to do was behave himself. Deimos knew enough about whips to do that. He'd stood rock still as required for the first part of the event, then answered obediently as Mitch had sent him trotting and cantering around the ring, the whip snapping back and forth, filling the arena with its gunshot cracks. Mitch hadn't asked too much of Deimos, and he hadn't been let down. They would not have the highest score in the event, but nor would they have the lowest. And for Mitch, the most important thing was that he show Deimos to good advantage. He wasn't going to win, but he was determined that some good would come of this for Liz.

It was beginning to look like his gamble was paying off. This morning Deimos had performed beautifully in both the bareback obstacle course and the stock handling. That was far more a tribute to Liz than it was to Mitch. She'd always been a good trainer and she'd trained this horse exceptionally well. The cross-country event Mitch and Deimos were now facing was by far the toughest event of the competition. A two-kilometre course with twenty jumps, mostly fallen trees and solid logs. Those jumps were unforgiving if either horse or rider made an error, and competitors had been known to suffer serious injury. But it was also the most important event for Deimos. His reputation could be made—or broken—on this event alone.

'I'll do the best I can for you,' Mitch told the colt as he tightened the saddle girth. 'And we have to both do our best for Liz. Got it?'

He led the horse out of the yard, swung himself into the saddle and rode to the cross-country side of the grounds. In the warm-up area, he put Deimos into a trot, followed by a gentle canter, and then turned him towards the practice jump. The horse pricked his ears and lengthened his stride to soar over the jump, clearing it easily. He landed, ducked his head and put in a joyful high kick then humped his back in a half-hearted attempt to dislodge his rider.

'Well, well.' Mitch pulled him to a trot and stroked his neck. 'You like this jumping business, don't you? Shall we try that again without the bucking?'

Deimos took the jump just as easily the second time, and settled down afterwards to a neat and controlled canter around the arena. As Mitch pulled him to a walk, another competitor drew alongside.

'That's a nice colt,' he said. 'He's young?'

'Yeah. A novice. But I think he'll go well.'

'I think so too. He's yours?'

'No. He's a Willowbrook horse.'

'Ah.' The man nodded in recognition. 'That old stallion was a fine animal. It's a shame I left it too late to send a mare to him.'

'This is his offspring,' Mitch said. 'He's standing his first season this year. It's a chance to get in early while the fee is cheap. In a couple more years, I think he'll be pulling pretty high fees.'

The man ran an experienced eye over Deimos. 'Worth thinking about.'

The cross-country steward waved Mitch forward.

'Good luck,' his companion said. 'I'll be watching.'

As he rode to the starting line, Mitch hoped he'd done the right thing, promoting Deimos like that. He wasn't entirely sure Liz would stand him at stud, but it was too late now to worry about that. He had more important things on his mind.

He glanced at the sloping ground ahead of him. The course was already visible, the grass flattened by riders walking it and by the first horses to compete. From here he couldn't see the place where he had found Liz lying unconscious. The steward shouted a warning and Mitch put Deimos into a canter, circling, waiting for the buzzer to sound.

Then he launched across the starting line at a gallop, and there was nothing else in the world but the course, the horse and his desire to help Liz.

CHAPTER
66

Kayla was carrying a cardboard box when she appeared in Liz's hospital room.

'They've taken the splint off.'

'Yes.' Liz stretched her leg. 'There's a good chance I can get out of here today.'

'That's good.'

'How is everything at home? Did you feed—'

'Everything is fine.'

'You checked the water in the yards like I told you?'

'Liz. I do know what I'm doing around horses too, you know.'

Liz caught her bottom lip between her teeth to hold back the words she'd been about to say. 'I know, but it's been a while for you.'

'Not that long. I looked after the place just fine when you took Deimos to Coonabarabran. In fact, I even went for a ride that weekend.'

'You did what? Who did you ride?'

'Zeke. We're old friends.'

'But—' Again Liz caught her words. Kayla wasn't a kid needing her protection and direction any more. If they were going to mend things between them, she had to remember that. She should also remember all the times they'd ridden together as kids. All the fun they'd had.

'How was it?'

'I ached all over the next day.'

'You're out of practice. Maybe we could ride together when I get out of here.'

'I'd like that.'

Small steps, but in the right direction. 'What's in the box?'

Without answering, Kayla put the box on the bed and opened it. Inside, Liz saw bits of broken china; the remains of the horse Kayla had given their father all those years ago.

'I'm really sorry that got broken.'

'Just because something is broken doesn't mean it can't be fixed. If we try hard enough.'

She was not talking about the horse.

Liz started taking bits of china out of the box and laying them out on her overbed table. There were a lot of them. 'You're doing this just to get back at me for boarding school, aren't you?'

Kayla picked up another broken piece of china. 'Maybe just a little.'

Liz lay against the hospital pillows.

'So, you're giving up.'

'Not on your life.' She pushed herself into a sitting position and surveyed the table. The pieces of broken china were starting to form the shape of a horse. The largest pieces were ready to be glued together, although the cracks would always be visible. Liz picked up a tiny piece of china. 'I think this might be an ear.'

Kayla pulled a bottle of glue out of the box and sat on the edge of the bed. 'Let's get started.'

'It'll never be quite the same again,' Liz pointed out.

'That's all right. Nothing ever is. Besides, I had to find a way to amuse you while you were here. Otherwise you'd have driven me and the nurses crazy.'

'I'm not so sure she hasn't.' One of the nurses appeared in the doorway. 'But this should make you feel a whole lot better.' She waved the paper she was carrying.

'I can go home?'

'Yes, you can.'

Liz almost jumped out of bed.

The nurse laughed. 'Not so fast. It's going to take a while to process the paperwork. But let's start by removing your cannula.'

Liz barely felt the needle being pulled from her skin. Her thoughts were already far from the hospital room where she'd spent the last three days.

The discharge paperwork moved at a snail's pace, and all the while, Liz sat dressed, ready to leave and fuming, on the edge of the bed. Even the horse project wasn't enough to distract her.

As soon as they were given the go-ahead, the sisters hurried to the car park and Kayla's little red car.

'It's not very big,' Liz said as she got in. 'It wouldn't be much use up here. Not much room for gear.'

'Well, it's a good thing I don't need it for that.'

'Anyway, I hope it's fast.'

'Oh, it's fast.'

Kayla drove steadily out of the hospital car park and through the suburban streets. Liz's impatience grew as they wended their way past the lines of motels and service stations. But as soon as they reached the highway, Kayla put her foot down and the little red

sports car surged forward like a racehorse. The kilometres began
to flash by.

'You're driving pretty fast,' Liz muttered.

'And you're complaining a lot,' Kayla said, 'but I forgive you.'

They both laughed and Liz was almost overawed by the wonder
of it. After so many years of anger and blame, of recriminations
and separation, she and Kayla were slipping back into their old
relationship. It wasn't quite that easy, and she was sure there were
disagreements aplenty ahead of them, but it felt good. As the paddocks and small towns slipped past, Liz vowed she wouldn't let
anything come between her and Kayla ever again.

She tried hard not to think about the years she'd lost. Kayla was
right—she was not to blame for the crash that killed their parents.
Yes, her family were following her and Mitch, but the accident
wasn't their fault. If blame was to be laid, there were others who
should claim a share. Perhaps even her father, for driving too fast.
But when it came down to it, the crash was just a horrible accident.
It had taken her a long time to accept that. She could only hope it
wasn't too long.

She had half expected Mitch to come to see her in the hospital,
but realistically, she knew he wouldn't. He had a competition that
was important to his business. Not only that, he'd promised Kayla
he would care for Liz's horses. And he would, that was the sort of
man he was. Even so, he could have found time to visit her but
she'd clearly driven him away too hard, too far and too many times.

I've had enough.

She wouldn't listen to that voice deep inside her that told her it
was too late and she had lost him. She hadn't heeded the doubts that
had plagued her as she wrestled to preserve her father's legacy, and
she wouldn't let fear stop her from saving something that meant so
much more than Willowbrook.

If only Mitch still felt the same. She pushed away the image of him kissing the cheek of the blonde woman. That kiss meant nothing more than friendship. It had to be that, because anything else was too heartbreaking to even consider.

She felt Kayla start to slow down, and a sign flashed past. They were in Murrurundi.

Kayla parked the car under a tree just up the road from the horse arena, and they got out. Liz was limping a bit, but she had no time to notice any pain in her leg. She didn't even think about going to check her campsite. The horses could manage without her for a bit longer. All she needed now was Mitch.

'Hey, Liz. Good to see you're okay.'

She raised a hand in acknowledgement each time someone greeted her, but she didn't stop. There was a lot of noise coming from the main arena. Maybe that's where Mitch would be.

She froze in her tracks when she saw him. He was leaning on a rail near the ring entrance, talking earnestly to another competitor. Her heart contracted in the strangest way and she felt as if she was seeing him clearly for the first time in years. Maybe she was.

This was Mitch, who she had loved since she was twelve years old. Mitch, with whom she had shared all the joys of childhood. With whom she had learned how to ride and train a horse; learned how to grow up and be more than she was. She had only ever kissed one man and that was Mitch. She had never wanted to be with any other man, and she knew now that she never would.

'Ladies and gentlemen, the awards will now be presented to the top scorers in the Stockman's Challenge individual events.'

Liz jumped as a speaker near her screeched into life.

'After the presentation, the finalists will go head to head. There's great action ahead this afternoon but right now, I'd like to call all competitors into the ring. Ladies and gentlemen, would you put your hands together please and give a big Hunter Valley welcome to the competitors in the Challenge Parade!'

Mitch had mounted the horse that had been standing behind him. Liz couldn't see him clearly as the horses and riders milled around, but then the gate swung open and one by one the riders entered the arena. They pushed their horses into a canter for their circuit. All around Liz, people were cheering for their favourites, but she didn't make a sound, or move her eyes from the gate.

Then she saw him.

A tall, dark brown horse walked through the gate and Mitch touched his hat to the steward as he sent the horse cantering around the track. Liz had always loved watching Mitch ride. His lean body was always so controlled and strong, while his hands on the reins were gentle. And his handsome face was always a mixture of joy and concentration. Liz's father had been one of the great horsemen of his generation, and as she watched Mitch circle the arena with the other competitors, Liz knew that he was too.

But he was so much more than that to her.

Someone tapped her on the shoulder, dragging her attention away from the arena. It was the man who'd been talking to Mitch.

'Liz, great to see you. As I was just telling Mitch, I've been watching that colt of yours over the last couple of days. I'm very impressed. I'd like to talk to you about sending a couple of mares to him this season.'

What was the man talking about? She didn't know and she didn't care. 'Sure,' she said. Whatever it took to make him leave her alone.

'Great. I'll be in touch. Good to see you out of hospital. Lucky escape, that.'

Liz wished the man would go away.

'Right then. Catch you later,' he said.

At last he was gone and she turned back to the ring, where prize ribbons were being presented. As she searched for Mitch in the line-up, the man's words came back to her. What did he mean, he'd been watching Deimos?

The speaker above her head crackled. 'And second place in the bareback obstacle course, Mitch Saunders riding Willowbrook Deimos.'

Liz blinked. What had the announcer said? It was only then that she actually looked at the horse Mitch was riding.

Deimos.

The award ceremony seemed to take forever, and Liz was practically hopping up and down on the spot when the riders finally set out on their victory lap. She was leaning over the rail when Mitch looked up and his eyes met hers. His face lit up, and Liz knew everything she needed to.

She pushed her way through the crowd milling around the arena gates. She could see Mitch, but he'd lost her in the melee. He looked around until, once again, their eyes locked.

All the noise and bustle of the place faded. Subconsciously, Liz did something she hadn't done in a very long time: ran her fingers through her hair to tidy it up. She wished she was wearing something other than the T-shirt and jeans Kayla had brought to the hospital to replace the torn and blood-spattered clothes she'd been wearing when she was admitted.

Somehow, the crowd parted and Liz took the last few steps to stand close to Mitch. She looked up into his face and suddenly didn't know what to say.

'I thought I had lost you.' His voice was so soft she hardly heard it break on the words. 'I couldn't bear it if—'

'Never.' She reached up to touch his cheek. 'Oh, Mitch, what did I do? I am so sorry. All these lost years. Can you ever forgive me?'

'How can I not?'

She was in his arms and he crushed her to his chest, speaking words she could barely hear. But she didn't have to, she could feel his love envelop her like a warm woollen blanket on a frosty morning. His lips brushed the top of her hair and she raised her face to his, and then he was kissing her lips. The years and the pain and anger dropped away and she was eighteen again, making a promise that—this time—she would keep.

A loud wolf whistle echoed around them, and Liz gently pushed Mitch away.

'There's so much I need to say, Mitch. But most of all I need to say I am sorry. I was wrong to do what I did. When Mum and Dad died, you lost people you loved too. You shouldn't have had to lose your wife as well. I should have known you were hurting. But I couldn't see past my own feelings.'

'You lost your parents, Liz. No matter how much I loved you, I knew I couldn't make up for that terrible loss. And it was my fault. If I hadn't suggested we run away and get married—'

'Stop.' She put her fingertips over his mouth. 'There's been enough blame and guilt. It has to stop now.'

Activity surged suddenly around them as the announcer called the start of the next event.

'Come on, Mitch.' Someone slapped him on the back. 'I'm going to beat you this time.'

'You haven't got a chance,' Liz said. 'Mitch and Deimos have got this one all sewn up.'

CHAPTER
67

Willowbrook was dressed for a wedding. Fairy lights decorated the garden and the bower was filled with tulips of every shade imaginable, red and yellow and white and pink. They had delicate petals, lacy edges and deep green leaves.

The rows of seats on the lawn were starting to fill with people. As she watched the guests take their places, Kayla noticed there were some very strong resemblances. Several of the men were tall, with dark, wavy hair. The women, and a couple of the girls, had rather large noses with a pronounced bump in the middle. This didn't make them ugly, it just showed they were family. The exception to the rule was, as always, Pascale. Her friend was as beautiful as ever as she found her seat. She wasn't working today, she was a guest. She was family.

And what a family it was. Four generations had come to witness the ceremony. All related to the bride and groom. And speaking of family ...

Kayla looked at the homestead where Liz and Mitch were standing, their heads close together. Her sister was—and this was something of a shock—wearing a cream skirt and top. Her newly-styled hair was waving a little in the breeze and there was a hint of colour on her lips. She looked ten years younger than when Kayla had returned to Willowbrook all those months ago. The look of defeat was gone from her face, and the hardness from her manner. She was smiling again. Kayla didn't have to think very hard to figure out why.

Mitch looked very handsome. Although he wasn't dressed like a stockman, he looked like one. From his tanned, lined face to the strength in his body and the way he walked, everything about Mitch said he belonged on the land. Belonged *to* the land. It was something that he and Liz shared and always would. As Kayla watched, Mitch bent his head and whispered in Liz's ear. Her sister smiled up at him, and even from where she was standing, Kayla could see the love that wrapped the two of them together in their own private world.

Kayla felt a twinge of envy. She had never felt anything like that. She glanced across at the marquee where the wedding guests would shortly be celebrating with drinks and canapés. Lachie wasn't catering this event. After last time, he'd vowed he would never leave Sydney again. The bush, he said, was unmitigated hell and he wouldn't work on another Willowbrook wedding. She hadn't seen much of him since then and she thought they had both probably started to move on. They would continue to work together professionally and they'd still be friends, but their romance was over. Strangely enough, Kayla wasn't bothered by that.

The last of the guests was seated now, and the marriage celebrant nodded at Kayla. Ken winked at her from his place, standing with camera in hand, ready to capture every moment. It was time. Kayla walked halfway to the house, until finally Liz and Mitch noticed her. She nodded and they walked up the steps onto the homestead veranda. There they separated, Liz to the bride's retreat, and Mitch to the groom's waiting room to tell the occupants that it was time.

Kayla caught the eye of the musicians standing discreetly to one side. The delicate notes of harp and flute filled the air as the guests stood and turned with expectation to see the happy couple.

They were possibly the loveliest couple Kayla had ever helped down the aisle.

Despite his age, Julien Bonet held himself straight and tall, cutting a dashing figure in his dark suit with its dark red bow tie. His grey hair was combed into place with almost military precision. But what caused Kayla's breath to catch was the way he looked at the woman by his side.

Marie Bonet was obviously the one who had gifted her offspring with large noses. Her grey hair was thinning, but for this event it had been carefully combed and curled. The hand lying on her husband's arm was almost painfully thin and sometimes, Kayla knew, that hand would shake as age and illness took its toll. But as Marie looked up at her husband of sixty years, Kayla could see the beautiful girl who had captured a dashing young man's heart.

The two gradually made their way to the bower, where, to celebrate their anniversary, they would renew their wedding vows in front of their family, including the great-niece who had planned the ceremony to perfection. Kayla was so pleased Pascale had chosen Willowbrook for this. It meant she had accepted Kayla's decision to move out of the city and back into her old family home. Now there definitely was a tear in Kayla's eye.

As she watched the scene unfold, she felt a deep sense of satisfaction. Willowbrook Weddings was rapidly becoming a success. She had enough events booked over the next few months to put the venture on a sound financial footing. Not only the wedding venture, but Willowbrook itself. Liz and Mitch had started to put the stud back on the map and Deimos was attracting bookings. Soon there would be mares and foals grazing in the paddocks that had become too bare.

Movement at the corner of the homestead caught her eye and she turned in time to see Liz and Mitch slip away. As they disappeared around the corner, Kayla saw that they were holding hands.

CHAPTER
68

The two figures walk up the gentle slope. Their hands are locked tightly together. It has rained recently and the grass is green and smells fresh. The summer is over and the worst of the heat is gone. Autumn is a beautiful time of year.

At the top of the hill, the lone tree casts a gentle shadow over the small graveyard and two stone crosses that are already showing signs of age.

Liz is holding a bunch of tulips.

'They'll never notice that I borrowed these,' she says, with a mischievous grin.

She places flowers at the foot of each cross, then turns to Mitch. He takes both her hands in his.

Although a month has passed since Mitch came third in the King of the Ranges competition, they haven't hurried this. There's been an unspoken agreement between them. They have been riding together every day and working side by side at Willowbrook and at Mitch's place. They have eaten together and they have laughed together. There may have been tears too, but no one else will ever know. They've planned a future for Willowbrook and for Deimos, but none for themselves. Until today.

They have taken the time to get over the hurt of the past.

They have taken the time to fall in love again.

Liz reaches into the pocket on her skirt and pulls out something small and shiny. She places it in Mitch's hands. It's a gold ring. The sort of ring a teenage boy would give to the girl he loves. It's as shiny as it was fifteen years ago and it still fits when Mitch slips it on her finger.

'Lizzie, I love you. You are my best friend and I cannot imagine a life without you. I promise to laugh with you, cry with you and grow old with you. I will love you when we are together and when we are apart. I will laugh with you when you are happy and comfort you when you cry. I promise that I will never let you down. With these words, and with all of my heart and soul, I marry you and join my life with yours.'

Tears prick her eyes as she remembers his vows. The words he spoke fifteen years ago now have deeper meaning. She and Mitch were children then. Today they are adults, and understand more about love than they did all those years ago.

'Mitch, I promise to love you in good times and in bad. I will love you when life is easy and when it's difficult; when being in love is simple, and when it's not. I will dream with you, work with you, celebrate with you and walk beside you through whatever our life together may bring. I take you as my husband—my love and my life, today and always.'

The look on Mitch's face tells her that he remembers her vows too. As she finishes speaking, tears roll down her face. Mitch kisses them away, and then he pulls her into his arms and kisses her with enough love to wash away all the lonely years.

They look down the hill to Willowbrook homestead, where the celebration is continuing. Faint music drifts up to them. The lights have come on and the place looks lovely. The soft evening colours enhance the graceful lines of the house. It is beautiful again, loved and cared for and echoing to the sound of laughter.

'Do you want to go and join the wedding?' Mitch asks.

'No. I don't think they need me there tonight.'

Their hearts begin to beat a little faster at the promise of what lies ahead.

'As you wish, Mrs Saunders.' Mitch is smiling as he takes her hand.

Together Mitch and Lizzie walk down the hill, towards the creek and the fallen tree that bridges two halves of the same dream.

ACKNOWLEDGEMENTS

While researching and writing this book, I was able to spend a lot of time in the Upper Hunter Valley, in and around Scone. Despite the ravages of drought, it is a beautiful part of the world. The people I met were warm and welcoming, and very happy to answer my questions about horses, history, mobile phone coverage, event competition rules and a thousand and one other things. My particular thanks go to George, Rosemary, Jon, Mary, Barry and Susie for telling me their stories and welcoming me into their homes.

Special thanks also go to the BelleBrook Country B&B—my home away from home and the perfect place to write a book.

Writing is a solitary occupation, but I never feel lonely. Not only do I have all these characters talking to me in my head, I am also blessed with wonderful friends, writers all, who know exactly what I am trying to do and how those successes and failures feel. Thank you, Jean, Jenny and Rachel for such supportive long lunches, and much love to the wonderful women of the Naughty Kitchen—Alison, Immi, Sheila, Ruth, Jeev and Kate—for always being somewhere out there in cyberspace whenever I need you.

I would also like to thank the wonderful team at HarperCollins, who have been a dream to work with, even when we are on opposite sides of the world. To my agent Julia—what can I say. You rock!

I'm not sure why my husband always appears at the bottom of this note. He shouldn't. Without you, John, I'm not sure how on earth I would ever write a book. I love you.

And to you, dear reader, I want to say thank you for coming with me on this journey.

Janet

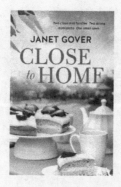

Turn over for a sneak peek.

CLOSE
to HOME

by

JANET GOVER

Available February 2021

mira

PROLOGUE

Nyringa, New South Wales
Spring, 1956

Alice gave a twirl as she closed the wooden gate behind her and turned towards the centre of town. Her grandmother's welcome cake had been safely delivered to the new teacher and now she was free for the rest of this special day. The circus was coming to town for the first time ever and she didn't want to miss any of the excitement. She started walking more quickly. Wayne was going to be there too, and they'd watch the parade together. Afterwards they might slip down to that spot by the creek. That thought was enough to send a little tingle through her. Granny didn't hold with fifteen-year-old girls having boyfriends, but Alice was almost sixteen, and Wayne *was* her boyfriend. They'd been going steady now for nearly three months. Yesterday he'd slipped his hand under her blouse while they were making out down by the creek. She'd told him off of course, because she didn't want to seem easy or a tramp like that Suzie at school—Suzie went with anyone and girls like that never got married. But next time Wayne was with her down by the creek, Alice would let him touch her breasts. Maybe even today. After the parade, though. She'd never seen a circus before.

Alice was determined to find a place at the front so she could see the parade up close. According to Granny, Nyringa was going to be more crowded today than ever before in the town's history, and Granny would know because she was ancient and had lived in this boring little town forever. Then tomorrow, the circus was going to do a show. She'd go with Wayne and wear the new yellow dress her mum had made for her. She'd talked her mother into taking the hem up another couple of inches, and she wanted to see what Wayne did when he saw her in it.

Alice heard a low rumble of noise coming from the main street, and then a cheer went up. The circus must be here already. She was late. She broke into a run and sprinted along the last row of houses, past the car park at the back of the store and into the crowd lining the main street, where the highway passed straight through the centre of town. Her mouth dropped open and she skidded to a stop.

Elephants! There were elephants in Nyringa.

They were big and grey and slow, swinging their trunks as they walked. Their skin looked like old leather, and their eyes seemed too small for such a big animal. Their feet though … their feet were huge. Imagine if one of them stood on you! All four creatures were adorned with brightly coloured headpieces and a man sat on each one, waving to the crowd. Alice waved back as she pushed her way forward. Her friend Martha had been to the cinema once in Newcastle. She'd seen a film with elephants in it and bragged about it for weeks. But this was better. These elephants were real! And they were so big! Alice felt a tiny frisson of fear that was exciting in its own way.

'Alice!' Wayne appeared next to her and grabbed her hand. He looked down at her, his whole face alive with excitement. 'Aren't they great?'

She nodded, too tongue-tied by everything to speak.

'Look, Alice. Look at the jugglers.'

Men wearing embroidered white shirts moved along the edge of the crowd, tossing small balls into the air with speed and precision and never dropping a single one.

'I could do that.'

The nearest juggler heard Wayne's words.

'Here you go, kid.' The man threw him a ball. 'Now try two. Like this.' The juggler tossed two balls into the air and kept them aloft with just one hand. He wasn't even really looking as he did it.

'Sure.' Wayne threw a ball in the air. Then a second. He caught one but the other bounced at his feet. The juggler swooped in to catch it with one hand and added it to his one-handed display.

'Good try, kid.' The juggler took the second ball from Wayne's hand and moved on.

'I would have done it next time,' Wayne muttered.

'Of course you would.' Alice took hold of his hand again and squeezed it. Wayne laced his fingers through hers and smiled down at her. For a moment Alice forgot the elephants and saw a future in which she and Wayne left Nyringa behind for good, and went out into the world. They would marry and have children one day, of course, but not before they had explored the whole world.

'Look, here come the horses!'

Alice followed Wayne's pointing finger. She loved horses. Most of the other girls in her class lived on farms and had their own ponies and horses. Living in town, Alice didn't have a pony. Every year since she was small she'd asked her parents for one for her birthday and for Christmas, but they never listened. The horses coming towards her were more beautiful than any she'd seen on the farms around Nyringa. They were all grey, with soft white manes and tails. Their harness glinted with silver as they tossed their heads. They didn't seem at all disturbed by the cheering people lining the street.

Then Alice saw the girl sitting sideways on the back of the lead horse. She was dressed in a tight pink costume like a bikini and a tiny skirt covered in sequins. She was wearing white ballet slippers and tights. They were jewels in her wavy blonde hair and dark mascara and shadow on her eyes, making her look very exotic. Granny would not have approved. As Alice watched, the girl stood on her horse's back and opened her arms to the crowd, who cheered loudly. Beside Alice, Wayne was cheering loudest of all. His eyes were shining and his attention was now entirely on the girl. He was ignoring everything else around him, including Alice. His fingers loosened in hers and their hands fell apart as he moved to get a better look at the girl on the horse, who suddenly leaped into the air in a graceful move that was almost like ballet, landing again on the horse without so much as a stumble. All around Alice, the crowd gasped and cheered even louder.

'The parade is nearly over.' Alice grabbed Wayne's hand and tugged at it. 'I have to get back soon. Why don't we go down to the creek and sit for a while?' She opened her eyes really wide and looked up at him through her eyelashes, because that's what the actresses did in the films, and everyone thought they were so sexy. Right now, Alice wanted to be sexy more than anything else in the world.

'I want to follow the parade,' Wayne said. 'I'll see you later.'

Never taking his eyes off the girl on the white horse, Wayne again pulled his hand away from hers and began to follow the parade.

Alice looked down at her empty hand. How could Wayne just leave her like that?

She felt a strange pain in her chest, like nothing she had ever felt before. It felt as if her heart was breaking.

CHAPTER
1

'The classroom layout is very different, as you can see, Miss Walker. It works better this way with the age range.'

Meg nodded. Everything about this school was different from the places she'd taught in Sydney. The desks were arranged in small squares, there wasn't a computer to be seen and the view outside the windows was just the dry yellow grass of a big oval surrounded by tall gum trees. The whole school was a single wooden building containing three classrooms, only two of which were being used for classes; the third was a combination store room and staff room. There was no library, gym or assembly hall. There were no lockers for the students, nor was there a lockable cabinet for the teacher. The gate she'd passed though when this tour began was only waist height and there were no security cameras. She wasn't sure if that was a good sign or a cause for concern. This place was about as far as she could get from the inner city schools she'd previously taught at. The schools where she had discovered her love of teaching—and then lost it again.

'Each group of tables represents a class year. You have grades seven to twelve. A lot of the older kids go off to boarding school, if their parents can afford it, so the groups are quite small,' Meg's tour guide said. 'I have quite a few more kids in the primary classroom.'

Meg nodded again. Her new colleague Anna was doing everything she could to make her feel at home. But she no longer felt at home in the classroom and wondered if she ever would again. This two-teacher school was very different to anywhere she'd taught before, but that wasn't what she was struggling with. She tugged the right sleeve of her blouse down over her wrist as she told herself everything would be different this time. The Nyringa school had about forty pupils split between primary and secondary classes. As she was taking the senior classes, she was, in effect, the headmistress of this tiny institution. She wasn't sure if she wanted the title, but she did want the job.

'We're so lucky you could join us for this term on such short notice, Miss Walker.' Anna beamed. 'Your predecessor left quite suddenly. Family matters.'

'Please, call me Meg. Tell me about the kids.'

'You must call me Anna. Some of our kids are from here in town but most are from nearby properties. There's a bus run every morning and afternoon that brings those kids in and takes them home. Attendance is good—there's not exactly much to tempt the kids to play truant around here.'

'I guess not.' Meg hadn't seen much of the town yet, she'd only arrived an hour ago. She had a couple of days to settle in and, on Monday, she would be standing in front of students again. She took another glance around the room, and it occurred to her that, as she moved between the desks, her back would be turned to one group while she attended to another. She felt her stomach churn and fought down her reaction. It would be fine. She could make it work. She had to. Because if she couldn't teach here, she would never teach anywhere, ever again. And if she couldn't teach, she didn't know what she would do.

'Perhaps we should go to the cottage now,' Meg said quickly. She'd come back to the classroom tomorrow and spend some time here alone. She could maybe change a few things or add some personal touches to make it seem like she belonged. To make it feel as though this was a safe place. But right now she needed to be somewhere else, where the screams in her head were not so loud and she could breathe again.

'Yes, of course.' The other teacher waved her hands around. 'How stupid of me. You must be tired and you'll want to settle in. All this could have waited until tomorrow.'

'It's fine, honestly. It's good to get a feel for the school.'

'Come on. I have the keys to the cottage.'

The school teacher's cottage was tucked away in a corner of the school grounds, set well back from the classrooms. It was one of those small wooden houses so common in towns like this. Set on stumps, it had the tiniest veranda and a peaked iron roof. It didn't have a garden worth the name, just a few native bushes and a sparse area of what might be called lawn in a better year, if one was being generous. One narrow gate led to the schoolyard and a second larger gate to the road. Meg's car, packed with cardboard boxes and suitcases, was parked in the driveway. Meg followed Anna up the short flight of stairs to the solid-looking front door.

'This lock is a bit tough,' Anna said. 'We probably should get someone to come and take a look at it. To be honest, around here a lot of people don't both too much about locking their doors.' She was so busy fighting with the lock, she didn't notice the way Meg tensed at her words.

At last, the door swung open. Meg stepped into a large, pleasant room. One window looked towards the school, the other towards a line of trees that Meg guessed was the creek shown on the town map she'd printed from Google. The room was furnished with a large sofa, bookshelves and a coffee table. There was even a television. In the middle of the ceiling, a fan awaited the start of the really hot weather. On the other side of the room was a small kitchen with a breakfast bar. It looked quite modern. Through the open door at the back of the room she could see a small hallway. That would lead to the bedroom, bathroom and laundry.

'I hope this will be all right for you,' Anna said hesitantly. 'I guess compared to what you had in the city, it's a bit …'

'No. No. It's fine. Thank you,' Meg assured her. And it really was fine. The last thing she wanted was a place that in any way reminded her of the city and what had happened there. 'Thank you so much. I guess I should start getting settled in.'

'Yes. Of course. It's just so nice to have a new person to talk to. You know where the shop is, right? You must have seen it as you drove in. But if you find yourself stuck, we live just a couple of streets away. You have my number. If there's anything I can do …'

'Thank you. That's very kind of you.' Meg held out her hand for the keys.

'Yes. Well …' Anna handed over the keys and, with many more offers of help, left.

Meg closed the door behind her with a sigh. She leaned against it for a few seconds, then spun and turned the key in the lock. Then she checked the rest of the house. The windows all had old but functioning locks. So did the back door. Like the kitchen, the bathroom appeared to have been recently refurbished. She looked at the double bed in the bedroom and told herself things would be different here. She would sleep well in that big, comfortable-looking bed.

She heard the distant cry of a crow and glanced at the window. It was already late afternoon. She needed to bring her things inside and then she'd have to do some shopping at the store. If she got to work now, she should have it all done before dark. She could ring her parents back home in Sydney, and unpack her boxes and suitcases after that—when she was safely inside and the doors were locked.

talk about it

Let's talk about books.

Join the conversation:

facebook.com/romanceanz

@romanceanz

romance.com.au

If you love reading and want to know about our authors and titles, then let's talk about it.